MEMOIRS OF AN ENGLISH OFFICER

MEMOIRS OF AN ENGLISH OFFICER

(The Military Memoirs of Capt. George Carleton)

with

THE HISTORY OF
THE REMARKABLE LIFE OF
JOHN SHEPPARD

and

THE MEMOIRS OF
MAJOR ALEXANDER RAMKINS,
A HIGHLAND OFFICER

by

DANIEL DEFOE

Introduction by James T. Boulton

Gollancz Classics

General Editor: Martin Seymour-Smith

LONDON
VICTOR GOLLANCZ LTD
1970

THE MILITARY MEMOIRS OF
CAPTAIN GEORGE CARLETON
first published 1728

THE HISTORY OF THE REMARKABLE LIFE
OF JOHN SHEPPARD
first published 1724

THE MEMOIRS OF MAJOR ALEXANDER RAMKINS,
A HIGHLAND OFFICER
first published 1718

Gollancz Classics Edition 1970
Introduction © James T. Boulton 1970
ISBN 0 575 00421 5

PRINTED IN GREAT BRITAIN
BY EBENEZER BAYLIS AND SON LTD
THE TRINITY PRESS, WORCESTER, AND LONDON

CONTENTS

PREFACE

'Lord Peterborough . . . is a favourite of mine, and is not
enough known' . . . 'But (said [Lord Eliot],) the best
account of Lord Peterborough that I have happened to meet
with, is in "Captain Carleton's Memoirs".' . . . Johnson
said, that he had never heard of the book. Lord Eliot . . .
procured a copy in London, and sent it to Johnson, who told
Sir Joshua Reynolds that he was going to bed when it came,
but was so much pleased with it, that he sat up till he had
read it through, and found in it such an air of truth, that he
could not doubt of its authenticity.[1]*

JOHNSON HATED DECEPTION; he would not have welcomed
the discovery that the *Memoirs of an English Officer* had been
fabricated. Had Defoean scholarship been as advanced in his
day as in ours, Johnson might at once have suspected that a book
published in 1728 purporting to be history, with 'an air of truth'
and seemingly 'authentic', was one of Defoe's over five hundred
works. Yet, though Defoe is long known to have written on the
remarkable John Sheppard, Carleton's *Memoirs* were confidently
attributed to him only in 1924, and Ramkins's even later. These
works exemplify (among other things) three important facets of
their author. *The History of John Sheppard* is the work of the
journalist who did not hesitate to exploit a current public interest
in some sensational person or event; in Carleton's *Memoirs* we
have the writer of works like the *Journal of the Plague Year* for
which neither 'history' nor 'fiction' are adequate descriptive
terms; and the author of Ramkins's *Memoirs* was Defoe the political campaigner, the man who had been briefly involved in
Monmouth's rebellion and, later, as a government undercover
agent had helped to influence public opinion. In whatever guise
he wrote Defoe invariably contrived an appearance of authenticity in his work.

* Notes on the Preface appear on p. 334.

In this respect he could scarcely have failed with *John Sheppard*: the man was still at large after his second incredible escape from prison. As for Carleton's *Memoirs*, they were regarded as genuine source material by most nineteenth-century historians of the Peninsular campaigns in the war of the Spanish Succession; largely on their evidence the supposed author was included in the *Dictionary of National Biography*. 'Major Alexander Ramkins' appears in the same Victorian collection of national worthies solely on the authority of his *Memoirs*. And a modern scholar, Donald Stauffer, in his monumental *Art of Biography in Eighteenth-Century England*, after extolling Ramkins's sophistication as a memoirist laments his death 'among the foreign rats of a French prison.'[2] In fact Ramkins's existence has not yet been established; in any case it is more likely that the real author of his memoirs died in 1731 in Ropemakers' Alley, London.

The *Memoirs of Major Alexander Ramkins* (dated 1719 but published in 1718) has a title-page which is instructive in some ways but deceptive in another. It informs the reader that the work, written by 'a Highland Officer now in Prison at *Avignon*', provides an account of 'several remarkable Adventures' experienced by the author in Britain and Europe over a period of 28 years. Such contents were very much to the taste of Defoe's contemporaries. Stimulated by several writers since the turn of the century, interest in recent English and European history was intense; it was no less so in travel literature. The Earl of Shaftesbury had remarked on the latter in his *Characteristicks* (1711):

> so enchanted we are with the *travelling Memoirs* of any casual Adventurer; that be his Character, or Genius, what it will, we have no sooner turn'd over a Page or two, than we begin to interest ourselves highly in his Affairs.[3]

Defoe exploited this public curiosity most memorably with *Robinson Crusoe* in 1719; the *Life and Adventures of Captain Singleton* and *Memoirs of a Cavalier* followed in 1720. Potential readers of Ramkins's *Memoirs* who looked for more than travel experiences could expect 'a very agreeable and instructive Lesson of Human Life, both in a Publick and Private Capacity, in several pleasant Instances of his Amours, Gallantry, Oeconomy, &c.' The title-page, then, promised a variety of pleasures. However, it concealed the author's main purpose which was political. The preface announces that though Ramkins was an 'active and diligent Servant' of James II, his book is designed to expose the treachery of the French king in merely pretending to support the exiled monarch. But in 1718 the English government reacted vigorously to any sign of Jacobitism. In 1719, for example, John Matthews was executed for high treason following the publication of his Jacobite pamphlet, *Vox Populi*;[4] and Defoe himself had suffered imprisonment in 1713 on account of three pamphlets in which he had employed irony to expose Jacobite casuistry. The pamphlets were interpreted at face value; Defoe's purpose was misunderstood; and only a pardon from the Queen herself secured his release from jail. These, then, were not times in which to risk misapprehension. To display on the title-page that the *Memoirs* were those of a former loyal supporter of James II would be to invite scrutiny from government agents; Defoe knew to his cost that such men were not sensitive to unusual literary methods.

Read with average care the *Memoirs* reveal their author's loyalties with great clarity. They record Ramkins's increasing suspicions about the French king's designs; he does not conceal his sympathy for James II whom he regards as a mere 'Property' of Louis, but his present support for George I is unquestionable. Indeed at the end of his book Ramkins proclaims his complete change of heart: whereas he had formerly believed that as a Roman Catholic he must be a Jacobite, he is now convinced that no Catholic should oppose the Protestant Succession either on principle or in practice. Harsh experience has prompted the change. It has proved that attempts to reinstate James create widespread misery and play into the hands of the French Machiavelli.

Defoe invariably sympathised with the pragmatic approach to human affairs. Just as Crusoe has to face repeated failure before he successfully makes his earthenware jar; or as Roxana has to suffer the consequences of bankruptcy before she recognises the importance of financial independence; so Ramkins has to endure battles, wounds and deprivation in order to acknowledge the folly of supporting a lost as well as a politically dangerous cause. With the benefit of hindsight he labels Jacobitism 'an incurable Distemper'; he dismisses Englishmen who believe Louis would actively support James II as men with 'no Notions of Foreign Affairs'; and he feels able to despise Louis as 'a juggler' with the fortunes of the Pretender. It was arduous experience which had provided his confidence.

Defoe intended that Ramkins's assurance should be shared by his readers. They had to be persuaded to participate imaginatively in the 'author's' adventures and to learn the same lessons. They had, then, to find Ramkins a credible autobiographer, not merely a puppet created to enliven a political tract. Defoe had already developed considerable skill in achieving this type of honourable deception: for example, in order to expose the inhumanity and folly of the Tory persecution of dissenters, he had assumed the guise of a High Anglican and written the famous pamphlet, *The Shortest Way with the Dissenters* (1702). Imaginatively he *became* a High Anglican and spoke with his unmistakable voice. When he *became* Ramkins Defoe had to think and write in the character of a professional soldier. That he succeeded is attested by the evidence already cited.

Part of the experience of reading the *Memoirs* is to believe in Ramkins's historical existence. The 'author' was not more than 17 in 1689, the date of the battle of Killiecrankie; his book was written 27 years later, that is just two years before it appeared. As a youth he abandoned his college studies in Aberdeen, went to the military academy in Strasbourg (which is reminiscent of the academy Defoe proposed in his *Essay upon Projects*, 1697), and after some adventures joined James II's army in Ireland. Captured at the battle of the Boyne (July 1690), Ramkins escaped and eventually returned to France. He was wounded at Landen (1693); he visited Antwerp and London. We hear of the death of James (1701), the battle of Malplaquet (1709), and the Peace of Utrecht (1713). There is, then, a credible historical framework. Closer examination alone reveals that there is no convincing evidence of the 'author's' presence at any of the battles he mentions. As in Carleton's *Memoirs* all the details which at first sight we accept as the fruit of personal experience could have come from secondary

sources. His account of the Boyne, for instance, is prefaced by
the remark:

> The History of that Battle has so many Eye Witnesses still
> alive for me to dwell upon it; I shall only make bold to relate
> what my Fate was upon that unfortunate Day.[5]

The description which follows, though vivid could be fictional.
Ramkins names no other officer who took part in the fighting,
and he explains his inability to describe the battle in detail on the
grounds that 'during the Fight, there is so much Noise, Smoak
and Confusion, that for my part, I scarce can give a true Narration
of what happen'd within a dozen Yards compass.'[6] It is plausible.
But when his captors, officers with whom Ramkins and his family
were well acquainted, are not named; when, rather preremptorily,
he declares that the reader 'must be content to be inform'd in
General' about other battles in Ireland; and when, later, because
he suffers another wound Ramkins is unable to describe the battle
of Landen—then suspicion increases. But it rarely occurs during
the act of reading the book, only in retrospect. To account for
this is to go some way towards explaining Defoe's control over
his readers' responses.

Ramkins is presented as a man who learns from experience how
to cope with a variety of situations. He does not, like Boswell,
concern himself with 'the feelings of his heart'.[7] Only once does
he approach the introspective skill we associate with his fellow-
countryman: in his description of the delirium brought on by
drinking Loraine beer after being wounded in Flanders, a *tour de
force* Donald Stauffer considered 'similar to the justly famous
close of Lytton Strachey's *Queen Victoria*'.[8] For the most part
Ramkins is an objective narrator and fully the devoted professional soldier. When he visits Paris, his brother-in-law shows
him 'several of the Curiosities that City abounds with'; but
it is in character that he neither relishes nor records them: 'my
Thoughts being chiefly upon War, I digested other Matters as a
nice [i.e. fastidious] Appetite does improper Food.'[9] Later, when
he is curious to see Antwerp he tells us nothing of the city; his
account is wholly occupied with his meeting a footman mas-
querading as an English aristocrat. Ramkins is a soldier and

adventurer; his insights into the motives and behaviour of others
are more important to him than those into his own; and it is
appropriate that he should pay special regard to that 'natural
precept of *Self-preservation*'. He distrusts emotion and tries to
avoid sexual entanglements: 'I was always so bent upon War,
that I cou'd never find spare Hours for such trifling Conversation
. . . A general Whining and Pining away for a Trolloping Girl,
was to me a very awker'd and inconsistent Piece of Pageantry.'[10]
Language and attitude are here all of a piece and proper to the
soldierly character. When a Spanish girl traps him into an intrigue
Ramkins is in greater consternation than 'in all the Skirmishes and
Sieges [he] had been at.' He is confused, suffers jealousy and recovers as only a soldier developing into a philosophical lover—
and perhaps only with Defoe as narrator—could recover from an
emotional crisis: by spending his time 'in a Treatise of Algebra and
Fortifications'.[11] On this occasion he is frightened of marriage;
later he seeks it but, characteristically—'I took a Singular Care
when any Thing was offer'd that way, to consult my Reason
more than my Passions.'[12] He meets a French widow with 'a large
Pension'; she charms him, but he remains prudent: 'our whole
Discourse . . . ran upon Oeconomy and Morals.' It is fitting
that such a man should make an intelligent choice of a wife,
emerge safely from numerous campaigns, and wish to communicate his amatory as well as his political shrewdness.

We accept the *Memoirs* as authentic, then, because of the
fascination of the autobiographer; the circumstantial detail of
Ramkins's various adventures—with highwaymen as well as an
adventuress, as a military spy as well as an officer, or in the company of as well as the near victim of confidence-men; and because
of the narrator's style. Some examples of this last have already
shown Ramkins's use of military metaphors and language which
has the gruff elegance of an officer who left college at 17. Life had
provided his education; ' 'tis only Experience that can School a
Husband', he remarks on one occasion; and it is from that school
that his most vivid phrases take their origin. Louis XIV's treachery
did not merely affect him as an abstract idea—it 'lay upon my
Stomach like an indigested Meal'; his fear that he might stumble
into marrying his Spanish mistress was well grounded—'for a

keen Hound is not easily call'd off from a hot Scent, till he has either caught or lost his Game'; and the sight of starving mercenaries begging where they had previously marched as conquerors reminds him that 'the Rod is often thrown away and burnt after the Child is Whip'd.'[13] Many such phrases are reminiscent of proverbs; they embody the wisdom available to all men from shared experience. They have our immediate assent. Similarly the supposed narrator, more familiar with the sword than the pen, gains our sympathy by his ingenuousness: 'But to proceed to my own concerns'; 'But to return to the Series of my own Story'; or, 'I have often observ'd my self to sweat and fret my self . . .' This is indeed the language of a man who would regard his savings as his 'excellent Friend' and would frankly admit: 'though I have frequently hazarded my Life, I never risqu'd my Substance.'[14] It is—as Defoe rightly believed—the language of a man who appears trustworthy and is therefore persuasive.

Ten years after—as we believe—Defoe fabricated Ramkins's *Memoirs*, he published the *Memoirs of an English Officer . . . By Capt. George Carleton* (1728). The second is the superior work. Not only was Defoe free of the political purpose which motivated him in the first, he was also a vastly more experienced writer. The great creative period of *Robinson Crusoe*, *Moll Flanders*, *Colonel Jack*, and *Roxana* was behind him; and his acquaintance with the problems facing the biographer and 'ghost writer' was now remarkably extensive. Among many other pieces he had written *The King of Pirates*, *The History of Mr. Duncan Campbell*, *Memoirs of a Cavalier*, *Captain Singleton*, *The History of Peter the Great*, and the *Life and Actions of Jonathan Wild*. By 1728 Defoe had narrated the lives of men noble and ignoble, honest and criminal, historical and fictitious.

We do not yet know in which of the last two categories to place Ramkins; but about Carleton there is no doubt. He was an historical personage. We are also certain—after the brilliant detective work of the late Arthur W. Secord—that Defoe's book is not a genuine memoir of the real Carleton. Secord amply substantiates his conclusions:

> Though containing a great deal of fact, it is, in its larger aspects,
> entirely a fiction, to which Carleton contributed only the

title and the path of the action; that is to say, it records many
events of history with a fair degree of accuracy, but the
accounts of those events are not the genuine reminiscences of
any one's experiences. The statements of the narrative are
based upon materials gathered painstakingly from Abel
Boyer's *History of King William III* (1702–3) and *Life of her
late Majesty Queen Anne* (1721), John Freind's *Account of the
Earl of Peterboro's Conduct in Spain* (1707), the Comtesse
d'Aulnoy's *Ingenious and Diverting Letters* (1708), and the
London Gazette. The fictions are embroidered around facts
mentioned in these sources.[15]

To separate the facts from the fiction is not the concern of this
essay—the interested reader will find that done for him by
Secord; rather is it our purpose to assess the *Memoirs* and to identify
their distinctive features.

Of course Defoe intended that, while reading the *Memoirs*, his
audience should accept them as genuine. To achieve this he did
not rely only on the historical works listed above; as in the case of
Ramkins, he created a narrator whose veracity we do not question. Carleton often assures his readers of the accuracy, even the
uniqueness, of his information. We are, however, more inclined
to believe a man who, in addition to insisting on his own truth-
fulness, reveals his honesty in less calculated ways. This Defoe
allows Carleton to do. For example, after briefly describing an
incident during the siege of Barcelona when the son of 'an old
cavalier' was decapitated, the writer comments: ' 'Twas a sad
spectacle, and truly it affects me now whilst I am writing.' That
Defoe had used a similar comment in his *Journal of the Plague Year*
(1722)—'I remember, and while I am writing this story I think I
hear the very sound of it' [16]—does not derogate from his achieve-
ment; it shows that he knew the technique worked. Again,
Carleton remarks, 'A Captain of the *English* Guards (whose
Name has slip'd my memory, though I well knew the Man)'; or,
'I had almost forgot another very common piece of barbarous
Pleasure . . .':[17] these are authenticating features of style of
which Defoe was a master. They prove that, when writing, he
had assumed the personality of his own imaginative creation.
Yet literary manner alone is not enough to secure conviction.

The central figure must command our attention, his experiences engage our interest, and his values enlist our respect perhaps also our approval.

Carleton's reminiscences were intended for an intelligent and serious-minded audience: 'these Memoirs are not design'd for the Low Amuzement of a Tea-Table, but rather of the Cabinet'[18] [i.e. the study]. The writer had, then, to appear as a man who could discriminate between trivial matters and those of consequence, one who would recount only what would significantly extend his readers' experience. Carleton is a writer of this calibre. He does more than chronicle a series of military adventures; like a multitude of Englishmen from the seventeenth century onwards, he is one who 'as they say *viaggiono con profitto*';[19] and like Mrs. Piozzi who made this remark, Carleton wishes to help his readers also to 'travel for improvement'. Defoe certainly shared the view later expressed by Richard Hurd (in *On the Uses of Foreign Travel*), that by travelling abroad men are 'polished by degrees into general and universal humanity'; Carleton's *Memoirs* were intended to foster this kind of liberal education. Thus he does not merely describe; he communicates his responses to the 'rare and strange' in such a way as to provoke general speculation. His account of Aranjuez, the summer residence of Spanish kings, is a case in point. Having described the gardens and in particular the remarkable 'waterworks', he introduces the question of the relation between art and nature: 'Where art imitates Nature well, Philosophers hold it a Perfection; Then what must she exact of us, where we find her transcendent in the Perfections of Nature?'[20] As he continues the reader is invited to ponder this philosophical issue. And Carleton never misses an opportunity to introduce his audience to exotic sights, people or customs. These range from a bull-fight and the magnificent pageant to greet Charles III in Barcelona, to the 'clothing' of a Spanish nun and the nauseous habits of the Spanish peasantry. Defoe evidently had in mind the belief expressed in his *Compleat English Gentleman* (written in the same year as the publication of Carleton's *Memoirs*): that 'men exalted in their curious search after knowledge above the ordinary sort of people look into things as these.'

If he had not travell'd in his youth, has not made the grand tour of Italy and France, [the gentleman] may make the tour of the world in books. . . . He may travell by land with the historian, by sea with the navigators . . . He may know the strength of towns and cityes by the descripcions of those that have storm'd and taken them. . . . Nor are these studyes profitable onely and improving, but delightfull and pleasant too to the last degree. No romances, playes, or diverting storyes can be equally entertaining to a man of sence; nay, they make a man be a man of sence.[21]

More especially, we might add, if the guide is himself such a man.

Carleton undoubtedly shows himself 'a man of sence' as he recounts his multitudinous adventures during his travels from the Lowlands where he fought (1674–8) under the Prince of Orange, to England, Scotland and Ireland; and thence, when the War of the Spanish Succession began, to Spain in 1705. It is not only that he is manifestly a frank reporter and a man of initiative; or that he relishes moments of grim humour and unusual human beings (like the lecherous priest at La Mancha). These features do engage our interest in him; but, together with other qualities, they ensure our respect for and acceptance of his values. Carleton proves himself a courageous man; more than that he can identify the source of courage in other men. 'True Courage cannot proceed from what Sir *Walter Raleigh* finely calls *the Art* or *Philosophy of Quarrel*. No! It must be the Issue of Principle, and can have no other Basis than a steady Tenet of Religion.' We share his astonishment at the people of Brussels who, during the bombardment of their city, 'stood stareing, and with their Hands impocketted, beheld their Houses gradually consume.' Or we sympathise with his reaction to the havoc created by a plague of locusts: 'Nature seem'd buried in her own Ruins; and the vegetable World to be Supporters only to her Monument.'[22] Most importantly, we come to accept Carleton's exalted view of his hero, the Earl of Peterborough, and accede to the grounds on which the view is based. Thus the earl gains his (and our) approval for intelligence, shrewdness, courage and discretion, essential qualities in a great commander. As a man Peterborough possesses a generous, forbearing spirit, a congenial personality, and a strong sense of chivalry. There is little wonder that Dr. Johnson found the portrait enthralling. And, finally, Carleton's good sense and judgment are attested by his direct, lucid, unpretentious style. With the possible exception of a half-paragraph on the ruins of Saguntun and parts of the description of the idyllic site of the hermits' cells at Monserat, the narrator avoids all 'literary' heightening of expression. Rather he normally relies on vivid comparisons—a dragoon struck off an enemy's head 'as a Man would do that of a Poppy'; on si milesappropriate to his profession —the French tried to surround the English army 'as to the very Fashion of a Horse's Shoe'; on phrases which, proper to a man with an awareness of providence, have a slight biblical overtone— highlanders disappearing into the fog seem'd rather to be People receiv'd up into Clouds, than flying from an Enemy.'[23] Or, as in several earlier quotations, he uses language which may occasionally falter grammatically but rarely fails to achieve its purpose: honest, clear and vigorous communication. It is a style which provides a warranty for the writer's integrity.

When we turn to the *History of John Sheppard* (1724) we quit the world of men of honour like Ramkins and Carleton, and, as in some of Defoe's major novels, enter the world of crime. Both as an individual and as a writer alert to public taste, Defoe found the criminal of absorbing interest. He had been personally involved in subterfuge. In his early career as a merchant he appears to have been guilty of fraudulent practices; later he certainly acted as a secret agent of the Tory government—his letters to Robert Harley, his political overlord, reveal his use of aliases and an elementary cipher. Defoe was, then, admirably qualified to understand and feel the fascination of the criminal mind. He was, moreover, well aware of the ready sale there would be for a life of the notorious Sheppard. Sensational, often scandalous biographies marketed by unscrupulous publishers were assured of a quick financial return: Dr. Arbuthnot told Swift that the fear of being the subject of such a biography was 'one of the new terrors of death'. But biographical treatment was no longer reserved for the eminent; its original purpose—moral instruction—was being eroded; and the genre had become a rich source of entertainment and varied human interest. Offerings were various. In 1723 George

James published his *Lives and Amours of the Empresses*; in the same
year as *Sheppard* appeared Defoe produced volume I of *The
General History of the Pyrates*; or, in 1748, one could buy for a
shilling the anonymous *Unfortunate Concubines* which related the
'lives, remarkable actions and unhappy ends' of the mistresses of
Henry II and Edward IV. Indeed in 1750 one writer commented:
'The lowest and most contemptible . . . find historians to record
their praise, and readers to wonder at their exploits. Even the
prisons and stews are ransacked to find materials for novels and
romances.'[24] Defoe's *John Sheppard*, then, fits comfortably into a
tradition of which we have not seen the end.

'His History will astonish! . . . Incredible, and yet Uncontestable': Defoe's sensationalism has a crude, modern ring. His
purpose is clear: to capitalize on the public's excitement and indig-
nation as well as their covert admiration for the successful criminal.
Though he later wrote a *Narrative* after Sheppard's execution,
which purported to be written by the man himself 'during his
confinement', Defoe published this earlier pamphlet while his
readers' alarm at Sheppard's second escape from the condemned
cell was at its height. The earlier version has been printed here to
show how the journalist in Defoe exploited his opportunity.

Yet to insist overmuch on the pamphlet's monetary significance
to Defoe might lead one to underestimate his literary skill. His
forte was to supply circumstantial detail and so provide both
vitality and veracity; the account of Sheppard's escapades is no
exception. Defoe's knowledge of the facts themselves cannot be
questioned; innumerable details proclaim it. But he was not
content simply to give factual evidence. His own admiration for
Sheppard, which becomes increasingly clear, enables him to enter
imaginatively into the several situations; thus his account avoids
dead accuracy and takes on a vivid immediacy. The scene of one
burglary, for example, comes alive when we learn that the victim,
Mr. Barton, 'slept Sounder than usual that Night, as having come
from a Merry-making with some Friends'; another victim, the
drunk Mr. Pargiter, is individualised by a single detail—'having a
great Coat on'. On other occasions the reporter in Defoe com-
bines with the experienced novelist; his account of the public
reaction to Sheppard's recapture after his first escape is one

example. Given from the viewpoint of an informed observer it concentrates on the behaviour of artisans, the profit made by ballad-writers, and the general speculation about Sheppard's imminent execution. Only with the announcement that he would be re-tried did public impatience recede: 'People began to grow calm and easy and got *Shav'd*, and their Shoes *finish'd* . . .'[25] With remarkable verbal economy Defoe momentarily creates a scene of impressionistic vividness. The detailed description of Sheppard's second escape is preceded by the astonished reaction of the prison staff; as other officials and citizens visit the jail we become gradually aware of the incredulity of the whole community.

What Defoe admired in Sheppard is common to Ramkins and Carleton. Each 'hero' is a man of action who displays ingenuity, resourcefulness and a capacity born of earlier experience to adapt to new situations. They are men whose ability to survive is tested by the rigorous demands which Defoe personally knew life could make. His participation in their activities was thoroughly grounded on accurate information from reliable sources; but it was not circumscribed by it. Defoe was a skilful imaginative historian and from the evidence in this volume alone merits the term he applied to Sheppard—'a Proteous'. But in the last resort his success depends on his efficient, spontaneous and unpretentious style which enables him to report vividly or to develop a speaking voice appropriate to the supposed memoirist. Thus imaginative ability in Defoe combined with factual knowledge to produce that 'air of truth' and 'authenticity' to which Dr. Johnson unwittingly paid tribute.

JAMES T. BOULTON

THE
Military Memoirs
OF
Capt. *George Carleton*

THE

Military Memoirs

OF

Capt. *George* Carleton

FROM THE

Dutch War, 1672.

In which he Serv'd, to the

Conclusion of the Peace at

Utrecht, 1713.

Illustrating

Some of the most Remarkable Transactions, both by Sea and Land, during the Reigns of King *Charles* and King *James* II. hitherto unobserved by all the Writers of those times.

Together with

An exact Series of the War in *Spain*; and a particular Description of the several Places of the Author's Residence in many Cities, Towns, and Countries; their Customs, Manners, &c. Also Observations on the Genius of the *Spaniards* (among whom he continued some Years a Prisoner) their Monasteries and Nunneries (especially that fine one at *Montferat*) and on their publick Diversions; more particularly their famous Bull-Feasts.

LONDON, Printed for E. Symon, over against the Royal Exchange, *Cornhill*, MDCCXXVIII.

'TWAS MY FORTUNE, my Lord, in my juvenile Years, *Musas cum
Marte commutare,* and truly I have Reason to blush, when I consider the small Advantage I have reap'd from that Change. But
lest it should be imputed to my Want of Merit, I have wrote these
Memoirs, and leave the World to judge of my Deserts. They are
not set forth by any fictitious Stories, nor imbelished with rhetori-
cal Flourishes; plain Truth is certainly most becoming the
Character of an old Soldier. Yet let them be never so meritorious,
if not protected by some noble Patron, some Persons may think
them to be of no Value.

To you therefore, my Lord, I present them; to you, who have
so eminently distinguished your self, and whose Wisdom has
been so conspicuous to the late Representatives of *Great Britain,*
that each revolving Age will speak in your Praise; and if you
vouchsafe to be the *Mecænas* of these Memoirs, your Name will
give them sufficient Sanction.

An old Soldier I may truly call my self, and my Family allows
me the Title of a Gentleman; yet I have seen many Favourites of
Fortune, without being able to discern why they should be so
happy, and my self so unfortunate; but let not that discourage
your Lordship from receiving these my Memoirs into your
Patronage; for the Unhappy cannot expect Favour but from
those who are endued with generous Souls.

Give me Leave, my Lord, to congratulate this good Fortune,
that neither Whig nor Tory (in this complaining Age) have found
fault with your Conduct. Your Family has produced Heroes, in

defence of injured Kings; and you, when 'twas necessary, have as nobly adher'd to the Cause of Liberty.

My LORD,

Your Lordship's

Most obedient

And most devoted

Humble Servant,

G. CARLETON.

TO THE

READER

THE Author of these Memoirs began early to distinguish himself in martial Affairs, otherwise he could not have seen such Variety of Actions both by Sea and Land. After the last Dutch War he went into Flanders, where he not only serv'd under the Command of his Highness the Prince of Orange, whilst he was Generalissimo of the Dutch Forces, but likewise all the time he reign'd King of Great Britain. Most of the considerable Passages and Events, which happened during that time, are contained in the former Part of this Book.

In the Year 1705, the Regiment in which he serv'd as Captain was order'd to embark for the West Indies; and he, having no Inclination to go thither, chang'd with an half-pay Captain; and being recommended to the Earl of Peterborow by the late Lord Cutts, went with him upon that noble Expedition into Spain.

When the Forces under his Lordship's Command were landed near Barcelona, the Siege of that Place was thought by several impracticable, not only for want of experienc'd Engineers, but that the Besieged were as numerous as the Besiegers; yet the Courage of that brave Earl surmounted those Difficulties, and the Siege was resolv'd upon.

Our Author having obtain'd, by his long Service, some Knowledge of the practick Part of an Engineer, and seeing at that critical Time the great Want of such, readily acted as one, which gave him the greater Opportunity of being an Eye-Witness of his Lordship's Actions; and consequently made him capable of setting them forth in these his Memoirs.

It may not be perhaps improper to mention that the Author of these Memoirs was born at Ewelme in Oxfordshire, descended from an ancient and an honourable Family. The Lord Dudley Carleton, who died Secretary of State to King Charles I. was his Great Uncle; and in the same Reign his Father was Envoy at the Court of Madrid, whilst his Uncle, Sir Dudley Carleton, was Embassador to the States of Holland, Men in those Days respected both for their Abilities and Loyalty.

MEMOIRS
OF AN
English Officer, &c.

IN THE YEAR one Thousand six Hundred seventy two, War being proclaimed with *Holland*, it was looked upon among Nobility and Gentry, as a Blemish, not to attend the Duke of *York* aboard the Fleet, who was then declared Admiral. With many others, I, at that Time about twenty Years of Age, enter'd my self a Voluntier on board the *London*, commanded by Sir *Edward Sprage*, Vice-Admiral of the *Red*.

The Fleet set Sail from the *Buoy of the Nore* about the beginning of *May*, in order to join the *French* Fleet, then at Anchor in St. *Hellen's Road*, under the Command of the *Count de Estrée*. But in executing this Design we had a very narrow Escape: For *De Ruyter*, the Admiral of the *Dutch* Fleet, having Notice of our Intentions, waited to have intercepted us at the Mouth of the River, but by the Assistance of a great Fog we pass'd *Dover* before he was aware of it; and thus he miscarried, with the poor Advantage of taking only one small Tender.

A Day or two after the joining of the *English* and *French*, we sailed directly towards the *Dutch* Coast, where we soon got sight of their Fleet; a Sand called the *Galloper* lying between. The *Dutch* seem'd willing there to expect an Attack from us: But in regard the *Charles* Man of War had been lost on those Sands the War before; and that our Ships drawing more Water than those of the Enemy, an Engagement might be render'd very disadvantagious; it was resolv'd in a Council of War to avoid coming to a Battle for the present, and to sail directly for *Solebay*, which was accordingly put in Execution.

We had not been in *Solebay* above four or five Days, when *De Ruyter*, hearing of it, made his Signal for sailing in order to surprize us; and he had certainly had his Aim, had there been any Breeze of Wind to favour him. But though they made use of all their Sails, there was so little Air stirring, that we could see their Fleet making towards us long before they came up; notwithstanding which, our Admirals found difficulty enough to form their Ships into a Line of Battle, so as to be ready to receive the Enemy.

It was about Four in the Morning of the 28th of *May*, being *Tuesday* in *Whitson Week*, when we first made the Discovery; and about Eight the same Morning the Blue Squadron, under the Command of the Earl of *Sandwich*, began to engage with Admiral *Van Ghent*, who commanded the *Amsterdam* Squadron; and about Nine the whole Fleets were under a general Engagement. The Fight lasted till Ten at Night, and with equal Fury on all Sides, the *French* excepted, who appeared stationed there rather as Spectators than Parties; and as unwilling to be too much upon the Offensive, for fear of offending themselves.

During the Fight the *English* Admiral had two Ships disabled under him; and was obliged about Four in the Afternoon to remove himself a third Time into the *London*, where he remain'd all the rest of the Fight, and till next Morning. Nevertheless, on his Entrance upon the *London*, which was the Ship I was in, and on our Hoisting the Standard, *De Ruyter* and his Squadron seem'd to double their Fire upon her, as if they resolv'd to blow her out of the Water. Notwithstanding all which, the Duke of *York* remain'd all the time upon Quarter Deck, and as the Bullets plentifully whizz'd around him, would often rub his Hands, and cry, *Sprage, Sprage, they follow us still.* I am very sensible later Times have not been over favourable in their Sentiments of that unfortunate Prince's Valour, yet I cannot omit the doing a Piece of Justice to his Memory, in relating a Matter of Fact, of which my own Eyes were Witnesses, and saying, That if Intrepidity, and Undauntedness, may be reckon'd any Parts of Courage, no Man in the Fleet better deserv'd the Title of Couragious, or behav'd himself with more Gallantry than he did.

The *English* lost the *Royal James*, commanded by the Earl of *Sandwich*, which about Twelve (after the strenuous Endeavours of her Sailors to disengage her from two *Dutch* Fire Ships plac'd on her, one athwart her Hawsers, the other on her Star-board

Side) took Fire, blew up, and perish'd; and with her a great many brave Gentlemen, as well as Sailors; and amongst the rest the Earl himself, concerning whom I shall further add, that in my Passage from *Harwich* to the *Brill*, a Year or two after, the Master of the Pacquet Boat told me, That having observ'd a great Flock of Gulls hovering in one particular Part of the Sea, he order'd his Boat to make up to it; when discovering a Corpse, the Sailors would have return'd it to the Sea, as the Corpse of a *Dutch Man*; but keeping it in his Boat, it proved to be that of the Earl of *Sandwich*. There was found about him between twenty and thirty Guineas, some Silver, and his Gold Watch; restoring which to his Lady, she kept the Watch, but rewarded their Honesty with all the Gold and Silver.

This was the only Ship the *English* lost in this long Engagement. For although the *Katherine* was taken, and her Commander, Sir *John Chicheley*, made Prisoner, her Sailors soon after finding the Opportunity they had watch'd for, seiz'd all the *Dutch* Sailors, who had been put in upon them, and brought the Ship back to our own Fleet, together with all the *Dutch Men* Prisoners; for which, as they deserv'd, they were well rewarded. This is the same Ship which the Earl of *Mulgrave* (afterwards Duke of *Buckingham*) commanded the next Sea Fight, and has caus'd to be painted in his House in St. *James's Park*.

I must not omit one very remarkable Occurrence which happened in this Ship, There was a Gentleman aboard her, a Voluntier, of a very fine Estate, generally known by the Name of *Hodge Vaughan*. This Person receiv'd, in the beginning of the Fight, a considerable Wound, which the great Confusion, during the Battle, would not give them leave to inquire into; so he was carried out of the Way, and disposed of in the Hold. They had some Hogs aboard, which the Sailor, under whose Care they were, had neglected to feed; these Hogs, hungry as they were, found out, and fell upon the wounded Person, and between dead and alive eat him up to his very Scull, which, after the Fight was over, and the Ship retaken, as before, was all that could be found of him.

Another Thing, less to be accounted for, happen'd to a Gentleman Voluntier who was aboard the same Ship with my self. He was of known personal Courage, in the vulgar Notion of it, his Sword never having fail'd him in many private Duels. But notwithstanding all his Land-mettle, it was observ'd of him at Sea, that when ever the Bullets whizz'd over his Head, or any way incommoded his Ears, he immediately quitted the Deck, and ran down into the Hold. At first he was gently reproach'd; but after many Repetitions he was laugh'd at, and began to be despis'd; sensible of which, as a Testimonial of his Valour, he made it his Request to be ty'd to the Main Mast. But had it been granted him, I cannot see any Title he could have pleaded from hence, to true Magnanimity; since to be ty'd from running away can import nothing less, than that he would have still continued these Signs of Cowardice, if he had not been prevented. There is a Bravery of Mind which I fansy few of those Gentlemen Duellists are possess'd of. True Courage cannot proceed from what Sir *Walter Raleigh* finely calls *the Art* or *Philosophy of Quarrel*. No! It must be the Issue of Principle, and can have no other Basis than a steady Tenet of Religion. This will appear more plain, if those Artists in Murder will give themselves leave cooly to consider, and answer me this Question, Why he that had ran so many Risques at his Sword's Point, should be so shamefully intimidated at the Whiz of a Cannon Ball?

The Names of those English Gentlemen who lost their Lives, as I remember, in this Engagement.

Commissioner Cox, Captain of the *Royal Prince*, under the Command of the Admiral; and Mr. *Travanian*, Gentleman to the Duke of *York*; Mr. *Digby*, Captain of the *Henry*, second Son to the Earl of *Bristol*; Sir *Fletchvile Hollis*, Captain of the *Cambridge*, who lost one of his Arms in the War before, and his Life in this; Captain *Saddleton*, of the *Dartmouth*; the Lord *Maidstone*, Son to the Earl of *Winchelsea*, a Voluntier on board the *Charles*, commanded by Sir *John Harman*, Vice-Admiral of the Red.

Sir *Philip Carteret*, Mr. *Herbert*, Mr. *Cotterel*, Mr. *Peyton*, Mr. *Gose*, with several other Gentlemen unknown to me, lost their Lives with the Earl of *Sandwich*, on board the *Royal James*; Mr. *Vaughan*, on board the *Katherine*, commanded by Sir *John Chicheley*.

In this Engagement, Sir *George Rook* was youngest Lieutenant to Sir *Edward Sprage*; Mr. *Russel*, afterwards Earl of *Orford*, was Captain of a small Fifth Rate, called the *Phnix*; Mr. *Herbert*, afterwards Earl of *Torrington*, was Captain of a small Fourth Rate, called the *Monck*; Sir *Harry Dutton Colt*, who was on board the *Victory*, commanded by the Earl of *Offery*, is the only Man now living that I can remember was in this Engagement.

But to proceed, the *Dutch* had one Man of War sunk, though so near the Shore, that I saw some part of her Main Mast remain above Water, with their Admiral *Van Ghent*, who was slain in the close Engagement with the Earl of *Sandwich*. This Engagement lasted fourteen Hours, and was look'd upon the greatest that ever was fought between the *English* and the *Hollander*.

I cannot here omit one Thing, which to some may seem trifling; though I am apt to think our Naturalists may have a different Opinion of it, and find it afford their Fansies no un-diverting Employment in more curious, and less perilous Re-flections. We had on board the *London* where, as I have said, I was a Voluntier, a great Number of Pidgeons, of which our Commander was very fond. These, on the first firing of our Cannon, dispers'd, and flew away, and were seen no where near us during the Fight. The next Day it blew a brisk Gale, and drove our Fleet some Leagues to the Southward of the Place where they forsook our Ship, yet the Day after they all returned safe aboard; not in one Flock, but in small Parties of four or five at a Time. Some Persons at that Time aboard the Ship admiring at the Manner of their Return, and speaking of it with some Surprize, Sir *Edward Sprage* told them, That he brought those Pidgeons with him from the *Streights*; and that when, pursuant to his Order, he left the *Revenge* Man of War, to go aboard the *London*, all those Pidgeons, of their own accord, and without the Trouble or Care of carrying, left the *Revenge* likewise, and removed with the Sailors on board the *London*, where I saw them; All which many of the Sailors afterwards confirm'd to me. What Sort of Instinct this could proceed from, I leave to the Curious.

Soon after this Sea Engagement I left the Fleet. And the Parliament, the Winter following, manifesting their Resentments against two of the Plenipotentiaries, *viz*. *Buckingham* and *Arling-ton*, who had been sent over into *Holland*; and expressing, withal, their great Umbrage taken at the prodigious Progress of the *French* Arms in the *United Provinces*; and warmly remonstrating the inevitable Danger attending *England* in their Ruin. King *Charles* from all this, and for want of the expected Supplies, found himself under a Necessity of clapping up a speedy Peace with *Holland*.

This Peace leaving those youthful Spirits, that had by the late Naval War been rais'd into a generous Ferment, under a perfect Inactivity at Home; they found themselves, to avoid a Sort of Life that was their Aversion, oblig'd to look out for one more active, and more suitable to their vigorous Tempers Abroad.

I must acknowledge my self one of that Number; and therefore in the Year 1674, I resolv'd to go into *Flanders*, in order to serve as Voluntier in the Army commanded by his Highness the Prince of *Orange*. I took my Passage accordingly at *Dover* for *Calais*, and so went by way of *Dunkirk* for *Brussels*.

Arriving at which Place, I was inform'd that the Army of the Confederates lay encamp'd not far from *Nivelle*; and under the daily Expectation of an Engagement with the Enemy. This News made me press forward to the Service; for which Purpose I carry'd along with me proper Letters of Recommendation to Sir *Walter Vane*, who was at that time a Major-General. Upon further Enquiry I understood, that a Party of Horse, which was to guard some Waggons that were going to Count *Montery*'s Army, were to set out next Morning; so I got an *Irish* Priest to introduce me to the Commanding Officer, which he readily oblig'd me in; and they, as I wish'd them, arriv'd in the Camp next day.

I had scarce been there an Hour, when happen'd one of the most extraordinary Accidents in Life. I observ'd in the East a strange dusty colour'd Cloud, of a pretty large Extent, riding, not before the Wind (for it was a perfect Calm) with such a pre-cipitate Motion, that it was got over our Heads almost as soon as seen. When the Skirts of that Cloud began to cover our Camp, there suddenly arose such a terrible Hurricaine, or Whirlwind, that all the Tents were carry'd aloft with great Violence into the

Air; and Soldiers' Hats flew so high and thick, that my Fansy can resemble it to nothing better than those Flights of Rooks, which at Dusk of Evening, leaving the Fields, seek their roosting Places. Trees were torn up by the very Roots; and the Roofs of all the Barns, &c. belonging to the Prince's Quarters, were blown quite away. This lasted for about half an Hour, until the Cloud was wholly past over us, when as suddenly ensued the same pacifik Calm as before the Cloud's Approach. Its Course was seemingly directly West; and yet we were soon after inform'd, that the fine Dome of the great Church at *Utrecht* had greatly suffer'd by it the same Day. And, if I am not must mistaken, Sir *William Temple*, in his Memoirs, mentions somewhat of it, which he felt at *Lillo*, on his Return from the Prince of *Orange's* Camp, where he had been a Day or two before.

As soon after this, as I could get an Opporunity, I deliver'd, at his Quarters, my recommendatory Letters to Sir *Walter Vane*; who receiv'd me very kindly, telling me at the same time, that there were six or seven *English* Gentlemen, who had enter'd themselves Voluntiers in the Prince's own Company of Guards: And added, that he would immediately recommend me to Count *Solmes*, their Colonel. He was not worse than his Word, and I was enter'd accordingly. Those six Gentlemen were as follows, —— *Clavers*, who since was better known by the Title of Lord *Dundee*; Mr. *Collier*, now Lord *Portmore*; Mr. *Rooke*, since Major-General; Mr. *Hales*, who lately died, and was for a long time Governor of *Chelsea-Hospital*; Mr. *Venner*, Son of that *Venner* remarkable for his being one of the Fifth-Monarchy Men; and Mr. *Boyce*. The four first rose to be very eminent; but Fortune is not to all alike favourable.

In about a Week's Time after, it was resolv'd in a Council of War, to march towards *Binch*, a small wall'd Town, about four Leagues from *Nivelle*; the better to cut off the Provisions from coming to the Prince of *Condé's* Camp that Way.

Accordingly, on the first Day of *August*, being *Saturday*, we began our March; and the *English* Voluntiers had the Favour of a Baggage Waggon appointed them. Count *Souches*, the Imperial General, with the Troops of that Nation, led the Van; the main Body was compos'd of *Dutch*, under the Prince of *Orange*.

as Generalissimo; and the *Spaniards*, under Prince *Vaudemont*, with some Detachments, made the Rear Guard.

As we were upon our March, I being among those Detachments which made up the Rear Guard, observ'd a great Party of the Enemy's Horse upon an Ascent, which, I then imagin'd, as it after prov'd, to be the Prince of *Condé* taking a View of our Forces under March. There were many Defiles, which our Army must necessarily pass; through which that Prince politickly enough permitted the *Imperial* and *Dutch* Forces to pass unmolested. But when Prince *Vaudemont*, with the *Spaniards*, and our Detachments, thought to have done the like, the Prince of *Condé* fell on our Rear Guard; and, after a long and sharp Dispute, entirely routed 'em; the Marquiss of *Assentar*, a *Spanish* Lieutenant-General, dying upon the spot.

Had the Prince of *Condé* contented himself with this Share of good Fortune, his Victory had been uncontested: But being pushed forward by a vehement Heat of Temper (which he was noted for) and flush'd with this extraordinary Success, he resolv'd to force the whole Confederate Army to a Battle. In order to which, he immediately led his Forces between our Second Line, and our Line of Baggage; by which means the latter were entirely cut off; and were subjected to the Will of the Enemy, who fell directly to plunder; in which they were not a little assisted by the routed *Spaniards* themselves, who did not disdain at that time to share with the Enemy in the plundering of their Friends and Allies.

The *English* Voluntiers had their Share of this ill Fortune with the rest; their Waggon appointed them being among those intercepted by the Enemy; and I, for my Part, lost every Thing but Life, which yet was saved almost as unaccountably as my Fellow-Soldiers had lost theirs. The Baggage, as I have said, being cut off, and at the Mercy of the Enemy, every one endeavour'd to escape through, or over the Hedges. And as in all Cases of like Confusion, one endeavours to save himself upon the Ruins of others: So here, he that found himself stopt by another in getting over the Cap of a Hedge, pull'd him back to make way for himself, and perhaps met with the same Fortune from a Third, to the Destruction of all. I was then in the Vigour of my Youth, and none of the least active, and perceiving how it had far'd with some before me, I clapt my left Leg upon the Shoulders of one who was thus contending with another, and with a Spring threw my self over both their Heads and the Hedge at the same time. By this Means I not only sav'd my Life (for they were all cut to Pieces that could not get over) but from an Eminence, which I soon after attain'd, I had an Opportunity of seeing, and making my Observations upon the remaining Part of that glorious Conflict.

It was from that advantagious Situation, that I presently discover'd that the Imperialists, who led the Van, had now join'd the main Body. And, I confess, it was with an almost inexpressible Pleasure, that I beheld, about three a-Clock, with what intrepid Fury they fell upon the Enemy. In short, both Armies were universally engag'd, and with great Obstinacy disputed the Victory till Eleven at Night. At which Time the *French*, being pretty well surfeited, made their Retreat. Nevertheless, to secure it by a Stratagem, they left their lighted Matches hanging in the Hedges, and waving with the Air, to conceal it from the Confederate Army.

About two Hours after, the Confederate Forces follow'd the Example of their Enemies, and drew off. And tho' neither Army had much Reason to boast; yet as the Prince of *Orange* remained last in the Field; and the *French* had lost what they before had gain'd, the Glory of the Day fell to the Prince of *Orange*; who, altho' but twenty-four Years of Age, had the Suffrage of Friend and Foe, of having play'd the Part of an old and experienc'd Officer.

There were left that Day on the Field of Battle, by a general Computation, not less than eighteen Thousand Men on both Sides, over and above those, who died of their Wounds: The Loss being pretty equal, only the *French* carried off most Prisoners. Prince *Waldeck* was shot through the Arm, which I was near enough to be an Eye-witness of; And my much lamented Friend, Sir *Walter Vane*, was carried off dead. A Wound in the Arm was all the Mark of Honour, that I as yet could boast of, though our Cannon in the Defiles had slain many near me.

The Prince of *Condé* (as we were next Day inform'd) lay all that Night under a Hedge, wrapp'd in his Cloke: And either from the

Mortification of being disappointed in his Hopes of Victory; or
from a Reflection of the Disservice, which is own natural over
Heat of Temper had drawn upon him, was almost inconsolable
many Days after. And thus ended the famous Battle of *Seneff*.

But though common Vogue has given it the Name of a Battle,
in my weak Opinion, it might rather deserve that of a confus'd
Skirmish; all Things having been forcibly carried on without
Regularity, or even Design enough to allow it any higher Denomination: For, as I have said before, notwithstanding I was
advantagiously stationed for Observation, I found it very often
impossible to distinguish one Party from another. And this was
more remarkably evident on the Part of the Prince of *Orange*,
whose Valour and Vigour having led him into the Middle of
the Enemy, and being then sensible of his Error, by a peculiar
Presence of Mind, gave the Word of Command in *French*,
which he spoke perfectly well. But the *French* Soldiers, who
took him for one of their own Generals, making Answer, that
their Powder was all spent, it afforded Matter of Instruction to
him to persist in his Attack; at the same Time, that it gave him a
Lesson of Caution, to withdraw himself, as soon as he could, to
his own Troops.

However, the Day after the Prince of *Orange* thought proper
to march to *Quarignan*, a Village within a League of *Mons*; where
he remain'd some Days, till he could be supply'd from *Brussells*
with those Necessaries which his Army stood in need of.

From thence we march'd to *Valenciennes*, where we again
encamp'd, till we could receive Things proper for a Siege. Upon
the Arrival whereof, the Prince gave Orders to decamp, and
march'd his Army with a Design to besiege *Aeth*. But having
Intelligence on our March, that the Mareschal *De Humiers* had
reinforc'd that Garrison, we march'd directly to *Oudenard*, and
immediately invested it.

This Siege was carried on with such Application and Success,
that the Besiegers were in a few Days ready for a Storm; but the
Prince of *Condé* prevented them, by coming up to its Relief.
Upon which the Prince of *Orange*, pursuant to the Resolution of a
Council of War the Night before, drew off his Forces in order to
give him Battle; and to that purpose, after the laborious Work

of filling up our Lines of Contravallation, that the Horse might pass more freely, we lay upon our Arms all Night. Next Morning we expected the Imperial General, Count *Souches*, to join us; but instead of that, he sent back some very frivolous Excuses, of the Inconveniency of the Ground for a Battle; and after that, instead of joining the Prince, marched off quite another way; the Prince of *Orange*, with the *Dutch* and *Spanish* Troops, marched directly for *Ghent*; exclaiming publickly against the Chicanery of *Souches*, and openly declaring, That he had been advertis'd of a Conference between a *French* Capuchin and that General, the Night before. Certain it is, that that General lay under the Displeasure of his Master, the Emperor, for that Piece of Management; and the Count *de Sporck* was immediately appointed General in his Place.

The Prince of *Orange* was hereupon leaving the Army in great Disgust, till prevail'd upon by the Count *de Montery*, for the general Safety, to recede from that Resolution. However, seeing no likelihood of any Thing further to be done, while *Souches* was in Command, he resolv'd upon a Post of more Action, though more dangerous; wherefore ordering ten Thousand Men to march before, he himself soon after follow'd to the Siege of *Grave*.

The *Grave*, a strong Place, and of the first Moment to the *Hollanders*, had been block'd up by the *Dutch* Forces all the Summer; the Prince of *Orange* therefore leaving the main Army under Prince *Waldeck* at *Ghent*, follow'd the Detachment he had made for the Siege of that important Place, resolving to purchase it at any Rate. On his Arrival before it, Things began to find new Motion; and as they were carried on with the utmost Application and Fury, the Besieged found themselves, in a little Time, oblig'd to change their haughty Summer Note for one more suitable to the Season.

The Prince, from his first coming, having kept those within hotly ply'd with Ball, both from Cannon and Mortars, Monsieur *Chamilly*, the Governor, after a few Days, being weary of such warm Work, desired to capitulate; upon which Hostages were exchanged, and Articles agreed on next Morning. Pursuant to which, the Garrison march'd out with Drums beating and

Colours flying, two Days after, and were conducted to *Charleroy*.

By the taking this Place, which made the Prince of *Orange* the more earnest upon it, the *French* were wholly expell'd their last Year's astonishing Conquests in *Holland*. And yet there was another Consideration, that render'd the Surrender of it much more considerable. For the *French* being sensible of the great Strength of this Place, had there deposited all their Cannon and Ammunition, taken from their other Conquests in *Holland*, which they never were able to remove or carry off, with tolerable Prospect of Safety, after that Prince's Army first took the Field.

The Enemy being march'd out, the Prince enter'd the Town, and immediately order'd public Thanksgivings for its happy Reduction. Then having appointed a Governor, and left a sufficient Garrison, he put an End to that Campaign, and return'd to the *Hague*, where he had not been long before he fell ill of the Small Pox. The Consternation this threw the whole Country into, is not to be express'd; Any one that had seen it would have thought, that the *French* had made another Inundation greater than the former. But when the Danger was over, their Joy and Satisfaction, for his Recovery, was equally beyond Expression.

The Year 1675 yielded very little remarkable in our Army. *Limburgh* was besieged by the *French*, under the Command of the Duke of *Enguien*, which the Prince of *Orange* having Intelligence of, immediately decamp'd from his fine Camp at *Bethlem*, near *Louvain*, in order to raise the Siege. But as we were on a full March for that purpose, and had already reach'd *Ruremond*, Word was brought, that the Place had surrender'd the Day before. Upon which Advice, the Prince, after a short Halt, made his little Army (for it consisted not of more than thirty Thousand Men) march back to *Brabant*. Nothing of moment, after this, occurr'd all that Campaign.

In the Year 1676, the Prince of *Orange* having, in concert with the *Spaniards*, resolv'd upon the important Siege of *Maestrich* (the only Town in the *Dutch* Provinces, then remaining in the Hands of the *French*) it was accordingly invested about the middle of *June*, with an Army of twenty Thousand Men, under the Command of his Highness Prince *Waldeck*, with the grand Army covering the Siege. It was some Time before the heavy Cannon, which we expected up the *Maes*, from *Holland*, arrived; which gave Occasion to a Piece of Raillery of Monsieur *Calvo*, the Governor, which was as handsomely repartee'd. That Governor, by a Messenger, intimating his Sorrow to find, we had pawn'd our Cannon for Ammunition Bread. Answer was made, That in a few Days we hoped to give him a Taste of the Loaves, which he should find would be sent him into the Town in extraordinary plenty. I remember another Piece of Raillery, which pass'd some Days after between the *Rhingrave* and the same *Calvo*. The former sending Word, that he hoped within three Weeks to salute that Governor's Mistress within the Place. *Calvo* reply'd, He'd give him leave to kiss her all over, if he kiss'd her any where in three Months.

But our long expected Artillery being at last arriv'd, all this Jest and Merriment was soon converted into earnest. Our Trenches were immediately open'd towards the *Dauphin* Bastion, against which were planted many Cannon, in order to make a Breach; my self as a Probationer being twice put upon the forlorn Hope to facilitate that difficult Piece of Service. Nor was it long before such a Breach was effected, as was esteem'd practicable, and therefore very soon after it was ordered to be attack'd.

The Disposition for the Attack was thus ordered; two Serjeants with twenty Grenadiers, a Captain with fifty Men, my self one of the Number; then a Party carrying Wool Sacks, and after them two Captains with one Hundred Men more; the Soldiers in the Trenches to be ready to sustain them, as Occasion should require.

The Signal being given, we left our Trenches accordingly, having about one Hundred Yards to run, before we could reach the Breach, which we mounted with some Difficulty and Loss; all our Batteries firing at the same instant to keep our Action in countenance, and favour our Design. When we were in Possession of the Bastion, the Enemy fir'd most furiously upon us with their small Cannon through a thin brick Wall, by which, and their hand Grenadoes, we lost more Men than we did in the Attack it self.

But well had it been had our ill Fortune stopp'd there; for as if Disaster must needs be the Concomitant of Success, we soon lost

2*

what we had thus gotten, by a small, but very odd Accident. Not being furnished with such Scoopes as our Enemies made use of, in tossing their hand Grenadoes some distance off, one of our own Soldiers aiming to throw one over the Wall into the Counterscarp among the Enemy, it so happen'd that he unfortunately miss'd his Aim, and the Grenade fell down again on our side the Wall, very near the Person who fir'd it. He starting back to save himself, and some others who saw it fall, doing the like, those who knew nothing of the Matter fell into a sudden Confusion, and imagining some greater danger than there really was, every body was struck with a panick Fear, and endeavour'd to be the first who should quit the Bastion, and secure himself by a real Shame from an imaginary Evil. Thus was a Bastion, that had been gloriously gain'd, inadvertently deserted; and that too, with the Loss of almost as many Men in the Retreat, as had been slain in the Onset, and the Enemy most triumphantly again took Possession of it.

Among the Slain on our Side in this Action, was an Ensign of Sir *John Fenwick*'s Regiment; and as an Approbation of my Services his Commission was bestowed upon me.

A few Days after it was resolv'd again to storm that Bastion, as before; out of three *English*, and one *Scotch* Regiment, then in the Camp, a Detachment was selected for a fresh Attack. Those Regiments were under the Command of Sir *John Fenwick* (who was afterwards beheaded) Colonel *Ralph Widdrington*, and Colonel *Ashley*, of the *English*; and Sir *Alexander Collier*, Father of the present Lord *Portmore*, of the *Scotch*. Out of every of these four Regiments, as before, were detach'd a Captain, a Lieutenant, and an Ensign, with fifty Men: Captain *Anthony Barnwell*, of Sir *John Fenwick*'s Regiment, who was now my Captain, commanding that Attack.

At break of Day the Attack was begun with great Resolution; and though vigorously maintain'd, was attended with the desir'd Success. The Bastion was again taken, and in it the commanding Officer, who in Service to himself, more than to us, told us, that the Center of the Bastion would soon be blown up being to his Knowledge undermin'd for that purpose. But this Secret prov'd of no other use, than to make us, by way of Precaution, to keep as much as we could upon the Rampart. In this Attack Captain *Barnwell* lost his Life; and it happened my new Commission was wetted (not, as too frequently is the Custom, with a Debauch) but with a Bullet through my Hand, and the Breach of my Collar Bone with the Stroke of a Halberd.

After about half an hour's Possession of the Bastion, the Mine under it, of which the *French* Officer gave us warning, was sprung; the Enemy at the same Time making a furious Sally upon us. The Mine did a little, though the less, Execution, for being discovered; but the Sally no way answer'd their End, for we beat them back, and immediately fix'd our Lodgment; which we maintain'd during the Time of the Siege. But to our double Surprize, a few Days after they fir'd another Mine under, or aside, the former, in which they had plac'd a quantity of Grena-does, which did much more Execution than the other: Notwith-standing all which, a Battery of Guns was presently erected upon that Bastion, which very considerably annoy'd the Enemy.

The Breach for a general Storm was now render'd almost practicable; yet before that could be advisably attempted, there was a strong Horn-work to be taken. Upon this Exploit the *Dutch* Troops only were to signalize themselves; and they an-swered the Confidence repos'd in them; for though they were twice repuls'd, at the third Onset they were more successful, and took Possession; which they likewise kept to the Raising of the Siege.

There was a Stratagem lay'd at this Time, which in its own Merit one would have thought should not have fail'd of a good Effect; but to shew the Vanity of the highest human Wisdom it miscarry'd. On the other side of the *Maes*, opposite to *Maestrich*, lies the strong Fortress of *Wyck*, to which it is join'd by a stone Bridge of six fair Arches. The design was, by a false Attack on that regular Fortification to draw the Strength of the Garrison to its Defence, which was but very natural to imagine would be the Consequence. Ready to attend that well concerted false Attack, a large flat bottom'd Boat, properly furnish'd with Barrels of Gun-Powder, and other Necessaries, was to fall down under one of the middle Arches, and when fix'd there, by firing the Powder to have blown up the Bridge, and by that means to have prevented the Return of the Garrison to oppose a real Attack at that instant of Time to be made upon the Town of *Maestrich* by the whole Army.

The false Attack on *Wyck* was accordingly made, which, as propos'd, drew the Main of the Garrison of *Maestrich* to its Defence, and the Boat so furnish'd fell down the River as projected, but unfortunately, before it could reach the Arch, from the Darkness of the Night, running upon a Shoal, it could not be got off; for which Reason the Men in the Boat were glad to make a hasty Escape for fear of being discovered; as the Boat was, next Morning; and the whole Design laid open.

This Stratagem thus miscarrying, all Things were immediately got ready for a general Storm, at the main Breach in the Town; and the rather, because the Prince of *Orange* had receiv'd incontestable Intelligence, That Duke *Schomberg*, at the Head of the *French* Army, was in full march to relieve the Place. But before every Thing could be rightly got ready for the intended Storm (though some there were who pretended to say, that a Dispute rais'd by the *Spaniards* with the *Dutch*, about the Propriety of the Town, when taken, was the Cause of that Delay) we heard at some distance several Guns fir'd as Signals of Relief; upon which we precipitately, and, as most imagin'd, shamefully drew off from before the Place, and join'd the grand Army under Prince *Waldeck*. But it was Matter of yet greater Surprize to most on the Spot, that when the Armies were so joyn'd, we did not stay to offer the Enemy Battle. The well known Courage of the Prince, then Generalissimo, was so far from solving this Riddle, that it rather puzzled all who thought of it; however, the prevailing Opinion was, that it was occasion'd by some great Misunderstanding between the *Spaniards* and the *Dutch*. And Experience will evince, that this was not the only Disappointment of that Nature, occasion'd by imperfect Understandings.

Besides the Number of common Soldiers slain in this Attack, which was not inconsiderable, we lost here the brave *Rhingrave*, a Person much lamented on account of his many other excellent Qualifications, as well as that of a General. Colonel *Ralph Widdrington*, and Colonel *Doleman* (who had not enjoy'd *Widdrington's* Commission above a Fortnight). Captain *Douglas*, Captain

Barnwell, and Captain *Lee*, were of the Slain among the *English*; who, indeed, had born the whole brunt of the Attack upon the *Dauphin*'s Bastion.

I remember the Prince of *Orange*, during the Siege, receiv'd a Shot through his Arm; which giving an immediate Alarm to the Troops under his Command, he took his Hat off his Head with the wounded Arm, and smiling, wav'd it, to shew them there was no danger. Thus, after the most gallant Defence against the most couragious Onsets, ended the Siege of *Maestrich*; and with it all that was material that Campaign.

Early in the Spring, in the Year 1677, the *French* Army, under the Duke of *Orleans*, besieged at once, both *Cambray* and *Saint Omers*. This last the Prince of *Orange* seem'd very intent and resolute to relieve. In order to which, well knowing by sad Experience, it would be to little purpose to wait the majestick Motions of the *Spaniards*, that Prince got together what Forces he could, all in *Dutch* Pay, and marching forward with all speed, resolv'd, even at the Hazard of a Battle, to attempt the Raising the Siege. Upon his appearing the Duke of *Orleans*, to whose particular Conduct the Care of that Siege was committed, drew off from before the Place, leaving scarce enough of his Men to defend the Trenches. The Prince was under the Necessity of marching his Forces over a Morass; and the Duke, well knowing it, took care to attack him near *Mont Cassel*, before half his little Army were got over. The Dispute was very sharp, but the Prince being much out number'd, and his Troops not able, by the Straitness of the Passage, to engage all at once, was oblig'd at last to retreat, which he did in pretty good Order. I remember the *Dutch* Troops did not all alike do their Duty; and the Prince seeing one of the Officers on his fullest speed, call'd to him over and over to halt; which the Officer in too must haste to obey, the Prince gave him a Slash over the Face, saying, *By this Mark I shall know you another Time*. Soon after this Retreat of the Prince, Saint *Omers* was surrender'd.

Upon this Retreat the Prince marching back, lay for some time among the Boors, who from the good Discipline, which he took care to make his Troops observe, did not give us their customary boorish Reception. And yet as secure as we might think our selves, I met with a little Passage that confirm'd in me the Notions, which the generality as well as I, had imbib'd of the private Barbarity of those People, whenever an Opportunity falls in their Way. I was stroling at a Distance from my Quarters, all alone, when I found my self near one of their Houses; into which, the Doors being open, I ventur'd to enter. I saw no body when I came in, though the House was, for that Sort of People, well enough furnish'd, and in pretty decent Order. I call'd, but no body answering, I had the Curiosity to advance a little farther, when, at the Mouth of the Oven, which had not yet wholly lost its Heat, I spy'd the Corpse of a Man so bloated, swoln and parch'd, as left me little room to doubt, that the Oven had been the Scene of his Destiny. I confess the Sight struck me with Horror; and as much Courage and Security as I enter'd with, I withdrew in haste, and with quite different Sentiments, and could not fansy my self out of Danger till I had reach'd our Camp. A wise Man should not frame an Accusation on Conjectures; but, on Inquiry, I was soon made sensible, that such barbarous Usage is too common among those People; especially if they meet with a Straggler, of what Nation soever.

This made me not very sorry when we decamp'd, and we soon after receiv'd Orders to march and invest *Charleroy*; before which Place we stay'd somewhat above a Week, and then drew off. I remember very well, that I was not the only Person then in the Camp that was at a Loss to dive into the Reason of this Investiture and Decampment: But since I at that time, among the Politicians of the Army, never heard a good one, I shall not venture to offer my Sentiments at so great a Distance.

We, after this march'd towards *Mons*; and, in our March, pass'd over the very Grounds on which the Battle of *Seneff* had been fought three Years before. It was with no little Pleasure, that I re-survey'd a Place, that had once been of so much Danger to me; and where my Memory and Fansy now repeated back all those Observations I had then made under some unavoidable Confusion. Young as I was, both in Years and Experience, from my own Reflections, and the Sentiments of others, after the Fight was over, methought I saw visibly before me the well order'd Disposition of the Prince of *Condé*; the inexpressible

Difficulties which the Prince of *Orange* had to encounter with; while at the same Moment I could not omit to repay my Debt to the Memory of my first Patron, Sir *Walter Vane*, who there loosing his Life, left me a solitary Wanderer to the wide World of Fortune.

But these Thoughts soon gave place to new Objects, which every Hour presented themselves in our continu'd March to *Enghien*, a Place famous for the finest Gardens in all *Flanders*, near which we encamp'd, on the very same Ground which the *French* chose some Years after at the Battle of *Steenkirk*: of which I shall speak in its proper Place. Here the Prince of *Orange* left our Army, as we afterwards found, to pass into *England*; where he marry'd the Princess *Mary*, Daughter of the Duke of *York*. And after his Departure, that Campaign ended without any thing further material.

Now began the Year 1678, famous for the Peace, and no less remarkable for an Action previous to it, which has not fail'd to employ the Talents of Men, variously, as they stood affected. Our Army, under the Prince of *Orange*, lay encamp'd at *Soignies*, where it was whisper'd that the Peace was concluded. Notwithstanding which, two Days after, being *Sunday* the 17th Day of *August*, the Army was drawn out, as most others as well as my self apprehended, in order to a *feux de Joye*; but in lieu of that, we found our March order'd towards St. *Dennis*, where the Duke of *Luxembourg* lay, as he imagin'd, safe in inaccessible Entrenchments.

About three of the Clock our Army arriv'd there, when we receiv'd Orders to make the Attack. It began with a most vigorous Spirit, that promis'd no less than the Success which ensu'd. The three *English* and three *Scotch* Regiments, under the Command of the ever renown'd Earl of *Ossory*, together with the Prince of *Orange*'s Guards, made their Attack at a Place call'd the *Château*; where the *French* took their Refuge among a Parcel of Hop-Poles; but their Resource was as weak as their Defence; and they were soon beaten out with a very great Slaughter.

It was here that a *French* Officer having his Pistol directed at the Breast of the Prince, Monsieur *D'Auverquerque* interpos'd, and shot the Officer dead upon the Spot.

The Fight lasted from three in the Afternoon till Nine at Night; when growing dark, the Duke of *Luxembourg* forsook his Entrenchments, into which we march'd next Morning. And to see the sudden Change of Things! that very Spot of Ground, where nothing but Fire and Fury appear'd the Day before, the yest saw solac'd with the Proclamation of a Peace.

About an Hour before the Attack began, the Duke of *Monmouth* arriv'd in the Army, being kindly receiv'd by the Prince of *Orange*, bravely fighting by his Side, all that Day. The Woods and the Unevenness of the Ground, render'd the Cavalry almost useless; yet I saw a Standard, among some others, which was taken from the Enemy, being richly embroidered with Gold and Silver, bearing the Sun in the Zodiack, with these haughty Words, *Nihil obstabit eunte*. On the News of this unexpected Victory, the States of *Holland* sent to congratulate the Prince; and to testify how much they valued his Preservation, they presented Monsieur *D'Auverquerque*, who had so bravely rescued him, with a Sword, whose Handle was of massy Gold set with Diamonds. I forgot to mention that this Gentleman receiv'd a Shot on his Head at the Battle of *Seneff*; and truly in all Actions, which were many, he nobly distinguished himself by his Bravery. He was Father of this present Earl of *Grantham*.

The Names of the English Officers which I knew to be killed in this Action.

Lieut. Col. Archer,	Capt. Pemfield,
Capt. Charleton,	Lieut. Charleton,
Capt. Richardson,	Lieut. Barton,
Capt. Fisher,	Ensign Colville.

With several others, whose Names I have forgot.

Lieut. Col. *Babington*, who began the Attack, by beating the *French* out of the Hop Garden, was taken Prisoner. Col. *Hales*, who was a long time Governor of *Chelsea College*, being then a Captain, received a Shot on his Leg, of which he went lame to his dying Day.

The War thus ended by the Peace of *Nimeugen*, The Regiment

in which I serv'd, was appointed to lie in Garrison at the *Grave*. We lay there near four Years, our Soldiers being mostly employ'd about the Fortifications. It was here, and by that Means, that I imbib'd the Rudiments of Fortification, and the practick Part of an Enginier, which in my more advanc'd Years was of no small Service to me.

Nevertheless, in the Year 1684, our Regiment receiv'd Orders to march to *Haren*, near *Brussels*, where, with other Forces, we encamp'd, till we heard that *Luxemburg*, invaded by the *French*, in a Time of the profoundest Peace, had surrender'd to them. Then we decamp'd, and march'd to *Mechlin*; where we lay in the Field till near *November*. Not that there was any War proclaim'd; but as not knowing, whether those who had committed such Acts of Hostility in time of Peace might not take it in their Heads to proceed yet further. In *November* we march'd into that Town, where Count *Nivelle* was Governor: The Marquiss *de Grana*, at the same time, governing the *Netherlands* in the Jurisdiction of *Spain*.

Nothing of any Moment happen'd after this, till the Death of King *Charles* II. The Summer after which, the three *English* and three *Scotch* Regiments receiv'd Orders to pass over into *England*, upon the Occasion of *Monmouth*'s Rebellion; where, upon our Arrival, we receiv'd Orders to encamp on *Hounslow-Heath*. But that Rebellion being soon stifled, and King *James* having no farther Need of us, those Regiments were order'd to return again to *Holland*, into the proper Service of those who paid them.

Tho' I am no stiff Adherer to the Doctrine of Predestination, yet to the full Assurance of a Providence I never could fail to adhere. Thence came it, that my natural Desire to serve my own native Country prevail'd upon me to quit the Service of another, though its Neighbour and Allie. Events are not always to direct the Judgment; and therefore whether I did best in following those fondling Dictates of Nature, I shall neither question nor determine.

However, it was not long after my Arrival in *England* before I had a Commission given me by King *James*, to be a Lieutenant in a new rais'd Regiment under the Command of Colonel *Tufton*, Brother to the Earl of *Thanet*. Under this Commission I sojourn'd out two peaceable Campaigns on *Hounslow-Heath*; where I was an Eye-Witness of one mock Siege of *Buda*: After which our Regiment was order'd to *Berwick*, where I remained till the Revolution.

King *James* having abdicated the Throne, and the Prince of *Orange* accepting the Administration, all Commissions were order'd to be renew'd in his Name. The Officers of our Regiment, as well as others, severally took out theirs accordingly, a very few excepted, of which Number was our Colonel; who refusing a Compliance, his Commission was given to Sir *James Lesley*.

The Prince of *Orange* presently after was declar'd and proclaim'd King, and his Princess Queen, with a conjunctive Power. Upon which our Regiment was order'd into *Scotland*, where Affairs appear'd under a Face of Disquietude. We had our Quarters at *Leith*, till the Time the Castle of *Edinburgh*, then under the Command of the Duke of *Gordon*, had surrender'd. After which, pursuant to fresh Orders, we march'd to *Inverness*, a Place of no great Strength, and as little Beauty; though yet I think I may say, without the least Danger of an *Hyperbole*, that it is as pleasant as most Places in that Country. Here we lay two long Winters, perpetually harrass'd upon Parties, and hunting of somewhat wilder than their wildest Game, namely, the *Highlanders*, who were, if not as nimble footed, yet fully as hard to be found.

But General *Mackay* having receiv'd Orders to build a Fort at *Inverlochy*, our Regiment, among others, was commanded to that Service. The two Regiments appointed on the same Duty, with some few Dragoons, were already on their March, which having join'd, we march'd together through *Louquebar*. This sure is the wildest Country in the *Highlands*, if not in the World. I did not see one House in all our March; and their Oeconomy, if I may call it such, is much the same with that of the *Arabs* or *Tartars*. Hutts, or Cabins of Trees and Trash, are their Places of Habitation; in which they dwell, till their half-horn'd Cattle have devour'd the Grass, and then remove, staying no where longer than that Convenience invites them.

In this March, or rather, if you please, most dismal Peregrination, we could be very rarely go two on a Breast; and oftner, like Geeze in a String, one after another. So that our very little Army had sometimes, or rather most commonly, an Extent of many Miles; our Enemy, the *Highlanders*, firing down upon us from their Summits all the Way. Nor was it possible for our Men, or very rarely at least, to return their Favours with any Prospect of Success; for as they pop'd upon us always on a sudden, they never stay'd long enough to allow any of our Soldiers a Mark; or even time enough to fire: And for our Men to march, or climb up those Mountains, which to them were natural Champion, would have been as dangerous as it seem'd to us impracticable. Nevertheless, under all these disheartning Disadvantages, we arriv'd at *Inverlochy*, and there perform'd the Task appointed, building a Fort on the same Spot where *Cromwell* had rais'd one before. And which was not a little remarkable, we had with us one *Hill*, a Colonel, who had been Governor in *Oliver*'s Time, and who was now again appointed Governor by General *Mackay*. Thus the Work on which we were sent being effected, we march'd back again by the Way of *Gillycrancky*, where that memorable Battle under *Dundee* had been fought the Year before.

Some time after, Sir *Thomas Levingston*, afterwards Earl of *Tiviot*, having receiv'd Intelligence that the *Highlanders* intended to fall down into the lower Countries, in a considerable Body, got together a Party of about five Hundred (the Dragoons, call'd the *Scotch Greys*, inclusive) with which he resolv'd, if possible, to give them a Meeting. We left *Inverness* the last Day of *April*, and encamp'd near a little Town call'd *Forrest*, the Place where, as Tradition still confidently avers, the Witches met *Mackbeth*, and greeted him with their diabolical Auspices. But this Story is so naturally display'd in a Play of the immortal *Shakespear*, that I need not descend here to any farther Particulars.

Here Sir *Thomas* receiv'd Intelligence, that the *Highlanders* design'd to encamp upon the *Spey*, near the Laird of *Grant*'s Castle. Whereupon we began our March about Noon; and the next Day, about the Break thereof, we came to that River, where we soon discover'd the *Highlanders* by their Fires. Sir *Thomas* immediately, on Sight of it, issued his Orders for our fording the River, and falling upon them as soon after as possible. Both were accordingly perform'd, and with so good Order, Secrecy and

Success, that *Cannon* and *Balfour*, their Commanders, were obliged to make their Escape naked.

They were about one Thousand in Number, of which were kill'd about three Hundred; we pursued them, till they got up *Crowdale-Hill*, where we lost them in a Fog. And, indeed so high is that Hill, that they, who perfectly knew it, assured me that it never is without a little dark Fog hanging over it. And to me, at that Instant of Time, they seem'd rather to be People receiv'd up into Clouds, than flying from an Enemy.

Near this there was an old Castle, call'd *Lethendy*, into which about Fifty of them made their Retreat, most of them Gentlemen, resolving there to defend themselves to the last. Sir *Thomas* sent a Messenger to them, with an Offer of Mercy, if they would surrender: But they refus'd the profer'd Quarter, and fir'd upon our Men, killing two of our Grenadiers, and wounding another. During my Quarters at the *Grave*, having learnt to throw a Grenado, I took three or four in a Bag, and crept down by the Side of a Ditch, or Dyke, to an old thatch'd House near the Castle, imagining, on my mounting the same, I might be near enough to throw them, so as to do execution. I found all Things answer my Expectation; and the Castle wanting a Cover, I threw in a Grenado, which put the Enemy immediately into Confusion. The Second had not so good Success, falling short, and the Third burst as soon as it was well out of my Hand, though without Damage to my self. But throwing the Fourth in at a Window, it so increas'd the Confusion, which the first had put them into, that they immediately call'd out to me, upon their Parole of Safety, to come to them.

Accordingly I went up to the Door, which they had barricaded, and made up with great Stones; when they told me they were ready to surrender upon Condition of obtaining Mercy. I return'd to Sir *Thomas*; and telling him what I had done, and the Consequence of it, and the Message they had desir'd me to deliver (a great many of the *Highland* Gentlemen, not of this Party, being with him) Sir *Thomas*, in a high Voice, and broad *Scotch*, best to be heard and understood, order'd me back to tell 'em, *He would cut them all to Pieces, for their Murder of two of his Grenadiers, after his Proffer of Quarter.*

I was returning full of these melancholy Tidings, when Sir *Thomas*, advancing after me a little Distance from the rest of the Company; *Hark ye, Sir*, says he, *I believe there may be among 'em some of our old Acquaintance* (for we had serv'd together in the Service of the *States* in *Flanders*) *therefore tell them they shall have good Quarter*. I very willingly carry'd back a Message to much chang'd to my Mind; and upon delivering of it, without the least Hesitation, they threw down the Barricado, open'd the Door, and out came one *Brody*, who, as he then told me, had had a Piece of his Nose taken off by one of my Grenadoes. I carry'd him to Sir *Thomas*, who confirming my Message, they all came out, and surrendered themselves Prisoners. This happen'd on *May Day* in the Morning; for which Reason we return'd to *Inverness* with our Prisoners, and Boughs in our Hats; and the *Highlanders* never held up their Heads so high after this Defeat.

Upon this Success Sir *Thomas* wrote to Court, giving a full Account of the whole Action. In which being pleas'd to make mention of my Behaviour, with some Particularities, I had soon after a Commission order'd me for a Company in the Regiment under the Command of Brigadier *Tiffin*.

My Commission being made out, sign'd, and sent to me, I repair'd immediately to *Portsmouth*, where the Regiment lay in Garrison. A few Days after I had been there, Admiral *Russel* arriv'd with the Fleet, and anchor'd at St. *Hellen's*, where he re-main'd about a Week. On the 18th of *May* the whole Fleet set Sail; and it being my Turn the same Day to mount the Main Guard, I was going the Rounds very early, when I heard great shooting at Sea. I went directly to acquaint the Governor, and told him my Sentiments, that the two contending Fleets were actually engag'd, which indeed prov'd true; for that very Night a Pinnace, which came from our Fleet, brought News that Admiral *Russel* had engag'd the *French* Admiral *Turvile*; and, after a long and sharp Dispute, was making after them to their own Coasts.

The next Day, towards Evening, several other Expresses arriv'd, one after another, all agreeing in the Defeat of the *French* Fleet, and in the Particulars of the burning their *Rising Sun*, together with many other of their Men of War, at *la Hogue*. All which Expresses were immediately forwarded to Court by Mr. *Gibson*, our Governor.

About two Months after this, our Regiment, among many others, was, according to Order, shipp'd off on a Secret Expedition, under the Command of the Duke of *Leinster*, no Man knowing to what Place we were going, or on what Design; no, not the Commander himself. However, when we were out at Sea, the General, according to Instructions, opening his Commission, we were soon put out of our Suspence, and inform'd, that our Orders were to attack *Dunkirk*. But what was so grand a Secret to those concern'd in the Expedition, having been intrusted to a Female Politician on Land, it was soon discover'd to the Enemy; for which Reason our Orders were countermanded, before we reach'd the Place of Action, and our Forces receiv'd Directions to land at *Ostend*.

Soon after this happen'd that memorable Battle at *Steenkirk*, which as very few at that Time could dive into the Reason of, and mistaken Accounts of it have pass'd for authentick, I will mention somewhat more particularly: The Undertaking was bold; and, as many thought, bolder than was consistent with the Character of the wise Undertaker. Nevertheless, the *French* having taken *Namure*; and, as the Malecontents alledg'd, in the very Sight of a superior Army; and nothing having been done by Land of any moment, Things were blown into such a dangerous Fermentation, by a malicious and lying Spirit, that King *William* found himself under a Necessity of attempting something that might appease the Murmurs of the People. He knew very well, though spoke in the Senate, that it was not true, that his Forces at the Siege of *Namure* exceeded those of the Enemy; no Man could be more afflicted than he at the overflowing of the *Mehaigne*, from the continual Rains, which obstructed the Relief he had designed for that important Place; yet since his Maligners made an ill Use of these false Topicks, to insinuate that he had no Mind to put an End to the War, he was resolv'd to evince the contrary, by shewing them that he was not afraid to venture his Life for the better obtaining what was so much desired.

To that Purpose, receiving Intelligence that the Duke of *Luxemburg* lay strongly encamp'd at *Steenkirk*, near *Enghien* (tho' he was sensible he must pass through many Defiles to engage him; and that the many Thickets between the two Armies would frequently afford him new Difficulties) he resolv'd there to attack him. Our Troops at first were forc'd to hew out their Passage for the Horse; and there was no one difficulty that his Imagination had drawn that was lessen'd by Experience; and yet so prosperous were his Arms at the Beginning, that our Troops had made themselves Masters of several Pieces of the Enemy's Cannon. But the farther he advanc'd, the Ground growing straiter, so strait as not to admit his Army's being drawn up in Battalia, the Troops behind could not give timely Succour to those engag'd, and the Cannon we had taken was forcibly left behind in order to make a good Retreat. The *French* had lost all their Courage in the Onset; for though they had too fair an Opportunity, they did not think fit to pursue it; or, at least, did it very languidly. However, the Malecontents at Home, I remember, grew very well pleas'd after this; for so long as they had but a Battle for their Money, like true *Englishmen*, lost or won, they were contented.

Several Causes, I remember, were assign'd for this Miscarriage, as they call'd it; Some there were who were willing to lay it upon the *Dutch*; and alledge a Saying of one of their Generals, who receiving Orders to relieve some *English* and *Scotch* that were over-power'd, was heard to say, *Dam 'em, since they love Fighting let 'em have their Bellies full.* But I should rather impute the Disappointment to the great Loss of so many of our bravest Officers at the very first Onset. General *Mackay*, Colonel *Lanier*, the Earl of *Angus*, with both his Field-Officers, Sir *Robert Douglas*, Colonel *Hodges*, and many others falling, it was enough to put a very considerable Army into Confusion. I remember one particular Action of Sir *Robert Douglas*, that I should think my self to blame should I omit: Seeing his Colours on the other Side the Hedge, in the Hands of the Enemy, he leap'd over, slew the Officer that had them, and then threw them over the Hedge to his Company; redeeming his Colours at the Expense of his Life. Thus the *Scotch* Commander improv'd upon the *Roman* General; for the brave *Posthumius* cast his Standard in the Middle of the Enemy for his Soldiers to retrieve, but *Douglas* retriev'd his from the Middle of the Enemy, without any Assistance, and cast it back to his Soldiers to retain, after he had so bravely rescued it out of the Hands of the Enemy.

From hence our Regiment receiv'd Orders to march to *Dixmuyd*, where we lay some time employ'd in fortifying that Place. While we were there, I had one Morning stedfastly fix'd my Eyes upon some Ducks, that were swimming in a large Water before me; when all on a sudden, in the Midst of a perfect Calm, I observ'd such a strange and strong Agitation in the Waters, that prodigiously surpriz'd me. I was at the same Moment seiz'd with such a Giddiness in my Head, that, for a Minute or two, I was scarce sensible, and had much a-do to keep on my Legs. I had never felt any thing of an Earthquake before, which, as I soon after understood from others, this was; and it left, indeed, very apparent Marks of its Force in a great Rent in the Body of the great Church, which remains to this Day.

Having brought the intended Fortifications into some tolerable Order, we receiv'd a Command out of hand to reimbarque for *England*. And, upon our Landing, Directions met us to march for *Ipswich*, where we had our Quarters all that Winter. From thence we were order'd up to *London*, to do Duty in the *Tower*. I had not been there long, before an Accident happen'd, as little to be accounted for, without a divine Providence, as some would make that Providence to be, that only can account for it.

There was at that Time, as I was assur'd by my Lord *Lucas*, Constable of it, upwards of twenty Thousand Barrels of Gunpowder, in that they call the *White-Tower*, when all at once the middle Flooring did not only give way, or shrink, but fell flat down upon other Barrels of Powder, together with many of the same combustible Matter which had been placed upon it. It was a Providence strangely neglected at that Time, and hardly thought of since; But let any considerate Man consult the Consequences, if it had taken fire; perhaps to the Destruction of the whole City, or, at least, as far as the *Bridge* and Parts adjacent. Let his Thoughts proceed to examine, why, or how, in that precipitate Fall, not one Nail, nor one Piece of Iron, in that large Fabrick, should afford one little Spark to enflame that Mass of sulphurous Matter it was loaded with; and if he is at a loss to find a Providence, I fear his Friends will be more at a loss to find his

Understanding. But the Battle of *Landen* happening while our Regiment was here on Duty, we were soon remov'd to our Satisfaction from that pacifick Station, to one more active in *Flanders*.

Notwithstanding that fatal Battle the Year preceding, namely, *A.D.* 1694, the Confederate Army under King *William* lay encamp'd at *Mont. St. André*, an open Place, and much expos'd; while the *French* were entrench'd up to their very Teeth, at *Vignamont*, a little Distance from us. This afforded Matter of great Reflection to the Politicians of those Times, who could hardly allow, that if the Confederate Army suffer'd so much, as it really did in the Battle of *Landen*, it could consist with right Conduct to tempt, or rather dare a new Engagement. But those sage Objectors had forgot the well-known Courage of that brave Prince, and were as little capable of fathoming his Designs. The Enemy, who to their Sorrow had by Experience been made better Judges, was resolv'd to traverse both; for which Purpose they kept close within their Entrenchments; so that after all his Efforts, King *William* finding he could no way draw them to a Battle, suddenly decamp'd, and march'd directly to *Pont Espiers*, by long Marches, with a Design to pass the *French* Lines at that Place.

But notwithstanding our Army march'd in a direct Line, to our great Surprize, we found the Enemy had first taken possession of it. They gave this the Name of the *Long March*, and very deservedly; for though our Army march'd upon the String, and the Enemy upon the Bow,* sensible of the Importance of the Post, and the Necessity of securing it, by double horseing with their Foot, and by leaving their Weary and Weak in their Garrisons, and supplying their Places with fresh Men out of them, they gain'd their Point in disappointing us. Though certain it is, that March cost 'em as many Men and Horses as a Battle. However their Master, the *French* King, was so pleas'd with their indefatigable and auspicious Diligence, that he wrote, with his own Hand, a Letter of Thanks to the Officers, for the great Zeal and Care they had taken to prevent the Confederate Army from entring into *French Flanders*.

* Notes on the text appear on p. 336.

King *William*, thus disappointed in that noble Design, gave immediate Orders for his whole Army to march through *Oudenard*, and then ecamp'd at *Rofendale*; after some little Stay at that Camp we were remov'd to the *Camerlins*, between *Newport* and *Ostend*, once more to take our Winter Quarters there among the Boors.

We were now in the Year 1695 when the strong Fortress of *Namur*, taken by the *French* in 1692 and since made by them much stronger, was invested by the Earl of *Athlone*. After very many vigorous Attacks, with the Loss of many Men, the Town was taken, the Garrison retiring into the Castle. Into which soon after, notwithstanding all the Circumspection of the Besiegers, Mareschal *Bouflers* found means, with some Dragoons, to throw himself.

While King *William* was thus engag'd in that glorious and important Siege, Prince *Vaudemont* being posted at *Watergaem*, with about fifty Battallions, and as many Squadrons, the Mareschal *Villeroy* laid a Design to attack him with the whole *French* Army. The Prince imagin'd no less, therefore he prepar'd accordingly, giving us Orders to fortify our Camp, as well as the little time we had for it would permit. Those Orders were pursu'd; nevertheless, I must confess, it was beyond the Reach of my little Reason to account for our so long Stay in the Sight of an Army so much superior to ours. The Prince in the Whole could hardly muster thirty Thousand; and *Villeroy* was known to value himself upon having one Hundred Thousand effective Men. However, the Prince provisionally sent away all our Baggage that very Morning to *Ghent*, and still made shew as if he resolv'd to defend himself to the last Extremity in our little Entrenchments. The enemy on their Side began to surround us; and in their Motions for that Purpose, blew up little Bags of Gun-powder, to give the readier Notice how far they had acomplish'd it. Another Captain, with my self, being plac'd on the Right, with one Hundred Men (where I found Monsieur *Montal* endeavouring, if possible, to get behind us) I could easily observe, they had so far attain'd their Aim of encompassing us, as to the very Fashion of a Horse's Shoe. This made me fix my Eyes so intently upon the advancing Enemy, that I never minded what my Friends were doing behind me; though I afterwards found that they had been fileing off so very artfully and privately, by that narrow Opening of the Horse-Shoe, that when the Enemy imagin'd us past a Possibility of Escape, our little Army at once, and of a sudden, was ready to disappear. There was a large Wood on the Right of our Army, through which lay the Road to *Ghent*, not broader than to admit of more than Four to march a breast. Down this the Prince had slid his Forces, except to that very small Party which the Captain and my self commanded, and which was designedly left to bring up the Rear. Nor did we stir till Captain *Collier*, then *Aid de Camp* to his Brother, now Earl of *Portmore*, came with the Word of Command for us to draw off.

When *Villeroy* was told of our Retreat, he was much surpriz'd, as thinking it a Thing utterly impossible. However, at last, being sensible of the Truth of it, he gave Orders for our Rear to be attack'd; but we kept fireing from Ditch to Ditch, and Hedge to Hedge, till Night came upon us; and so our little Army got clear of its gigantick Enemy with very inconsiderable Loss. However, the *French* fail'd not, in their customary Way, to express the Sense of their vexation, at this Disappointment, with Fire and Sword in the Neighbourhood round. Thus Prince *Vaudemont* acquir'd more Glory by that Retreat than an intire Victory could have given him; and it was not, I confess, the least Part of Satisfaction in Life, that my self had a Share of Honour under him to bring off the Rear at that his glorious Retreat at *Arfeel*.

However, in further Revenge of this political Chicane of the Prince of *Vaudemont*, and to oblige, if possible, King *William* to raise the Siege from before *Namur*, *Villeroy* enter'd into the Resolution of Bombarding *Brussells*. In order to which he encamp'd at *Anderleck*, and then made his Approaches as near as was convenient to the Town. There he caus'd to be planted thirty Mortars, and rais'd a Battery of ten Guns to shoot hot Bullets into the Place.

But before they fir'd from either, *Villeroy*, in complement to the Duke of *Bavaria*, sent a Messenger to know in what Part of the Town his Dutchess chose to reside, that they might, as much as possible, avoid incommoding her, by directing their Fire to other Parts. Answer was return'd that she was at her usual Place of Residence, the Palace; and accordingly their fireing from Battery or Mortars little incommoded them that Way.

Five Days the Bombardment continu'd; and with such Fury, that the Centre of that noble City was quite lay'd in Rubbish. Most of the Time of Bombarding I was upon the Counterscarp, where I could best see and distinguish; and I have often counted in the Air, at one time, more than twenty Bombs; for they shot whole Vollies out of their Mortars all together. This, as it must needs be terrible, threw the Inhabitants into the utmost Confusion. Cartloads of Nuns, that for many Years before had never been out of the Cloister, were now hurry'd about from Place to Place, to find Retreats of some Security. In short, the Groves, and Parts remote, were all crowded; and the most spacious Streets had hardly a Spectator left to view their Ruins. Nothing was to be seen like that Dexterity of our People in extinguishing the Fires; for where the red-hot Bullets fell, and rais'd new Conflagrations, not Burghers only, but the vulgar Sort, stood stareing, and with their Hands impocketted, beheld their Houses gradually consume; and without offering prudent or charitable Hand to stop the growing Flames.

But after they had almost thus destroy'd that late fair City, *Villeroy*, finding he could not raise the Siege of *Namur*, by that vigorous Attack upon *Brussels*, decamp'd at last from before it, and put his Army on the March, to try if he could have better Success by exposing to Show his Pageant of one Hundred Thousand Men. Prince *Vaudemont* had timely Intelligence of the Duke's Resolution and Motion; and resolv'd, if possible to get there before him. Nor was the Attempt fruitless: He fortunately succeeded, though with much Fatigue, and no little Difficulty, after he had put a Trick upon the Spies of the Enemy, by pretending to encamp, and so soon as they were gone ordering a full March.

The Castle of *Namur* had been all this Time under the Fire of the Besieger's Cannon; and soon after our little Army under the Prince was arriv'd, a Breach, that was imagin'd practicable, being made in the *Terra Nova* (which, as the Name imports, was a new Work, rais'd by the *French*, and added to the Fortifications, since it fell into their Hands in 1692 and which very much increas'd the Strength of the Whole) a Breach, as I have said, being made in this *Terra Nova*, a Storm, in a Council of War, was resolv'd upon. Four entire Regiments, in conjunction with some Draughts made out of several others, were order'd for that Work, my self commanding that Part of 'em which had been drawn out of Colonel *Tiffin*'s. We were all to rendevouze at the Abbey of *Salsines*, under the Command of the Lord Cutts; the Signal, when the Attack was to be made, being agreed to be the blowing up of a Bag of Gun-powder upon the Bridge of Boats that lay over the *Sambre*.

So soon as the Signal was made, we march'd up to the Breach with a decent Intrepidity, receiving all the Way we advanc'd the full Fire of the *Cohorn* Fort. But as soon as we came near enough to mount, we found it vastly steep and rugged. Notwithstanding all which, several did get up, and enter'd the Breach; but not being supported as they ought to have been, they were all made Prisoners. Which, together with a Wound my Lord *Cutts* receiv'd, after he had done all that was possible for us, necessitated us to retire with the Loss of many of our Men.

VILLEROY all this while lay in fight, with his Army of One Hundred Thousand Men, without making the least Offer to incommode the Besiegers; or even without doing any thing more than make his Appearance in favour of the Besieged, and reconnoitring our Encampment: And, at last, seeing, or imagining that he saw, the Attempt would be to little purpose, with all the good Manners in the World, in the Night, he withdrew that terrible Meteor, and reliev'd our poor Horses from feeding on Leaves, the only Inconvenience he had put us to.

This Retreat leaving the Garrison without all Hope of Relief, they in the Castle immediately capitulated. But after one of the Gates had been, according to Articles, delivered up and Count *Guiscard* was marching out at the Head of the Garrison, and *Bouflers* at the Head of the Dragoons; the latter was, by order of King *William*, arrested, in reprize of the Garrison of *Dixmuyd* (who, contrary to the *Cartel*, had been detain'd Prisoners) and remain'd under Arrest till they were set free.

At the very Beginning of the Year 1696 was discover'd a Plot, fit only to have had its Origin from Hell or *Rome*. A Plot, which would have put *Hottentots* and Barbarians out of Countenance. This was call'd the *Assassination Plot*, from the Design of it, which was to have assassinated King *William* a little before the Time of his usual leaving *England* to head the Army of the Confederates in *Flanders*. And as nothing could give a nobler Idea of the great Character of that Prince than such a nefarious Combination against him; so, with all considerate Men, nothing could more depreciate the Cause of his inconsiderate Enemies. If I remember what I have read, the Sons of ancient *Rome*, though Heathens, behav'd themselves against an Enemy in a quite different Manner. Their Historians afford us more Instances than a few of their generous Intimations to Kings and Generals, under actual Hostilities, of barbarous Designs upon their Lives. I proceed to this of our own Countrymen.

Soon after the Discovery had been made, by Persons actually engag'd in that inhuman Design, the Regiment, in which I served, with some others then in *Flanders*, receiv'd Orders, with all Expedition, to embarque for *England*; though, on our Arrival at *Gravesend*, fresh Orders met us to remain on board the Transports, till we had surther Directions.

On my going to *London*, a few Days after, I was told, that two Regiments only were now design'd to come a-shore; and that the rest would be remanded to *Flanders*, the Danger apprehended being pretty well over. I was at *White Hall* when I receiv'd this Notice; where meeting my Lord *Cutts* (who had ever since the storming of the *Terra Nova* at *Namur* allow'd me a Share in his Favour) he express'd himself in the most obliging Manner; and at parting desir'd he might not fail of seeing me next Morning at his House; for he had somewhat of an extraordinary Nature to communicate to me.

At the time appointed, I waited on his Lorship, where I met Mr. *Steel* (now Sir *Richard*, and at that time his Secretary) who immediately introduc'd me. I found in company with him three Gentlemen; and after common Salutations, his Lordship deliver'd into my Hands, an Order from the King in Council to go along with Captain *Porter*, Mr. *de la Rue*, and Mr. *George Harris* (who prov'd to be those three with him) to search all the

Transports at *Gravesend*, in order to prevent any of the Conspirators getting out of *England* that Way. After answering, that I was
ready to pay Obedience, and receiving, in private, the further
necessary Instructions, we took our Leave, and Oars soon after
for *Gravesend*. 'Twas in our Passage down, that I understood that
they had all been of the Conspiracy, but now reluctant, were
become Witnesses.

When we came to *Gravesend*, I produc'd my Authority to the
Commanding Officer, who very readily paid Obedience, and
gave Assistance; But after our most diligent Search, finding
nothing of what we look'd for, we return'd that very Night to
London.

Next Day a Proclamation was to come out for the apprehending three of four Troopers, who were sent over by King *James*,
with a thousand Pounds Reward for each: Mr. *George Harris*,
who was the fourth, being the only Evidence against the other
three. No sooner were we return'd from *Gravesend*, but *Harris*
had Intelligence brought him, that *Cassells*, one of the three, was
at Mr. *Allens* in the *Savoy*, under the Name of *Green*. Upon
which we went directly to the Place; and enquiring for Mr.
Green, we were told he lodg'd there, and was in his Room.

I was oblig'd by my Order to go along with them, and assist
'em; and very well was it that I was so: For in consideration of
the Reward in the Proclamation, which, as I have said, was to
come out the next Day, *Harris* and the rest were for deferring his
Seizure, till the coming out of that Proclamation; but making
answer, that in case of his Escape that Night, I must be responsible to my Superiors; who, under the most favourable Aspect,
would construe it a Neglect of Duty, they were forc'd to comply;
and so he was taken up, and his Name that Night struck out of the
Proclamation. It is very true, by this faithful Discharge of my
Trust, I did save the Government one Thousand Pounds; but it is
equally so, that I never had of my Governors one Farthing Consideration for what others term'd an over-officious Piece of Service; though in Justice it must be own'd a Piece of exact and
disinterested Duty.

Some few Days after, attending by Direction at the Secretary's
Office, with Mr. *Harris*, there came in a *Dutchman*, spluttering and

making a great Noise, that he was sure he could discover one of
the Conspirators; but the Mein and the Behaviour of the Man,
would not give any Body Leave to give him any Credit or
Regard. However, the Man persisting in his Assertions, I spoke
to Mr. *Harris* to take him aside, and ask him what Sort of a Person he was; *Harris* did so; and the *Dutchman* describing him, says
Harris, returning to me, I'll be hang'd if it be not *Blackburn*. Upon
which we had him question'd somewhat more narrowly; when
having no room to doubt, and understanding where he was,
Colonel *Rivet* of the Guards was sent for, and order'd to go
along with us to seize him. We went accordingly; and it proving
to be *Blackburn*, the *Dutchman* had five Hundred Pounds, and the
Colonel and others the Remainder. *Cassels* and *Blackburn*, if still
alive, are in *Newgate*, confin'd by Act of Parliament, one only
Witness, which was *Harris*, being producible against them.

When *Blackburn* was seiz'd, I found in the Chamber with him,
one *Davison*, a Watch-maker, living in *Holbourn*. I carry'd him
along with me to the Secretary of State; but nothing on his
Examination appearing against him, he was immediately discharg'd. He offer'd afterwards to present me with a fine Watch
of his own making, which I refus'd; and he long after own'd the
Obligation.

So soon as the Depth of this Plot was fathom'd, and the intended Evil provided against, as well as prevented, King *William*
went over into *Flanders*, and our Regiment thereupon receiv'd
Orders for their immediate Return. Nothing of any Moment
occurr'd till our Arrival at our old Quarters, the *Camerlins*,
where we lay dispers'd amongst the Country Boors or Farmers,
as heretofore. However, for our better Security in those Quarters,
and to preserve us from the Excursions of the neighbouring
Garrison of Furnes, we were oblig'd to keep an Out-guard at a
little Place call'd *Shoerbeck*. This Guard was every forty-eight
Hours chang'd, and remounted with a Captain, a Lieutenant, an
Ensign, and threescore Men.

When it came to my Turn to relieve that Guard, and for that
Purpose I was arriv'd at my Post, it appear'd to me with the Face
of a Place of Debauch, rather than Business; there being too
visible Tokens, that the hard Duty of both Officers and Soldiers

had been that of hard Drinking, the foulest Error that a Soldier can commit, especially when on his Guard.

To confirm my Apprehensions, a little after I had taken Possession of my Guard, the Man of the House related to me such Passages, and so many of 'em, that satisfy'd me, that if ten sober Men had made the Attack, they might have fairly knock'd all my Predecessors of the last Guard on the Head, without much Difficulty. However, his Account administer'd Matter of Caution to me, and put me upon taking a narrower View of our Situation. In consequence whereof, at Night I plac'd a Centinel a Quarter of a Mile in the Rear, and such other Centinels as I thought necessary and convenient in other Places; with Orders, that upon Sight of an Enemy the Centinel near should fire; and that upon hearing that, all the other Centinels, as well as he, should hasten in to strengthen our Main Guard.

What my Jealousy, on my Landlord's Relation, had suggested, happen'd accordingly: For about one in the Morning I was alarm'd with the Cry of one of my Centinels, *Turn out for God's sake*; which he repeated, with Vehemence, three or four times over. I took the Alarm, got up suddenly; and with no little Difficulty got my Men into their Ranks, when the Person who made the Outcry came running in, almost spent, and out of Breath. It was the Centinel, that I had luckily plac'd about a Quarter of a Mile off, who gave the Alarm, and his Musket flashing in the Pan, without going off, he endeavour'd to supply with his Voice the Defect of his Piece. I had just got my Men into their Ranks, in order to receive the Enemy, when by the Moonlight, I discover'd a Party advancing upon us. My out Centinel challeng'd 'em, and as I had precaution'd, they answer'd, *Hispanioli*; though I knew 'em to be *French*.

However, on my Survey of our Situation by Day-light, having mark'd in my Mind a proper Place for drawing up my Men in Case of an Attack, which was too narrow to admit of more than two on a Breast; and which would secure between us and the Enemy a Ditch of Water: I resolv'd to put in practice what had entertain'd me so well in the Theory. To that Purpose I order'd my first Rank to keep their Post, stand still and face the Enemy, while the other two Ranks stooping should follow me to gain the

3

intended Station; which done, the first Rank had Orders to file off and fall behind. All was perform'd in excellent Order; and I confess it was with no little Pleasure, that I beheld the Enemy, for the best Part of an Hour, in Consultation whether they should attack us or no. The result, nevertheless, of that Consultation ended in this; that, seeing us so well upon our Guard, it was most adviseable to draw off. They soon put their Resolution into practice, which I was very glad to see; on Examination a little before having found that my Predecessor, as in other Things, had fail'd of Conduct in leaving me a Garrison without Ammunition.

Next Morning I was very pleasingly surpriz'd with a handsome Present of Wine, and some other necessary Refreshments. At first I made a little Scruple and Hesitation whether or no to receive 'em; till the Bearer assur'd me, that they were sent me from the Officers of the next Garrison, who had made me a Visit the Night before, as a candid Acknowledgment of my Conduct and good Behaviour. I return'd their Compliment, that I hop'd I should never receive Men of Honour otherwise than like a Man of Honour; which mightily pleas'd them. Every of which Particulars the *Ghent Gazettier* the Week after publish'd.

We had little to do except Marching and Counter-marching all the Campaign after; till it was resolv'd in a Council of War, for the better preserving of *Brussels* from such Insults, as it had before sustain'd from the *French*, during the Siege of *Namur*, to fortify *Anderlech*; upon which our Regiment, as well as others, were commanded from our more pacifick Posts to attend that Work. Our whole Army was under Movement to cover that Resolution; and the Train fell to my Care and Command in the March. There accompany'd the Train a Fellow, seemingly ordinary, yet very officious and courteous, being ready to do any thing for any Person, from the Officer to the common Soldier. He travell'd along and mov'd with the Train, sometimes on Foot, and sometimes getting a Ride in some one or other of the Waggons; but ever full of his Chit-chat and Stories of Humour. By these insinuating Ways he had screw'd himself into the general good Opinion; but the Waggoners especially grew particularly fond of him. At the End of our March all our Powder-Waggons were plac'd breast a-breast, and so close, that one miscarrying would leave little doubt of the Fate of all the rest. This in the Camp we commonly call *the Park*; and here it was that our new Guest, like another *Phaeton*, though under Pretence of Weariness, not Ambition, got Leave of the very last Carter to the Train to take a Nap in his Waggon. One who had entertain'd a Jealousy of him, and had watch'd him, gave Information against him; upon which he was seiz'd and brought to me as Captain of the Guard. I caus'd him to be search'd; and upon search, finding Match, Touchwood, and other dangerous Materials upon him; I sent him and them away to the Provoe. Upon the Whole, a Council of War was call'd, at which, upon a strict Examination, he confess'd himself a hir'd Incendiary; and as such receiv'd his Sentence to be burnt in the Face of the Army. The Execution was a Day or two after: When on the very Spot, he further acknowledged, that on Sight or Noise of the Blow, it had been concerted, that the *French* Army should fall upon the Confederates under those lamentable Circumstances.

The Peace of *Riswick* soon after taking place, put an End to all Incendiarisms of either Sort. So that nothing of a Military Kind, which was now become my Province, happen'd of some Years after. Our Regiment was first order'd into *England*; and presently after into *Ireland:* But as these Memoirs are not design'd for the Low Amuzement of a Tea-Table, but rather of the Cabinet, a Series of inglorious Inactivity can furnish but very little towards 'em.

Yet as little as I admir'd a Life of Inactivity, there are some Sorts of Activity, to which a wise Man might almost give Supineness the Preference: Such is that of barely encountring Elements, and wageing War with Nature; and such, in my Opinion, would have been the spending my Commission, and very probably my Life with it, in the *West Indies*. For though the Climate (as some would urge) may afford a Chance for a very speedy Advance in Honour, yet, upon revolving in my Mind, that those Rotations of the Wheel of Fortune are often so very quick, as well as uncertain, that I my self might as well be the First as the Last; the Whole of the Debate ended in somewhat like that Couplet of the excellent *Hudibras:*

Then he, that ran away and fled,
Must lie in Honour's Truckle-bed.

However, my better Planets soon disannull'd those melancholy
Ideas, which a Rumour of our being sent into the *West Indies* had
crowded my Head and Heart with: For being call'd over into
England, upon the very Affairs of the Regiment, I arriv'd there
just after the Orders for their Transportation went over; by
which Means the Choice of going was put out of my Power,
and the Danger of Refusing, which was the Case of many, was
very luckily avoided.

It being judg'd, therefore, impossible for me to return soon
enough to gain my Passage, one in Power propos'd to me, that I
should resign to an Officer then going over; and with some other
contingent Advantages, to my great Satisfaction, I was put upon
the Half-pay List. This was more agreeable, for I knew, or at
least imagin'd my self wise enough to foretel, from the over hot
Debate of the House of Commons upon the Partition Treaty,
that it could not be long before the present Peace would, at least,
require patching.

Under this Sort of uncertain Settlement I remain'd with the
Patience of a *Jew*, though not with Judaical Absurdity, a faithful
Adherer to my Expectation. Nor did the Consequence fail of
answering, a War was apparent, and soon after proclaim'd. Thus
waiting for an Opportunity, which I flatter'd my self would soon
present, the little Diversions of *Dublin*, and the moderate Conversation of that People, were not of Temptation enough to
make my Stay in *England* look like a Burden.

But though the War was proclaim'd, and Preparations accordingly made for it, the Expectations from all receiv'd a sudden
Damp, by the as sudden Death of King *William*. That Prince,
who had stared Death in the Face in many Sieges and Battles,
met with his Fate in the Midst of his Diversions, who seiz'd his
Prize in an Hour, to human Thought, the least adapted to it. He
was a Hunting (his customary Diversion) when, by an unhappy
Trip of his Horse, he fell to the Ground; and in the Fall displac'd
his Collar-bone. The News of it immediately alarm'd the Court,
and all around; and the sad Effects of it soon after gave all *Europe*

the like Alarm. *France* only, who had not disdain'd to seek it sooner by ungenerous Means, receiv'd new Hope, from what gave others Motives for Despair. He flatter'd himself, that that long liv'd Obstacle to his Ambition thus remov'd, his Successor would never fall into those Measures, which he had wisely concerted for the Liberties of *Europe*; but he, as well as others of his Adherents, was gloriously deceiv'd; that God-like Queen, with a Heart entirely *English*, prosecuted her royal Predecessor's Counsels; and to remove all the very Faces of Jealousy, immediately on her Accession dispatch'd to every Court of the great Confederacy, Persons adequate to the Importance of the Message, to give Assurances thereof.

This gave new Spirit to a Cause, that at first seem'd to languish in its Founder, as it struck its great Opposers with a no less mortifying Terror; And well did the great Successes of her Arms answer the Prayers and Efforts of that royal Soul of the Confederacies; together with the Wishes of all, that, like her, had the Good, as well as the Honour of their Country at Heart, in which the Liberties of *Europe* were included. The first Campaign gave a noble Earnest of the Future. *Bon, Keyserwaert, Venlo*, and *Ruremond*, were sound Forerunners only of *Donawert, Hochstet*, and *Blenheim*. Such a March of *English* Forces to the Support of the tottering Empire, as it gloriously manifested the ancient Genius of a warlike People; so was it happily celebrated with a Success answerable to the Glory of the Undertaking, which concluded in Statues and princely Donatives to an *English* Subject, from the then only Emperor in *Europe*. A small Tribute, it's true, for ransom'd Nations and captiv'd Armies, which justly enough inverted the Exclamations of a *Roman* Emperor to the *French* Monarch, who deprecated his Legions lost pretty near the same Spot; but to a much superior Number, and on a much less glorious Occasion.

But my good Fortune not allowing me to participate in those glorious Appendages of the *English* Arms in *Flanders*, nor on the *Rhine*, I was resolv'd to make a Push for it the first Opportunity, and waste my Minutes no longer on Court Attendances. And my Lord *Cutts* returning with his full Share of Laurels, for his never to be forgotten Services at *Venlo, Ruremond*, and *Hochstet*, found his active Genius now to be repos'd, under the less agreeable Burden of unhazardous Honour, where Quiet must provide a Tomb for one already past any Danger of Oblivion; deep Wounds and glorious Actions having anticipated all that could be said in Epitaphs or litteral Inscriptions. Soon after his Arrival from *Germany*, he was appointed General of all her Majesty's Forces in *Ireland*; upon which going to congratulate him, he was pleas'd to enquire of me several Things relating to that Country; and particularly in what Part of *Dublin* I would recommend his Residence; offering at the same time, if I would go over with him, all the Services that should fall in his Way.

But Inactivity was a Thing I had too long lamented; therefore, after I had, as decently as I could, declin'd the latter Part, I told his Lordship, that as to a Place of Residence, I was Master of a House in *Dublin*, large enough, and suitable to his great Quality, which should be at his Service, on any Terms he thought fit. Adding withal, that I had a Mind to see *Spain*, where my Lord *Peterborow* was now going; and that if his Lordship would favour me with a Recommendation, it would suit my present Inclinations much better than any further tedious Recess. His Lordship was so good to close with both my Overtures; and spoke so effectually in my Favour, that the Earl of *Peterborow*, then General of all the Forces order'd on that Expedition, bad me speedily prepare my self; and so when all Things were ready I embarqu'd with that noble Lord for *Spain*, to pursue his well concerted Undertaking; which, in the Event, will demonstrate to the World, that little Armies, under the Conduct of auspicious Generals, may sometimes produce prodigious Effects.

The *Jews*, in whatever Part of the World, are a People industrious in the increasing of *Mammon*; and being accustom'd to the universal Methods of Gain, are always esteem'd best qualify'd for any Undertaking, where that bears a Probability of being a Perquisite. Providing Bread, and other Requisites for an Army, was ever allow'd to carry along with it a Profit answerable; and *Spain* was not the first Country where that People had engag'd in such an Undertaking. Besides, on any likely Appearance of great Advantage, it is in the Nature as well as Practice of that Race, strenuously to assist one another; and that with the utmost

Confidence and prodigious Alacrity. One of that Number, both competent and willing enough to carry on an Undertaking of that kind, fortunately came at that Juncture to solicit the Earl of *Peterborow* to be employ'd as Proveditor to the Army and Troops, which were, or should be sent into *Spain*.

It will easily be admitted, that the Earl, under his present Exigencies, did not decline to listen. And a very considerable Sum being offer'd, by way of Advance, the Method common in like Cases was pursu'd, and the Sum propos'd accepted; by which Means the Earl of *Peterborow* found himself put into the happy Capacity of proceeding upon his first concerted Project. The Name of the *Jew*, who sign'd the Contract, was *Curtisos*; and he and his Friends, with great Punctuality, advanc'd the expected Sum of One Hundred Thousand Pounds Sterling, or very near it; which was immediately order'd into the Hands of the Pay-master of the Forces. For though the Earl took Money of the *Jews*, it was not for his own, but public Use. According to Agreement, Bills were drawn for the Value from *Lisbon*, upon the Lord *Godolphin* (then Lord Treasurer) all which were, on that Occasion, punctually comply'd with.

The Earl of *Peterborow* having thus fortunately found Means to supply himself with Money, and by that with some Horse, after he had obtain'd Leave of the Lord *Galoway* to make an Exchange of two Regiments of Foot, receiv'd the Arch-Duke, and all those who would follow him, aboard the Fleet; and, at his own Expense, transported him and his whole Retinue to *Barcelona*: For all which prodigious Charge, as I have been very lately inform'd, from very good Hands, that noble Earl never to this Day receiv'd any Consideration from the Government, or any Person whatsoever.

We sail'd from *Lisbon*, in order to join the Squadron under Sir *Cloudsley Shovel*: Meeting with which at the appointed Station off *Tangier*, the Men of War and Transports thus united, made the best of their Way for *Gibraltar*. There we stay'd no longer than to take aboard two Regiments out of that Garrison, in lieu of two out of our Fleet. Here we found the Prince of *Hesse*, who immediately took a Resolution to follow the Arch-Duke in this Expedition. He was a Person of great Gallantry; and having been

Vice-Roy of *Catalonia*, was receiv'd on board the Fleet with the utmost Satisfaction, as being a Person capable of doing great Service in a Country where he was well known, and as well belov'd.

Speaking *Latin* then pretty fluently, it gave me frequent Opportunies of conversing with the two Father Confessors of the Duke of *Austria*; and upon that Account I found my self honour'd with some Share in the Favour of the Arch-Duke himself. I mention this, not to gratify any vain Humour, but as a corroborating Circumstance, that my Opportunities of Information, in Matters of Consequence, could not thereby be suppos'd to be lessen'd; but that I might more reasonably be imagin'd to arrive at Intelligence, that not very often, or at least not so soon, came to the Knowledge of others.

From *Gibraltar* we sail'd to the Bay of *Altea*, not far distant from the City of *Valencia*, in the Road of which we continu'd for some Days. While we were there, as I was very credibly inform'd, the Earl of *Peterborow* met with some fresh Disappointment; but what it was, neither I nor any Body else, as far as I could perceive, could ever dive into: Neither did it appear by any outward Tokens, in that noble General, that it lay so much at his Heart, as those about him seem'd to assure me it did.

However, while we lay in *Altea* Bay, two Bomb-Vessels, and a small Squadron, were order'd against *Denia*, which had a small Castle; but rather fine than strong. And accordingly, upon our Offer to bring to bear with our Cannon, and preparing to fix our Bomb-Vessels, in order to bombard the Place, it surrender'd; and acknowledg'd the Arch-Duke as lawful King of *Spain*, and so proclaim'd him. From this time, therefore, speaking of that Prince, it shall be under that Title. General *Ramos* was left Commander here; a Person who afterwards acted a very extraordinary Part in the War carry'd on in the Kingdom of *Valencia*.

But notwithstanding no positive Resolutions had been taken for the Operations of the Campaign, before the Arch Duke's Departure from *Lisbon*, the Earl of *Peterborow*, ever solicitous of the Honour of his Country, had premeditated another Enterprize, which, had it been embrac'd, would in all Probability, have brought that War to a much more speedy Conclusion; and at the same time have obviated all those Difficulties, which were but too apparent in the Siege of *Barcelona*. He had justly and judiciously weigh'd, that there were no Forces in the Middle Parts of *Spain*, all their Troops being in the extream Parts of the Kingdom, either on the Frontiers of *Portugal*, or in the City of *Barcelona*; that with King *Philip*, and the royal Family at *Madrid*, there were only some few Horse, and those in a bad Condition, and which only serv'd for Guards: if therefore, as he rightly projected within himself, by the taking of *Valencia*, or any Sea-Port Town, that might have secur'd his Landing, he had march'd directly for *Madrid*; what could have oppos'd him? But I shall have occasion to dilate more upon this Head a few Pages hence; and therefore shall here only say, that though that Project of his might have brought about a speedy and wonderful Revolution, what he was by his Orders afterwards oblig'd to, against his Inclinations, to pursue, contributed much more to his great Reputation, as it put him under a frequent Necessity of overcoming Difficulties, which, to any other General, would have appear'd unsurmountable.

VALENCIA is a City towards the Centre of *Spain*, to the Seaward, seated in a rich and most populous Country, just fifty Leagues from *Madrid*. It abounds in Horses and Mules; by reason of the great Fertility of its Lands, which they can, to great Advantage, water when, and as they please. This City and Kingdom was as much inclin'd to the Interest of King *Charles* as *Catalonia* it self; for even on our first Appearance, great Numbers of People came down to the Bay of *Altea*, with not only a bare Offer of their Services, but loaded with all Manner of Provisions, and loud Acclamations of *Viva Carlos tercero, Viva*. There were no regular Troops in any of the Places round about it, or in the City it self. The nearest were those few Horse in *Madrid*, one hundred and fifty Miles distant; nor any Foot nearer than *Barcelona*, or the Frontiers of *Portugal*.

On the contrary, *Barcelona* is one of the largest and most populous Cities in all *Spain*, fortify'd with Bastions; one Side thereof is secur'd by the Sea; and the other by a strong Fortification call'd *Monjouick*. The Place is of so large a Circumference, that thirty thousand Men would scarce suffice to form the Lines of Circumvallation. It once resisted for many Months an Army of

3*

that Force; and is almost at the greatest Distance from *England* of any Place belonging to that *Monarchy*.

This short Description of these two Places will appear highly necessary, if it be consider'd, that no Person without it would be able to judge of the Design which the Earl of *Peterborow* intended to pursue, when he first took the Arch-Duke aboard the Fleet. Nevertheless the Earl now found himself under a Necessity of quitting that noble Design, upon his Receipt of Orders from *England*, while he lay in the Bay of *Altea*, to proceed directly to *Catalonia*; to which the Arch-Duke, as well as many Sea and Land Officers, were most inclin'd; and the Prince of *Hesse* more than all the rest.

On receiving those Orders, the Earl of *Peterborow* seem'd to be of Opinion, that from an Attempt, which he thought under a Probability of Success, he was condemn'd to undertake what was next to an Impossibility of effecting; since nothing appear'd to him so injudicious as an Attempt upon *Barcelona*. A Place at such a Distance from receiving any Reinforcement or Relief; the only Place in which the *Spaniards* had a Garrison of regular Forces; and those in Number rather exceeding the Army he was to undertake the Siege with, was enough to cool the Ardour of a Person of less Penetration and Zeal than what the Earl had on all Occasions demonstrated. Whereas if the General, as he intended, had made an immediate March to *Madrid*, after he had secur'd *Valencia*, and the Towns adjacent, which were all ready to submit and declare for King *Charles*; or if otherwise inclin'd, had it not in their Power to make any considerable Resistance; to which, if it be added, that he could have had Mules and Horses immediately provided for him, in what Number he pleas'd, together with Carriages necessary for Artillery, Baggage, and Ammunition; in few Days he could have forc'd King *Philip* out of *Madrid*, where he had so little Force to oppose him. And as there was nothing in his Way to prevent or obstruct his marching thither, it is hard to conceive any other Part King *Philip* could have acted in such an Extremity, than to retire either towards *Portugal* or *Catalonia*. In either of which Cases he must have left all the middle Part of *Spain* open to the Pleasure of the Enemy; who in the mean time would have had it in their Power to prevent any Communication of those Bodies at such opposite Extreams of the Country, as were the Frontiers of *Portugal* and *Barcelona*, where only, as I said before, were any regular Troops.

And on the other Side, as the Forces of the Earl of *Peterborow* were more than sufficient for an Attempt where there was so little Danger of Opposition; so if their Army on the Frontiers of *Portugal* should have march'd back upon him into the Country; either the *Portugueze* Army could have enter'd into *Spain* without Opposition; or, at worst, supposing the General had been forc'd to retire, his Retreat would have been easy and safe into those Parts of *Valencia* and *Andaluzia*, which he previously had secur'd. Besides, *Gibraltar*, the strongest Place in *Spain*, if not in the whole World, was already in our Possession, and a great Fleet at Hand ready to give Assistance in all Places near the Sea. From all which it is pretty apparent, that in a little time the War on our Side might have been supported without entering the *Mediterranean*; by which Means all Reinforcements would have been much nearer at Hand, and the Expences of transporting Troops and Ammunition very considerably diminish'd.

But none of these Arguments, though every one of them is founded on solid Reason, were of Force enough against the prevailing Opinion for an Attempt upon *Catalonia*. Mr. *Crow*, Agent for the Queen in those Parts, had sent into *England* most positive Assurances, that nothing would be wanting, if once our Fleet made an invasion amongst the *Catalans*: The Prince of *Hesse* likewise abounded in mighty Offers and prodigious Assurances; all which enforc'd our Army to that Part of *Spain*, and that gallant Prince to those Attempts in which he lost his Life. Very much against the Inclination of our General, who foresaw all those Difficulties, which were no less evident afterwards to every one; and the Sense of which occasion'd those Delays, and that Opposition to any Effort upon *Barcelona*, which ran thro' so many successive Councils of War.

However, pursuant to his Instructions from *England*, the repeated Desires of the Arch-Duke, and the Importunities of the Prince of *Hesse*, our General gave Orders to sail from *Altea* towards the Bay of *Barcelona*, the chief City of *Catalonia*. Nevertheless, when we arriv'd there, he was very unwilling to land any of the Forces, till he saw some Probability of that Assistance and Succour so must boasted of, and so often promis'd. But as nothing appear'd but some small Numbers of Men, very indifferently arm'd, and without either Gentlemen or Officers at the Head of them; the Earl of *Peterborow* was of Opinion, this could not be deem'd sufficient Encouragement for him to engage in an Enterprize, which carry'd so poor a Face of Probability of Success along with it. In answer to this it was urg'd, that till a Descent was made, and the Affairs thoroughly engag'd in, it was not to be expected that any great Numbers would appear, or that Persons of Condition would discover themselves. Upon all which it was resolv'd the Troops should be landed.

Accordingly, our Forces were disembark'd, and immediately encamp'd; notwithstanding which the Number of Succours increas'd very slowly, and that after the first straggling Manner. Nor were those that did appear any way to be depended on; coming when they thought fit, and going away when they pleas'd, and not to be brought under any regular Discipline. It was then pretended, that until they saw the Artillery landed as well as Forces, they would not believe any Siege actually intended. This brought the General under a sort of Necessity of complying in that also. Though certainly so to do must be allow'd a little unreasonable, while the Majority in all Councils of War declar'd the Design to be impracticable; and the Earl of *Peterborow* had positive Orders to proceed according to such Majorities.

At last the Prince of *Hesse* was pleas'd to demand Pay for those Stragglers, as Officers and Soldiers, endeavouring to maintain, that it could not be expected that Men should venture their Lives for nothing. Thus we came to *Catalonia* upon Assurances of universal Assistance; but found, when we came there, that we were to have none unless we paid for it. And as we were sent thither without Money to pay for any thing, it had certainly been for us more tolerable to have been in a Country where we might have taken by Force what we could not obtain any other way.

However, to do the *Miquelets* all possible Justice, I must say, that notwithstanding the Number of 'em, which hover'd about the Place, never much exceeded fifteen Hundred Men; if sometimes more, oftner less; and though they never came under any

Command, but planted themselves where and as they pleas'd; yet did they considerable Service in taking Possession of all the Country Houses and Convents, that lay between the Hills and the Plain of *Barcelona*; by means whereof they render'd it impossible for the Enemy to make any *Sorties* or Sallies at any Distance from the Town.

And now began all those Difficulties to bear, which long before by the General had been apprehended. The Troops had continu'd under a State of Inactivity for the Space of three Weeks, all which was spent in perpetual Contrivances and Disputes amongst our selves, not with the Enemy. In six several Councils of War the Siege of *Barcelona*, under the Circumstances we then lay, was rejected as a Madness and Impossibility. And though the General and Brigadier *Stanhope* (afterward Earl *Stanhope*) consented to some Effort should be made to satisfy the Expectation of the World, than with any Hopes of Success. However, no Consent at all could be obtain'd from any Council of War; and the *Dutch* General in particular declar'd, that he would not obey even the Commands of the Earl of *Peterborow*, if he should order the Sacrifice of the Troops under him in so unjustifiable a Manner, without the Consent of a Council of War.

And yet all those Officers, who refus'd their Consent to the Siege of *Barcelona*, offer'd to march into the Country, and attempt any other Place, that was not provided with so strong and numerous a Garrison; taking it for granted, that no Town in *Catalonia*, *Barcelona* excepted, could make long Resistance; and in case the Troops in that Garrison should pursue them, they then might have an Opportunity of fighting them at less Disadvantage in the open Field, than behind the Walls of a Place of such Strength. And, indeed, should they have issu'd out on any such Design, a Defeat of those Troops would have put the Province of *Catalonia*, together with the Kingdoms of *Aragon* and *Valencia*, into the Hands of King *Charles* more effectually than the taking of *Barcelona* it self.

Let it be observ'd, *en passant*, that by those Offers of the Land Officers in a Council of War, it is easy to imagine what would have been the Success of our Troops, had they march'd directly from *Valencia* to *Madrid*. For if after two Months Alarm, it was

thought reasonable, as well as practicable, to march into the open
Country rather than attempt the Siege of *Barcelona*, where Forces
equal, if not superior in Number, were ready to follow us at the
Heels; what might not have been expected from an Invasion by
our Troops when and where they could meet with little Opposition? But leaving the Consideration of what might have been,
I shall now endeavour at least with great Exactness to set down
some of the most remarkable Events from our taking to the
Relief of *Barcelona*.

The repeated Refusals of the Councils of War for undertaking
the Siege of so strong a Place, with a Garrison so numerous, and
those Refusals grounded upon such solid Reasons, against a
Design so rash, reduc'd the General to the utmost Perplexity. The
Court of King *Charles* was immerg'd in complaint; all belonging
to him lamenting the hard Fate of that Prince, to be brought into
Catalonia only to return again, without the Offer of any one
Effort in his Favour. On the other Hand, our own Officers and
Soldiers were highly dissatisfy'd, that they were reproach'd,
because not dispos'd to enter upon and engage themselves in
Impossibilities. And, indeed, in the Manner that the Siege was
propos'd and insisted upon by the Prince of *Hesse*, in every of
the several Councils of War, after the Loss of many Men, thrown
away to no other purpose, but to avoid the Shame (as the Expression ran of coming like Fools and going away like Cowards,
it could have ended in nothing but a Retreat at last.

It afforded but small Comfort to the Earl to have foreseen all
these Difficulties, and to have it in his Power to say, that he
would never have taken the Arch-Duke on Board, nor have propos'd to him the Hopes of a Recovery of the *Spanish* Monarchy
from King *Philip*, if he could have imagin'd it probable, that he
should not have been at liberty to pursue his own Design,
according to his own Judgment. It must be allow'd very hard for
him, who had undertaken so great a Work, and that without any
Orders from the Government; and by so doing could have had
no Justification but by Success; I say, it must be allow'd to be very
hard (after the Undertaking had been approv'd in *England*) that he
should find himself to be directed in this Manner by those at a
Distance, upon ill grounded and confident Reports from Mr.

Crow; and compell'd, as it were, though General, to follow the Sentiments of Strangers, who either had private Views of Ambition, or had no immediate Care or Concern for the Troops employ'd in this Expedition.

Such were the present unhappy Circumstanches of the Earl of *Peterborow* in the Camp before *Barcelona:* Impossibilities propos'd; no Expedients to be accepted; a Court reproaching; Councils of War rejecting; and the *Dutch* General refusing the Assistance of the Troops under his Command; and what surmounted all, a Despair of bringing such Animosities and differing Opinions to any tolerable Agreement. Yet all these Difficulties, instead of discouraging the Earl, set every Faculty of his more afloat; and, at last, produc'd a lucky Thought, which was happily attended with Events extraordinary, and Scenes of Success much beyond his Expectation; such, as the General himself was heard to confess, it had been next to Folly to have look'd for; as certainly, *in prima facie*, it would hardly have born proposing, to take by Surprize a Place much stronger than *Barcelona* it self. True it is, that his only Hope of succeeding consisted in this: That no Person could suppose such an Enterprize could enter into the Imagination of Man; and without doubt the General's chief Dependence lay upon what he found true in the Sequel; that the Governor and Garrison of *Monjouick*, by reason of their own Security, would be very negligent, and very little upon their Guard.

However, to make the Experiment, he took an Opportunity, unknown to any Person but an *Aid de Camp* that attended him, and went out to view the Fortifications: And there being no Horse in that strong Fortress; and the *Miquelets* being possess'd of all the Houses and Gardens in the Plain, it was not difficult to give himself that Satisfaction, taking his Way by the Foot of the Hill. The Observation he made of the Place it self, the Negligence and Supineness of the Garrison, together with his own uneasy Circumstances, soon brought the Earl to a Resolution of putting his first Conceptions in Execution, satisfy'd as he was, from the Situation of the Ground between *Monjouick* and the Town, that if the first was in our Possession, the Siege of the latter might be undertaken with some Prospect of Success.

From what has been said, some may be apt to conclude that the

Siege afterward succeeding, when the Attack was made from the Side of *Monjouick*, it had not been impossible to have prevail'd, if the Effort had been made on the East Side of the Town, where our Forces were at first encamp'd, and where only we could have made our Approaches, if *Monjouick* had not been in our Power. But a few Words will convince any of common Experience of the utter Impossibility of Success upon the East Part of the Town, although many almost miraculous Accidents made us succeed when we brought our Batteries to bear upon that Part of *Barcelona* towards the West. The Ground to the East was a perfect Level for many Miles, which would have necessitated our making our Approaches in a regular Way; and consequently our Men must have been expos'd to the full Fire of their whole Artillery. Besides, the Town is on that Side much stronger than any other; there is an Out-work just under the Walls of the Town, flank'd by the Courtin and the Faces of two Bastions, which might have cost us half our Troops to possess, before we could have rais'd a Battery against the Walls. Or supposing, after all, a competent Breach had been made, what a wise Piece of Work must it have been to have attempted a Storm against double the Number of regular Troops within?

On the contrary, we were so favoured by the Situation, when we made the Attack from the Side of *Monjouick*, that the Breach was made and the Town taken without opening of Trenches, or without our being at all incommoded by any Sallies of the Enemy; as in truth they made not one during the whole Siege. Our great Battery, which consisted of upwards of fifty heavy Cannon, supply'd from the Ships, and manag'd by the Seamen, were plac'd upon a Spot of rising Ground, just large enough to contain our Guns, with two deep hollow Ways on each Side the Field, at each End whereof we had rais'd a little Redoubt, which serv'd to preserve our Men from the Shot of the Town. Those little Redoubts, in which we had some Field Pieces, flank'd the Battery, and render'd it intirely secure from any Surprize of the Enemy. There were feveral other smaller Batteries rais'd upon the Hills adjacent, in Places not to be approach'd, which, in a manner, render'd all the Artillery of the Enemy useless, by reason their Men could not play 'em, but with the utmost Danger; whereas ours were secure, very few being kill'd, and those mostly by random Shot.

But to return to the General; forc'd, as he was, to take this extraordinary Resolution, he concluded, the readiest Way to surprize his Enemies was to elude his Friends. He therefore call'd a Council of War ashore, of the Land Officers; and aboard, of the Admirals and Sea Officers: In both which it was resolv'd, that in case the Siege of *Barcelona* was judg'd impracticable, and that the Troops should be re-imbark'd by a Day appointed, an Effort should be made upon the Kingdom of *Naples*. Accordingly, the Day affix'd being come, the heavy Artillery landed for the Siege was return'd aboard the Ships, and every thing in appearance prepar'd for a Re-imbarkment. During which, the General was oblig'd to undergo all the Reproaches of a dissatisfy'd Court; and what was more uneasy to him, the Murmurings of the Sea Officers, who, not so competent Judges in what related to Sieges, were one and all inclin'd to a Design upon *Barcelona*; and the rather, because as the Season was so far spent, it was thought altogether improper to engage the Fleet in any new Undertaking. However, all Things were so well disguis'd by our seeming Preparations for a Retreat, that the very Night our Troops were in March towards the Attack of *Monjouick*, there were publick Entertainments and Rejoicings in the Town for the raising of the Siege.

The Prince of *Hesse* had taken large Liberties in complaining against all the Proceedings in the Camp before *Barcelona*; even to Insinuations, that though the Earl gave his Opinion for some Effort in public, yet us'd he not sufficient Authority over the other General Officers to incline them to comply; throwing out withal some Hints, that the General from the Beginning had declar'd himself in favour of other Operations, and against coming to *Catalonia*; the latter Part whereof was nothing but Fact. On the other Side, the Earl of *Peterborow* complain'd, that the boasted Assistance was no way made good; and that in failure thereof, his Troops were to be sacrificed to the Humours of a Stranger; one who had no Command; and whose Conduct might bear a Question whether equal to his Courage. These Reproaches of one another had bred so much ill Blood between those two

great Men, that for above a Fortnight they had no Correspondence, nor ever exchang'd one Word.

The Earl, however, having made his proper Dispositions, and
deliver'd out his Orders, began his March in the Evening with
twelve Hundred Foot and two Hundred Horse, which of necessity were to pass by the Quarters of the Prince of *Hesse*. That
Prince, on their Appearance, was told that the General was come
to speak with him; and being brought into his Apartment, the
Earl acquainted him, that he had at last resolv'd upon an Attempt
against the Enemy; adding, that now, if he pleas'd, he might be
a Judge of their Behaviour, and see whether his Officers and
Soldiers had deserv'd that Character which he had so liberally
given 'em. The Prince made answer, that he had always been
ready to take his Share; but could hardly believe, that Troops
marching that way could make any Attempt against the Enemy
to satisfaction. However, without further Discourse he call'd for
his Horse.

By this we may see what Share Fortune has in the greatest
Events. In all probability the Earl of *Peterborow* had never engag'd in such a dangerous Affair in cold Blood and unprovok'd;
and if such an Enterprize had been resolv'd on in a regular Way,
it is very likely he might have given the Command to some of the
General Officers; since it is not usual, nor hardly allowable, for
one, that commands in chief, to go in Person on such kind of
Services. But here we see the General and Prince, notwithstanding
their late indifferent Harmony, engag'd together in this most
desperate Undertaking.

Brigadier *Stanhope* and Mr. *Methuen* (now Sir *Paul*) were the
General's particular Friends, and those he most consulted, and
most confided in; yet he never imparted this Resolution of his
to either of them; for he was not willing to engage them in a
Design so dangerous, and where there was so little Hope of
Success; rather choosing to reserve them as Persons most capable
of giving Advice and Assistance in the Confusion, great enough
already, which yet must have been greater, if any Accident had
happen'd to himself. And I have very good Reason to believe,
that the Motive, which mainly engag'd the Earl of *Peterborow* in
this Enterprize, was to satisfy the Prince of *Hesse* and the World,

that his Diffidence proceeded from his Concern for the Troops committed to his Charge, and not for his own Person. On the other Hand, the great Characters of the two Gentlemen just mention'd are so well known, that it will easily gain Credit, that the only Way the General could take to prevent their being of the Party, was to conceal it from them, as he did from all Mankind, even from the Archduke himself. And certainly there never was a more universal Surprize than when the firing was heard next Morning from *Monjouick*.

But I now proceed to give an exact Account of this great Action; of which no Person, that I have heard of, ever yet took upon him to deliver to Posterity the glorious Particulars; and yet the Consequences and Events, by what follows, will appear so great, and so very extraordinary, that few, if any, had they had it in their Power, would have deny'd themselves the Pleasure or the World the Satisfaction of knowing it.

The Troops, which march'd all Night along the Foot of the Mountains, arriv'd two Hours before Day under the Hill of *Monjouick*, not a Quarter of a Mile from the outward Works: For this Reason it was taken for granted, whatever the Design was which the General had propos'd to himself, that it would be put in Execution before Day-light; but the Earl of *Peterborow* was now pleas'd to inform the Officers of the Reasons why he chose to stay till the Light appear'd. He was of opinion that any Success would be impossible, unless the Enemy came into the outward Ditch under the Bastions of the second Enclosure; but that if they had time allow'd them to come thither, there being no Palisadoes, our Men, by leaping in upon them, after receipt of their first Fire, might drive 'em into the upper Works; and following them close, with some Probability, might force them, under that Confusion, into the inward Fortifications.

Such were the General's Reasons then and there given; after which, having promis'd ample Rewards to such as discharg'd their Duty well, a Lieutenant, with thirty Men, was order'd to advance towards the Bastion nearest the Town; and a Captain, with fifty Men, to support him. After the Enemy's Fire they were to leap into the Ditch, and their Orders were to follow 'em close, if they retir'd into the upper Works: Nevertheless, not to pursue 'em farther, if they made into the inner Fort; but to endeavour to cover themselves within the Gorge of the Bastion.

A Lieutenant and a Captain, with the like Number of Men and the same Orders, were commanded to a Demi-Bastion at the Extremity of the Fort towards the West, which was above Musket-Shot from the inward Fortification. Towards this Place the Wall, which was cut into the Rock, was not fac'd for about twenty Yards; and here our own Men got up; where they found three Pieces of Cannon upon a Platform, without many Men to defend them.

Those appointed to the Bastion towards the Town were sustain'd by two hundred Men; with which the General and Prince went in Person. The like Number, under the Directions of Colonel *Southwell*, were to sustain the Attack towards the West; and about five hundred Men were left under the Command of a *Dutch* Colonel, whose Orders were to assist, where, in his own Judgment, he should think most proper; and these were drawn up between the two Parties appointed to begin the Assault. My Lot was on the Side where the Prince and Earl were in Person; and where we sustain'd the only Loss from the first Fire of the Enemy.

Our men, though quite expos'd, and though the Glacis was all escarp'd upon the live Rock, went on with an undaunted Courage; and immediately after the first Fire of the Enemy, all, that were not kill'd or wounded, leap'd in, *pel-mel*, amongst the Enemy; who, being thus boldly attack'd, and seeing others pouring in upon 'em, retir'd in great Confusion; and some one Way, some another, ran into the inward Works.

There was a large Port in the Flank of the principal Bastion, towards the North-East, and a cover'd Way, through which the General and the Prince of *Hesse* follow'd the flying Forces; and by that Means became possess'd of it. Luckily enough here lay a Number of great Stones in the Gorge of the Bastion, for the Use of the Fortification; with which we made a Sort of Breast-Work, before the Enemy recover'd of their Amaze, or made any considerable Fire upon us from their inward Fort, which commanded the upper Part of that Bastion.

We were afterwards inform'd, that the Commander of the

Citadel, expecting but one Attack, had call'd off the Men from the most distant and western Part of the Fort, to that Side which was next the Town; upon which our Men got into a Demi-Bastion in the most extream Part of the Fortification. Here they got Possession of three Pieces of Cannon, with hardly any Opposition; and had Leisure to cast up a little Retrenchment, and to make use of the Guns they had taken to defend it. Under this Situation, the Enemy, when drove into the inward Fort, were expos'd to our Fire from those Places we were possess'd of, in case they offer'd to make any Sally, or other Attempt against us. Thus we every Moment became better and better prepar'd against any Effort of the Garrison. And as they could not pretend to assail us without evident Hazard; so nothing remain'd for us to do, till we could bring up our Artillery and Mortars. Now it was that the General sent for the thousand Men under Brigadier *Stanhope*'s Command, which he had posted at a Convent, half-way between the Town and *Monjouick*.

There was almost a total Cessation of Fire, the Men on both Sides being under Cover. The General was in the upper Part of the Bastion; the Prince of *Hesse* below, behind a little Work at the Point of the Bastion, whence he could only see the Heads of the Enemy over the Parapet of the inward Fort. Soon after an Accident happen'd which cost that gallant Prince his Life.

The Enemy had Lines of Communication between *Barcelona* and *Monjouick*. The Governor of the former, upon hearing the firing from the latter, immediately sent four hundred Dragoons on Horseback, under Orders, that two Hundred dismounting should reinforce the Garrison, and the other two Hundred should return with their Horses back to the Town.

When those two Hundred Dragoons were accordingly got into the inward Fort, unseen by any of our Men, the *Spaniards*, waving their Hats over their Heads, repeated over and over, *Viva el Rey, Viva*. This the Prince of *Hesse* unfortunately took for a Signal of their Desire to surrender. Upon which, with too much Warmth and Precipitancy, calling to the Soldiers following, *They surrender, they surrender*, he advanc'd with near three Hundred Men (who follow'd him without any Orders from their General) along the

Curtain² which led to the Ditch of the inward Fort. The Enemy suffered them to come into the Ditch, and there surrounding 'em, took two Hundred of them Prisoners, at the same time making a Discharge upon the rest, who were running back the Way they came. This firing brought the Earl of *Peterborow* down from the upper Part of the Bastion, to see what was doing below. When he had just turn'd the Point of the Bastion, he saw the Prince of *Hesse* retiring, with the Men that had so rashly advanc'd. The Earl had exchang'd a very few Words with him, when, from a second Fire, that Prince receiv'd a Shot in the great Artery of the Thigh, of which he died immediately, falling down at the General's Feet, who instantly gave Orders to carry off the Body to the next Convent.

Almost the same Moment an Officer came to acquaint the Earl of *Peterborow*, that a great Body of Horse and Foot, at least three Thousand, were on their March from *Barcelona* towards the Fort. The Distance is near a Mile, all uneven Ground; so that the Enemy was either discoverable, or not to be seen, just as they were marching on the Hills or in the Vallies. However, the General directly got on Horse-back, to take a View of those Forces from the rising Ground without the Fort, having left all the Posts, which were already taken, well secur'd with the allotted Numbers of Officers and Soldiers.

But the Event will demonstrate of what Consequence the Absence or Presence of one Man may prove on great Occasions; No sooner was the Earl out of the Fort, the Care of which he had left under the Command of the Lord *Charlemont* (a Person of known Merit and undoubted Courage, but somewhat too flexible in his Temper) when a panick Fear (tho' the Earl, as I have said, was only gone to take a View of the Enemy) seiz'd upon the Soldiery, which was a little too easily comply'd with by the Lord *Charlemont*, then commanding Officer. True it is; for I heard an Officer, ready enough to take such Advantages, urge to him, that none of all those Posts we were become Masters of, were tenable; that to offer at it would be no better than wilfully sacrificing human Lives to Caprice and Humour; and just like a Man's knocking his Head against Stone Walls, to try which was hardest. Having over-heard this Piece of Lip-Oratory, and finding by the Answer that it was too likely to prevail, and that all I was like to say would avail nothing. I slipt away as fast as I could, to acquaint the General with the Danger impending.

As I pass'd along, I took notice that the Panick was upon the Increase, the general Rumor affirming, that we should be all cut off by the Troops that were come out of *Barcelona*, if we did not immediately gain the Hills, or the Houses possess'd by the *Miquelets*. Officers and Soldiers, under this prevailing Terror, quitted their Posts; and in one united Body (the Lord *Charlemont* at the Head of them) march'd, or rather hurry'd out of the Fort; and were come half way down the Hill before the Earl of *Peterborow* came up to them. Though on my acquainting him with the shameful and surprizing Accident he made no Stay, but answering, with a good deal of Vehemence, *Good God, is it possible?* hastened back as fast as he could.

I never thought my self happier than in this Piece of Service to my Country. I confess I could not but value it, as having been therein more than a little instrumental in the glorious Successes which succeeded; since immediately upon this Notice from me, the Earl gallop'd up the Hill, and lighting when he came to Lord *Charlemont*, he took his Half-pike out of his Hand; and turning to the Officers and Soldiers, told them, if they would not face about and follow him, they should have the Scandal and eternal Infamy upon them of having deserted their Posts, and abandon'd their General.

It was surprizing to see with what Alacrity and new Courage they fac'd about and follow'd the Earl of *Peterborow*. In a Moment they had forgot their Apprehensions; and, without doubt, had they met with any Opposition, they would have behav'd themselves with the greatest Bravery. But as these Motions were unperceiv'd by the Enemy, all the Posts were regain'd, and anew possess'd in less than half an Hour, without any Loss: Though, had our Forces march'd half Musket-shot farther, their Retreat would have been perceiv'd, and all the Success attendant on this glorious Attempt must have been intirely blasted.

Another Incident which attended this happy Enterprize was this: The two hundred Men which fell into the Hands of the Enemy, by the unhappy Mistake of the Prince of *Hesse*, were carry'd directly into the Town. The Marquis of *Risburg*, a Lieutenant-General, who commanded the three thousand Men which were marching from the Town to the Relief of the Fort, examin'd the Prisoners, as they pass'd by; and they all agreeing that the General and the Prince of *Hesse* were in Person with the Troops that made the Attack on *Monjouick*, the Marquis gave immediate Orders to retire to the Town; taking it for granted, that the main Body of the Troops attended the Prince and General; and that some Design therefore was on foot to intercept his Return, in case he should venture too far. Thus the unfortunate Loss of our two hundred Men turn'd to our Advantage, in preventing the Advance of the Enemy, which must have put the Earl of *Peterborow* to inconceivable Difficulties.

The Body of one Thousand, under Brigadier *Stanhope*, being come up to *Monjouick*, and no Interruption given us by the Enemy, our Affairs were put into very good Order on this Side; while the Camp on the other Side was so fortify'd, that the Enemy, during the Siege, never made one Effort against it. In the mean time, the Communication between the two Camps was secure enough; although our Troops were obliged to a tedious March along the Foot of the Hills, whenever the General thought fit to relieve those on Duty on the Side of the Attack, from those Regiments encamp'd on the West Side of *Barcelona*.

The next Day, after the Earl of *Peterborow* had taken Care to secure the first Camp to the Eastward of the Town, he gave Orders to the Officers of the Fleet to land the Artillery and Ammunition behind the Fortress to the Westward. Immediately upon the Landing whereof, two Mortars were fix'd; from both which we ply'd the Fort of *Monjouick* furiously with our Bombs. But the third or fourth Day, one of our Shells fortunately lighting on their Magazine of Powder, blew it up; and with it the Governor, and many principal Officers who were at Dinner with him. The Blast, at the same Instant, threw down a Face of one of the smaller Bastions; which the vigilant *Miquelets*, ready enough to take all Advantages, no sooner saw (for they were under the Hill, very near the Place) but they readily enter'd, while the Enemy were under the utmost Confusion. If the Earl, no less watchful than they, had not at the same Moment thrown himself in with some regular Troops, and appeas'd the general Disorder, in all probability the Garrison had been put to the Sword. However, the General's Presence not only allay'd the Fury of the *Miquelets*; but kept his own Troops under strictest Discipline: So that in a happy Hour for the frighted Garrison, the General gave Officers and Soldiers Quarters, making them Prisoners of War.

How critical was that Minute wherein the General met his retreating Commander? a very few Steps farther had excluded us our own Conquests, to the utter Loss of all those greater Glories which ensu'd. Nor would that have been the worst; for besides the Shame attending such an ill concerted Retreat from our Acquests on *Monjouick*, we must have felt the accumulative Disgrace of infamously retiring aboard the Ships that brought us; but Heaven reserv'd for our General amazing Scenes both of Glory and Mortification.

I cannot here omit one Singularity of Life, which will demonstrate Men's different Way of Thinking, if not somewhat worse; when many Years after, to one in Office, who seem'd a little too dead to my Complaints, and by that Means irritating my human Passions, in Justice to my self, as well as Cause, I urged this Piece of Service, by which I not only preserv'd the Place, but the Honour of my Country; that *Minister petite*, to mortify my Expectations and baffle my Plea, with a Grimace as odd as his Logick, return'd, that, in his Opinion, the Service pretended was a Disservice to the Nation; since Perseverance had cost the Government more Money than all our Conquests were worth, could we have kept 'em. So irregular are the Conceptions of Man, when even great Actions thwart the Bent of an interested Will!

The Fort of *Monjouick* being thus surprizingly reduc'd, furnish'd a strange Vivacity to Mens Expectations, and as extravagantly flatter'd their Hopes; for as Success never fails to excite weaker Minds to pursue their good Fortune, though many times to their own Loss; so is it often too apt to push on more elevated Spirits to renew the Encounter for atchieving new Conquests, by hazarding too rashly all their former Glory. Accordingly, every Body now began to make his utmost Efforts; and look'd upon himself as a Drone, if he was not employ'd in doing something or other towards pushing forward the Siege of *Barcelona* it self, and raising proper Batteries for that Purpose. But, after all, it must in Justice be acknowledg'd, that notwithstanding this prodigious Success that attended this bold Enterprize, the Land Forces of themselves, without the Assistance of the Sailors, could never have reduc'd the Town. The Commanders and Officers of the Fleet had always evinc'd themselves Favourers of this Project upon *Barcelona*. A new Undertaking so late in the Year, as I have said before, was their utter Aversion, and what they hated to hear of. Elated therefore with a Beginning so auspicious, they gave a more willing Assistance than could have been ask'd, or judiciously expected. The Admirals forgot their Element, and acted as General Officers at Land: They came every Day from their Ships, with a Body of Men form'd into Companies, and regularly marshall'd and commanded by Captains and Lieutenants of their own. Captain *Littleton* in particular, one of the most advanced Captains in the whole Fleet, offer'd of himself to take care of the Landing and Conveyance of the Artillery to the Camp. And answerable to that his first Zeal was his Vigour all along, for finding it next to an Impossibility to draw the Cannon and Mortars up such vast Precipices by Horses, if the Country had afforded them, he caus'd Harnesses to be made for two hundred Men; and by that Means, after a prodigious Fatigue and Labour, brought the Cannon and Mortars necessary for the Siege up to the very Batteries.

In this Manner was the Siege begun; nor was it carry'd on with any less Application; the Approaches being made by an Army of Besiegers, that very little, if at all, exceeded the Number of the Besieg'd; not altogether in a regular Manner, our few Forces would not admit it; but yet with Regularity enough to secure our two little Camps, and preserve a Communication between both, not to be interrupted or incommoded by the Enemy. We had soon erected three several Batteries against the Place, all on the West Side of the Town, *viz.* one of nine Guns, another of Twelve, and the last of upwards of Thirty. From all which we ply'd the Town incessantly, and with all imaginable Fury; and very often in whole Vollies.

Nevertheless it was thought not only adviseable, but necessary, to erect another Battery, upon a lower Piece of Ground under a small Hill; which lying more within Reach, and opposite to those Places where the Walls were imagin'd weakest, would annoy the Town the more; and being design'd for six Guns only, might soon be perfected. A *French* Engeneer had the Direction; and indeed very quickly perfected it. But when it came to be consider'd which way to get the Cannon to it, most were of opinion that it would be absolutely impracticable, by reason of the vast Descent; tho' I believe they might have added a stronger Reason, and perhaps more intrinsick, that it was extremely expos'd to the Fire of the Enemy.

Having gain'd some little Reputation in the Attack of *Monjouick*, this Difficulty was at last to be put upon me; and as some, not my Enemies, suppos'd, more out of Envy than good Will. However, when I came to the Place, and had carefully taken a View of it, though I was sensible enough of the Difficulty, I made my main Objection as to the Time for accomplishing it; for it was then between Nine and Ten, and the Guns were to be mounted by Day-light. Neither could I at present see any other Way to answer their Expectations, than by casting the Cannon down the Precipice, at all Hazards, to the Place below, where that fourth Battery was erected.

This wanted not Objections to; and therefore to answer my Purpose, as to point of Time, sixty Men more were order'd me, as much as possible to facilitate the Work by Numbers; and accordingly I set about it. Just as I was setting all Hands to work, and had given Orders to my Men to begin some Paces back, to make the Descent more gradual, and thereby render the Task a little more feasible, Major *Collier*, who commanded the Train, came to me; and perceiving the Difficulties of the Undertaking, in a Fret told me, I was impos'd upon; and vow'd he would go and find out Brigadier *Petit*, and let him know the Impossibility, as well as the Unreasonableness of the Task I was put upon. He had scarce utter'd those Words, and turn'd himself round to perform his Promise, when an unlucky Shot with a Musket-Ball wounded him through the Shoulder; upon which he was carry'd off, and I saw him not till some considerable time after.

By the painful Diligence, and the additional Compliment of Men, however, I so well succeeded (such was my great good

Fortune) that the Way was made, and the Guns, by the Help of Fascines[3], and other lesser Preparations below, safely let down and mounted; so that that fourth Battery began to play upon the Town before Break of Day; and with all the Success that was propos'd.

In short, the Breach in a very few Days after was found wholly practicable; and all Things were got ready for a general Storm. Which Don *Valasco* the Governor being sensible of, immediately beat a Parley; upon which it was, among other Articles, concluded, that the Town should be surrender'd in three Days; and the better to ensure it, the Bastion, which commanded the Port St. *Angelo*, was directly put into our Possession.

But before the Expiration of the limited three Days, a very unexpected Accident fell out, which hasten'd the Surrender. Don *Valasco*, during his Government, had behav'd himself very arbitrarily, and thereby procur'd, as the Consequence of it, a large Proportion of ill will, not only among the Townsmen, but among the *Miquelets*, who had, in their Zeal to King *Charles*, flock'd from all Parts of *Catalonia* to the Siege of their Capital; and who, on the Signing of the Articles of Surrender, had found various Ways, being well acquainted with the most private Avenues, to get by Night into the Town: So that early in the Morning they began to plunder all that they knew Enemies to King *Charles*, or thought Friends to the Prince his Competitor.

Their main Design was upon *Valasco* the Governor, whom, if they could have got into their Hands, it was not to be question'd, but as far as his Life and Limbs would have serv'd, they would have sufficiently satiated their Vengeance upon. He expected no less; and therefore concealed himself, till the Earl of *Peterborow* could give Orders for his more safe and private Conveyance by Sea to *Alicant*.

Nevertheless, in the Town all was in the utmost Confusion; which the Earl of *Peterborow*, at the very first hearing, hastened to appease; with his usual Alacrity he rid all alone to Port St. *Angelo*, where at that time my self happen'd to be; and demanding to be admitted, the Officer of the Guard, under Fear and Surprise, open'd the Wicket, through which the Earl enter'd, and I after him.

Scarce had we gone a hundred Paces, when we saw a Lady of apparent Quality, and indisputable Beauty, in a strange, but most affecting Agony, flying from the apprehended Fury of the *Miquelets*; her lovely Hair was all flowing about her Shoulders, which, and the Consternation she was in, rather added to, than any thing diminish'd from the Charms of an Excess of Beauty. She, as is very natural to People in Distress, made up directly to the Earl, her Eyes satisfying her he was a Person likely to give her all the Protection she wanted. And as soon as ever she came near enough, in a Manner that declar'd her Quality before she spoke, she crav'd that Protection, telling him, the better to secure it, who it was that ask'd it. But the generous Earl presently convinc'd her, he wanted no Intreaties, having, before he knew her to be the Dutchess of *Popoli*, taken her by the Hand, in order to convey her through the Wicket which he enter'd at, to a Place of Safety without the Town.

I stay'd behind, while the Earl convey'd the distress'd Dutchess to her requested *Asylum*; and I believe it was much the longest Part of an Hour before he return'd. But as soon as ever he came back, he, and my self, at his Command, repair'd to the Place of most Confusion, which the extraordinary Noise full readily directed us to; and which happened to be on the Parade before the Palace. There it was that the *Miquelets* were making their utmost Efforts to get into their Hands the almost sole Occasion of the Tumult, and the Object of their raging Fury, the Person of Don *Valasco*, the late Governor.

It was here that the Earl preserv'd that Governor from the violent, but perhaps too just Resentments of the *Miquelets*; and, as I said before, convey'd him by Sea to *Alicant*. And, indeed, I could little doubt the Effect, or be any thing surpriz'd at the Easiness of the Task, when I saw, that wherever he appear'd the popular Fury was in a Moment allay'd, and that every Dictate of that General was assented to with the utmost Chearfulness and Deference. *Valasco*, before his Embarkment, had given Orders, in Gratitude to his Preserver, for all the Gates to be deliver'd up, tho' short of the stipulated Term; and they were accordingly so delivered, and our Troops took Possession so soon as ever that Governor was aboard the Ship that was to convey him to *Alicant*.

During the Siege of *Barcelona*, Brigadier *Stanhope* order'd a Tent to be pitch'd as near the Trenches as possibly could be with Safety; where he not only entertain'd the chief Officers who were upon Duty, but likewise the *Catalonian* Gentlemen who brought *Miquelets* to our Assistance. I remember I saw an old Cavalier, having his only Son with him, who appear'd a fine young Gentleman, about twenty Years of Age, go into the Tent, in order to dine with the Brigadier. But whilst they were at Dinner, an unfortunate Shot came from the Bastion of St. *Antonio*, and intirely struck off the Head of the Son. The father immediately rose up, first looking down upon his headless Child, and then lifting up his Eyes to Heaven, whilst the Tears ran down his Cheeks, he cross'd himself, and only said, *Fiat voluntas tua*, and bore it with a wonderful Patience. 'Twas a sad Spectacle, and truly it affects me now whilst I am writing.

The Earl of *Peterborow*, tho' for some time after the Revolution he had been employ'd in civil Affairs, return'd to the military Life with great Satisfaction, which was ever his Inclination. Brigadier *Stanhope*, who was justly afterwards created an Earl, did well deserve this Motto, *Tam Marte quam Mercurio*; for truly he behav'd, all the time he continu'd in *Spain*, as if he had been inspir'd with Conduct; for the Victory at *Almanar* was intirely owing to him; and likewise at the Battle of *Saragosa* he distinguish'd himself with great Bravery. That he had not Success at *Bruhega* was not his Fault; for no Man can resist Fate; for 'twas decreed by Heaven that *Philip* should remain King of *Spain*, and *Charles* to be Emperor of *Germany*. Yet each of these Monarchs have been ungrateful to the Instruments which the Almighty made use of to preserve them upon their Thrones; for one had not been King of *Spain* but for *France*; and the other had not been Emperor but for *England*.

Barcelona, the chief Place in *Catalonia*, being thus in our Hands, as soon as the Garrison, little inferior to our Army, had march'd out with Drums beating, Colours flying, &c. according to the Articles, *Charles* the Third made his publick Entry, and was proclaim'd King, and receiv'd with the general Acclamations, and all other Demonstrations of Joy suitable to that great Occasion. Some Days after which, the Citizens, far from being satiated with their former Demonstrations of their Duty, sent a Petition to the King, by proper Deputies for that Purpose appointed, desiring Leave to give more ample Instances of their Affections in a public *Cavalcade*. The King granted their Request, and the Citizens, pursuant thereto, made their Preparations.

On the Day appointed, the King, plac'd in a Balcony belonging to the House of the Earl of *Peterborow*, appear'd ready to honour the Show. The Ceremonial, to speak nothing figuratively, was very fine and grand: Those of the first Rank made their Appearance in decent Order, and upon fine Horses; and others under Arms, and in Companies, march'd with native Gravity and Grandeur, all saluting his Majesty as they pass'd by, after the *Spanish* Manner, which that Prince return'd with the Movement of his Hand to his Mouth; for the Kings of *Spain* are not allow'd to salute, or return a Salute, by any Motion to, or of, the Hat.

After these follow'd several Pageants; the first of which was drawn by Mules, set off to the Height with stateliest Feathers, and adorn'd with little Bells. Upon the Top of this Pageant appear'd a Man dress'd all in Green; but in the Likeness of a Dragon. The Pageant making a Stop just over-against the Balcony where the King sate, the Dragonical Representative diverted him with great Variety of Dancings, the Earl of *Peterborow* all the time throwing out Dollars by Handfuls among the Populace, which they as constantly receiv'd with the loud Acclamation and repeated Cries of *Viva, Viva, Carlos Terceros, Viva la Casa d'Austria*.

When that had play'd its Part, another Pageant, drawn as before, made a like full Stop before the same Balcony. On this was plac'd a very large Cage, or Aviary, the Cover of which, by Springs contriv'd for that Purpose, immediately flew open, and out of it a surprizing Flight of Birds of various Colours. These, all amaz'd at their sudden Liberty, which I took to be the Emblem intended, hover'd a considerable space of time over and about their Place of Freedom, chirping, singing, and otherwise testifying their mighty Joy for their so unexpected Enlargement.

There were many other Pageants; but having little in them very remarkable, I have forgot the Particulars. Nevertheless, every one of them was dismiss'd with the like Acclamations of

Viva, Viva; the Whole concluding with Bonfires and Illumina-
tions common on all such Occasions.

I cannot here omit one very remarkable Instance of the Catholick Zeal of that Prince, which I was soon after an Eye-witness of.
I was at that time in the Fruit-Market, when the King passing
by in his Coach, the Host (whether by Accident or Contrivance
I cannot say) was brought, at that very Juncture, out of the great
Church, in order, as I after understood, to a poor sick Woman's
receiving the Sacrament. On Sight of the Host the King came out
of his Coach, kneel'd down in the Street, which at that time
prov'd to be very dirty, till the Host pass'd by; then rose up, and
taking the lighted Flambeau from him who bore it, he follow'd
the Priest up a streight nasty Alley, and there up a dark ordinary
Pair of Stairs, where the poor sick Woman lay. There he stay'd
till the whole Ceremony was over, when, returning to the Door
of the Church, he very faithfully restor'd the lighted Flambeau
to the Fellow he had taken it from, the People all the while crying out *Viva, Viva*; an Acclamation, we may imagine, intended
to his Zeal, as well as his Person.

Another remarkable Accident, of a much more moral Nature,
I must, in justice to the Temperance of that, in this truly inimit-
able People, recite. I was one Day walking in one of the most
populous Streets of that City, where I found an uncommon Concourse of People, of all Sorts, got together; and imagining so
great a Croud could not be assembled on a small Occasion, I
prest in among the rest; and after a good deal of Struggling and
Difficulty, reach'd into the Ring and Centre of that mix'd Multitude. But how did I blush? with what Confusion did I appear?
when I found one of my own Countrymen, a drunken Granadier,
the attractive Loadstone of all that high and low Mob, and the
Butt of all their Merriment? It will be easily imagin'd to be a
Thing not a little surprizing to one of our Country, to find that
a drunken Man should be such a wonderful Sight; However, the
witty Sarcasms that were then by high and low thrown upon that
senseless Creature, and as I interpreted Matters, me in him, were
so pungent, that if I did not curse my Curiosity, I thought it best
to withdraw my self as fast as Legs could carry me away.

BARCELONA being now under King *Charles*, the Towns of

Gironne, Tarragona, Tortosa, and *Lerida,* immediately declar'd for him. To every one of which Engeneers being order'd, it was my Lot to be sent to *Tortosa.* This Town is situated on the Side of the River *Ebro,* over which there is a fair and famous Bridge of Boats. The Waters of this River are always of a dirty red Colour, somewhat fouler than our Moorish Waters; yet is it the only Water the Inhabitants drink, or covet to drink; and every House providing for its own Convenience Cisterns to preserve it in, by a few Hours standing it becomes as clear as the clearest Rock-water, but as soft as Milk. In short, for Softness, Brightness, and Pleasantness of Taste, the Natives prefer it to all the Waters in the World. And I must declare in favour of their Opinion, that none ever pleas'd me like it.

This Town was of the greater Moment to our Army, as opening a Passage into the Kingdom of *Valencia* on one Side, and the Kingdom of *Arragon* on the other: And being of it self tolerably defensible, in human Appearance might probably repay a little Care and Charge in its Repair and Improvement. Upon this Employ was I appointed, and thus was I busy'd, till the Arrival of the Earl of *Peterborow* with his little Army, in order to march to *Valencia,* the Capital of that Province. Here he left in Garrison Colonel *Hans Hamilton's* Regiment; the Place, nevertheless, was under the Command of a *Spanish* Governor, appointed by King *Charles.*

While the Earl stay'd a few Days at this Place, under Expectation of the promis'd Succours from *Barcelona,* he receiv'd *a Proprio* (or Express) from the King of *Spain,* full of Excuses, instead of Forces. And yet the very same Letter, in a paradoxical Manner, commanded him, at all Events, to attempt the Relief of *Santo Mattheo,* where Colonel *Jones* commanded, and which was then under Siege by the *Conde de los Torres* (as was the Report) with upwards of three thousand Men. The Earl of *Peterborow* could not muster above one thousand Foot, and about two hundred Horse; a small Force to make an Attempt of that Nature upon such a superior Power: Yet the Earl's Vivacity[4] (as will be occasionally further observ'd in the Course of these Memoirs) never much regarded Numbers, so there was but room, by any Stratagem, to hope for Success. True it is, for his greater Encouragement and Consolation, the same Letter intimated, that a great

4

Concourse of the Country People being up in Arms, to the
Number of many Thousands, in Favour of King *Charles*, and
wanting only Officers, the Enterprize would be easy and un-
attended with much Danger. But upon mature Enquiry, the Earl
found that great Body of Men all *in nubibus*; and that the *Conde*,
in the plain Truth of the Matter, was much stronger than the
Letter at first represented.

SANTO Mattheo was a Place of known Importance; and that
from its Situation, which cut off all Communication between
Catalonia and *Valencia*; and, consequently, should it fall into the
Hands of the Enemy, the Earl's Design upon the latter must
inevitably have been postpon'd. It must be granted, the Commands for attempting the Relief of it were pressing and peremptory; nevertheless, the Earl was very conscious to himself, that
as the promis'd Reinforcements were suspended, his Officers
would not approve of the Attempt upon the Foot of such vast
Inequalities; and their own declar'd Sentiments soon confirm'd
the Dictates of the Earl's Reason. He therefore addresses himself
to those Officers in a different Manner: He told 'em he only
desir'd they would be passive, and leave it to him to work his
own Way. Accordingly, the Earl found out and hired two
Spanish Spies, for whose Fidelity (as his great Precaution always
led him to do) he took sufficient Security; and dispatch'd 'em
with a Letter to Colonel *Jones*, Governor of the Place, intimating
his Readiness, as well as Ability, to relieve him; and, above all,
exhorting him to have the *Miquelets* in the Town ready, on Sight
of his Troops, to issue out, pursue, and plunder; since that would
be all they would have to do, and all he would expect at their
Hands. The Spies were dispatch'd accordingly; and, pursuant to
Instructions, one betray'd and discover'd the other who had the
Letter in charge to deliver to Colonel *Jones*. The Earl, to carry on
the Feint, having in the mean time, by dividing his Troops, and
marching secretly over the Mountains, drawn his Men together,
so as to make their Appearance on the Height of a neighbouring
Mountain, little more than Cannot-shot from the Enemy's
Camp. The Tale of the Spies was fully confirm'd, and the *Conde*
(though an able General) march'd off with some Precipitation
with his Army; and by that Means the Earl's smaller Number of

twelve Hundred had Liberty to march into the Town without Interruption. I must not let slip an Action of Colonel *Jones's* just before the Earl's Delivery of them: The *Conde*, for want of Artillery, had set his Miners to work; and the Colonel, finding they had made some dangerous Advances, turned the Course of a Rivulet, that ran through the Middle of the Town, in upon them, and made them quit a Work they thought was brought to Perfection.

SANTO Mattheo being reliev'd, as I have said, the Earl, though he had so far gain'd his Ends, left not the flying Enemy without a Feint of Pursuit; with such Caution, nevertheless, that in case they should happen to be better inform'd of his Weakness, he might have a Resource either back again to *Santo Mattheo*, or to *Vinaros* on the Sea-side; or some other Place, as occasion might require. But having just before receiv'd fresh Advice, that the Reinforcements he expected were anew countermanded; and that the Duke of *Anjou* had increas'd his Troops to twelve thousand Men; the Officers, not enough elated with the last Success to adventure upon new Experiments, resolv'd, in a Council of War, to advise the Earl, who had just before receiv'd a discretionary Commission in lieu of Troops, so to post the Forces under him, as not to be cut off from being able to assist the King in Person; or to march to the Defence of *Catalonia*, in case of Necessity.

Pursuant to this Resolution of the Council of War, the Earl of *Peterborow*, tho' still intent upon his Expedition into *Valencia* (which had been afresh commanded, even while his Supplies were countermanded) orders his Foot, in a truly bad Condition, by tedious Marches Day and Night over the Mountains, to *Vinaros*; and with his two hundred Horse, set out to prosecute his pretended Design of pursuing the flying Enemy; resolv'd, if possible, notwithstanding all seemingly desperate Circumstances, to perfect the Security of that Capital.

To that Purpose, the Earl, with his small Body of Patrolers, went on frightning the Enemy, till they came under the Walls of *Nules*, a Town fortify'd with the best Walls, regular Towers, and in the best Repair of any in that Kingdom. But even here, upon the Appearance of the Earl's Forlorn (if they might not properly at that time all have pass'd under that Character) under the same Panick they left that sensible Town, with only one Thousand of the Town's People, well arm'd, for the Defence of it. Yet was it scarce to be imagin'd, that the Earl, with his small Body of two hundred Horse, should be able to gain Admission; or, indeed, under such Circumstances, to attempt it. But bold as the Undertaking was, his good Genius went along with him; and so good a Genius was it, that it rarely left him without a good Effect. He had been told the Day before, that the Enemy, on leaving *Nules*, had got Possession of *Villa Real*, where they put all to the Sword. What would have furnish'd another with Terror, inspir'd his Lordship with a Thought as fortunate as it was successful. The Earl rides up to the very Gates of the Town, at the Head of his Party, and peremptorily demands the chief Magistrate, or a Priest, immediately to be sent out to him; and that under Penalty of being all put to the Sword, and us'd as the Enemy had us'd those at *Villa-Real* the Day or two before. The Troops, that had so lately left the Place, had left behind 'em more Terror than Men; which, together with the peremptory Demand of the Earl, soon produc'd some Priests to wait upon the General. By their Readiness to obey, the Earl very justly imagin'd Fear to be the Motive; wherefore, to improve their Terror, he only allow'd them six Minutes time to resolve upon a Surrender, telling them, that otherwise, so soon as his Artillery was come up, he would lay them under the utmost Extremities. The Priests return'd with this melancholy Message into the Place; and in a very short time after the Gates were thrown open. Upon the Earl's Entrance he found two hundred Horse, which were the Original of his Lordship's forming that Body of Horse, which afterwards prov'd the saving of *Valencia*.

The News of the taking of *Nules* soon overtook the flying Enemy; and so increas'd the Apprehensions of their Danger, that they renew'd their March, the same Day; though what they had taken before would have satisfy'd them much better without it. On the other hand, the Earl was so well pleas'd with his Success, that leaving the Enemy to fly before their Fears, he made a short Turn towards *Castillon de la Plana*, a considerable, but open Town, where his Lordship furnish'd himself with four hundred Horses more; and all this under the Assurance that his Troops were driving the Enemy before them out of the Kingdom. Hence he sent Orders to Colonel *Pierce*'s Regiment at *Vinaros* to meet him at *Oropesa*, a Place at no great Distance; where, when they came, they were very pleasingly surpriz'd at their being well mounted, and furnish'd with all Accoutrements necessary. After which, leaving 'em canton'd in wall'd Towns, where they could not be disturb'd without Artillery, that indefatigable General, leaving them full Orders, went on his way towards *Tortosa*.

At *Vinaros* the Earl met with Advice, that the *Spanish* Militia of the Kingdom of *Valencia* were assembled, and had already advanc'd a Day's March at least into that Country. Upon which, collecting, as fast as he could, the whole Corps together, the Earl resolv'd to penetrate into *Valencia* directly; notwithstanding this whole collected Body would amount to no more than six hundred Horse and two thousand Foot.

But there was a strong Pass over a River, just under the Walls of *Molviedro*, which must be first disputed and taken. This Brigadier *Mahoni*, by the Orders of the Duke of *Arcos*, who commanded the Troops of the Duke of *Anjou* in the Kingdom of *Valencia*, had taken care to secure. *Molviedro*, though not very strong, is a wall'd Town, very populous of it self; and had in it, besides a Garrison of eight hundred Men, most of *Mahoni*'s Dragoons. It lies at the very Bottom of a high Hill; on the upper Part whereof they shew the Ruins of the once famous SAGUN-TUM; famous sure to Eternity, if Letters shall last so long, for an inviolable Fidelity to a negligent Confederate, against an implacable Enemy. Here yet appear the visible *Vestigia* of awful Antiquity, in half standing Arches, and the yet unlevell'd Walls and Towers of that once celebrated City. I could not but look upon all these with the Eyes of Despight, in regard to their Enemy *Hannibal*; with those of Disdain, in respect to the uncommon and unaccountable Supineness of its Confederates, the *Romans*; but with those of Veneration, as to the Memory of a glorious People, who rather than stand reproach'd with a Breach of Faith, or the Brand of Cowardice, chose to sacrifice themselves, their Wives, Children, and all that was dear to them, in the Flames of their expiring City.

In *Molviedro*, as I said before, *Mahoni* commanded, with eight hundred Men, besides Inhabitants; which, together with our having but little Artillery, induc'd the Officers under the Earl of *Peterborow* reasonably enough to imagine and declare, that there could be no visible Appearance of surmounting such Difficulties. The Earl, nevertheless, instead of indulging such Despondencies, gave them Hope, that what Strength serv'd not to accomplish, Art might possibly obtain. To that Purpose he proposed an Interview between himself and *Mahoni*; and accordingly sent an Officer with a Trumpet to intimate his Desire. The Motion was agreed to; and the Earl having previously station'd his Troops to advantage, and his little Artillery at a convenient Distance, with Orders they should appear on a slow March on the Side of a rising Hill, during the time of Conference, went to the Place appointed; only, as had been stipulated, attended with a small Party of Horse. When they were met, the Earl first offer'd all he could to engage *Mahoni* to the Interest of King *Charles*; proposing some Things extravagant enough (as *Mahoni* himself some time after told me) to stagger the Faith of a Catholick; but all to little Purpose: *Mahoni* was inflexible, which oblig'd the Earl to new Measures.

Whereupon the Earl frankly told him, that he could not however but esteem the Confidence he had put in him; and therefore, to make some Retaliation, he was ready to put it in his Power to avoid the Barbarities lately executed at *Villa-Real*.

"My Relation to you," continued the General, "inclines me to spare a Town under your Command. You see how near my Forces are; and can hardly doubt our soon being Masters of the Place: What I would therefore offer you, said the Earl, is a Capitulation, that my Inclination may be held in Countenance by my Honour. Barbarities, however justified by Example, are my utter Aversion, and against my Nature; and to testify so much, together with my good Will to your Person, was the main Intent of this Interview."

This Frankness so far prevail'd on *Mahoni*, that he agreed to return an Answer in half an Hour. Accordingly, an Answer was returned by a *Spanish* Officer, and a Capitulation agreed upon; the Earl at the same time endeavouring to bring over that Officer to King *Charles*, on much the same Topicks he us'd with *Mahoni*.

But finding this equally fruitless, whether it was that he tacitly reproach'd the Officer with a Want of Consideration in neglecting to follow the Example of his Commander, or what else, he created in that Officer such a Jealousy of *Mahoni*, that was afterward very serviceable to him in his further Design.

To forward which to a good Issue, the Earl immediately made choice of two Dragoons, who, upon promise of Promotion, undertook to go as Spies to the Duke of *Arcos*, whose Forces lay not far off, on the other Side a large Plain, which the Earl must unavoidably pass, and which would inevitably be attended with almost insuperable Dangers, if there attack'd by a Force so much superior. Those Spies, according to Instructions, were to discover to the Duke, that they over-heard the Conference between the Earl and *Mahoni*; and at the same time saw a considerable Number of Pistoles deliver'd into *Mahoni*'s Hands, large Promises passing at that Instant reciprocally: But above all, that the Earl had recommended to him the procuring the March of the Duke over the Plain between them. The Spies went and deliver'd all according to Concert; concluding, before the Duke, that they would ask no Reward, but undergo any Punishment, if *Mahoni* did not very soon send to the Duke a Request to march over the Plain, in order to put the concerted Plot in execution. It was not long after this pretended Discovery before *Mahoni* did send indeed an Officer to the Duke, desiring the March of his Forces over the Plain; but, in reality, to obstruct the Earl's Passage, which he knew very well must be that and no other way. However, the Duke being prepossess'd by the Spies, and what those *Spanish* Officers that at first escap'd had before infus'd, took Things in their Sense; and as soon as *Mahoni*, who was forc'd to make the best of his way over the Plain before the Earl of *Peterborow*, arriv'd at his Camp, he was put under Arrest and sent to *Madrid*. The Duke having thus imbib'd the Venom, and taken the Alarm, immediately decamp'd in Confusion, and took a different Rout than at first he intended; leaving that once formidable Plain open to the Earl, without an Enemy to obstruct him. In some little time after he arriv'd at *Madrid*, *Mahoni* made his Innocence appear, and was created a General; while the Duke of *Arcos* was recall'd from his Post of Honour.

The Day after we arriv'd at *Valencia*, the Gates of which fine City were set open to us with the highest Demonstrations of Joy. I call'd it a fine City; but sure it richly deserves a brighter Epithet, since it is a common Saying among the *Spaniards*, that the Pleasures of *Valencia* would make a *Jew* forget *Jerusalem*. It is most sweetly situated in a very beautiful Plain, and within half a League of the *Mediterranean* Sea. It never wants any of the Fragrancies of Nature, and always has something to delight the most curious Eye. It is famous to a Proverb for fine Women; but as infamous, and only in that so, for the Race of Bravoes, the common Companions of the Ladies of Pleasure in this Country. These Wretches are so Case-hardened, they will commit a Murder for a Dollar, tho' they run their Country for it when they have done. Not that other Parts of this Nation are uninfested with this sort of Animals; but here their Numbers are so great, that if a Catalogue was to be taken of those in other Parts of that Country, perhaps nine in ten would be found by Birth to be of this Province.

But to proceed, tho' the Citizens, and all Sorts of People, were redundant in their various Expressions of Joy, for an Entry so surprizing, and utterly lost to their Expectation, whatever it was to their Wishes, the Earl had a secret Concern for the Publick, which lay gnawing at his Heart, and which yet he was forced to conceal. He knew that he had not four thousand Soldiers in the Place, and not Powder or Ammunition for those; nor any Provisions lay'd in for any thing like a Siege. On the other Hand, the Enemy without were upwards of seven Thousand, with a Body of four Thousand more, not fifteen Leagues off, on their March to join them. Add to this, the Marechal de *Thesse* was no farther off than *Madrid*, a very few Days' March from *Valencia*; a short Way indeed for the Earl (who, as was said before, was wholly unprovided for a Siege, which was reported to be the sole End of the Mareschal's moving that Way.) But the Earl's never-failing Genius resolv'd again to attempt that by Art, which the Strength of his Forces utterly disallow'd him. And in the first Place, his Intelligence telling him that sixteen twenty-four Pounders, with Stores and Ammunition answerable for a Siege, were ship'd off for the Enemy's Service at *Alicant*, the Earl forthwith lays a Design, and with his usual Success intercepts 'em all, supplying that way his own Necessities at the Expence of the Enemy.

The four thousand Men ready to reinforce the Troops nearer *Valencia*, were the next Point to be undertaken; but *hic labor, hoc opus*; since the greater Body under the Conde *de las Torres* (who, with *Mahoni*, was now reinstated in his Post) lay between the Earl and those Troops intended to be dispers'd. And what inhaunc'd the Difficulty, the River *Xucar* must be passed in almost the Face of the Enemy. Great Disadvantages as these were, they did not discourage the Earl. He detach'd by Night four hundred Horse and eight hundred Foot, who march'd with such hasty Silence, that they surpriz'd that great Body, routed 'em, and brought into *Valencia* six hundred Prisoners very safely, notwithstanding they were oblig'd, under the same Night-Covert, to pass very near a Body of three Thousand of the Enemy's Horse. Such a prodigious Victory would hardly have gain'd Credit in that City, if the Prisoners brought in had not been living Witnesses of the Action as well as the Triumph. The Conde *de las Torres*, upon these two military Rebuffs, drew off to a more convenient Distance, and left the Earl a little more at ease in his new Quarters.

Here the Earl of *Peterborow* made his Residence for some time. He was extreamly well belov'd, his affable Behaviour exacted as much from all; and he preserv'd such a good Correspondence with the Priests and the Ladies, that he never fail'd of the most early and best Intelligence, a thing by no means to be slighted in the common Course of Life; but much more commendable and necessary in a General, with so small an Army, at open War, and in the Heart of his Enemy's Country.

The Earl, by this Means, some small time after, receiving early Intelligence that King *Philip* was actually on his March to *Barcelona*, with an Army of upwards of twenty five thousand Men, under the Command of a Mareschal of *France*, began his March towards *Catalonia*, with all the Troops that he could gather together, leaving in *Valencia* a small Body of Foot, such as in that Exigence could best be spar'd. The whole Body thus collected made very little more than two thousand Foot and six hundred Horse; yet resolutely with these he sets out for *Barcelona*: In the

4*

Neighbourhood of which, as soon as he arriv'd, he took care to post himself and his diminutive Army in the Mountains which inviron that City; where he not only secur'd 'em against the Enemy; but found himself in a Capacity of putting him under perpetual Alarms. Nor was the Mareschal, with his great Army, capable of returning the Earl's Compliment of Disturbance; since he himself, every six or eight Hours, put his Troops into such a varying Situation, that always when most arduously fought, he was farthest off from being found. In this Manner the General bitterly harrass'd the Troops of the Enemy; and by these Means struck a perpetual Terror into the Besiegers. Nor did he only this way annoy the Enemy; the Precautions he had us'd, and the Measures he had taken in other Places, with a View to prevent their Return to *Madrid*, though the Invidious endeavour'd to bury them in Oblivion, having equally contributed to the driving of the Mareschal of *France*, and his Catholick King, out of the *Spanish* Dominions.

But to go on with the Siege: The Breaches in the Walls of that City, during its Siege by the Earl, had been put into tolerable Repair; but those of *Monjouick*, on the contrary, had been as much neglected. However, the Garrison made shift to hold out a Battery of twenty-three Days, with no less than fifty Pieces of Cannon; when, after a Loss of the Enemy of upwards of three thousand Men (a Moiety of the Army employ'd against it when the Earl took it) they were forc'd to surrender at Discretion. And this cannot but merit our Observation, that a Place, which the *English* General took in little more than an Hour, and with inconsiderable Loss, afforded the Mareschal of *France* a Resistance of twenty-three Days.

Upon the taking of Fort *Monjouick*, the Marechal *de Thess* gave immediate Orders for Batteries to be rais'd against the Town. Those Orders were put in Execution with all Expedition; and at the same time his Army fortify'd themselves with such Entrenchments, as would have ruin'd the Earl's former little Army to have rais'd, or his present much lesser Army to have attempted the forcing them. However, they sufficiently demonstrated their Apprehensions of that watchful General, who lay hovering over their Heads upon the Mountains. Their main Effort was to make a Breach between Port St. *Antonio* and that Breach which our Forces had made the Year before; to effect which they took care to ply them very diligently both from Cannon and Mortars; and in some few Days their Application was answer'd with a practicable Breach for a Storm. Which however was prudently deferr'd for some time, and that thro' fear of the Earl's falling on the Back of them whenever they should attempt it; which, consequently, they were sensible might put them into some dangerous Disorder.

And now it was that the Earl of *Peterborow* resolv'd to put in practice the Resolution he had some time before concerted within himself. About nine or ten Days before the Raising of the Siege, he had receiv'd an Express from Brigadier *Stanhope* (who was aboard Sir *John Leake*'s Fleet appointed for the Relief of the Place, with the Reinforcements from *England*) acquainting the Earl, that he had us'd all possible Endeavours to prevail on the Admiral to make the best of his way to *Barcelona*. But that the Admiral, however, persisted in a positive Resolution not to attempt the *French* Fleet before that Place under the Count *de Thoulouse*, till the Ships were join'd him which were expected from *Ireland*, under the Command of Sir *George Bing*. True it was, the Fleet under Admiral *Leake* was of equal Strength with that under the *French* Admiral; but jealous of the Informations he had receiv'd, and too ready to conclude that People in Distress were apt to make Representations too much in their own Favour; he held himself, in point of Discretion, oblig'd not to hazard the Queen's Ships, when a Reinforcement of both cleaner and larger were under daily Expectation.

This unhappy Circumstance (notwithstanding all former glorious Deliverances) had almost brought the Earl to the Brink of Despair; and to increase it, the Earl every Day receiv'd such Commands from the King within the Place, as must have sacrificed his few Forces, without the least Probability of succeeding. Those all tended to his forcing his Way into the Town; when, in all human Appearance, not one Man of all that should make the Attempt could have done it, with any Hope or Prospect of sursurviving. The *French* were strongly encamp'd at the Foot of the Mountains, distant two Miles from *Barcelona*; towards the Bottom of those Hills, the Avenues into the Plain were possess'd and fortify'd by great Detachments from the Enemy's Army. From all which it will be evident, that no Attempt could be made without giving the Enemy time to draw together what Body of Foot they pleas'd. Or supposing it feasible, under all these difficult Circumstances, for some of them to have forc'd their Passage, the Remainder, that should have been so lucky to have escap'd their Foot, would have found themselves expos'd in open Field to a Pursuit of four thousand Horse and Dragoons; and that for two Miles together; when in case of their inclosing them, the bravest Troops in the World, under such a Situation, would have found it their best way to have surrender'd themselves Prisoners of War.

Nevertheless, when Brigadier *Stanhope* sent that Express to the Earl, which I just now mention'd, he assur'd him in the same, that he would use his utmost Diligence, both by Sea and Land, to let him have timely Notice of the Conjunction of the Fleets, which was now all they had to depend upon. Adding withal, that if the Earl should at any time receive a Letter, or Paper, though directed to no Body, and with nothing in it, but a half Sheet of Paper cut in the Middle, he, the Earl, might certainly depend upon it, that the two Fleets were join'd, and making the best of their Way for *Barcelona*. It will easily be imagin'd the Express was to be well paid; and being made sensible that he ran little or no Hazard in carrying a Piece of blank Paper, he undertook it, and as fortunately arriv'd with it to the Earl, at a Moment when Chagrin and Despair might have hurry'd him to some Resolution that might have prov'd fatal. The Messenger himself, however, knew nothing of the Joining of the Fleets, or the Meaning of his Message.

As soon as the Earl of *Peterborow* receiv'd this welcome Message from Brigadier *Stanhope*, he march'd the very same Night, with his whole little Body of Forces, to a Town on the Sea-Shore, call'd *Sigeth*. No Person guess'd the Reason of his March, or knew any thing of what the Intent of it was. The Officers, as formerly, obey'd without Enquiry; for they were led to it by so many unaccountable Varieties of Success, that Affiance became a second Nature, both in Officer and Soldier.

The Town of *Sigeth* was about seven Leagues to the Westward of *Barcelona*; where, as soon as the Earl with his Forces arriv'd, he took care to secure all the small Fishing-Boats, *Feluccas*, and *Sattées*; nay, in a Word, every Machine in which he could transport any of his Men: So that in two Days' time he had got together a Number sufficient for the Conveyance of all his Foot.

But a Day or two before the Arrival of the *English* Fleet off *Sigeth*, The Officers of his Troops were under a strange Consternation at a Resolution their General had taken. Impatient of Delay, and fearful of the Fleets passing by without his Knowledge, the Earl summon'd them together a little before Night, at which time he discover'd to the whole Assembly, that he himself was oblig'd to endeavour to get aboard the *English* Fleet; and that, if possible, before the *French* Scouts should be able to make any Discovery of their Strength: That finding himself of no further Use on Shore, having already taken the necessary Precautions for their Transportation and Security, they had nothing to do but to pursue his Orders, and make the best of their Way to *Barcelona*, in the Vessels which he had provided for them: That they might do this in perfect Security when they saw the *English* Fleet pass by; or if they should pass by in the Night, an Engagement with the *French*, which would give them sufficient Notice what they had to do further.

This Declaration, instead of satisfying, made the Officers ten times more curious: But when they saw their General going with a Resolution to lie out all Night at Sea, in an open Boat, attended with only one Officer; and understood that he intended to row out in his *Felucca* five or six Leagues distance from the Shore, it is hardly to be express'd what Amazement and Concern surpriz'd them all. Mr. *Crow*, the Queen's Minister, and others, express'd a particular Dislike and Uneasiness; but all to no purpose, the Earl had resolv'd upon it. Accordingly, at Night he put out to Sea in his open *Felucca*, all which he spent five Leagues from Shore, with no other Company than one Captain and his Rowers.

In the Morning, to the great Satisfaction of all, Officers and others, the Earl came again to Land; and immediately began to put his Men into the several Vessels which lay ready in Port for that Purpose. But at Night their Amaze was renew'd, when they found their General ready to put in execution his old Resolution, in the same Equipage, and with the same Attendance. Accordinly, he again *felucca'd* himself; and they saw him no more till they were landed on the Mole in *Barcelona*.

When the Earl of *Peterborow* first engag'd himself in the Expedition to *Spain*, he propos'd to the Queen and her Ministry, that Admiral *Shovel* might be join'd in Commission with him in the Command of the Fleet. But this Year, when the Fleet came through the Straites, under Vice-Admiral *Leake*, the Queen had sent a Commission to the Earl of *Peterborow* for the full Command, whenever he thought fit to come aboard in Person. This it was that made the General endeavour, at all Hazards, to get aboard the Fleet by Night; for he was apprehensive, and the Sequel prov'd his Apprehensions too well grounded, that *Admiral Leake* would make his Appearance with the whole Body of the Fleet, which made near twice the Number of the Ships of the Enemy; in which Case it was natural to suppose, that the Count *de Tholouse*, as soon as ever the *French* Scouts should give Notice of our Strength, would cut his Cables and put out to Sea, to avoid an Engagement. On the other hand, the Earl was very sensible, that if a Part of his Ships had kept a-stern, that the Superiority might have appear'd on the *French* Side, or rather if they had bore away in the Night towards the Coast of *Africa*, and fallen to the Eastward of *Barcelona* the next Day, a Battle had been inevitable, and a Victory equally certain; since the Enemy by this Means had been tempted into an Engagement, and their Retreat being cut off, and their whole Fleet surrounded with almost double their Number, there had hardly been left for any of them a Probability of Escaping.

Therefore, when the Earl of *Peterborow* put to Sea again the second Evening, fearful of loosing such a glorious Opportunity, and impatient to be aboard to give the necessary Orders, he order'd his Rowers to obtain the same Station, in order to discover the *English* Fleet. And according to his Wishes he did fall in with it; but unfortunately the Night was so far advanc'd, that it was impossible for him then to put his Project into practice. Captain *Price*, a Gentleman of *Wales*, who commanded a Third Rate[5], was the Person he first came aboard of; but how amaz'd was he to find, in an open Boat at open Sea, the Person who had

Commission to command the Fleet? So soon as he was enter'd the Ship, the Earl sent the Ship's Pinnace with Letters to Admiral *Leake*, to acquaint him with his Orders and Intentions; and to Brigadier *Stanhope* with a Notification of his safe Arrival; but the Darkness of the Night prov'd so great an Obstacle, that it was a long time before the Pinnace could reach the Admiral. When Day appear'd, it was astonishing to the whole Fleet to see the *Union* Flag waving at the Main-top-mast Head. No body could trust his own Eyes, or guess at the Meaning, till better certify'd by the Account of an Event so singular and extraordinary.

When we were about six Leagues Distance from *Barcelona*, the Port we aim'd at, one of the *French* Scouts gave the Alarm, who making the Signal to another, he communicated it to a Third, and so on, as we afterward sorrowfully found, and as the Earl had before apprehended: The *French* Admiral being thus made acquainted with the Force of our Fleet, hoisted sail, and made the best of his Way from us, either pursuant to Orders, or under the plausible Excuse of a Retreat.

This favourable Opportunity thus lost, there remain'd nothing to do but to land the Troops with all Expedition; which was executed accordingly: The Regiments, which the Earl of *Peterborow* embark'd the Night before, being the first that got into the Town. Let the Reader imagine how pleasing such a Sight must be to those in *Barcelona*, reduc'd as they were to the last Extremity. In this Condition, to see an Enemy's Fleet give way to another with Reinforcements from *England*, the Sea at the same Instant cover'd with little Vessels crouded with greater Succours; what was there wanting to compleat the glorious Scene, but what the General had projected, a Fight at Sea, under the very Walls of the invested City, and the Ships of the Enemy sinking, or tow'd in by the victorious *English*? But Night, and a few Hours, defeated the latter Part of that well intended Landskip.

King *Philip*, and the Mareschal of *France*, had not fail'd to push on the Siege with all imaginable Vigour; but this Retreat of the Count *de Tholouse*, and the News of those Reinforcements, soon chang'd the Scene. Their Courage without was abated proportionably, as theirs within was elated. In these Circumstances, a Council of War being call'd, it was unanimously resolv'd to raise the Siege. Accordingly, next Morning, the first of *May*, 1706, while the Sun was under a total Eclypse, in a suitable Hurry and Confusion, they broke up, leaving behind them most of their Cannon and Mortars, together with vast Quantities of all sorts of Ammunition and Provisions, scarce stopping to look back till they had left all but the very Verge of the disputed Dominion behind them.

King *Charles* look'd with new Pleasure upon this lucky Effort of his old Deliverers. Captivity is a State no way desirable to Persons however brave, of the most private Station in Life; but for a King, within two Days of falling into the Hands of his Rival, to receive so seasonable and unexpected a Deliverance, must be supposed, as it really did, to open a Scene to universal Rejoicing among us, too high for any Words to express, or any Thoughts to imagine, to those that were not present and Partakers of it. He forthwith gave Orders for a Medal to be struck suitable to the Occasion; one of which, set round with Diamonds, he presented to Sir *John Leake*, the *English* Admiral. The next Orders were for re-casting all the damag'd brass Cannon which the Enemy had left; upon every one of which was, by order, a Sun eclyps'd, with this Motto under it: *Magna parvis obscurantur.*

I have often wonder'd that I never heard any Body curious enough to enquire what could be the Motives to the King of *Spain*'s quitting his Dominions upon the raising of this Siege; very certain it is that he had a fine Army, under the Command of a Mareschal of *France*, not very considerably decreas'd, either by Action or Desertion: But all this would rather increase the Curiosity than abate it. In my Opinion then, though Men might have Curiosity enough, the Question was purposely evaded, under an Apprehension that an honest Answer must inevitably give a higher Idea of the General than their Inclinations led them to. At first View this may carry the Face of a Paradox; yet if the Reader will consider, that in every Age Virtue has had its Shaders or Maligners, he will himself easily solve it, at the same time that he finds himself compell'd to allow, that those, who found themselves unable to prevent his great Services, were willing, in a more subtil Manner, to endeavour at the annulling of them by Silence and Concealment.

This will appear more than bare Supposition, if we compare the present Situation, as to Strength, of the two contending Powers: The *French*, at the Birth of the Siege, consisted of five thousand Horse and Dragoons, and twenty-five thousand Foot, effective Men. Now grant, that their kill'd and wounded, together with their Sick in the Hospitals, might amount to five Thousand; yet as their Body of Horse was entire, and in the best Condition, the Remaining will appear to be an Army of twenty-five Thousand at least. On the other Side, all the Forces in *Barcelona*, even with their Reinforcements, amounted to no more than seven thousand Foot and four hundred Horse. Why then, when they rais'd their Siege, did not they march back into the Heart of *Spain*, with their so much superior Army? or, at least, towards their Capital? The Answer can be this, and this only; Because the Earl of *Peterborow* had taken such provident Care to render all secure, that it was thereby render'd next to an Impossibility for them so to do. That General was satisfy'd, that the Capital of *Catalonia* must, in course, fall into the Hands of the Enemy, unless a superior Fleet remov'd the Count *de Tholouse*, and threw in timely Succours into the Town: And as that could not depend upon him, but others, he made it his chief Care and assiduous Employment to provide against those Strokes of Fortune to which he found himself again likely to be expos'd, as he often had been; and therefore had he Resource to that Vigilance and Precaution which had often retriev'd him, when to others his Circumstances seem'd to be most desperate.

The Generality of Mankind, and the *French* in particular, were of opinion that the taking *Barcelona* would prove a decisive Stroke, and put a Period to the War in *Spain*; and yet at that very Instant I was inclin'd to believe, that the General flatter'd himself it would be in his Power to give the Enemy sufficient Mortification, even though the Town should be oblig'd to submit to King *Philip*. The wise Measures taken induc'd me so to believe, and the Sequel approv'd it; for the Earl had so well expended his Caution, that the Enemy, on the Disappointment, found himself under a Necessity of quitting *Spain*; and the same would have put him under equal Difficulties had he carry'd the Place. The *French* could never have undertaken that Siege without depending on their Fleet, for their Artillery, Ammunition, and Provisions; since they must be inevitably forc'd to leave behind them the strong Towns of *Tortosa*, *Lerida*, and *Taragona*. The Earl, therefore, whose perpetual Difficulties seem'd rather to render him more sprightly and vigorous, took care himself to examine the whole Country between the *Ebro* and *Barcelona*; and, upon his doing so, was pleasingly, as well as sensibly satisfy'd, that it was practicable to render their Return into the Heart of *Spain* impossible, whether they did or did not succeed in the Siege they were so intent to undertake.

There were but three Ways they could attempt it: The first of which was by the Sea-side, from *Taragona* towards *Tortosa*; the most barren, and consequently the most improper Country in the Universe to sustain an Army; and yet to the natural, the Earl had added such artificial Difficulties, as render'd it absolutely impossible for an Army to subsist or march that Way.

The middle Way lay through a better Country indeed, yet only practicable by the Care which had been taken to make the Road so. And even here there was a Necessity of marching along the Side of a Mountain, where by vast Labour and Industry, a high Way had been cut for two Miles at least out of the main Rock. The Earl therefore, by somewhat of the same Labour, soon made it impassable. He employ'd to that End many Thousands of the Country People, under a few of his own Officers and Troops, who cutting up twenty several Places, made so many Precipices, perpendicular almost as a Wall, which render'd it neither safe, or even to be attempted by any single Man in his Wits, much less by an Army. Besides, a very few Men, from the higher Cliffs of the Mountain, might have destroy'd an Army with the Arms of Nature only, by rolling down large Stones and Pieces of the Rock upon the Enemy passing below.

The last and uppermost Way, lay thro' the hilly Part of *Catalonia*, and led to *Lerida*, towards the Head of the *Ebro*, the strongest Place we had in all *Spain*, and which was as well furnish'd with a very good Garrison. Along this Road there lay many old Castles and little Towns in the Mountains, naturally strong; all which would not only have afforded Opposition, but at the same time had entertain'd an Enemy with variety of Difficulties; and especially as the Earl had given Orders and taken Care that all Cattle, and every Thing necessary to sustain an Army, should be convey'd into Places of Security, either in the Mountains or thereabouts. These three Ways thus precautiously secur'd, what had the Earl to apprehend but the Safety of the Arch-Duke; which yet was through no Default of his, if in any Danger from the Siege?

For I well remember, on Receipt of an Express from the Duke of *Savoy* (as he frequenly sent such to enquire after the Proceedings in *Spain*) I was shew'd a Letter, wrote about this time by the Earl of *Peterborow* to that Prince, which rais'd my Spirits, though then at a very low Ebb. It was too remarkable to be forgot; and the Substance of it was, That his Highness might depend upon it, that he (the Earl) was in much better Circumstances than he was thought to be: That the *French* Officers, knowing nothing of the Situation of the Country, would find themselves extreamly disappointed, since in case the Siege was rais'd, their Army should be oblig'd to abandon *Spain:* Or in case the Town was taken, they should find themselves shut up in that Corner of *Catalonia*, and under an Impossibility of forcing their Way back, either through *Aragon* or *Valencia:* That by this Means all *Spain*, to the *Ebro*, would be open to the Lord *Galoway*, who might march to *Madrid*, or any where else, without Opposition. That he had no other Uneasiness or Concern upon him, but for the Person of the Arch-Duke, whom he had nevertheless earnestly solicited not to remain in the Town on the very first Appearance of the intended Siege.

BARCELONA being thus reliev'd, and King *Philip* forc'd out of *Spain*, by these cautious Steps taken by the Earl of *Peterborow*, before we bring him to *Valencia*, it will be necessary to intimate, that as it always was the Custom of that General to settle, by a Council of War, all the Measures to be taken, whenever he was oblig'd for the Service to leave the Arch-Duke; a Council of War was now accordingly held, where all the General Officers, and those in greatest Employments at Court assisted. Here every thing was in the most solemn Manner concerted and resolv'd upon; here Garrisons were settled for all the strong Places, and Governors appointed: But the main Article then agreed upon was, that King *Charles* should immediately begin his

Journey to *Madrid*, and that by the Way of *Valencia*. The Reason assign'd for it was, because that Kingdom being in his Possession, no Difficulties could arise which might occasion Delay, if his Majesty took that Rout. It was likewise agreed in the same Council, that the Earl of *Peterborow* should embark all the Foot, not in Garrisons, for their more speedy, as well as more easy Conveyance to *Valencia*. The same Council of War agreed, that all the Horse in that Kingdom should be drawn together, the better to insure the Measures to be taken for the opening and facilitating his Majesty's Progress to *Madrid*.

Accordingly, after these Resolutions were taken, the Earl of *Peterborow* embarks his Forces and sails for *Valencia*, where he was doubly welcom'd by all Sorts of People upon Account of his safe Arrival, and the News he brought along with it. By the Joy they express'd, one would have imagin'd that the General had escap'd the same Danger with the King; and, in truth, had their King arriv'd with him in Person, the most loyal and zealous would have found themselves at a loss how to have express'd their Satisfaction in a more sensible Manner.

Soon after his Landing, with his customary Vivacity, he apply'd himself to put in execution the Resolutions taken in the Councils of War at *Barcelona*; and a little to improve upon them, he rais'd an intire Regiment of Dragoons, bought them Horses, provided them Cloaths, Arms, and Acoutrements; and in six Weeks time had them ready to take the Field; a thing though hardly to be parallell'd, is yet scarce worthy to be mentioned among so many nobler Actions of his; yet in regard to another General it may merit Notice, since while he had *Madrid* in Possession near four Months, he neither augmented his Troops, nor lay'd up any Magazines; neither sent he all that time any one Express to concert any Measures with the Earl of *Peterborow*; but lay under a perfect Inactivity, or which was worse, negotiating that unfortunate Project of carrying King *Charles* to *Madrid* by the round-about and ill-concerted Way of *Aragon*; a Project not only contrary to the solemn Resolutions of the Council of War; but which in reality was the Root of all our succeeding Misfortunes; and that only for the wretched Vanity of appearing to have had some Share in bringing the King to his Capital; but how minute a

Share it was will be manifest, if it be consider'd that another
General had first made the Way easy, by driving the Enemy out of
Spain; and that the French General only stay'd at *Madrid* till the
Return of those Troops which were in a manner driven out of
Spain.

And yet that Transaction, doughty as it was, took up four most
precious Months, which most certainly might have been much
better employ'd in rendering it impossible for the Enemy to
re-enter *Spain*; nor had there been any Great Difficulty in so
doing, but the contrary, if the General at *Madrid* had thought
convenient to have join'd the Troops under the Earl of *Peterborow*, and then to have march'd directly towards *Pampelona*, or
the Frontiers of *France*. To this the Earl of *Peterborow* solicited
the King, and those about him; he advis'd, desir'd, and intreated
him to lose no time, but to put in Execution those Measures resolv'd on at *Barcelona*. A Council of War in *Valencia* renew'd the
same Application; but all to no Purpose, his Rout was order'd
him, and that to meet his Majesty on the Frontiers of *Arragon*.
There, indeed, the Earl did meet the King; and the *French* General
an Army, which, by Virtue of a decrepid Intelligence, he never
saw or heard of till he fled from it to his Camp at *Guadalira*. Inexpressible with the Confusion in this fatal Camp: The King
from *Arragon*, The Earl of *Peterborow* from *Valencia* arriving in it
the same Day, almost the same Hour that the Earl of *Galoway*
enter'd under a hasty Retreat before the *French* Army.

But to return to Order, which a Zeal of Justice has made me
somewhat anticipate; the Earl had not been long at *Valencia*
before he gave Orders to Major-General *Windham* to march with
all the Forces he had, which were not above two thousand Men,
and lay Siege to *Requina*, a Town ten Leagues distant from
Valencia, and in the Way to *Madrid*. The Town was not very
strong, nor very large; but sure the odliest fortify'd that ever
was. The Houses in a Circle connectively compos'd the Wall;
and the People, who defended the Town, instead of firing from
Hornworks, Counterscarps, and Bastions, fir'd out of the Windows of their Houses.

Notwithstanding all which, General *Windham* found much
greater Opposition than he at first imagin'd; and therefore finding

he should want Ammunition, he sent to the Earl of *Peterborow* for a Supply; at the same time assigning, as a Reason for it, the unexpected Obstinacy of the Town. So soon as the Earl receiv'd the Letter he sent for me; and told me I must repair to *Requina*, where they would want an Engineer; and that I must be ready next Morning, when he should order a Lieutenant, with thirty Soldiers and two Matrosses[6], to guard some Powder for that Service. Accordingly, the next Morning we set out, the Lieutenant, who was a *Dutchman*, and Commander of the Convoy, being of my Acquaintance.

We had reach'd Saint *Jago*, a small Village about midway between *Valencia* and *Requina*, when the Officer, just as he was got without the Town, resolving to take up his Quarters on the Spot, order'd the Mules to be unloaded. The Powder, which consisted of forty-five Barrels, was pil'd up in a Circle, and cover'd with Oil-cloth, to preserve it from the Weather; and though we had agreed to sup together at my Quarters within the Village, yet being weary and fatigu'd, he order'd his Field-Bed to be put up near the Powder, and so lay down to take a short Nap. I had scarce been at my Quarters an Hour, when a sudden Shock attack'd the House so violently, that it threw down Tiles, Windows, Chimneys and all. It presently came into my Head what was the Occasion; and as my Fears suggested so it prov'd: For running to the Door I saw a Cloud ascending from the Spot I left the Powder pitch'd upon. In haste making up to which, nothing was to be seen but the bare Circle upon which it had stood. The Bed was blown quite away, and the poor Lieutenant all to pieces, several of his Limbs being found separate, and at a vast Distance each from the other; and particularly an Arm, with a Ring on one of the Fingers. The Matrosses were, if possible, in a yet worse Condition, that is, as to Manglement and Laceration. All the Soldiers who were standing, and any thing near, were struck dead. Only such as lay sleeping on the Ground escap'd, and of those one assur'd me, that the Blast remov'd him several Foot from his Place of Repose. In short, enquiring into this deplorable Disaster, I had this Account: That a Pig running out of the Town, the Soldiers endeavour'd to intercept its Return; but driving it upon the Matrosses, one of them, who was jealous of its getting back into the Hands of the Soldiers, drew his Pistol to shoot it, which was the Source of this miserable Catastrophe. The Lieutenant carry'd along with him a Bag of Dollars to pay the Soldiers' Quarters, of which the People, and the Soldiers that were sav'd, found many; but blown to an inconceivable Distance.

With those few Soldiers that remain'd alive, I proceeded, according to my Order, to *Requina*; where, when I arriv'd, I gave General *Windham* an Account of the Disaster at St. *Jago*. As such it troubled him, and not a little on account of the Disappointment. However, to make the best of a bad Market, he gave Orders for the forming of a Mine under an old Castle, which was part of the Wall. As it was order'd, so it was begun, more *in Terrorem*, than with any Expectation of Success from it as a Mine. Nevertheless, I had scarce began to frame the Oven of the Mine, when those within the Town desir'd to capitulate. This being all we could aim at, under the Miscarriage of our Powder at St. *Jago* (none being yet arriv'd to supply that Defect) Articles were readily granted them; pursuant to which, that Part of the Garrison, which was compos'd of *Castilian* Gentry, had Liberty to go wherever they thought best, and the rest were made Prisoners of War. *Requina* being thus reduc'd to the Obedience of *Charles* III a new rais'd Regiment of *Spaniards* was left in Garrison, the Colonel of which was appointed Governor; and our Supply of Powder having at last got safe to us, General *Windham* march'd his little Army to *Cuenca*.

CUENCA is a considerable City and a Bishoprick; therefore to pretend to sit down before it with such a Company of Forragers, rather than an Army, must be plac'd among the hardy Influences of the Earl of *Peterborow*'s auspicious Administration. On the out Part of *Cuenca* there stood an old Castle, from which, upon our Approach, they play'd upon us furiously: But as soon as we could bring two Pieces of our Cannon to bear, we answered their Fire with so good Success, that we soon oblig'd them to retire into the Town. We had rais'd a Battery of twelve Guns against the City, on their Rejection of the Summons sent them to come under the Obedience of King *Charles*; going to which from the old Castle last reduc'd, I receiv'd a Shot on the Toe of one of my Shoes, which carry'd that Part of the Shoe intirely away, without any further Damage.

When I came to that Battery we ply'd them warmly (as well as from three Mortars) for the Space of three Days, their Nights included; but observing, that in one particular House, they were remarkably busy; People thronging in and out below; and those above firing perpetually out of the Windows, I was resolv'd to have one Shot at that Window, and made those Officers about me take Notice of it. True it was, the Distance would hardly allow me to hope for Success; yet as the Experiment could only be attended with the Expence of a single Ball, I made it. So soon as the Smoak of my own Cannon would permit it, we could see Clouds of Dust issuing from out of the Window, which, together with the People's crouding out of Doors, convinc'd the Officers, whom I had desir'd to take Notice of it, that I had been no bad Marksman.

Upon this, two Priests were sent out of the Place with Proposals; but they were so triflingly extravagant, that as soon as ever the General heard them, he order'd their Answer in a fresh Renewal of the Fire of both Cannon and Mortars. And it happen'd to be with so much Havock and Execution, that they were soon taught Reason; and sent back their Divines, with much more moderate Demands. After the General had a little modell'd these last, they were accepted; and according to the Articles of Capitulation, the City was that very Day surrender'd into our Possession. The Earl of *Duncannon*'s Regiment took Guard of all the Gates; and King *Charles* was proclaim'd in due Form.

The Earl of *Peterborow*, during this Expedition, had left *Valencia*, and was arriv'd at my Lord *Galway*'s Camp at *Guadalaxara*; who for the Confederates, and King *Charles* in particular, unfortunately was order'd from *Portugal*, to take the Command from a General, who had all along been almost miraculously successful, and by his own great Actions pav'd the Way for a safe Passage to that his Supplanter.

Yet even in this fatal Place the Earl of *Peterborow* made some Proposals, which, had they been embrac'd, might, in all Probability, have secur'd *Madrid* from falling into the Hands of the Enemy; But, in opposition thereto, the Lord *Galway*, and all his

Portugueze Officers, were for forcing the next Day the Enemy to Battle. The almost only Person against it was the Earl of *Peterborow*; who then and there took the Liberty to evince the Impossibility of coming to an Engagement. This the next Morning too evidently made apparent, when upon the first Motion of our Troops towards the River, which they pretended to pass, and must pass, before they could engage, they were so warmly saluted from the Batteries of the Enemy, and their small Shot, that our Regiments were forc'd to retire in Confusion to their Camp. By which Rebuff all heroical Imaginations were at present laid aside, to consider how they might make their Retreat to *Valencia*.

The Retreat being at last resolv'd on, and a Multiplicity of Generals rendering our bad Circumstances much worse, the Earl of *Peterborow* met with a fortunate Reprieve, by Solicitations from the Queen, and Desires tantamount to Orders, that he would go with the Troops left in *Catalonia* to the Relief of the Duke of *Savoy*. It is hardly to be doubted that that General was glad to withdraw from those Scenes of Confusion, which were but too visible to Eyes even less discerning than his. However, he forebore to prepare himself to put her Majesty's Desires in execution, as they were not peremptory, till it had been resolv'd by the unanimous Consent of a Council of War, where the King, all the Generals and Ministers were present. That it was expedient for the Service that the Earl of *Peterborow*, during the Winter Season, should comply with her Majesty's Desires, and go for *Italy*; since he might return before the opening of the Campaign, if it should be necessary. And return indeed he did, before the Campaign open'd, and brought along with him one hundred thousand Pounds from *Genoa*, to the great Comfort and Support of our Troops, which had neither Money nor Credit. But on his Return, that noble Earl found the Lord *Galway* had been near as successful against him, as he had been unsuccessful against the Enemy. Thence was the Earl of *Peterborow* recall'd to make room for an unfortunate General, who the next Year suffer'd himself to be decoy'd into that fatal Battle of *Almanza*.

The Earl of *Peterborow*, on his leaving *Valencia*, had order'd his Baggage to follow him to the Camp at *Guadalaxara*; and it arriv'd in our little Camp, so far safe in its way to the greater at *Guadalaxara*. I think it consisted of seven loaded Waggons; and General *Windham* gave Orders for a small Guard to escorte it; under which they proceeded on their Journey: But about eight Leagues from *Cuenca*, at a pretty Town call'd *Huette*, a Party from the Duke of *Berwick*'s Army, with Boughs in their Hats, the better to appear what they were not (for the Bough in the Hat is the Badge of the *English*, as white Paper is the Badge of the *French*) came into the Town, crying all the way, *Viva Carlos Tercero, Viva*. With these Acclamations in their Mouths, they advanc'd up to the very Waggons; when attacking the Guards, who had too much deluded themselves with Appearances, they routed 'em, and immediately plunder'd the Waggons of all that was valuable, and then march'd off.

The Noise of this soon reach'd the Ears of the Earl of *Peterborow* at *Guadalaxara*. When leaving my Lord *Galway*'s Camp, pursuant to the Resolutions of the Council of War, with a Party only of fourscore of *Killigrew*'s Dragoons, he met General *Windham*'s little Army within a League of *Huette*, the Place where his Baggage had been plunder'd. The Earl had strong Motives of Suspicion, that the Inhabitants had given Intelligence to the Enemy; and, as is very natural, giving way to the first Dictates of Resentment, he resolv'd to have lay'd the Town in Ashes: But when he came near it, the Clergy and Magistrates upon their Knees, disavowing the Charge, and asserting their Innocence, prevail'd on the good Nature of that generous Earl, without any great Difficulty, to spare the Town, at least not to burn it.

We march'd however into the Town, and that Night took up our Quarters there; and the Magistrates, under the Dread of our avenging our selves, on their part took Care that we were well supplied. But when they were made sensible of the Value of the Loss, which the Earl had sustain'd; and that on a moderate Computation it amounted to at least eight thousand Pistoles; they voluntarily presented themselves next Morning, and of their own accord offer'd to make his Lordship full Satisfaction, and that, in their own Phrase, *de Contado*, *in Ready Money*. The Earl was not displeas'd at their Offer; but generously made Answer, That he was just come from my Lord *Galway*'s Camp at *Chincon*, where he found they were in a likelihood of wanting Bread; and as he imagin'd it might be easier to them to raise the Value in Corn, than in ready Money; if they would send to that Value in Corn to the Lord *Galway*'s Camp, he would be satisfy'd. This they with Joy embrac'd, and immediately complied with.

I am apt to think the last Century (and I very much fear the Current will be as deficient) can hardly produce a parallel Instance of Generosity and true public Spiritedness; And the World will be of my Opinion, when I have corroborated this with another Passage some Years after. The Commissioners for Stating the Debts due to the Army, meeting daily for that Purpose at their House in *Darby* Court in *Channel Row*, I there mentioned to Mr. *Read*, Gentleman to his Lordship, this very just and honourable Claim upon the Government, as Monies advanced for the Use of the Army. Who told me in a little Time after, that he had mention'd it to his Lordship, but with no other Effect than to have it rejected with a generous Disdain.

While we stayed at *Huette* there was a little Incident in Life, which gave me great Diversion. The Earl, who had always maintain'd a good Correspondence with the fair Sex, hearing from one of the Priests of the Place, That on the Alarm of burning the Town, one of the finest Ladies in all *Spain* had taken Refuge in the Nunnery, was desirous to speak with her.

The Nunnery stood upon a small rising Hill within the Town; and to obtain the View, the Earl had presently in his Head this Stratagem; he sends for me, as Engineer, to have my Advice, how to raise a proper Fortification upon that Hill out of the Nunnery. I waited upon his Lordship to the Place, where declaring the Intent of our coming, and giving plausible Reasons for it, the Train took, and immediately the Lady Abbess, and the fair Lady, came out to make Intercession, That his Lordship would be pleas'd to lay aside that Design. The divine Oratory of one, and the beautiful Charms of the other, prevail'd; so his Lordship left the Fortification to be the Work of some future Generation.

From *Huette* the Earl of *Peterborow* march'd forwards for *Valencia*, with only those fourscore Dragoons, which came with him from *Chincon*, leaving General *Windham* pursuing his own Orders to join his Forces to the Army then under the Command of the

Lord *Galway*. But stopping at *Campilio*, a little Town in our Way, his Lordship had Information of a most barbarous Fact committed that very Morning by the *Spaniards*, at a small *Villa*, about a League distant, upon some *English* Soldiers.

A Captain of the *English* Guards (whose Name has slip'd my Memory, tho' I well knew the Man) marching in order to join the Battalion of the Guards, then under the Command of General *Windham*, with some of his Soldiers, that had been in the Hospital, took up his Quarters in that little *Villa*. But on his marching out of it, next Morning, a Shot in the Back laid that Officer dead upon the Spot: And as it had been before concerted, the *Spaniards* of the Place at the same Time fell upon the poor, weak Soldiers, killing several; not even sparing their Wives. This was but a Prelude to their Barbarity; their savage Cruelty was only whetted, not glutted. They took the surviving few; hurried and dragg'd them up a Hill, a little without the *Villa*. On the Top of this Hill there was a Hole, or Opening, somewhat like the Mouth of one of our Coal-Pits, down this they cast several, who, with hideous Shrieks and Cries, made more hideous by the Ecchoes of the Chasm, there lost their Lives.

This Relation was thus made to the Earl of *Peterborow*, at his Quarters at *Campilio*; who immediately gave Orders for to sound to Horse. At first we were all surpriz'd; but were soon satisfy'd, that it was to revenge, or rather, do Justice, on this barbarous Action.

As soon as we enter'd the *Villa* we found that most of the Inhabitants, but especially the most Guilty, had withdrawn themselves on our Approach. We found, however, many of the dead Soldiers Cloaths, which had been convey'd into the Church, and there hid. And a strong Accusation being laid against a Person belonging to the Church, and full Proof made, that he had been singularly Industrious in the Execution of that horrid Piece of Barbarity on the Hill, his Lordship commanded him to be hang'd up at the Knocker of the Door.

After this piece of military Justice, we were led up to the fatal Pit or Hole, down which many had been cast headlong. There we found one poor Soldier alive, who, upon his throwing in, had catch'd fast hold of some impending Bushes, and sav'd himself on a little Jutty within the Concavity. On hearing us talk *English* he cry'd out; and Ropes being let down, in a little Time he was drawn up; when he gave us an ample Detail of the whole Villany. Among other Particulars, I remember he told me of a very narrow Escape he had in that obscure Recess. A poor Woman, one of the Wives of the Soldiers, who were thrown down after him, struggled, and roared so much, that they could not, without all their Force, throw her cleaverly in the Middle; by which means falling near the Side, in her Fall she almost beat him from his Place of Security.

Upon the Conclusion of this tragical Relation of the Soldier thus saved, his Lordship gave immediate Orders for the Firing of the *Villa*, which was executed with due Severity: After which his Lordship march'd back to his Quarters at *Campilio*; from whence, two Days after, we arriv'd at *Valencia*, Where, the first Thing presented to that noble Lord, was all the Papers taken in the Plunder of his Baggage, which the Duke of *Berwick* had generously order'd to be return'd him, without waste or opening.

It was too manifest, after the Earl's arrival at this City, that the Alteration in the Command of the *English* Forces, which before was only receiv'd as a Rumour, had deeper Grounds for Belief, than many of his Friends in that City could have wish'd. His Lordship had gain'd the Love of all by a Thousand engaging Condescensions; even his Gallantries being no way prejudicial, were not offensive; and though his Lordships did his utmost to conceal his Chagrin, the Sympathy of those around him made such Discoveries upon him, as would have disappointed a double Portion of his Caution. They had seen him un-elated under Successes, that were so near being unaccountable, that in a Country of less Superstition than *Spain*, they might almost have pass'd for miraculous; they knew full well, that nothing, but that Series of Successes had pav'd a Passage for the General that was to supersede him; those only having removed all the Difficulties of his March from *Portugal* to *Madrid*; they knew him the older General; and therefore not knowing, that in the Court he came from, Intrigue was too often the Soul of Merit, they could not but be amazed at a Change, which his Lordship was unwilling any body should perceive by himself.

It was upon this Account, that, as formerly, he treated the
Ladies with Balls, and to pursue the Dons in their own Humour,
order'd a *Tawridore* or *Bull-Feast*. In *Spain* no sort of public
Diversions are esteemed equal with this. But the Bulls provided
at *Valencia*, not being of the right Breed, nor ever initiated in the
Mysteries, did not acquit themselves at all masterly; and consequently, did not give the Diversion, or Satisfaction expected. For
which Reason I shall omit giving a Description of this Bull-Feast;
and desire my Reader to suspend his Curiosity till I come to some,
which, in the *Spanish* Sense, were much more entertaining; that
is, attended with much greater Hazards and Danger.

But though I have said, the Gallantries of the General were
mostly political at least very inoffensive; yet there happen'd
about this Time, and in this Place, a piece of Gallantry, that gave
the Earl a vast deal of Offence and Vexation; as a Matter, that in
its Consequences might have been fatal to the Interest of King
Charles, if not to the *English* Nation in general; and which I the
rather relate, in that it may be of use to young Officers, and
others; pointing out to them the Danger, not to say Folly, of
inadvertent and precipitate Engagements, under unruly Passions.

I have said before, that *Valencia* is famous for fine Women. It
indeed abounds in them; and among those, are great Numbers
of Courtezans not inferior in Beauty to any. Nevertheless, two
of our *English* Officers, not caring for the common Road, however safe, resolv'd to launch into the deeper Seas, though attended
with much greater Danger. Amours, the common Failing of that
fair City, was the Occasion of this Accident, and two Nuns the
Objects. It is customary in that Country for young People in an
Evening to resort to the Grates of the Nunneries, there to divert
themselves, and the Nuns, with a little pleasant and inoffensive
Chitchat. For though I have heard some relate a World of nauseous Passages at such Conversations, I must declare, that I never
saw, or heard any Thing unseemly; and therefore whenever I
have heard any such from such Fabulists, I never so much wrong'd
my Judgment as to afford them Credit.

Our two Officers were very assiduous at the Grates of a
Nunnery in this Place; and having there pitch'd upon two Nuns,
prosecuted their Amours with such Vigour, that, in a little time,

they had made a very great Progress in their Affections, without in the least considering the Dangers that must attend themselves and the Fair; they had exchang'd Vows, and prevail'd upon the weaker Vessels to endeavour to get out to their Lovers. To effect which, soon after, a Plot was lay'd; the Means, the Hour, and every thing agreed upon.

It is the Custom of that Nunnery, as of many others, for the Nuns to take their weekly Courses in keeping the Keys of all the Doors. The two Love-sick Ladies giving Notice to their Lovers at the Grate, that one of their Turns was come, the Night and Hour was appointed, which the Officers punctually observing, carry'd off their Prey without either Difficulty or Interruption.

But next Morning, when the Nuns were missing, what an Uproar was there over all the City? The Ladies were both of Quality; and therefore the Tidings were first carry'd to their Relations. They receiv'd the News with Vows of utmost Vengeance; and, as is usual in that Country, put themselves in Arms for that Purpose. There needed no great canvassing for discovering who were the Aggressors: The Officers had been too frequent, and too publick, in their Addresses, to leave any room for question. Accordingly, they were complain'd of and sought for, but sensible at last of their past Temerity, they endeavour'd, and with a great deal of Difficulty perfected their Escape.

Less fortunate were the two fair Nuns; their Lovers, in their utmost Exigence, had forsaken them; and they, poor Creatures, knew not where to fly. Under this sad Dilemma they were taken; and, as in like Offences, condemn'd directly to the Punishment of *immuring*. And what greater Punishment is there on Earth than to be confin'd between four narrow Walls, only open at the Top; and thence to be half supported with Bread and Water, till the Offenders gradually starve to Death?

The Earl of *Peterborow*, though highly exasperated at the Proceedings of his Officers, in compassion to the unhappy Fair, resolv'd to interpose by all the moderate Means possible. He knew very well, that no one Thing could so much prejudice the *Spaniard* against him, as the countenancing such an Action; wherefore he inveigh'd against the Officers, at the same time that he endeavour'd to mitigate in favour of the Ladies: But all was in vain; it was urg'd against those charitable Intercessions, that they had broke their Vows; and in that had broke in upon the Laws of the Nunnery and Religion; the Consequence of all which could be nothing less than the Punishment appointed to be inflicted. And which was the hardest of all, the nearest of their Relations most oppos'd all his generous Mediations; and those, who according to the common Course of Nature should have thank'd him for his Endeavours to be instrumental in rescuing them from the impending Danger, grew more and more enrag'd, because he oppos'd them in their Design of a cruel Revenge.

Notwithstanding all which the Earl persever'd; and after a deal of Labour, first got the Penalty suspended; and, soon after, by the Dint of a very considerable Sum of Money (a most powerful Argument, which prevails in every Country) sav'd the poor Nuns from immuring; and at last, though with great Reluctance, he got them receiv'd again into the Nunnery. As to the Warlike Lovers, one of them was the Year after slain at the Battle of *Almanza*; the other is yet living, being a Brigadier in the Army.

While the Earl of *Peterborow* was here with his little Army of great Hereticks, neither Priests nor People were so open in their superstitious Fopperies, as I at other times found them. For which Reason I will make bold, and by an Antichronism[7] in this Place, a little anticipate some Observations that I made some time after the Earl left it. And as I have not often committed such a Transgression, I hope it may be the more excusable now, and no way blemish my Memoirs, that I break in upon the Series of my Journal.

VALENCIA is a handsome City, and a Bishoprick; and is considerable not only for the Pleasantness of its Situation and beautiful Ladies; but (which at some certain Times, and on some Occasions, to them is more valuable than both those put together) for being the Birth-place of Saint *Vincent*, the Patron of the Place; and next for its being the Place where *Santo Domingo*, the first Institutor of the *Dominican* Order had his Education. Here, in honour of the last, is a spacious and very splendid Convent of the *Dominicans*. Walking by which, I one Day observ'd over the Gate, a Figure of a man in stone; and near it a Dog with a lighted

Torch in his Mouth. The Image I rightly enough took to intend that of the Saint; but inquiring of one of the Order, at the Gate, the Meaning of the Figures near it, he very courteously ask'd me to walk in, and then entertain'd me with the following Relation:

When the Mother of *Santo Domingo*, said that Religious, was with Child of that future Saint, she had a Dream which very much afflicted her. She dreamt that she heard a Dog bark in her Belly; and inquiring (at what Oracle is not said) the Meaning of her Dream, she was told, *That that Child should bark out the Gospel* (excuse the Bareness of the Expression, it may run better in *Spanish*; tho', if I remember right, *Erasmus* gives it in *Latin* much the same Turn) *which should thence shine out like that lighted Torch.* And this is the Reason, that wherever you see the Image of that Saint, a Dog and a lighted Torch is in the Group.

He told me at the same time, that there had been more Popes and Cardinals of that Order than of any, if not all the other. To confirm which, he led me into a large Gallery, on each Side whereof he shew'd me the Pictures of all the Popes and Cardinals that had been of that Order; among which, I particularly took Notice of that of Cardinal *Howard*, great Uncle to the present Duke of *Norfolk*. But after many *Encomiums* of their Society, with which he interspers'd his Discourse, he added one that I least valu'd it for; That the sole Care and Conduct of the Inquisition was intrusted with them.

Finding me attentive, or not so contradictory as the *English* Humour generally is, he next brought me into a fair and large Cloister, round which I took several Turns with him; and, indeed, The Place was too delicious to tire, under a Conversation less pertinent or courteous than that he entertain'd me with. In the Middle of the Cloister was a small but pretty and sweet Grove of Orange and Lemon-trees; these bore Fruit ripe and green, and Flowers, all together on one Tree; and their Fruit was so very large and beautiful, and their Flowers so transcendently odoriferous, that all I had ever seen of the like Kind in *England* could comparatively pass only for Beauty in Epitome, or Nature imitated in Wax-work. Many Flocks also of pretty little Birds, with their chearful Notes, added not a little to my Delight. In short, in

5

Life I never knew or found three of my Senses at once so exquisitely gratify'd.

Not far from this, Saint *Vincent*, the Patron, as I said before, of this City, has a Chapel dedicated to him. Once a Year they do him Honour in a sumptuous Procession. Then are their Streets all strow'd with Flowers, and their Houses set off with their richest Tapestries, every one strives to excel his Neighbour in distinguishing himself by the Honour he pays to that Saint; and he is the best Catholick, as well as the best Citizen, in the Eye of the *religious*, who most exerts himself on this Occasion.

The Procession begins with a Cavalcade of all the Friars of all the Convents in and about the City. These walk two and two with folded Arms, and Eyes cast down to the very Ground, and with the greatest outward Appearance of Humility imaginable; nor, though the Temptation from the fine Women that fill'd their Windows, or the rich Tapestries that adorn'd the Balconies might be allow'd sufficient to attract, could I observe that any one of them all ever mov'd them upwards.

After the Friars is borne, upon the Shoulders of twenty Men at least, an Imagine of that Saint of solid Silver, large as the Life; It is plac'd in a great Chair of Silver likewise; the Staves that bear him up, and upon which they bear him, being of the same Metal. The whole is a most costly and curious Piece of Workmanship, such as my Eyes never before or since beheld.

The Magistrates follow the Image and its Supporters, dress'd in their richest Apparel, which is always on this Day, and on this Occasion, particularly sumptuous and distinguishing. Thus is the Image, in the greatest Splendor, borne and accompany'd round that fine City; and at last convey'd to the Place from whence it came: And so concludes that annual Ceremony.

The *Valencians*, as to the Exteriors of Religion, are the most devout of any in *Spain*, though in common Life you find them amorous, gallant, and gay, like other People; yet on solemn Occasions there shines out-right such a Spirit as proves them the very Bigots of Bigotry: As a Proof of which Assertion, I will now give some Account of such Observations, as I had time to make upon them, during two *Lent* Seasons, while I resided there.

The Week before the *Lent* commences, commonly known by

the Name of *Carnaval Time*, the whole City appears a perfect *Bartholomew* Fair; the Streets are crouded, and the Houses empty; nor is it possible to pass along without some Gambol or Jack-pudding Trick offer'd to you; Ink, Water, and sometimes Ordure, are sure to be hurl'd at your Face or Cloaths; and if you appear concern'd or angry, they rejoyce at it, pleas'd the more, the more they displease; for all other Resentment is at that time out of Season, though at other times few in the World are fuller of Resentment or more captious.

The younger Gentry, or Dons, to express their Gallantry, carry about them Egg-shells, fill'd with Orange or other sweet Water, which they cast at Ladies in their Coaches, or such other of the fair Sex as they happen to meet in the Streets.

But after all, if you would think them extravagant to Day, as much transgressing the Rules of common Civility, and neither regarding Decency to one another, nor the Duty they owe to Almighty God; yet when *Ash-Wednesday* comes you will imagine them more unaccountable in their Conduct, being then as much too excessive in all outwards Indications of Humility and Repentance. Here you shall meet one, bare-footed, with a Cross on his Shoulder, a Burden rather fit for somewhat with four Feet, and which his poor Two are ready to sink under, yet the vain Wretch bears and sweats, and sweats and bears, in hope of finding Merit in an Ass's Labour.

Others you shall see naked to their Wastes, whipping themselves with Scourges made for the Purpose, till the Blood follows every Stroke; and no Man need be at a Loss to follow them by the very Tracks of Gore they shed in this frentick Perambulation. Some, who from the Thickness of their Hides, or other Impediments, have not Power by their Scourgings to fetch Blood of themselves, are follow'd by Surgeons with their Lancets, who at every Turn, make use of them, to evince the Extent of their Patience and Zeal by the Smart of their Folly. While others, mingling Amour with Devotion, take particular Care to present themselves all macerated before the Windows of their Mistresses; and even in that Condition, not satisfy'd with what they have barbarously done to themselves, they have their Operators at hand, to evince their Love by the Number of their Gashes and

Wounds; imagining the more Blood they lose, the more Love they shew, and the more they shall gain. These are generally Devoto's of Quality; though the Tenet is universal, that he that is most bloody is most devout.

After these Street-Exercises, these ostentatious Castigations are over, these Self-sacrificers repair to the great Church, the bloodier the better; there they throw themselves, in a Condition too vile for the Eye of a Female, before the Image of the Virgin *Mary*; though I defy all their Race of Fathers, and their infallible holy Father into the Bargain, to produce any Authority to fit it for Belief, that she ever delighted in such sanguinary Holocausts.

During the whole Time of *Lent*, you will see in every Street some Priest or Frier, upon some Stall or Stool, preaching up Repentance to the People; and with violent Blows on his Breast crying aloud, *Mia Culpa, mia maxima Culpa*, till he extract reciprocal Returns from the Hands of his Auditors on their own Breasts.

When *Good Friday* is come they entertain it with the most profound Show of Reverence and Religion, both in their Streets and in their Churches. In the last, particularly, they have contriv'd about twelve a-Clock suddenly to darken them, so as to render them quite gloomy. This they do to intimate the Eclipse of the Sun, which at that time happen'd. And to signify the Rending of the Vail of the Temple, you are struck with a strange artificial Noise at the very same Instant.

But when *Easter* Day appears, you find it in all Respects with them a Day of Rejoicing; for though Abstinence from Flesh with them, who at no time eat much, is not so great a Mortification as with those of the same Persuasion in other Countries, who eat much more, yet there is a visible Satisfaction darts out at their Eyes, which demonstrates their inward Pleasure in being set free from the Confinement of Mind to the Dissatisfaction of the Body. Every Person you now meet greets you with a *Resurrexit Jesus*; a good Imitation of the primitive Christians, were it the real Effect of Devotion. And all Sorts of the best Musick (which here indeed is the best in all *Spain*) proclaim an auspicious Valediction to the departed Season of superficial Sorrow and stupid Superstition. But enough of this: I proceed to weightier Matters.

While we lay at *Valencia*, under the Vigilance and Care of the indefatigable Earl, News was brought that *Alicant* was besieg'd by General *Gorge* by Land, while a Squadron of Men of War batter'd it from the Sea; from both which the Besiegers play'd their Parts so well, and so warmly ply'd them with their Cannon, that an indifferent practicable Breach was made in a little time.

MAHONI commanded in the Place, being again receiv'd into Favour; and clear'd as he was of those political Insinuations before intimated, he now seem'd resolv'd to confirm his Innocence by a resolute Defence. However, perceiving that all Preparations tended towards a Storm, and knowing full well the Weakness of the Town, he withdrew his Garrison into the Castle, leaving the Town to the Defence of its own Inhabitants.

Just as that was doing, the Sailors, not much skill'd in Sieges, nor at all times capable of the coolest Consideration, with a Resolution natural to them, storm'd the Walls to the Side of the Sea; where not meeting with much Opposition (for the People of the Town apprehended the least Danger there) they soon got into the Place; and, as soon as got in, began to Plunder. This oblig'd the People, for the better Security of themselves, to open their Gates, and seek a Refuge under one Enemy, in opposition to the Rage of another.

General *Gorge*, as soon as he enter'd the Town, with a good deal of seeming Lenity, put a stop to the Ravages of the Sailors; and ordered Proclamation to be made throughout the Place, that all the Inhabitants should immediately bring in their best Effects into the great Church for their better Security. This was by the mistaken Populace, as readily comply'd with; and neither Friend nor Foe at all disputing the Command, or questioning the Integrity of the Intention; the Church was presently crouded with Riches of all sorts and sizes. Yet after some time remaining there, they were all taken out, and disposed of by those, that had as little Property in 'em, as the Sailors, they were pretended to be preserv'd from.

The Earl of *Peterborow* upon the very first News of the Siege had left *Valencia*, and taken Shipping for *Alicant*; where he arrived soon after the Surrender of the Town, and that Outcry of the Goods of the Towns-men. Upon his Arrival, *Mahoni*,

who was block'd up in the Castle, and had experienced his indefatigable Diligence, being in want of Provisions, and without
much hope of Relief, desired to capitulate. The Earl granted him
honourable Conditions, upon which he delivered up the Castle,
and *Gorge* was made Governor.

Upon his Lordship's taking Ship at *Valencia*, I had an Opportunity of marching with those Dragoons, which escorted him
from *Castile*, who had received Orders to march into *Murcia*.
We quarter'd the first Night at *Alcira*, a Town that the River
Segra almost surrounds, which renders it capable of being made
a Place of vast Strength, though now of small Importance.

The next Night we lay at *Xativa*, a Place famous for its steadi-
ness to King *Charles*. General *Basset*, a *Spaniard*, being Governor;
it was besieg'd by the Forces of King *Philip*; but after a noble
Resistance, the Enemy were beat off, and the Siege raised; for
which Effort, it is supposed, that on the Retirement of King
Charles out of this Country, it was depriv'd of its old Name
Xativa, and is now called *San Felippo*; though to this day the
People thereabouts much dissallow by their Practice, that novel
Denomination.

We march'd next Morning by *Monteza*; which gives Name
to the famous Title of Knights of *Monteza*. It was at the Time
that Colonel O *Guaza*, an *Irishman*, was Governor, besieg'd by
the People of the Country, in favour of King *Charles*; but very
ineffectually, so it never chang'd its Sovereign. That Night
we quarter'd at *Fonte dalas Figuras*, within one League of *Almanza*;
where that fatal and unfortunate Battle, which I shall give an
Account of in its Place, was fought the Year after, under the Lord
Galway.

On our fourth days March we were oblig'd to pass *Villena*,
where the Enemy had a Garrison. A Party of *Mahoni*'s Dragoons
made a part of that Garrison, and they were commanded by
Major O. *Rairk* an *Irish* Officer, who always carried the Reputation of a good Soldier, and a brave Gentleman.

I had all along made it my Observation, that Captain *Matthews*,
who commanded those Dragoons, that I march'd with, was a
Person of much more Courage than Conduct; and he us'd as little
Precaution here, though just marching under the Eye of the

Enemy, as he had done at other Times. As I was become intimately acquainted with him, I rode up to him, and told him the Danger, which, in my Opinion, attended our present March. I pointed out to him just before *Villena* a jutting Hill, under which we must unavoidably pass; at the turning whereof, I was apprehensive the Enemy might lie, and either by Ambuscade or otherwise, surprize us; I therefore intreated we might either wait the coming of our Rear Guard; or at least march with a little more leisure and caution. But he taking little notice of all I said, kept on his round March; seeing which, I press'd forward my Mule, which was a very good one, and rid as fast as her Legs could carry her, till I had got on the top of the Hill. When I came there, I found both my Expectation, and my Apprehensions answered: For I could very plainly discern three Squadrons of the Enemy ready drawn up, and waiting for Us at the very winding of the Hill.

Hereupon I hastened back to the Captain with the like Speed, and told him the Discovery I had made; who nevertheless kept on his March, and it was with a good deal of Difficulty, that I at last prevail'd on him to halt, till our Rear Guard of twenty Men had got up to us. But those joining us, and a new Troop of *Spanish* Dragoons, who had march'd towards us that Morning, appearing in Sight; our Captain, as if he was afraid of their rivalling him in his Glory, at the very turn of the Hill, rode in a full Gallop, with Sword in Hand, up to the Enemy. They stood their Ground, till we were advanc'd within two hundred Yards of them, and then in Confusion endeavoured to retire into the Town.

They were obliged to pass over a small Bridge, too small to admit of such a Company in so much haste; their crouding upon which obstructed their Retreat, and left all that could not get over, to the Mercy of our Swords, which spar'd none. However narrow as the Bridge was, Captain *Matthews* was resolved to venture over after the Enemy; on doing which, the Enemy made a halt, till the People of the Town, and the very Priests came out to their Relief with fire Arms. On so large an Appearance, Captain *Matthews* thought it not adviseable to make any further Advances; so driving a very great flock of Sheep from under the Walls, he continued his March towards *Elda*. In this Action we lost Captain *Topham*, and three Dragoons.

I remember we were not marched very far from the Place, where this Rencounter happen'd; when an *Irish* Dragoon overtook the Captain, with a civil Message from Major *O Rairk*, desiring that he would not entertain a mean Opinion of him for the Defence that was made; since could he have got the *Spaniards* to have stood their Ground, he should have given him good Reason for a better. The Captain return'd a complimental Answer, and so march'd on. This Major *O Rairk*, or *O Roork*, was the next Year killed at *Alkay*, being much lamented, for he was esteemed both for his Courage and Conduct, one of the best of the *Irish* Officers in the *Spanish* Service. I was likewise informed that he was descended from one of the ancient Kings of *Ireland*; the Mother of the honourable Colonel *Paget*, one of the Grooms of the Bedchamber to his present Majesty, was nearly related to this Gallant Gentleman.

One remarkable Thing I saw in that Action, which affected and surprised me; A *Scotch* Dragoon, of but a moderate Size, with his large basket-hilted Sword, struck off a *Spaniard's* Head at one stroke, with the same ease, in appearance, as a Man would do that of a Poppy.

When we came to *Elda* (a Town much in the Interest of King *Charles*, and famous for its fine Situation, and the largest Grapes in *Spain*) the Inhabitants received us in a manner as handsome as it was peculiar; all standing at their Doors with lighted Torches; which considering the Time we enter'd was far from an unwelcome or disagreeable Sight.

The next Day several requested to be the Messengers of the Action at *Villena* to the Earl of *Peterborow* at *Alicant*; but the Captain return'd this Answer to all, that in consideration of the Share that I might justly claim in that Day's Transactions, he could not think of letting any other Person be the Bearer. So giving me his Letters to the Earl, I the next Day deliver'd them to him at *Alicant*. At the Delivery, Colonel *Killigrew* (whose Dragoons they were) being present, he expressed a deal of Satisfaction at the Account, and his Lordship was pleased at the same time to appoint me sole Engineer of the Castle of *Alicant*.

Soon after which, that successful General embark'd for *Genoa*, according to the Resolutions of the Council of War at *Guadalaxara*, on a particular Commission from the Queen of *England*, another from *Charles* King of *Spain*, and charged at the same time with a Request of the Marquiss *das Minas*, General of the *Portugueze* Forces, to negotiate Bills for one hundred thousand Pounds for the use of his Troops. In all which, tho' he was (as ever) successful; yet may it be said without a figure, that his Departure, in a good measure, determin'd the Success of the confederate Forces in that Kingdom. True it is, the General return'd again with the fortunate, Fruits of those Negotiations; but never to act in his old auspicious Sphere: And therefore, as I am now to take leave of this fortunate General, let me do it with Justice, in an Appeal to the World, of the not to be parallel'd Usage (in these latter Ages, at least) that he met with for all his Services; such a vast variety of Enterprizes, all successful, and which had set all *Europe* in amaze; Services that had given occasion to such solemn and public Thanksgivings in our Churches, and which had received such very remarkable Approbations, both of Sovereign and Parliament; and which had been represented in so lively a Manner, in a Letter wrote by the King of *Spain*, under his own Hand, to the Queen of *England*, and communicated to both Houses in the Terms following:

Madam, my Sister,

I should not have been so long e'er I did my self the Honour to repeat the Assurances of my sincere Respects to you, had I not waited for the good Occasion which I now acquaint you with, that the City of *Barcelona* is surrendered to me by Capitulation. I doubt not but you will receive this great News with intire Satisfaction, as well, because this happy Success is the Effect of your Arms, always glorious, as from the pure Motives of that Bounty and maternal Affection you have for me, and for every Thing which may contribute to the Advancement of my Interest.

I must do this Justice to all the Officers and common Soldiers, and particularly to my Lord *Peterborow*, that he has shown

5*

in this whole Expedition, a Constancy, Bravery, and Conduct, worthy of the Choice that your Majesty has made of him, and that he could no ways give me better Satisfaction than he has, by the great Zeal and Application, which he has equally testified for my Interest, and for the Service of my Person. I owe the same Justice to Brigadier *Stanhope*, for his great Zeal, Vigilance, and very wise Conduct, which he has given Proofs of upon all Occasions: As also to all your Officers of the Fleet, particularly to your worthy Admiral *Shovel*, assuring your Majesty, that he has assisted me in this Expedition, with an inconceivable Readiness and Application, and that no Admiral will be ever better able to render me greater Satisfaction, than he has done. During the Siege of *Barcelona*, some of your Majesty's Ships, with the Assistance of the Troops of the Country, have reduc'd the Town of *Tarragona*, and the officers are made Prisoners of War. The Town of *Girone* has been taken at the same time by Surprize, by the Troops of the Country. The Town of *Lerida* has submitted, as also that of *Tortosa* upon the *Ebro;* so that we have taken all the Places of *Catalonia*, except *Roses*. Some Places in *Aragon* near *Sarrogosa* have declared for me, and the Garrison of the Castle of *Denia* in *Valencia* have maintained their Post, and repulsed the Enemy; 400 of the Enemies Cavalry have enter'd into our Service, and a great number of their Infantry have deserted.

This, Madam, is the State that your Arms, and the Inclination of the People have put my Affairs in. It is unnecessary to tell you what stops the Course of these Conquests, it is not the Season of the Year, nor the Enemy; these are no Obstacles to your Troops, who desire nothing more than to act under the Conduct that your Majesty has appointed them. The taking of Barcelona, with so small a Number of Troops, is very remarkable; and what has been done in this Siege is almost without Example; that with seven or eight thousand Men of your Troops, and two hundred Miquelets, we should surround and invest a Place, that thirty thousand *French* could not block up.

After a March of thirteen Hours, the Troops climb'd up the Rocks and Precipices, to attack a Fortification stronger than the Place, which the Earl of *Peterborow* has sent you a

Plan of; two Generals, with the Grenadiers, attack'd it Sword
in Hand. In which Action the Prince of *Hesse* died gloriously,
after so many brave Actions: I hope his Brother and his Family
will always have your Majesty's Protection. With eight hundred Men they forc'd the cover'd Way, and all the Intrench-
ments and Works, one after another, till they came to the last
Work which surrounded it, against five hundred Men of
regular Troops which defended the Place, and a Reinforcement
they had receiv'd; and three Days afterwards we became
Masters of the Place. We afterwards attack'd the Town on the
Side of the Castle. We landed again our Cannon, and the other
Artillery, with inconceivable Trouble, and form'd two Camps,
distant from each other three Leagues, against a Garrison almost
as numerous as our Army, whose Cavalry was double the
Strength of ours. The first Camp was so well intrench'd, that
'twas defended by two thousand Men and the Dragoons;
whilst we attack'd the Town with the rest of our Troops. The
Breach being made, we prepar'd to make a general Assault
with all the Army. These are Circumstances, Madam, which
distinguish this Action, perhaps, from all others.

Here has happen'd an unforeseen Accident. The Cruelty
of the pretended Viceroy, and the Report spread abroad, that
he would take away the Prisoners, contrary to the Capitulation, provok'd the Burghers, and some of the Country People,
to take up Arms against the Garrison, whilst they were busy
in packing up their Baggage, which was to be sent away the
next Day; so that every thing tended to Slaughter: But your
Majesty's Troops, entering into Town with the Earl of *Peterborow*, instead of seeking Pillage, a Practice common upon
such Occasions, appeas'd the Tumult, and have sav'd the
Town, and even the Lives of their Enemies, with a Discipline
and Generosity without Example.

What remains is, that I return you my most hearty Thanks
for sending so great a Fleet, and such good and valiant Troops
to my Assistance. After so happy a Beginning, I have thought
it proper, according to the Sentiments of your Generals and
Admirals, to support, by my Presence, the Conquests that we
have made; and to shew my Subjects, so affectionate to my

Person, that I cannot abandon them. I receive such succours from your Majesty, and from your generous Nation, that I am loaded with your Bounties; and am not a little concern'd to think that the Support of my Interest should cause so great an Expence. But, Madam, I sacrifice my Person, and my Subjects in Catalonia expose also their Lives and Fortunes, upon the Assurances they have of your Majesty's generous Protection. Your Majesty and your Council knows better than we do, what is necessary for our Conservation. We shall then expect your Majesty's Succours, with an entire Confidence in your Bounty and Wisdom. A further Force is necessary: We give no small Diversion to *France*, and without doubt they will make their utmost Efforts against me as soon as possible; but I am satisfy'd, that the same Efforts will be made by my Allies to defend me. Your Goodness, Madam, inclines you, and your Power enables you, to support those that the Tyranny of France would oppress. All that I can insinuate to your Wisdom, and that of your Allies, is, that the Forces employ'd in this Country will not be unprofitable to the public Good, but will be under an Obligation and Necessity to act with the utmost Vigour against the Enemy. I am,

With an inviolable Affection,

Respect, and most

Sincere Acknowledgment,

Madam, my Sister,

Your most affectionate

Brother,

CHARLES.

And yet, after all, was this noble General not only recall'd, the Command of the Fleet taken from him, and that of the Army given to my Lord *Galway*, without Assignment of Cause; but all Manner of Falsities were industriously spread abroad, not only to dimish, if they could, his Reputation, but to bring him under Accusations of a malevolent Nature. I can hardly imagine it necessary here to take Notice, that afterward he disprov'd all those idle Calumnies and ill-invented Rumours; or to mention what Compliments he receiv'd, in the most solemn Manner,

from his Country, upon a full Examination and thorough canvassing of his Actions in the House of Lords. But this is too
notorious to be omitted, That all Officers coming from *Spain*
were purposely intercepted in their Way to *London*, and craftily
examin'd upon all the idle Stories which had pass'd tending to
lessen his Character: And when any Officers had asserted the
Falsity of those Inventions (as they all did, except a military
Sweetner or two) and that there was no Possibility of laying any
thing amiss to the Charge of that General- they were told, that
they ought to be careful however, not to speak advantagiously
of that Lord's Conduct, unless they were willing to fall Martyrs
in his Cause —— A Thing scarce to be credited even in a popish
Country. But *Scipio* was accus'd —— tho' (as my Author finely
observes) by Wretches only known to Posterity by that stupid
Accusation.

As a mournful Valediction, before I enter upon any new
Scene, the Reader will pardon this melancholy Expostulation.
How mortifying must it be to an *Englishman*, after he has found
himself solac'd with a Relation of so many surprising Successes
of her Majesty's Arms, under the Earl of *Peterborow*; Successes
that have lay'd before our Eyes Provinces and Kingdoms reduc'd,
and Towns and Fortresses taken and reliev'd; where we have seen
a continu'd Series of happy Events, the Fruits of Conduct and
Vigilance; and Caution and Foresight preventing Dangers that
were held, at first View, certain and unsurmountable: to change
this glorious Landskip, I say, for Scenes every way different, even
while our Troops were as numerous as the Enemy, and better
provided, yet always baffled and beaten, and flying before the
Enemy till fatally ruin'd in the Battle of *Almanza:* How mortifying must this be to any Lover of his Country! But I proceed
to my Memoirs.

ALICANT is a Town of the greatest Trade of any in the
Kingdom of *Valencia*, having a strong Castle, being situated on a
high Hill, which commands both Town and Harbour. In this
Place I resided a whole Year; but it was soon after my first
Arrival, that Major *Collier* (who was shot in the Back at *Barcelona*, as I have related in the Siege of that Place) hearing of me,
sought me out at my Quarters; and, after a particular Enquiry

into the Success of that difficult Task that he left me upon, and my answering all his Questions to satisfaction (all which he receiv'd with evident Pleasure) he threw down a Purse of Pistoles upon the Table; which I refusing, he told me, in a most handsome Manner, his Friendship was not to be preserv'd but by my accepting it.

After I had made some very necessary Repairs, I pursu'd the Orders I had receiv'd from the Earl of *Peterborow*, to go upon the erecting a new Battery between the Castle and the Town. This was a Task attended with Difficulties, neither few in Number, nor small in Consequence; for it was to be rais'd upon a great Declivity, which must render the Work both laborious and precarious. However, I had the good Fortune to effect it much sooner than was expected; and it was call'd *Gorge*'s Battery, from the Name of the Governor then commanding; who, out of an uncommon Profusion of Generosity, wetted that Piece of Gossiping with a distinguishing Bowl of Punch. Brigadier *Bougard*, when he saw this Work some time after, was pleas'd to honour it with a singular Admiration and Approbation, for its Compleatness, notwithstanding its Difficulties.

This Work, and the Siege of *Cartagena*, then in our Possession, by the Duke of *Berwick*, brought the Lord *Galway* down to this place. *Cartagena* is of so little Distance from *Alicant*, that we could easily hear the Cannon playing against, and from it, in our Castle, where I then was. And I remember my Lord *Galway*, on the fourth Day of the Siege, sending to know if I could make any useful Observations, as to the Success of it; I return'd, that I was of Opinion the Town was surrender'd, from the sudden Cessation of the Cannon, which, by our News next Day from the Place, prov'd to be fact. *Cartagena* is a small Sea-Port Town in *Murcia*; but has so good an Harbour, that when the famous Admiral *Doria* was ask'd, which were the three best Havens in the *Mediterranean*, he readily return'd, *June, July*, and *Cartagena*.

Upon the Surrender of this Place, a Detachment of Foot was sent by the Governor, with some Dragoons, to *Elsha*; but it being a Place of very little Strength they were soon made Prisoners of War.

The Siege of *Cartagena* being over, the Lord *Galway* return'd to his Camp; and the Lord *Duncannon* dying in *Alicant*, the first Guns that were fir'd from *Gorge's* Battery, were the Minute-Guns for his Funeral. His Regiment had been given to the Lord *Montandre*, who lost it before he had Possession, by an Action as odd as it was scandalous.

That Regiment had received Orders to march to the Lord *Galway's* Camp, under the Command of their Lieutenant-Colonel *Bateman*, a Person before reputedly a good Officer, tho' his Conduct here gave People, not invidious, too much Reason to call it in Question. On his March, he was so very careless and negligent (though he knew himself in a Country surrounded with Enemies, and that he was to march through a Wood, where they every Day made their Appearance in great Numbers) that his Soldiers march'd with their Muskets slung at their Backs, and went one after another (as necessity had forc'd us to do in *Scotland*) himself at the Head of 'em, in his Chaise, riding a considerable way before.

It happened there was a Captain, with threescore Dragoons, detach'd from the Duke of *Berwick's* Army, with a Design to intercept some Cash, that was order'd to be sent to Lord *Galway's* Army from *Alicant*. This Detachment, missing of that intended Prize, was returning very disconsolately, *Re infecta*; when their Captain, observing that careless and disorderly March of the *English*, resolv'd, boldly enough, to attack them in the Wood. To that Purpose he secreted his little Party behind a great Barn; and so soon as they were half passed by, he falls upon 'em in the Center with his Dragoons, cutting and slashing at such a violent Rate, that he soon dispersed the whole Regiment, leaving many dead and wounded upon the Spot. The three Colours were taken; and the gallant Lieutenant-Colonel taken out of his Chaise, and carried away Prisoner with many others; only one Officer who was an Ensign, and so bold as to do his Duty, was kill'd.

The Lieutenant who commanded the Granadiers, received the Alarm time enough to draw his Men into a House in their way; where he bravely defended himself for a long Time; but being killed, the rest immediately surrender'd. The Account of this Action I had from the Commander of the Enemy's Party himself, some Time after, while I was a Prisoner. And Captain *Mahoni*,

who was present when the News was brought, that a few *Spanish*
Dragoons had defeated an *English* Regiment, which was this
under *Bateman*, protested to me, that the Duke of *Berwick* turn'd
pale at the Relation; and when they offer'd to bring the Colours
before him, he would not so much as see them. A little before the
Duke went to Supper, *Bateman* himself was brought to him, but
the Duke turn'd away from him without any further Notice
than coldly saying, that *he thought he was very strangely taken*. The
Wags of the Army made a thorough jest of him, and said his
military Conduct was of a piece with his Oeconomy, having two
Days before this March, sent his young handsome Wife into
England, under the Guardship of the young Chaplain of the
Regiment.

April 15. In the Year 1707, being *Easter Monday*, we had in the
Morning a flying Report in *Alicant*, that there had been the Day
before a Battle at *Almanza*, between the Army under the Command of the Duke of *Berwick*, and that of the *English*, under Lord
Galway, in which the latter had suffer'd an entire Defeat. We at
first gave no great Credit to it: But, alas, we were too soon woe-
fully convinced of the Truth of it, by Numbers that came flying
to us from the conquering Enemy. Then indeed we were satisfied
of Truths, too difficult before to be credited. But as I was not
present in that calamitous Battle, I shall relate it, as I received it
from an Officer then in the Duke's Army.

To bring the Lord *Galway* to a Battle, in a Place most commo-
dious for his purpose, the Duke made use of this Stratagem: He
ordered two *Irishmen*, both Officers, to make their way over to the
Enemy as Deserters; putting this Story in their Mouths, that the
Duke of *Orleans* was in a full March to join the Duke of *Berwick*
with twelve thousand Men; that this would be done in two Days,
and that then they would find out the Lord *Galway*, and force
him to Fight, where-ever they found him.

Lord *Galway*, who at this Time lay before *Villena*, receiving
this Intelligence from those well instructed Deserters, immediately rais'd the Siege; with a Resolution, by a hasty March, to
force the Enemy to Battle, before the Duke of *Orleans* should be
able to join the Duke of *Berwick*. To effect this, after a hard March
of three long *Spanish* Leagues in the heat of the Day; he appears

a little after Noon in the face of the Enemy with his fatigu'd Forces. Glad and rejoyc'd at the Sight, for he found his Plot had taken; *Berwick*, the better to receive him, draws up his Army in a half Moon, placing at a pretty good Advance three Regiments to make up the Centre, with express Order, nevertheless, to retreat at the very first Charge. All which was punctually observ'd, and had its desired Effect; For the three Regiments, at the first Attack gave way, and seemingly fled towards their Camp; the *English*, after their customary Manner, pursuing them with Shouts and Hollowings. As soon as the Duke of *Berwick* perceiv'd his Trap had taken, he order'd his right and left Wings to close; by which Means, he at once cut off from the rest of their Army all those who had so eagerly pursu'd the imaginary Runaways. In short, the Rout was total, and the most fatal Blow that ever the *English* receiv'd during the whole War with *Spain*. Nor, as it is thought, with a great probability of Reason, had those Troops that made their Retreat to the Top of the Hills, under Major General *Shrimpton*, met with any better Fate than those on the Plain, had the *Spaniards* had any other General in the Command than the Duke of *Berwick*; whose native Sympathy[8] gave a check to the Ardour of a victorious Enemy. And this was the sense of the *Spaniards* themselves after the Battle. Verifying herein that noble Maxim, *That Victory to generous Minds is only an Inducement to Moderation.*

The Day after this fatal Battle (which gave occasion to a *Spanish* piece of Wit, *that the English General had routed the French*) the Duke of *Orleans* did arrive indeed in the Camp, but with an Army of only fourteen Attendants.

The fatal Effects of this Battle were soon made visible, and to none more than those in *Alicant*. The Enemy grew every Day more and more troublesome; visiting us in Parties more boldly than before: and often hovering about us so very near, that with our Cannon we could hardly teach 'em to keep a proper Distance. *Gorge* the Governor of *Alicant* being recall'd into *England*, Major General *Richards* was by King *Charles* appointed Governor in his Place. He was a Roman Catholick, and very much belov'd by the Natives on that Account; tho' to give him his due, he behaved himself extremely well in all other Respects. It was in his Time, that a Design was laid of surprising *Guardamere*, a small Sea-port Town, in *Murcia*: But the military Bishop (for he was in a literal Sense excellent *tam Marte, quam Mercurio*, among his many others Exploits, by a timely Expedition, prevented that.

Governor *Richards*, my Post being always in the Castle, had sent to desire me to give notice whenever I saw any Parties of the Enemy moving. Pursuant to this Order, discovering one Morning a considerable body of Horse towards *Elsha*, I went down into the Town, and told the Governor what I had seen; and without any delay he gave his Orders, that a Captain with threescore Men should attend me to an old House about a Mile distance. As soon as we had got into it, I set about barricading all the open Places, and Avenues, and put my Men in a Posture ready to receive an Enemy, as soon as he should appear; upon which the Captain, as a feint, ordered a few of his men to shew them-selves on a rising Ground just before the House. But we had like to have caught a Tartar: For tho' the Enemy took the Train I had laid, and on sight of our small Body on the Hill, sent a Party from their greater Body to intercept them, before they could reach the Town; yet the Sequel prov'd, we had mistaken their Number and it soon appeared to be much greater than we at first imagin'd However our Out-scouts, as I may call 'em, got safe into the House; and on the Appearance of the Party, we let fly a full Volly, which laid dead on the Spot three Men and one Horse. Hereupon the whole Body made up to the House, but stood a-loof upon the Hill without reach of our Shot. We soon saw our Danger from the number of the Enemy: And well for us it was, that the watchful Governor had taken notice of it, as well as we in the House. For observing us surrounded with the Enemy, and by a Power so much superior, he marched himself with a good part of the Garrison to our Relief. The Enemy stood a little time as if they would receive 'em; but upon second thoughts they retir'd; and to our no little Joy left us at Liberty to come out of the House and join the Garrison.

Scarce a Day pass'd but we had some visits of the like kind attended sometimes with Rencounters of this Nature; in so much that there was hardly any stirring out in Safety for small Parties, tho' never so little away. There was within a little Mile of the

Town, an old Vineyard, environed with a loose stone Wall: An Officer and I made an Agreement to ride thither for an Airing. We did so, and after a little riding, it came into my Head to put a Fright upon the Officer. And very lucky for us both was that unlucky Thought of mine; pretending to see a Party of the Enemy make up to us, I gave him the Alarm, set Spurs to my Horse, and rid as fast as Legs could carry me. The Officer no way bated of his Speed; and we had scarce got out of the Vineyard but my Jest prov'd Earnest, twelve of the Enemy's Horse pursuing us to the very Gates of the Town. Nor could I ever after prevail upon my Fellow-Traveller to believe that he ow'd his Escape to Merriment more than Speed.

Soon after my Charge, as to the Fortifications, was pretty well over, I obtain'd Leave of the Governor to be absent for a Fortnight, upon some Affairs of my own at *Valencia*. On my Return from whence, at a Town call'd *Venissa*, I met two Officers of an *English* Regiment, going to the Place from whence I last came. They told me, after common Congratulations, that they had left Major *Boyd*, at a little Place call'd *Capel*, hiring another Mule, that he rode on thither having tir'd and fail'd him; desiring withal, that if I met him, I would let him know that they would stay for him at that Place. I had another Gentleman in my Company, and we had travell'd on not above a League further, whence, at a little Distance, we were both surpriz'd with a Sight that seem'd to have set all Art at defiance, and was too odd for any thing in Nature. It appear'd all in red, and to move; but so very slowly, that if we had not made more way to that than it did to us, we should have made it a Day's Journey before we met it. My Companion could as little tell what to make of it as I; and, indeed, the nearer it came the more monstrous it seem'd, having nothing of the Tokens of Man, either Walking, Riding, or in any Posture whatever. At last, coming up with this strange Figure of a Creature (for now we found it was certainly such) what, or rather who, should it prove to be, but Major *Boyd?* He was a Person of himself far from one of the least Proportion, and mounted on a poor little Ass, with all his warlike Accoutrements upon it, you will allow must make a Figure almost as odd as one of the old *Centaurs*. The Morocco Saddle that cover'd the Ass was of Burden enough for the Beast without its Master; and the additional Holsters and Pistols made it much more weighty. Nevertheless, a Curb Bridle of the largest Size cover'd his little Head, and a long red Cloak, hanging down to the Ground, cover'd Jackboots, Ass, Master and all. In short, my Companion and I, after we could specifically declare it to be a Man, agreed we never saw a Figure so comical in all our Lives. When we had merrily greeted our Major (for a *Cynick* could not have forborn Laughter) He excus'd all as well as he could, by saying he could get no other Beast. After which, delivering our Message, and condoling with him for his present Mounting, and wishing him better at his next Quarters, he settled into his old Pace, and we into ours, and parted.

We lay that Night at *Altea*, famous for its Bay for Ships to water at. It stands on a high Hill; and is adorn'd, not defended, with an old Fort.

Thence we came to *Alicant*, where having now been a whole Year, and having effected what was held necessary, I once more prevail'd upon the Governor to permit me to take another Journey. The Lord *Galway* lay at *Tarraga*, while *Lerida* lay under the Siege of the Duke of *Orleans*; and having some Grounds of Expectation given me, while he was at *Alicant*, I resolv'd at least to demonstrate I was still living. The Governor favour'd me with Letters, not at all to my Disadvantage; so taking Ship for *Barcelona*, just at our putting into the Harbour, we met with the *English* Fleet, on its Return from the Expedition to *Toulon* under Sir *Cloudsly Shovel*.

I stay'd but very few Days at *Barcelona*, and then proceeded on my intended Journey to *Tarraga*; arriving at which Place I deliver'd my Packet to the Lord *Galway*, who receiv'd me with very great Civility; and to double it, acquainted me at the same time, that the Governor of *Alicant* had wrote very much in my Favour: But though it was a known Part of that noble Lord's Character, that the first Impression was generally strongest, I had Reason soon after to close with another Saying, equally true, *That general Rules always admit of some Exception.* While I was here we had News of the taking of the Town of *Lerida*; the Prince of *Hesse* (Brother to that brave Prince who lost his Life before

Monjouick) retiring into the Castle with the Garrison, which he bravely defended a long time after.

When I was thus attending my Lord *Galway* at *Tarraga*, he receiv'd Intelligence that the Enemy had a Design to lay Siege to *Denia*; whereupon he gave me Orders to repair there as Engineer. After I had receiv'd my Orders, and taken Leave of his Lordship, I set out, resolving, since it was left to my Choice, to go by way of *Barcelona*, and there take Shipping for the Place of my Station; by which I propos'd to save more time than would allow me a full Opportunity of visiting *Montserat*, a Place I had heard much Talk of, which had fill'd me with a longing Desire to see it. To say Truth, I had been told such extravagant Things of the Place, that I could hardly impute more than one half of it to any thing but *Spanish* Rhodomontado's, the Vice of extravagant Exaggeration being too natural to that Nation.

MONTSERAT is a rising lofty Hill, in the very Middle of a spacious Plain, in the Principality of *Catalonia*, about seven Leagues distant from *Barcelona* to the Westward, somewhat inclining to the North. At the very first Sight, its Oddness of Figure promises something extraordinary; and given at that Distance the Prospect makes somewhat of a grand Appearance: Hundreds of aspiring Pyramids presenting themselves all at once to the Eye, look, if I may be allowed so to speak, like a little petrify'd Forrest; or, rather, like the awful Ruins of some capacious Structure, the Labour of venerable Antiquity. The nearer you approach the more it affects; but till you are very near you can hardly form in your Mind any thing like what you find it when you come close to it. Till just upon it you would imagine it a perfect Hill of Steeples; but so intermingled with Trees of Magnitude, as well as Beauty, that your Admiration can never be tir'd, or your Curiosity surfeited. Such I found it on my Approach; yet much less than what I found it, was so soon as I enter'd upon the very Premises.

Now that stupendious Cluster of Pyramids affected me in a Manner different to all before; and I found it so finely group'd with verdant Groves, and here and there interspers'd with aspiring, but solitary Trees, that it no way lessened my Admiration, while it increased my Delight. Those Trees, which I call solitary, as standing single, in opposition to the numerous Groves, which are close and thick (as I observ'd when I ascended to take a View of the several Cells) rise generally out of the very Clefts of the main Rock, with nothing, to Appearance, but a Soil or bed of Stone for their Nurture. But though some few Naturalists may assert, that the Nitre in the Stone may afford a due Proportion of Nourishment to Trees and Vegetables; these, in my Opinion, were all too beautiful, their Bark, Leaf, and Flowers, carry'd too fair a Face of Health, to allow them even to be the Foster-children of Rock and Stone only.

Upon this Hill, or if you please, Grove of Rocks, are thirteen Hermits Cells, the last of which lies near the very Summit. You gradually advance to every one, from Bottom to Top, by a winding Ascent; which to do would otherwise be Impossible, by reason of the Steepness; but though there is a winding Ascent to every Cell, as I have said, I would yet set at defiance the most observant, if a Stranger, to find it feasible to visit them in order, if not precaution'd to follow the poor *Borigo*, or old Ass, that with Paniers hanging on each Side of him, mounts regularly, and daily, up to every particular Cell. The Manner is as follows:

In the Paniers there are thirteen Partitions; one for every Cell. At the Hour appointed, the Servant having plac'd the Paniers on his Back, the Ass, of himself, goes to the Door of the Convent at the very Foot of the Hill, where ever Partition is supply'd with their several Allowances of Victuals and Wine. Which, as soon as he has receiv'd, without any further Attendance, or any Guide, he mounts and takes the Cells gradually, in their due Course, till he reaches the very uppermost. Where having discharg'd his Duty, he descends the same Way, lighter by the Load he carry'd up. This the poor stupid Drudge fails not to do, Day and Night, at the stated Hours.

Two Gentlemen, who had join'd me on the Road, alike led by Curiosity, seem'd alike delighted, that the End of it was so well answer'd. I could easily discover in their Countenances a Satisfaction, which, if it did not give a Sanction to my own, much confirm'd it, while they seem'd to allow with me that these reverend Solitaries were truly happy Men; I then thought them such; and a thousand times since, reflecting within my self, have wish'd, bating their Errors, and lesser Superstitions, my self as happily station'd: For what can there be wanting to a happy Life, where all things necessary are provided without Care? Where the Days, without Anxiety or Troubles, may be gratefully passed away, with an innocent Variety of diverting and pleasing Objects, and where their Sleep sand Slumbers are never interrupted with any thing more offensive, than murmuring Springs, natural Cascades, or the various Songs of the pretty feather'd Quiristers.

But their Courtesy to Strangers is no less engaging than their Solitude. A recluse Life, for the Fruits of it, generally speaking, produces Moroseness; Pharisaical Pride too often sours the Temper; and a mistaken Opinion of their own Merit too naturally leads such Men into a Contempt of others; But on the contrary, these good Men (for I must call them as I thought them) seem'd to me the very Emblems of Innocence; so ready to oblige others, that at the same Instant they seem'd laying Obligations upon themselves. This is self-evident, in that Affability and Complaisance they use in shewing the Rarities of their several Cells; where, for fear you should slip any thing worthy Observation, they endeavour to instil in you as quick a Propensity of asking, as you find in them a prompt Alacrity in answering such Questions of Curiosity as their own have inspir'd.

In particular, I remember one of those reverend old Men, when we were taking Leave at the Door of his Cell, to which out of his great Civility he accompany'd us, finding by the Air of our Faces, as well as our Expressions, that we thought ourselves pleasingly entertain'd; to divert us afresh, advanc'd a few Paces from the Door, when giving a Whistle with his Mouth, a surprising Flock of pretty little Birds, variegated, and of different Colours, immediately flock'd around him. Here you should see some alighting upon his Shoulders, some on his awful Beard; others took Refuge on his snow-like Head, and many feeding, and more endeavouring to feed out of his Mouth; each appearing emulous and under an innocent Contention, how best to express their Love and Respect to their no less pleased Master.

Nor did the other Cells labour under any Deficiency of Variety: Every one boasting in some particular, that might distinguish it in something equally agreeable and entertaining. Nevertheless, crystal Springs spouting from the solid Rocks were, from the highest to the lowest, common to them all; and, in most of them, they had little brass Cocks, out of which, when turn'd, issu'd the most cool and crystalline Flows of excellent pure Water. And yet what more affected me, and which I found near more Cells than one, was the natural Cascades of the same transparent Element; these falling from one Rock to another, in that warm, or rather hot Climate, gave not more delightful Astonishment to the Eye, than they afforded grateful Refreshment to the whole Man. The Streams falling from these, soften, from a rougher tumultuous Noise, into such affecting Murmurs, by Distance, the Intervention of Groves, or neighbouring Rocks, that it were impossible to see or hear them and not be charm'd.

Neither are those Groves grateful only in a beautiful Verdure; Nature renders them otherwise delightful, in loading them with Clusters of Berries of a perfect scarlet Colour, which, by a beautiful Intermixture, strike the Eye with additional Delight. In short, it might nonplus a Person of the nicest Taste, to distinguish or determine, whether the Neatness of their Cells within, or the beauteous Varieties without, most exhaust his Admiration. Nor is the Whole, in my Opinion, a little advantag'd by the frequent View of some of those pyramidical Pillars, which seem, as weary of their own Weight, to recline and seek Support from others in the Neighbourhood.

When I mention'd the outside Beauties of their Cells, I must be thought to have forgot to particularize the glorious Prospects presented to your Eye from every one of them; but especially from that nearest the Summit. A Prospect, by reason of the Purity of the Air, so extensive, and so very entertaining that to dilate upon it properly to one that never saw it, would baffle Credit; and naturally to depaint it, would confound Invention. I therefore shall only say, that on the *Mediterranean* Side, after an agreeable Interval of some fair Leagues, it will set at defiance the strongest Opticks; and although *Barcelona* bounds it on the Land, the Eyes are feasted with the Delights of such an intervening Champion (where beauteous Nature does not only smile, but riot) that the Sense must be very temperate, or very weak, that can be soon or easily satisfy'd.

Having thus taken a View of all their refreshing Springs, their grateful Groves, and solitary Shades under single Trees, whose Clusters prov'd that even Rocks were grown fruitful; and having ran over all the Variety of Pleasures in their several pretty Cells, decently set off with Gardens round the, equally fragrant and beautiful, we were brought down again to the Convent, which, though on a small Ascent, lies very near the Foot of this terrestrial Paradise, there to take a Survey of their sumptuous Hall, much more sumptuous Chapel, and its adjoining Repository; and feast our Eyes with Wonders of a different Nature; and yet as entertaining as any, or all, we had seen before.

Immediately on our Descent, a Priest presented himself at the Door of the Convent, ready to shew us the hidden Rarities. And though, as I understood, hardly a Day passes without the Resort of some Strangers to gratify their Curiosity with the Wonders of the Place; yet is there, on every such Occasion, a superior Concourse of Natives ready to see over again, out of meer Bigotry and Superstition, what they have seen, perhaps, a hundred times before. I could not avoid taking notice, however, that the Priest treated those constant Visitants with much less Ceremony, or more Freedom, if you please, than any of the Strangers of what Nation soever; or, indeed, he seem'd to take as much Pains to disoblige those, as he did Pleasure in obliging us.

The Hall was neat, large and stately; but being plain and unadorn'd with more than decent Decorations, suitable to such a Society, I hasten to the other.

When we enter'd the Chapel, our Eyes were immediately attracted by the Image of our Lady of *Montserat* (as they call it) which stands over the Altar-Piece. It is about the natural Stature; but as black and shining as Ebony it self. Most would imagine it made of that Material; though her Retinue and Adorers will allow nothing of the Matter. On the contrary, Tradition, which with them is, on some Occasions, more than tantamount to Religion, has assur'd them, and they relate it as undoubted Matter of Fact, that her present Colour, if I may so call it, proceeded from her Concealment, in the Time of the *Moors*, between those two Rocks on which the Chapel is founded; and that her long lying in that dismal Place chang'd her once lovely White into its present opposite. Would not a Heretick here be apt to say, That it was greaty pity that an Image which still boasts the Power of acting so many Miracles, could no better conserve her own Complexion? At least it must be allow'd, even by a good Catholick, to carry along with it Matter of Reproach to the fair Ladies, Natives of the Country, for their unnatural and excessive Affection of adulterating, if not defacing, their beautiful Faces, with the ruinating Dauberies of *Carmine?*

As the Custom of the Place is (which is likewise allow'd to be a distinguishing Piece of Civility to Strangers) when we approach the black Lady (who, I should have told you, bears a Child in her Arms; but whether maternally Black, or of the *Mulatto* Kind, I protest I did not mind) the Priest, in great Civility, offers you her Arm to salute; at which Juncture, I, like a true blue Protestant, mistaking my Word of Command, fell foul on the fair Lady's Face. The Displeasure in his Countenance (for he took more Notice of the Rudeness than the good Lady her self) soon convinc'd me of my Error; However, as a greater Token of his Civility, having admitted no *Spaniards* along with my Companions and me, is pass'd off the better; and his after Civilities manifested, that he was willing to reform my Ignorance by his Complaisance.

To demonstrate which, upon my telling him that I had a Set of Beads, which I must entreat him to consecrate for me, he readily, nay eagerly comply'd; and having hung them on her Arm for the Space of about half, or somewhat short of a whole Minute, he return'd me the holy Baubles with a great deal of Address and most evident Satisfaction. The Reader will be apt to admire at this curious Piece of Superstition of mine, till I have told him, that even rigid Protestants have, in this Country, thought it but prudent to do the like; and likewise having so done, to carry them about their Persons, or in their Pockets: For Experience has convinc'd us of the Necessity of this most Catholick Precaution; since those who have here, travelling or otherwise, come to their Ends, whether by Accident, Sickness, or the Course of Nature, not having these sanctifying Seals found upon them, have ever been refus'd Christian Burial, under a superstitious Imagination, that the Corps of a Heretick will infect every thing near it.

Two instances of this kind fell within my Knowledge; one before I came to *Montserat*, the other after. The first was of one *Slunt*, who had been *Bombardier* at *Monjouick*; but being kill'd while we lay at *Campilio*, a Priest, whom I advis'd with upon the Matter, told me, that if he should be buried where any Corn grew, his Body would not only be taken up again, but ill treated, in revenge of the Destruction of so much Corn, which the People would on no account be persuaded to touch; for which Reason we took care to have him lay'd in a very deep Grave, on a very barren Spot of Ground. The other was of one Captain *Bush*, who was a Prisoner with me on the Surrender of *Denia*; who being sent, as I was afterwards, to Saint *Clemente la Mancha*, there dy'd; and, as I was inform'd, tho' he was privately, and by Night, bury'd in a Corn-Field, he was taken out of his Grave by those superstitious People, as soon as ever they could discover the Place where his Body was deposited. But I return to the Convent at *Montserat*.

Out of the Chapel, behind the High-Altar, we descended into a spacious Room, the Repository of the great Offerings made to the Lady. Here, though I thought in the Chapel it self I had seen the Riches of the Universe, I found a prodigious Quantity of more costly Presents, the superstitious Tribute of most of the Roman-Catholick Princes in *Europe*. Among a Multitude of others, they show'd me a Sword set with Diamonds, the Offering of *Charles* the Third, then King of *Spain*, but now Emperor of *Germany*. Though I must confess, being a Heretick, I could much easier find a Reason for a fair Lady's presenting such a Sword to a King of *Spain*, than for a King of *Spain*'s presenting such a Sword to a fair Lady: And by the Motto upon it, *Pulchra tamen nigra*, it was plain such was his Opinion. That Prince was so delighted with the Pleasure's of this sweet Place, that he, as well as I, stay'd as long as ever he could; though neither of us so long as either could have wish'd.

But there was another Offering from a King of *Portugal*, equally glorious and costly; but much better adapted; and therefore in its Propriety easier to be accounted for. That was a Glory for the Head of her Ladiship, every Ray of which was set with Diamonds, large at the Bottom, and gradually lessening to the very Extremity of every Ray. Each Ray might be about half a Yard Long; and I imagin'd in the Whole there might be about one Hundred of them. In short, if ever her Ladiship did the Offerer the Honour to put it on, I will though a Heretick, venture to aver, she did not at that present time look like a humane Creature.

To enumerate the rest, if my Memory would suffice, would exceed Belief. As the upper Part was a plain Miracle of Nature, the lower was a compleat Treasury of miraculous Art.

If you ascend from the lowest Cell to the very Summit, the last of all the thirteen, you will perceive a continual Contention between Pleasure and Devotion; and at last, perhaps, find your self at a Loss to decide which deserves the Preheminence: For you are not here to take Cells in the vulgar Acceptation, as the little Dormitories of solitary Monks: No! Neatness, Use, and Contrivance appear in every one of them; and though in an almost perfeèt Equality, yet in such Perfeótion, that you will find it difficult to discover in any one of them any thing wanting to the Pleasure of Life.

If you descend to the Convent near the Foot of that venerable Hill; you may see more, much more of the Riches of the World; but less, far less Appearance of a celestial Treasure. Perhaps, it might be only the Sentiment of a Heretick; but that Awe and Devotion, which I found in my Attendant from Cell to Cell grew languid, and lost in meer empty Bigotry and foggy Superstition, when I came below. In short, there was not a great Difference in their Heights, than in the Sentiments they inspir'd me with.

Before I leave this Emblem of the beatific Vision, I must correèt some thing like a Mistake, as to the poor *Borigo*. I said at the Beginning that his Labour was daily; but the *Sunday* is to him a Day of rest, as it is to the Hermits, his Masters, a Day of Refeótion. For to save the poor faithful Brute the hard Drudgery of that Day, the thirteen Hermits, if Health permit, descend to their *Canobium*, as they call it; that is, to the Hall of the Convent; where they dine in common with the Monks of the Order, who are *Benediótines*.

After seven Days Variety of such innocent Delight (the Space allow'd for the Entertainment of Strangers. I took my Leave of this pacifick Hermitage, to pursue the more boisterous Duties of my Calling. The Life of a Soldier is in every Respect the full *Antithesis* to that of a Hermit; and I know not, whether it might not be a Sense of that, which inspir'd me with very great Reluctancy at parting. I confess, while on the Spot, I over and over bandy'd in my Mind the Reasons which might prevail upon *Charles* the Fifth to relinquish his Crown; and the Arguments on his Side never fail'd of Energy, I could persuade my self that this, or some like happy Retreat, was the Reward of abdicated Empire.

Full of these Contemplations (for they lasted there) I arriv'd at *Barcelona*; where I found a Vessel ready to sail, on which I embarked for *Denia*, in pursuance of my Orders. Sailing to the Mouth of the *Mediterranean*, no Place along the *Christian* Shore affords a Prospect equally delightful with the Castle of *Denia*. It was never designed for a Place of great Strength, being built, and first design'd, as a Seat of Pleasure to the Great Duke of *Lerma*. In that Family it many Years remain'd; tho', within less than a Century, that with two other Dukedoms, have devolv'd upon the Family of the Duke *de Medina Celi*, the richest Subject at this time in all *Spain*.

DENIA was the first Town, that in our Way to *Barcelona*, declar'd for King *Charles*; and was then by his Order made a Garrison. The Town is but small, and surrounded with a thin Wall; so thin, that I have known a Cannon-Ball pierce through it at once.

When I arriv'd at *Denia*, I found a *Spaniard* Governor of the Town, whose Name has slipt my Memory; tho' his Behaviour merited everlasting Annals. Major *Percival*, an *Englishman*, commanded in the Castle, and on my coming there, I understood, it had been agreed between 'em, that in case of a Siege, which they apprehended, the Town should be defended wholly by *Spaniards*, and the Castle by the *English*.

I had scarce been there three Weeks before those Expectations were answered. The Place was invested by Count *D' Alfelt*, and Major General *Mahoni*; two Days after which, they open'd Trenches on the East Side of the Town. I was necessitated upon their so doing, to order the Demolishment of some Houses on that Side, that I might erect a Battery to point upon their Trenches, the better to annoy them. I did so; and it did the intended Service;

for with that, and two others, which I rais'd upon the Castle
'from all which we fir'd incessantly, and with great Success) the
Besiegers were sufficiently incommoded.

The Governor of the Town (a *Spaniard* as I said before, and
with a *Spanish* Garrison) behav'd very gallantly; insomuch,
that what was said of the Prince of *Hesse*, when he so bravely
defended *Gibraltar* against the joint Forces of *France* and *Spain*,
might be said of him, that he was Governor, Engineer, Gunner,
and Bombardier all in one; For no Man could exceed him, either
in Conduct or Courage; nor were the *Spaniards* under him less
valiant or vigilant; for in case the Place was taken, expecting
but indifferent Quarter, they fought with Bravery, and defended
the Place to Admiration.

The Enemy had answer'd our Fire with all the Ardour imaginable; and having made a Breach, that, as we thought was
practicable, a Storm was expected every Hour. Preparing against
which to the great Joy of all the Inhabitants, and the Surprize of
the whole Garrison, and without our being able to assign the least
Cause, the Enemy suddenly raised the Siege, and withdrew
from a Place, which those within imagined in great Danger.

The Siege thus abdicated (if I may use a modern Phrase) I was
resolved to improve my Time, and make the best Provision I
could against any future Attack. To that purpose I made several
new Fortifications, together with proper Casemets[9] for our
Powder, all which render'd the Place much stronger, tho' Time
too soon show'd me that Strength it self must yield to Fortune.

Surveying those works, and my Workmen, I was one Day
standing on the great Battery, when casting my Eye toward the
Barbary Coast, I observ'd an odd sort of greenish Cloud making
to the *Spanish* Shoar. Not like other Clouds with Rapidity or
Swiftness, but with a Motion so slow, that Sight itself was a long
time before it would allow it such. At last, it came just over my
Head, and interposing between the Sun and me, so thickened the
Air, that I had lost the very Sight of Day. At this moment it had
reach'd the Land; and tho' very near me in my Imagination, it
began to dissolve, and lose of its first Tenebrity, when all on a
sudden there fell such a vast multitude of Locusts, as exceeded
the thickest storm of Hail or Snow that I ever saw. All around me

was immediately cover'd with those crauling Creatures; and they yet continu'd to fall so thick, that with the swing of my Cane I knock'd down thousands. It is scarce imaginable the Havock I made in a very little space of time; much less conceivable is the horrid Desolation which attended the Visitation of those *Animalcula*. There was not in a Day or two's time, the least Leaf to be seen upon a Tree, nor any green Thing in a Garden. Nature seem'd buried in her own Ruins; and the vegetable World to be Supporters only to her Monument. I never saw the hardest Winter, in those Parts, attended with any equal Desolation. When, glutton like, they had devoured all that should have sustained them, and the more valuable Part of God's Creation (whether weary with gorging, or over thirsty with devouring, I leave to Philosophers) they made to Ponds, Brooks, and standing Pools, there revenging their own Rape upon Nature, upon their own vile Carkasses. In every of these you might see them lie in Heaps like little Hills; drown'd indeed, but attended with Stenches so noisome, that it gave the distracted Neighbourhood too great Reason to apprehend yet more fatal Consequences. A Pestilential Infection is the Dread of every Place, but especially of all Parts upon the *Mediterranean*. The Priests therefore repair'd to a little Chapel, built in the open Fields, to be made use of on such like Occasions, there to deprecate the miserable Cause of this dreadful Visitation. In a Week's time, or there abouts, the Stench was over, and every Thing but verdant Nature in its pristin Order.

Some few Months after this, and about eight Months from the former Siege, Count *D'Alfelt* caus'd *Denia* to be again invested; and being then sensible of all the Mistakes he had before committed, he now went about his Business with more Regularity and Discretion. The first Thing he set upon, and it was the wisest Thing he could do, was to cut off our Communication with the Sea. This he did, and thereby obtained what he much desired. Next, he caus'd his Batteries to be erected on the West side of the Town, from which he ply'd it so furiously, that in five Days' time a practicable Breach was made; upon which they stormed and took it. The Governor, who had so bravely defended it in the former Seige, fortunately for him had been remov'd; and *Francis*

Valero, now in his Place, was made Prisoner of War with all his Garrison.

After the taking the Town, they erected Batteries against the Castle, which they kept ply'd with incessant Fire, both from Cannon and Mortars. But what most of all plagu'd us, and did us most Mischief, was the vast showers of Stones sent among the Garrison from their Mortars. These, terrible in Bulk and Size, did more Execution than all the rest put together. The Garrison could not avoid being somewhat disheartened at this uncommon way of Rencounter; yet, to a Man, declar'd against hearkening to any Proposals of Surrender, the Governor excepted; who having selected more Treasure than he could properly, or justly call his own, was the only Person that seem'd forward for such a Motion. He had more than once thrown out Expressions of such a Nature, but without any effect. Nevertheless, having at last secretly obtained a peculiar Capitulation for himself, Bag, and Baggage; the Garrison was sacrific'd to his private Interest, and basely given up Prisoners of War. By these Means indeed he saved his Money, but lost his Reputation; and soon after, Life it self. And sure every Body will allow the latter loss to be least, who will take Pains to consider, that it screened him from the consequential Scrutinies of a Council of War, which must have issued as the just Reward of his Demerits.

The Garrison being thus unaccountably delivered up and made Prisoners, were dispersed different ways: Some into *Castile*, others as far as *Oviedo*, in the Kingdom of *Leon*. For my own part, having received a Contusion in my Breast; I was under a necessity of being left behind with the Enemy, till I should be in a Condition to be remov'd, and when that time came, I found my self agreeably ordered to *Valencia*.

As Prisoner of War I must now bid adieu to the active Part of the military Life; and hereafter concern my self with Descriptions of Countries, Towns, Palaces, and Men, instead of Battles. However, if I take in my way Actions of War, founded on the best Authorities, I hope my Interspersing such will be no disadvantage to my now more pacifick MEMOIRS.

So soon as I arriv'd at *Valencia*, I wrote to our Pay-master Mr. *Mead*, at *Barcelona*, letting him know, that I was become a

Prisoner, wounded, and in want of Money. Nor could even all those Circumstances prevail on me to think it long before he returned a favourable Answer, in an Order to Monsieur *Zoulicafre*, a Banker, to pay me on Sight fifty Pistoles. But in the same Letter he gave me to understand, that those fifty Pistoles were a Present to me from General (afterward Earl) *Stanhope*; and so indeed I found it, when I return'd into *England*, my Account not being charged with any part of it: But this was not the only Test I received of that generous Earl's Generosity. And where's the Wonder, as the World is compell'd to own, that Heroick Actions and Largeness of Soul ever did discover and amply distinguish the genuine Branches of that illustrious Family.

This Recruit to me however was the more generous for being seasonable. Benefits are always doubled in their being easily conferr'd and well tim'd; and with such an Allowance as I constantly had by the order of King *Philip*, as Prisoner of War, *viz.* eighteen Ounces of Mutton *per diem* for my self, and nine for my Man, with Bread and Wine in proportion, and especially in such a Situation; all this I say was sufficient to invite a Man to be easy, and almost forget his want of Liberty, and much more so to me if it be consider'd, that, that want of Liberty consisted only in being debarr'd from leaving the pleasantest City in all *Spain*.

Here I met with the *French* Engineer, who made the Mine under the Rock of the Castle at *Alicant*. That fatal Mine, which blew up General *Richards*, Colonel *Syburg*, Colonel *Thornicroft*, and at least twenty more Officers. And yet by the Account, that Engineer gave me, their Fate was their own choosing: The General, who commanded at that Siege being more industrious to save them, than they were to be sav'd: He endeavour'd it many ways: He sent them word of the Mine, and their readiness to spring it; he over and over sent them Offers of Leave to come, and take a view of it, and inspect it: Notwithstanding all which, tho' Colonel *Thornicroft*, and Captain *Page*, a *French* Engineer, in the Service of King *Charles*, pursued the Invitation, and were permitted to view it, yet would they not believe; but reported on their Return, that it was a sham Mine, a feint only to intimidate 'em to a Surrender, all the Bags being fill'd with Sand instead of Gunpowder.

6

The very Day on which the Besiegers design'd to spring the
Mine, they gave Notice of it; and the People of the Neighbourhood ran up in Crowds to an opposite Hill in order to see it:
Nevertheless, altho' those in the Castle saw all this, they still
remain'd so infatuated, as to imagine it all done only to affright
'em. At length the fatal Mine was sprung, and all who were
upon that Battery lost their Lives; and among them those I first
mentioned. The very Recital hereof made me think within my
self, *who can resist his Fate?*

That Engineer added further, that it was with an incredible
Difficulty, that he prepar'd that Mine; that there were in the
Concavity thirteen hundred Barrels of Powder; notwithstanding
which, it made no great Noise without, whatever it might do
inwardly; that only taking away what might be not improperly
term'd an Excrescence in the Rock, the Heave on the Blast had
render'd the Castle rather stronger on that Side than it was before,
a Crevice or Crack which had often occasioned Apprehensions
being thereby wholly clos'd and firm.

Some further Particulars I soon after had from Colonel *Syburg's*
Gentleman; who seeing me at the Play-house, challenged me,
tho' at that Time unkown to me. He told me, that the Night
preceeding the unfortunate Catastrophe of his Master, he was
waiting on him in the Casemet, where he observed, sometime
before the rest of the Company took notice of it, that General
Richards appeared very pensive and thoughtful, that the whole
Night long he was pester'd with, and could not get rid of a great
Flie, which was perpetually buzzing about his Ears and Head, to
the vexation and disturbance of the rest of the Company, as well
as the General himself; that in the Morning, when they went
upon the Battery, under which the Mine was, the General made
many offers of going off; but Colonel *Syburg*, who was got a
little merry, and the rest out of a Bravado, would stay, and would
not let the General stir; that at last it was propos'd by Colonel
Syburg to have the other two Bottles to the Queen's Health, after
which he promised they would all go off together.

Upon this my Relator, *Syburg*'s Gentleman, said, he was sent
to fetch the stipulated two Bottles; returning with which, Captain *Daniel Weaver*, within thirty or forty Yards of the Battery,

ran by him, vowing, he was resolv'd to drink the Queen's Health with them; but his Feet were scarce on the Battery, when the Mine was sprung, which took him away with the rest of the Company; while Major *Harding* now a Justice in *Westminster* coming that very Moment off Duty, exchang'd Fates.

If Predestination, in the Eyes of many, is an unaccountable Doctrine, what better Account can the wisest give of this Fatality? Or to what else shall we impute the Issue of this whole Transaction? That Men shall be solicited to their Safety; suffered to survey the Danger they were threatened with; among many other Tokens of its approaching Certainty, see such a Concourse of People crowding to be Spectators of their impending Catastrophe; and after all this, so infatuated to stay on the fatal Spot the fetching up of the other two Bottles; whatever it may to such as never think, to such as plead an use of Reason, it must administer Matter worthy of the sedatest Consideration.

Being now pretty well recover'd of my Wounds, I was by Order of the Governor of *Valencia*, removed to *Sainte Clemente de la Mancha*, a Town somewhat more Inland, and consequently esteem'd more secure than a Semi-Seaport. Here I remain'd under a sort of Pilgrimage upwards of three Years. To me as a Stranger divested of Acquaintance or Friend (for at that instant I was sole Prisoner there) at first it appear'd such, tho' in a very small compass of Time, I luckily found it made quite otherwise by an agreeable Conversation.

SAINTE Clemente de la Mancha, is rendered famous by the renown'd *Don Michael Cerviantes*, who in his facetious but satyrical Romance, has fix'd it the Seat and Birth Place of his Hero *Don Quixot*.

The Gentlemen of this Place are the least Priest-ridden or Sons of Bigotry, of any that I met with in all *Spain*; of which in my Conversation with them I had daily Instances. Among many others, an Expression that fell from *Don Felix Pacheco*, a Gentleman of the best Figure thereabout, and of a very plentiful Fortune, shall now suffice. I was become very intimate with him; and we us'd often to converse together with a Freedom too dangerous to be common in a Country so enslav'd by the Inquisition. Asking me one Day in a sort of a jocose manner, who, in my

Opinion, had done the greatest Miracles that ever were heard of? I answer'd, Jesus Christ.

"It is very true," says he, "Jesus Christ did great Miracles, and a great one it was to feed five Thousand People with two or three small Fishes, and a like number of Loaves: But *Saint Francis*, the Founder of the *Franciscan* Order, has found out a way to feed daily one hundred Thousand Lubbards with nothing at all";

meaning the *Franciscans*, the Followers of Saint *Francis*, who have no visible Revenues; yet in their way of Living come up to, if they do not exceed any other Order.

Another Day talking of the Place, it naturally led us into a Discourse of the Knight of *la Mancha, Don Quixot*. At which time he told me, that in his Opinion, that Work was a perfect Paradox, being the best and the worst Romance, that ever was wrote.

"For," says he, "tho' it must infallibly please every Man, that has any taste of Wit; yet has it had such a fatal Effect upon the Spirits of my Countrymen, that every Man of Wit must ever resent; for," continu'd he, "before the Appearance in the World of that Labour of *Cerviantes*, it was next to an Impossibility for a Man to walk the Streets with any Delight, or without Danger. There were seen so many Cavaliero's prancing and curvetting before the Windows of their Mistresses, that a Stranger would have imagin'd the whole Nation to have been nothing less than a Race of Knight Errants. But after the World became a little acquainted with that notable History; the Man that was seen in that once celebrated Drapery, was pointed at as a *Don Quixot*, and found himself the Jest of High and Low. And I verily believe," added he, "that to this, and this only we owe that dampness and poverty of Spirit, which has run thro' all our Councils for a Century past, so little agreeable to those nobler Actions of our famous Ancestors."

After many of these lesser sorts of Confidences, *Don Felix* recommended me to a Lodging next Door to his own. It was at a Widow's, who had one only Daughter, her House just opposite to a *Francisan* Nunnery. Here I remain'd somewhat upwards of two Years; all which time, lying in my Bed, I could hear the Nuns early in the Morning at their *Matins*, and late in the Evening at their *Vespers*, with Delight enough to my self, and without the least Indecency in the World in my Thoughts of them. Their own Divine Employ too much employ'd every Faculty of mine to entertain any Thing inconsentaneous or offensive.

This my Neighbourhood to the Nunnery gave me an opportunity of seeing two Nuns invested; and in this I must do a Justice to the whole Country, to acknowledge, that a Stranger who is curious (I would impute it rather to their hopes of Conversion, than to their Vanity) shall be admitted to much greater Freedoms in their religious Pageantries, than any Native.

One of these Nuns was of the first Quality, which render'd the Ceremony more remarkably fine. The manner of investing them was thus: In the Morning her Relations and Friends all met at her Father's House; whence, she being attir'd in her most sumptuous Apparel, and a Coronet plac'd on her Head, they attended her, in Cavalcade, to the Nunnery, the Streets and Windows being crowded, and fill'd with Spectators of all sorts.

So soon as she enter'd the Chapel belonging to the Nunnery, she kneel'd down, and with an appearance of much Devotion, saluted the Ground; then rising up, she advanced a Step or two farther, when on her Knees she repeated the Salutes: This done she approached to the Altar, where she remained till Mass was over: After which, a Sermon was preach'd by one of the Priests in Praise, or rather in an exalted Preference of a single Life. The Sermon being over, the Nun elect fell down on her Knees before the Altar; and after some short mental Oraisons, rising again, she withdrew into an inner Room, where stripping off all her rich Attire, she put on her Nun's Weeds: In which making her Appearance, she, again kneeling, offer'd up some private Devotions; which being over, she was led to the Door of the Nunnery, where the Lady and the rest of the Nuns stood ready to receive her with open Arms. Thus enter'd, the Nuns conducted her into the Quire, where after they had entertained her with Singing, and playing upon the Organ, the Ceremony concluded, and every one departed to their proper Habitations.

The very same Day of the Year ensuing the Relations and Friends of the fair Novitiate meet again in the Chapel of the Nunnery, where the Lady Abbess brings her out, and delivers her to them. Then again is there a Sermon preach'd on the same Subject as at first; which being over, she is brought up to the Altar, in a decent, but plain Dress, the fine Apparel, which she put off on her Initiation, being deposited on one side of the Altar, and her Nun's Weeds on the other. Here the Priest in Latin cries, *Utrum horum mavis, accipe*: to which she answers, as her Inclination, or as her Instruction directs her. If she, after this her Year of Probation, show any Dislike, she is at Liberty to come again into the World: But if aw'd by Fear (as too often is the Case) or won by Expectation, or present real Inclination, she makes choice of the Nun's Weeds, she is immediately invested, and must never expect to appear again in the World out of the Walls of the Nunnery. The young Lady I thus saw invested was very beautiful, and sang the best of any in the Nunnery.

There are in the Town three Nunneries, and a Convent to every one of them; *viz.* one of *Jesuits*, one of *Carmelites*, and the other of *Franciscans*. Let me not be so far mistaken to have this taken by way of Reflection. No! Whatever some of our Rakes of the Town may assert, I freely declare, that I never saw in any of the Nunneries (of which I have seen many both in *Spain* and other Parts of the World) any thing like indecent Behaviour, that might give occasion for Satyr or Disesteem. It is true, there may be Accidents, that may lead to a Misinterpretation, of which I remember a very untoward Instance in *Alicant*.

When the *English* Forces first laid Siege to that Town, the Priests, who were apprehensive of it, having been long since made sensible of the profound Regard to Chastity and Modesty of us Hereticks, by the ignominious Behaviour of certain Officers at *Rota* and *Porta St. Maria*, the Priests, I say, had taken care to send away privately all the Nuns to *Majorca*. But that the Heretick Invaders might have no Jealousy of it, the fair *Curtezans* of the Town were admitted to supply their Room. The Officers, both of Land and Sea, as was by the Friars pre-imagin'd, on taking the Town and Castle, immediately repair'd to the Grates of the Nunnery, toss'd over their Handkercheifs, Nosegays, and other pretty Things; all which were, doubtless, very graciously received by those imaginary Recluses. Thence came it to pass, that in the space of a Month or less, you could hardly fall into Comany of any one of our younger Officers, of either sort, but the Discourse, if it might deserve the Name, was concerning these beautiful Nuns; and you wou'd have imagin'd the Price of these Ladies as well known as that of Flesh in their common Markets. Others, as well as my self, have often endeavour'd to disabuse those Glorioso's, but all to little purpose, till more sensible Tokens convinced them, that the Nuns, of whose Favours they so much boasted, could hardly be perfeǎ Virgins, tho' in a Cloyster. And I am apt to think, those who would palm upon the World like vicious Relations of Nuns and Nunneries, do it on much like Grounds. Not that there are wanting Instances of Nunneries disfranchis'd, and even demolish'd, upon very flagrant Accounts; but I confine myself to *Spain*.

In this Town of *la Mancha* the *Corrigidore* always has his Presidence, having sixteen others under his Jurisdiǎion, of which Almanza is one. They are changed every three Years, and their Offices are the Purchase of an excessive Price; which occasions the poor People's being extravagantly fleeced, nothing being to be sold but at the Rates they impose; and every Thing that is sold paying the *Corrigidore* an Acknowledgment in specie, or an Equivalent to his liking.

While I was here, News came of the Battle of *Almanar* and *Saragosa*; and giving the Viǎory to that Side, which they espous'd (that of King *Philip*) they made very great Rejoycings. But soon, alas, for them, was all that Joy converted into Sorrow: The next Courier evincing, that the Forces of King *Charles* had been viǎorious in both Engagements. This did not turn to my present Disadvantage: For Convents and Nunneries, as well as some of those Dons, whom afore I had not stood so well with, strove now how most to oblige me; not doubting, but if the viǎorious Army should march that way, it might be in my Power to double the most signal of their Services in my Friendship.

Soon after an Accident fell out, which had like to have been of an unhappy Consequence to me. I was standing in Company, upon the Parade, when a most surprizing flock of Eagles flew over our Heads, where they hover'd for a considerable time. The Novelty struck them all with Admiration, as well as my self. But I, less accustomed to like Speǎacles, innocent saying, that in my Opinion, it could not bode any good to King *Philip*, because the

Eagle compos'd the Arms of *Austria*; some busie Body, in hearing, went and inform'd the *Corrigidore* of it. Those most magisterial Wretches embrace all Occasions of squeezing Money; and more especially from Strangers. However finding his Expectations disappointed in me, and that I too well knew the length of his Foot, to let my Money run freely; he sent me next Day to *Alercon*; but the Governor of that Place having had before Intelligence, that the *English* Army was advancing that way, refus'd to receive me, so I return'd as I went; only the Gentlemen of the Place, as they had condol'd the first, congratulated the last; for that *Corrigidore* stood but very indifferently in their Affections. However, it was a warning to me ever after, how I made use of *English* Freedom in a *Spanish* Territory.

As I had attain'd the Acquaintance of most of the Clergy, and Religious of the Place; so particularly I had my aim in obtaining that of the Provincial of the *Carmelites*. His Convent, tho' small, was exceeding neat; but what to me was much more agreeable, There were very large Gardens belonging to it, which often furnished me with Sallading and Fruit, and much oftner with Walks of Refreshment, the most satisfactory Amusement in this warm Climate. This Acquaintance with the Provincial was by a little Incident soon advanced into a Friendship; which was thus: I was one Day walking, as I us'd to do, in the long Gallery of the Convent, when observing the Images of the Virgin *Mary*, of which there was one at each end; I took notice that one had an Inscription under it, which was this, *Ecce, Virgo peperit filium*: but the other had no Inscription at all; upon which, I took out my Pencil, and wrote underneath, this Line:

Sponsa Dei, patrisque parens, & filia filii.

The Friars, who at a little distance had observed me, as soon as I was gone, came up and read what I had writ; reporting which to the Provincial, he order'd them to be writ over in Letters of Gold, and plac'd just as I had put 'em; saying, doubtless, such a fine Line cou'd proceed from nothing less than Inspiration. This secur'd me ever after his and their Esteem; the least advantage of which, was a full Liberty of their Garden for all manner of Fruit,

Sallading, or whatever I pleased: And as I said before, the Gardens were too fine not to render such a Freedom acceptable.

They often want Rain in this Country: To supply the Defect of which, I observed in this Garden, as well as others, an Invention not unuseful. There is a Well in the Middle of the Garden, and over that a Wheel with many Pitchers, or Buckets, one under another, which Wheel being turned round by an Ass, the Pitchers scoop up the Water on one Side, and throw it out on the other into a Trough, that by little Channels conveys it, as the Gardiner directs, into every part of the Garden. By this Means their Flowers and their Sallading are continually refresh'd, and preserved from the otherwise over-parching Beams of the Sun.

The Inquisition, in almost every Town in *Spain* (and more especially, if of any great Account) has its Spies, or Informers, for treacherous Intelligence. These make it their Business to ensnare the simple and unguarded; and are more to be avoided by the Stranger, than the Rattle Snake. Nature have appointed no such happy Tokens in the former to foreshew the Danger. I had Reason to believe, that one of those Vermin once made his Attack upon me in this place: And as they are very rarely, if ever known to the Natives themselves, I being a Stranger, may be allowed to make a guess by Circumstances.

I was walking by my self, when a Person, wholly unknown to me, giving me the civil Salute of the Day, endeavour'd to draw me into Conversation. After Questions had passed on general Heads, the fellow ensnaringly asked me, how it came to pass, that I show'd so little Respect to the Image of the crucify'd Jesus, as I pass'd by it in such a Street, naming it? I made Answer, that I had, or ought to have him always in my Heart crucified. To that he made no Reply: But proceeding in his Interrogatories, question'd me next, whether I believ'd a Purgatory? I evaded the Question, as I took it to be ensnaring; and only told him, that I should be willing to hear him offer any Thing that might convince me of the Truth, or Probability of it. Truth? He reply'd in a Heat: There never yet was Man so Holy as to enter Heaven without first passing through Purgatory. In my Opinion, said I, there will be no Difficulty in convincing a reasonable Man to the contrary. What mean you by that, cry'd the Spy? I mean, said I, that I can

6*

name one, and a great Sinner too, who went into Bliss without
any Visit to Purgatory. Name him, if you can, reply'd my
Querist. What think you of the Thief upon the Cross, said I?
to whom our dying Saviour said, *Hodie eris mecum in Paradiso*. At
which being silenced tho' not convicted, he turned from me in a
violent Rage, and left me to my self.

What increas'd my first Suspicion of him was, that a very short
time after, my Friend the Provincial sent to speak with me; and
repeating all Passages between the holy Spy and me, assur'd me
that he had been forc'd to argue in my Favour, and tell him that
I had said nothing but well: *For* says he, *all ought to have the Holy
Jesus crucified in their Hearts*.

"Nevertheless," continu'd he, "it is a commendable and good Thing
to have him represented in the high Ways: For, suppose," said he, "a
Man was going upon some base or profligate Design, the very Sight
of a crucified Saviour may happen to subvert his Resolution, and
deter him from committing Theft, Murder, or any other of the deadly
Sins." And thus ended that Conference.

I remember upon some other occasional Conversation after,
the Provincial told me, that in the *Carmelite* Nunnery next to his
Convent, and under his Care, there was a Nun, that was Daughter
to *Don Juan* of *Austria*; if so, her Age must render her venerable,
as her Quality.

Taking notice one Day, that all the People of the Place fetch'd
their Water from a Well without the Town, altho' they had
many seemingly as good within; I spoke to *Don Felix* of it, who
gave me, under the Seal of Secrecy, this Reason for it:

"When the Seat of the War," said he, "lay in these Parts, the *French*
Train of Artillery was commonly quarter'd in this Place; the Officers
and Soldiers of which were so very rampant and rude, in attempting to
debauch our Women, that there is not a Well within the Town,
which has not some *French* Mens Bones at the bottom of it; therefore
the Natives, who are sensible of it, choose rather to go farther a field."

By this Well there runs a little Rivulet, which gives head to
that famous River call'd the *Guadiana*; which running for some
Leagues under Ground, affords a pretence for the Natives to boast
of a Bridge on which they feed many Thousands of Sheep.

When it rises again, it is a fine large River, and after a Currency of many Leagues, empties it self into the *Atlantick* Ocean.

As to military Affairs, *Almanar* and *Saragosa* were Victories so compleat, that no Body made the least doubt of their settling the Crown of *Spain* upon the Head of *Charles* the Third, without a Rival. This was not barely the Opinion of his Friends, but his very Enemies resign'd all Hope or Expectation in favour of King *Philip*. The *Castilians*, his most faithful Friends, entertain'd no other Imagination; for after they had advis'd, and prevail'd that the Queen with the Prince of *Asturias* should be sent to *Victoria*; under the same Despondency, and a full Dispiritedness, they gave him so little Encouragement to stay in *Madrid*, that he immediately quitted the Place, with a Resolution to retire into his Grandfather's Dominions, the Place of his Nativity.

In his way to which, even on the last Day's Journey, it was his great good Fortune to meet the Duke of *Vendome*, with some few Troops, which his Grandfather *Lewis* XIV. of *France* had order'd to his Succour, under that Duke's Command. The Duke was grievously affected at such an unexpected Catastrophe; nevertheless, he left nothing unsaid or undone, that might induce that Prince to turn back; and at length prevailing, after a little Rest, and a great deal of Patience, by the Coming in of his scatter'd Troops, and some few he could raise, together with those the Duke brought with him, he once more saw himself at the Head of twenty thousand Men.

While Things were in this Manner, under Motion in King *Philip*'s Favour, *Charles* the third, with his victorious Army, advances forward, and enters into *Madrid*, of which he made General *Stanhope* Governor. And even here the *Castilians* gave full Proof of their Fidelity to their Prince; even at the Time when, in their Opinion, his Affairs were past all Hopes of Retrieve, they themselves having, by their Advice, contributed to his Retreat. Instead of prudential Acclamations therefore, such as might have answered the Expectations of a victorious Prince, now entering into their Capital, their Streets were all in a profound Silence, their Balconies un-adorn'd with costly Carpets, as was customary on like Occasions; and scarce an Inhabitant to be seen in either Shop or Window.

This doubtless was no little Mortification to a conquering Prince; however his Generals were wife enough to keep him from shewing any other Tokens of Resentment, than marching through the City with Unconcern, and taking up his Quarters at *Villa-verda*, about a League from it.

Nevertheless King *Charles* visited, in his March, the Chapel of the Lady *de Atocha*, where finding several *English* Colours and Standards, taken in the Battle of *Almanza*, there hung up; he ordered 'em to be taken down, and restor'd 'em to the *English* General.

It was the current Opinion then, and almost universal Consent has since confirm'd it, that the falsest Step in that whole War was this Advancement of King *Charles* to *Madrid*. After those two remarkable Victories at *Almanar* and *Saragosa*, had he directed his March to *Pampeluna*, and obtain'd Possession of that Place, or some other near it, he had not only stopt all Succours from coming out of *France*, but he would, in a great Measure, have prevented the gathering together of any of the routed and dispers'd Forces of King *Philip*: And it was the general Notion of the *Spaniards*, I convers'd with while at *Madrid*, that had King *Philip* once again set his Foot upon *French* Land, *Spain* would never have been brought to have re-acknowledged him.

King *Charles* with his Army having stay'd some Time about *Madrid*, and seeing his Expectations of the *Castilians* joining him not at all answered, at last resolved to decamp, and return to *Saragosa*: Accordingly with a very few Troops that Prince advanced thither; while the main Body, under the Command of the Generals *Stanhope* and *Staremberg*, passing under the very Walls of *Madrid*, held on their March towards *Aragon*.

After about three Days' March, General *Stanhope* took up his Quarters at *Breuhiga*, a small Town half wall'd; General *Staremberg* marching three Leagues farther, to *Cisuentes*. This choice of Situation of the two several Armies not a little puzzled the Politicians of those Times, who could very indifferently account for the *English* General's lying expos'd in an open Town, with his few *English* Forces, of which General *Harvey's* Regiment of fine Horse might be deem'd the Main; and General *Staremberg* encamping three Leagues farther off the Enemy. But to see the

Vicissitudes of Fortune, to which the Actions of the bravest, by an untoward Sort of Fatality, are often forced to contribute! None, who had been Eye-witnesses of the Bravery of either of those Generals at the Battles of *Almanar* and *Saragosa*, could find Room to call in question either their Conduct or their Courage; and yet in this March, and this Encampment will appear a visible ill Consequence to the Affairs of the Interest they fought for.

The Duke of *Vendome* having increas'd the Forces which he brought from *France*, to upwards of twenty thousand Men, marches by *Madrid* directly for *Breuhiga*, where his Intelligence inform'd him General *Stanhope* lay, and that so secretly as well as swiftly, that that General knew nothing of it, nor could be persuaded to believe it, till the very Moment their Bullets from the Enemy's Cannon convinc'd him of the Truth. *Breuhiga*, I have said, was wall'd only on one Side, and yet on that very side the Enemy made their Attack. But what could a Handful do against a Force so much superior, though they had not been in want of both Powder and Ball; and in want of these were forc'd to make use of Stones against all Sorts of Ammunition, which the Enemy ply'd them with? The Consequence answered the Deficiency; they were all made Prisoners of War, and *Harvey*'s Regiment of Horse among the rest; which, to augment their Calamity, was immediately remounted by the Enemy, and march'd along with their Army to attack General *Staremberg*.

That General had heard somewhat of the March of *Vendome*; and waited with some Impatience to have the Confirmation of it from General *Stanhope*, who lay between, and whom he lay under an Expectation of being joined with: However he thought it not improper to make some little Advance towards him; and accordingly breaking up from his Camp at *Cisuentes*, he came back to *Villa viciosa*, a little Town between *Cisuentes* and *Breuhiga*; there he found *Vendome* ready to attack him, before he could well be prepared for him, but no *English* to join him, as he had expected; nevertheless, the Battle was hot, and obstinately fought; although *Staremberg* had visibly the Advantage, having beat the Enemy at least a League from their Cannon; at which Time hearing of the Misfortune of *Breuhiga*, and finding himself thereby frustrated of those expected Succours to support him, he made a handsome

Retreat to *Barcelona*, which in common Calculation is about one hundred Leagues, without any Disturbance of an Enemy that seem'd glad to be rid of him. Nevertheless his Baggage having fallen into the Hands of the Enemy, at the Beginning of the Fight, King *Philip* and the Duke of *Vendome* generously returned it unopen'd, and untouched, in acknowledgement of his brave Behaviour.

I had like to have omitted one material Passage, which I was very credibly informed of; That General *Carpenter* offered to have gone, and have join'd General *Staremberg* with the Horse, which was refus'd him. This was certainly an Oversight of the highest Nature; since his going would have strengthen'd *Staremberg* almost to the Assurance of an intire Victory; whereas his Stay was of no manner of Service, but quite the contrary: For, as I said before, the Enemy, by re-mounting the *English* Horse (which perhaps were the compleatest of any Regiment in the World) turn'd, if I may be allowed the Expression, the Strength of our Artillery upon our Allies.

Upon this Retreat of *Staremberg*, and the Surprize at *Breuhiga*, there were great Rejoicings at *Madrid*, and everywhere else, where King *Philip*'s Interest prevailed. And indeed it might be said, from that Day the Interest of King *Charles* look'd with a very lowering Aspect. I was still a Prisoner at *la Mancha*, when this News arriv'd; and very sensibly affected at that strange Turn of Fortune. I was in bed, when the Express pass'd through the Town, in order to convey it farther; and in the Middle of the Night I heard a certain *Spanish* Don, with whom, a little before, I had had some little Variance, thundering at my Door, endeavouring to burst it open, with, as I had Reason to suppose, no very favourable Design upon me. But my Landlady, who hitherto had always been kind and careful, calling Don *Felix*, and some others of my Friends together, sav'd me from the Fury of his Designs, whatever they were.

Among other Expressions of the general Joy upon this Occasion, there was a Bull-Feast at *la Mancha*; which being much beyond what I saw at *Valencia*, I shall here give a Description of. These Bull-Feasts are not so common now in *Spain* as formerly, King *Philip* not taking much Delight in them. Nevertheless, as soon as it was publish'd here, that there was to be one, no other Discourse was heard; and in the Talk of the Bulls, and the great Preparations for the Feast, Men seem'd to have lost, or to have lay'd aside, all Thoughts of the very Occasion. A Week's time was allow'd for the Building of Stalls for the Beasts, and Scaffolds for the Spectators; and other necessary Preparations for the setting off their Joy with the most suitable Splendour.

On the Day appointed for the bringing the Bulls into Town, the *Cavalieroes* mounted their Horses, and, with Spears in their Hands, rode out of Town about a League, or somewhat more to meet them: If any of the Bulls break from the Drove, and make an Excursion (as they frequently do) the *Cavaliero* that can make him return again to his Station among his Companions, is held in Honour, suitable to the Dexterity and Address he performs it with. On their Entrance into the Town, all the Windows are fill'd with Spectators; a Pope passing in grand Procession could not have more; for what can be more than all? And he or she who should neglect so rare a Show, would give Occasion to have his or her Legitimacy call'd in Question.

When they come to the *Plaza*, where the Stalls and Scaffolds are built, and upon which the Feats of Chivalry are to be performed, it is often with a great deal of Difficulty that the Brutes are got in; for there are twelve Stalls, one for every Bull, and as their Number grows less by the enstalling of some, the Remainder often prove more untractable and unruly: In these Stalls they are kept very dark, to render them fiercer for the Day of Battle.

On the first of the Days appointed (for a Bull-Feast commonly lasts three) all the Gentry of the Place, or near adjacent, resort to the *Plaza* in their most gaudy Apparel, every one vieing in making the most glorious Appearance. Those in the lower Ranks provide themselves with Spears, or a great many small Darts in their Hands, which they fail not to cast or dart, whenever the Bull by his Nearness gives them an Opportunity. So that the poor Creature may be said to fight, not only with the Tauriro (or Bull-hunter, a Person always hired for that Purpose) but with the whole Multitude in the lower Class at least.

All being seated, the uppermost Door is open'd first; and as soon as ever the Bull perceives the Light, out he comes, snuffing up the Air, and stareing about him, as if in admiration of his attendants; and with his Tail cock'd up, he spurns the Ground with his Forefeet, as if he intended a Challenge to his yet unappearing Antagonist. Then at a Door appointed for that purpose, enters the Tauriro all in white, holding a Cloak in one Hand, and a sharp two edged Sword in the other. The Bull no sooner sets Eyes upon him, but wildly staring, he moves gently towards him; then gradually mends his pace, till he is come within about the space of twenty Yards of the Tauriro; when, with a sort of Spring, he makes at him with all his might. The Tauriro knowing by frequent Experience, that it behoves him to be watchful, slips aside just when the Bull is at him; when casting his Cloak over his Horns, at the same Moment he gives him a slash or two, always aiming at the Neck, where there is one particular Place, which if he hit, he knows he shall easily bring him to the Ground. I my Self observ'd the truth of this Experiment made upon one of the Bulls, who receiv'd no more than one Cut, which happening upon the fatal Spot, so stun'd him, that he remain'd perfectly stupid, the Blood flowing out from the Wound, till after a violent Trembling he dropt down stone dead.

But this rarely happens, and the poor Creature oftner receives many Wounds, and numberless Darts, before he dies. Yet whenever he feels a fresh Wound either from Dart, Spear, or Sword, his Rage receives addition from the Wound, and he pursues his Tauriro with an Increase of Fury and Violence. And as often as he makes at his Adversary, the Tauriro takes care with the utmost of his Agility to avoid him, and reward his kind Intention with a new Wound.

Some of their Bulls will play their Parts much better than others: But the best must die. For when they have behav'd themselves with all the commendable Fury possible; if the Tauriro is spent, and fail of doing Execution upon him, they set Dogs upon him: Hough[10] him and stick him all over with Darts, till with very loss of Blood he puts an end to their present Cruelty.

When dead, a Man brings in two Mules dress'd out with Bells and Feathers, and fastening a Rope about his Horns, draws off the Bull with the Shouts and Acclamations of the Spectators; as if the Infidels had been drove from before *Ceuta*.

I had almost forgot another very common piece of barbarous Pleasure at these Diversions. The Tauriro will sometimes stick one of their Bull Spears fast in the Ground, aslant, but levell'd as near as he can at his Chest; then presenting himself to the Bull, just before the point of the Spear, on his taking his run at the Tauriro, which, as they assur'd me, he always does with his Eyes closed, the Tauriro slips on one side, and the poor Creature runs with a violence often to stick himself, and sometimes to break the Spear in his Chest, running away with part of it till he drop.

This *Tauriro* was accounted one of the best in *Spain*; and indeed I saw him mount the back of one of the Bulls, and ride on him, slashing and cutting, till he had quite wearied him; at which time dismounting, he kill'd him with much Ease, and to the acclamatory Satisfaction of the whole Concourse: For variety of Cruelty, as well as Dexterity, administers to their Delight.

The *Tauriroes* are very well paid; and in Truth so they ought to be; for they often lose their Lives in the Diversion, as this did the Year after in the way of his Calling. Yet is it a Service of very great Profit when they perform dextrously: For when ever they do any Thing remarkable, deserving the Notice of the Spectators, they never fail of a generous Gratification, Money being thrown down to 'em in plenty.

This Feast (as they generally do) lasted three Days; the last of which was, in my Opinion, much before either of the other. On this, a young Gentleman, whose Name was *Don Pedro Ortega*, a Person of great Quality, perform'd the Exercise on Horseback. The Seats, if not more crowded, were filled with People of better Fashion, who came from Places at a distance to grace the noble *Tauriro*.

He was finely mounted, and made a very graceful Figure; but as when the Foot *Tauriro* engages, the Bull first enters, so in the Contest the *Cavaliero* always makes his Appearance on the *Plaza* before the Bull. His Steed was a manag'd Horse; mounted on which he made his Entry, attended by four Footmen in rich Liveries; who, as soon as their Master had rid round, and paid his Devoirs to all the Spectators, withdrew from the Dangers they left him expos'd to. The *Cavaliero* having thus made his Bows, and received the repeated Vivas of that vast Concourse, march'd with a very stately Air to the very middle of the *Plaza*, there standing ready to receive his Enemy at coming out.

The Door being open'd, the Bull appeared; and as I thought with a fiercer and more threatning Aspect that any of the former. He star'd around him for a considerable time, snuffing up the Air, and spurning the Ground, without in the least taking notice of his Antagonist. But at last fixing his Eyes upon him, he made a full run at the *Cavaliero*, which he most dexterously avoided, and at the same moment of time, passing by, he cast a Dart that stuck in his Shoulders. At this the Shouts and *Vivas* were repeated; and I observed a Handkerchief wav'd twice or thrice, which, as I afterwards understood, was a Signal from the Lady of his Affections, that she had beheld him with Satisfaction. I took notice that the *Cavaliero* endeavour'd all he could to keep aside the Bull, for the Advantage of the Stroke, when putting his Horse on a full Career, he threw another Dart, which fix'd in his Side, and so enrag'd the Beast, that he seem'd to renew his Attacks with greater Fury. The *Cavaliero* had behav'd himself to Admiration, and escap'd many Dangers; with the often repeated Acclamations of *Viva, Viva*; when at last the enraged Creature getting his Horns between the Horse's hinder Legs, Man and Horse came both together to the Ground.

I expected at that Moment nothing less than Death could be the Issue; when to the general Surprize, as well as mine, the very civil Brute, Author of all the Mischief, only withdrew to the other Side of the *Plaza*, where he stood still, staring about him as if he knew nothing of the Matter.

The *Cavaliero* was carry'd off not much hurt, but his delicate Beast suffer'd much more. However I could not but think afterward, that the good natur'd Bull came short of fair Play. If I may be pardon'd the Expression, he had us'd his Adversary with more Humanity than he met with; at least, since, after he had the *Cavaliero* under, he generously forsook him; I think he might have pleaded, or others for him, for better Treatment than he after met with.

For as the *Cavaliero* was disabled and carry'd off, the Foot *Tauriro* enter'd in white Accoutrements, as before; but he flatter'd himself with an easier Conquest than he found: there is always on these Occasions, when he apprehends any imminent Danger, a Place of Retreat ready for the Foot *Tauriro*; and well for him there was so; this Bull oblig'd him over and over to make Use of it. Nor was he able at last to dispatch him, without a general Assistance; for I believe I speak within Compass, when I say, he had more than an hundred Darts stuck in him. And so barbarously was he mangled, and flash'd[11] besides, that, in my Mind, I could not but think King *Philip* in the Right, when he said, *That it was a Custom deserv'd little Encouragement.*

Soon after this *Tauridore*, or Bull-Feast was over, I had a Mind to take a pleasant Walk to a little Town, call'd *Minai*, about three Leagues off; but I was scarce got out of *la Mancha*, when an Acquaintance meeting me, ask'd where I was going? I told him to *Minai*; when taking me by the Hand, *Friend* Gorgio, says he in *Spanish, Come back with me; you shall not go a Stride further; there are* Picarons[12] *that Way; you shall not go.* Inquiring, as we went back, into his Meaning, he told me, that the Day before, a Man, who had received a Sum of Money in Pistoles at *la Mancha*, was, on the road, set upon by some, who had got notice of it, and murdered him; that not finding the Money expected about him (for he had cautiously enough left it in a Friend's Hands at *la Mancha*) they concluded he had swallowed it; and therefore they ript up his Belly, and open'd every Gut; but all to as little Purpose. This diverted my Walk for that time.

But some little Time after, the same Person inviting me over to the same Place, to see his Melon-Grounds, which in that Country are wonderful fine and pleasant; I accepted his Invitation, and under the Advantage of his Company, went thither. On the Road I took notice of a Cross newly erected, and a Multitude of small stones around the Foot of it: Asking the Meaning whereof, my Friend told me, that it was rais'd for a Person there murder'd (as is the Custom throughout *Spain*) and that every good Catholick passing by, held it his Duty to cast a Stone upon the Place, in Detestation of the Murder. I had often before taken Notice of many such Crosses: but never till then knew the Meaning of their Erection, or the Reason of the Heaps of Stones around them.

There is no Place in all *Spain* more famous for good Wine than *Sainte Clemente de la Mancha*; nor is it any where sold cheaper:

For as it is only an inland Town, near no navigable River, and the People temperate to a Proverb, great Plenty, and a small Vend must consequently make it cheap. The Wine here is so famous, that, when I came to *Madrid*, I saw wrote over the Doors of host Houses that sold Wine, *Vino Sainte Clemente*. As to the Temperance of the People, I must say, that notwithstanding those two excellent Qualities of good and cheap, I never saw, all the three Years I was Prisoner there, any one Person overcome with Drinking.

It is true, there may be a Reason, and a political one, assign'd for that Abstemiousness of theirs, which is this, That if any Man, upon any Occasion, should be brought in as an Evidence against you, if you can prove that he was ever drunk, it will invalidate his whole Evidence. I could not but think this a grand Improvement upon the *Spartans*. They made their Slaves purposely drunk, to shew their Youth the Folly of the Vice by the sottish Behaviour of their Servants under it: But they never reach'd to that noble height of laying a Penalty upon the Aggressor, or of discouraging a voluntary Impotence of Reason by a disreputable Impotence of Interest. The *Spaniard* therefore, in my Opinion, in this exceeds the *Spartan*, as much as a natural Beauty exceeds one procured by Art; for tho' Shame may somewhat influence some few, Terrour is of force to deter all. A Man, we have seen it, may shake Hands with Shame; but *Interest*, says another Proverb, *will never lye*. A wise Institution therefore doubtless is this of the *Spaniard*; but such as I fear will never take Place in *Germany*, *Holland*, *France*, or *Great Britain*.

But though I commend their Temperance, I would not be thought by any Means to approve of their Bigotry. If there may be such a Thing as Intemperance in Religion, I much fear their Ebriety in that will be found to be over-measure. Under the notion of Devotion, I have seen Men among 'em, and of Sense too, guilty of the grossest Intemperancies. It is too common to be a rarity to see their Dons of the prime Quality as well as those of the lower Ranks, upon meeting a Priest in the open Streets, condescend to take up the lower part of his Vestment, and salute it with Eyes erected as if they look'd upon it as the Seal of Salvation.

When the *Ave-Bell* is heard, the Hearer must down on his Knees upon the very Spot; nor is he allowed the small Indulgence of deferring a little, till he can recover a clean Place; Dirtiness excuses not, nor will dirty Actions by any means exempt. This is so notorious, that even at the Play-house, in the middle of a Scene, on the first sound of the Bell, the Actors drop their Discourse, the Auditors supersede the indulging of their unsanctified Ears, and all on their Hearts, quite a different way, to what they just before had been employ'd in. In short, tho' they pretend in all this to an extraordinary Measure of Zeal and real Devotion; no Man, that lives among them any time, can be a Proselyte to them without immolating his Senses and his Reason: Yet I must confess, while I have seen them thus deludeing themselves with *Ave Marias*, I cou'd not refrain throwing up my Eyes to the only proper Object of Adoration, in commiseration of such Delusions.

The Hours of the *Ave Bell*, are eight and twelve in the Morning, and six in the Evening. They pretend at the first to fall down in beg that God would be pleas'd to prosper them in all things they go about that Day. At twelve they return Thanks for their Preservation to that time; and at six for that of the whole Day. After which, one would think that they imagine themselves at perfect Liberty; and their open Gallantries perfectly countenance the Imagination: for tho' Adultery is look'd upon as a grievous Crime, and punish'd accordingly; yet Fornication is softened with the title of a Venial Sin, and they seem to practise it under that Persuasion.

I found here, what *Erasmus* ridicules with so much Wit and Delicacy, the custom of burying in a *Franciscan*'s Habit, in mighty request. If they can for that purpose procure an old one at the price of a new one; the Purchaser wil look upon himself a provident Chap, that has secur'd to his deceased Friend or Relation, no less than Heaven by that wise Bargain.

The Evening being almost the only time of Enjoyment of Company, or Conversation, every body in *Spain* then greedily seeks it; and the Streets are at that time crowded like our finest Gardens or most private Walks. On one of those Occasions, I met a Don of my Acquaintance walking out with his Sisters; and as I thought it became an *English* Cavalier, I saluted him: But to my Surprize he never return'd the Civility. When I met him the Day after, instead of an Apology, as I had flattered my self, I received a Reprimand, tho' a very civil one; telling me it was the Custom in *Spain*, nor well taken of any one, that took Notice of any who were walking in the Company of Ladies at Night.

But a Night or two after, I found by Experience, that if the Men were by Custom prohibited taking Notice, Women were not. I was standing at the Door, in the cool of the Evening, when a Woman seemingly genteel, passing by, call'd me by my Name, telling me she wanted to speak with me: She had her *Mantilio* on; so that had I had Day-light, I could have only seen one Eye of her. However I walk'd with her a good while, without being able to discover any thing of her Business, nor pass'd there between us any thing more than a Conversation upon indifferent Matters. Nevertheless, at parting she told me she should pass by again the next Evening; and if I would be at the Door, she would give me the same Advantage of a Conversation, That seem'd not to displease me. Accordingly the next Night she came, and as before we walk'd together in the privatest parts of the Town: For tho' I knew her not, her Discourse was always entertaining and full of Wit, and her Enquiries not often improper. We had continu'd this Intercourse many Nights together, when my Landlady's Daughter having taken Notice of it, stopt me one Evening, and would not allow me to stand at the usual Post of Intelligence, saying, with a good deal of heat, *Don Gorgio, take my Advice; go no more along with that Woman: You may soon be brought home deprived of your Life if you do*. I cannot say, whether she knew her; but this I must say, she was very agreeable in Wit as well as Person. However my Landlady and her Daughter took that Opportunity of giving me so many Instances of the fatal Issues of such innocent Conversations, (for I could not call it an Intrigue) that apprehensive enough of the Danger, on laying Circumstances together, I took their Advice, and never went into her Company after.

Sainte Clemente de la Mancha, where I so long remain'd a Prisoner of War, lies in the Road from *Madrid* to *Valencia*; and the Duke of *Vendome* being ordered to the latter, great Preparations were made for his Entertainment, as he pass'd through. He stay'd here only one Night, where he was very handsomely treated by the *Corrigidore*. He was a tall fair Person, and very fat, and at the time I saw him wore a long black Patch over his left Eye; but on what Occasion I could not learn. The afterwards famous *Alberoni* (since made a Cardinal) was in his Attendance; as indeed the Duke was very rarely without him. I remember that very Day three Weeks, they return'd through the same Place; the Duke in his Herse, and *Alberoni* in a Coach, paying his last Duties. That Duke was a prodigious Lover of Fish, of which having eat over heartily at *Veneros*, in the Province of *Valencia*, he took a Surfeit, and died in three Days' time. His Corps was carrying to the *Escurial*, there to be buried in the *Panthæon* among their Kings.

The *Castilians* have a Privilege by Licence from the Pope, which, if it could have been converted into a Prohibition, might have sav'd that Duke's Life: In regard their Country is wholly inland, and the River *Tagus* famous for its Poverty, or rather Barrenness; their Holy Father indulges the Natives with the Liberty, in lieu of that dangerous Eatable, of eating all Lent time the Inwards of Cattle. When I first heard this related, I imagin'd, that the Garbidge had been intended, but I was soon after this rectify'd, *by Inwards* (for so expressly says the Licence it self) *is meant the Heart, the Liver, and the Feet.*

They have here as well as in most other Parts of *Spain*, *Valencia* excepted, the most wretched Musick in the Universe. Their *Guitars*, if not their *Sole*, are their darling Instruments, and what they most delight in: Tho' in my Opinion our *English* Sailors are not much amiss in giving them the Title of *Strum Strums*. They are little better than our *Jews-harps*, tho' hardly half so Musical. Yet are they perpetually at Nights disturbing their Women with the Noise of them, under the notion and name of Serenadoes. From the Barber to the Grandee the Infection spreads, and very often with the same Attendant, Danger: Night Quarrels and Rencounters being the frequent Result. The true born *Spaniards* reckon it a part of their Glory, to be jealous of their Mistresses, which is too often the Forerunner of Murders; at best attended with many other very dangerous Inconveniences. And yet bad as their Musick is, their Dancing is the reverse. I have seen a Country Girl manage her Castanets with the graceful Air of a Dutchess,

and that not to common Musick; but to Peoples beating or drum-
ing a Tune with their Hands on a Table. I have seen half a Dozen
couple at a time dance to the like in excellent order.

I just now distinguish'd, by an Exception, the Music of *Valencia*,
where alone I experienced the use of the Violin; which tho' I cannot,
in respect to other Countries, call good; yet in respect to the other
parts of *Spain*, I must acknowledge it much the best. In my Account
of that City, I omitted to speak of it; therefore now to supply that
Defect, I will speak of the best I heard, which was on this unfortunate Occasion: Several Natives of that Country having
received Sentence of Death for their Adherence to King *Charles*,
were accordingly ordered to the Place of Execution. It is the
Custom there, on all such Occasions, for all the Musick of the
City to meet near the Gallows, and play the most affecting and
melancholy Airs, to the very approach of the Condemn'd; and
really the Musick was so moving, it heightened the Scene of
Sorrow, and brought Compassion into the Eyes of even Enemies.

As to the Condemn'd, they came stript of their own Cloaths,
and cover'd with black Frocks, in which they were led along the
Streets to the Place of Execution, the Friars praying all the way.
When they came through any Street, were any public Images
were fix'd, they stay'd before 'em some reasonable time in
Prayer with the Friars. When they are arriv'd at the fatal Place,
those Fathers leave 'em not, but continue praying and giving them
ghostly Encouragement, standing upon the rounds of the Ladder
till they are turn'd off. The Hangman always wears a silver Badge
of a Ladder to distinguish his Profession: But his manner of executing his Office had somewhat in it too singular to allow of
Silence. When he had ty'd fast the Hands of the Criminal, he
rested his Knee upon them, and with one Hand on the Criminal's
Nostrils, to stop his Breath the sooner, threw himself off the
Ladder along with the dying Party. This he does to expedite his
Fate; tho' considering the Force, I wonder it does not tear Head
and Body asunder; which yet I never heard that it did.

But to return to *la Mancha*; I had been there now upwards of
two Years, much diverted with the good Humour and Kindness
of the Gentlemen, and daily pleased with the Conversation of the
Nuns of the Nunnery opposite to my Lodgings; when walking

one Day alone upon the *Plaza*, I found my self accosted by a *Clerico*. At the first Attack, he told me his Country: But added, that he now came from *Madrid* with a *Potent*, that was his Word, from *Pedro de Dios*, Dean of the Inquisition, to endeavour the Conversion of any of the *English* Prisoners; that being an *Irishman*, as a sort of a Brother, he had conceived a Love for the *English*, and therefore more eagerly embraced the Opportunity which the Holy Inquisition had put into his Hands for the bringing over to Mother Church as many Hereticks as he could; that having heard a very good Character of me, he should think himself very happy, if he could be instrumental in my Salvation;

"It is very true, continu'd he, I have lately had the good Fortune to convert many; and besides the Candour of my own Disposition, I must tell you, that I have a peculiar knack at Conversion, which very few, if any, ever could resist. I am going upon the same work into *Murcia*; but your good Character is fix'd me in my Resolution of preferring your Salvation to that of others."

To this very long, and no less surprising Address, I only return'd, that it being an Affair of moment, it would require some Consideration; and that by the time he return'd from *Murcia*, I might be able to return him a proper Answer. But not at all satisfy'd with this Reply;

"Sir," says he, "God Almighty is all-sufficient: This moment is too precious to be lost; he can turn the Heart in the twinkling of an Eye, as well as in twenty Years. Hear me then; mind what I say to you: I will convince you immediately. You Hereticks do not believe in Transubstantiation, and yet did not our Saviour say in so many Words, *Hoc est corpus meum?* And if you don't believe him, don't you give him the Lye? Besides, does not one of the Fatherss ay, *Deus, qui est omnis Veritas, non potest dicere falsum?*"

He went on at the same ridiculous rate; which soon convinced me, he was a thorough Rattle.[13] However, as a *Clerico*, and consequently in this Country, a Man dangerous to disoblige, I invited him home to Dinner; where when I had brought him, I found I had no way done an unacceptable thing; for my Landlady and her Daughter, seeing him to be a Clergyman, receiv'd him with a vast deal of Respect and Pleasure.

Dinner being over, he began to entertain me with a Detail of the many wonderful Conversions he had made upon obstinate Hereticks; that he had convinced the most Stubborn, and had such a *Nostrum*, that he would undertake to convert any one. Here he began his old round, intermixing his Harangue with such scraps and raw sentences of fustian *Latin*, that I grew weary of his Conversation; so pretending some Business of consequence, I took leave, and left him and my Landlady together.

I did not return till pretty late in the Evening, with Intent to give him Time enough to think his own Visit tedious; but to my great Surprize, I found my *Irish* Missionary still on the Spot, ready to dare me to the Encounter, and resolv'd, like a true Son of the Church militant, to keep last on the Field of Battle. As soon as I had seated my self, he began again to tell me, how good a Character my Landlady had given me, which had prodigiously increased his Ardour of saving my Soul; that he could not answer it to his own Character, as well as mine, to be negligent; and therefore he had enter'd into a Resolution to stay my Coming, though it had been later. To all which, I return'd him Abundance of Thanks for his good Will, but pleading Indisposition and want of Rest, after a good deal of civil Impertinence, I once more got rid of him; at least, I took my Leave, and went to Bed, leaving him again Master of the Field; for I understood next Morning, that he stay'd some Time after I was gone, with my good Land-lady.

Next Morning the Nuns of the Nunnery opposite, having taken Notice of the *Clerico*'s Ingress, long Visit, and late Egress, sent to know whether he was my Country-man; with many other Questions, which I was not then let into the Secret of. To all which I return'd, that he was no Country-man of mine, but an *Irish-man*, and so perfectly a Stranger to me, that I knew no more of him than what I had from his own Mouth. that he was going into *Murcia*. What the Meaning of this Enquiry was, I could never learn; but I could not doubt, but it proceeded from their great Care of their *Vicino*, as they call'd me; a Mark of their Esteem, and of which I was not a little proud.

As was my usual Custom, I had been taking my Morning Walk, and had not been long come home in order to Dinner, when in again drops my *Irish Clerico*; I was confounded, and vexed, and he could not avoid taking Notice of it; nevertheless, without the least Alteration of Countenance, he took his Seat; and on my saying, in a cold and indifferent Tone, that I imagin'd he had been got to *Murcia* before this; he reply'd, with a natural Fleer,[14] that truely he was going to *Murcia*, but his Conscience pricked him, and he did find that he could not go away with any Satisfaction, or Peace of Mind, without making me a perfect Convert; that he had plainly discovered in me a good Disposition, and had, for that very Reason, put himself to the Charge of Man and Mule, to the Bishop of *Cuenca* for a Licence, under his Hand, for my Conversion: For in *Spain*, all private Missionaries are obliged to ask Leave of the next Bishop, before they dare enter upon any Enterprize of this Nature.

I was more confounded at this last Assurance of the Man than at all before; and it put me directly upon reflecting, whether any, and what Inconveniences might ensue, from a Rencounter that I, at first, conceiv'd ridiculous, but might now reasonably begin to have more dangerous Apprehensions of. I knew, by the Articles of War, all Persons are exempted from any Power of the Inquisition; but whether carrying on a Part in such a Farce, might not admit, or at least be liable to some dangerous Construction, was not imprudently now to be considered. Though I was not fearful, yet I resolv'd to be cautious. Wherefore not making any Answer to his Declaration about the Bishop, he took Notice of it; and to raise a Confidence, he found expiring, began to tell me, that his Name was *Murtough Brennan*, that he was born near *Kilkenny*, of a very considerable Family. This last part indeed, when I came to *Madrid*, I found pretty well confirm'd in a considerable Manner. However, taking Notice that he had alter'd his Tone of leaving the Town, and that instead of it, he was advancing somewhat like an Invitation of himself to Dinner the next Day, I resolv'd to show my self shy of him; and thereupon abruptly, and without taking any Leave, I left the Room, and my Landlady and him together.

Three or four Days had passed, every one of which, he never fail'd my Lodgings; not at Dinner Time only, but Night and Morning too; from all which I began to suspect, that instead of

my Conversion, he had fix'd upon a Re-conversion of my Landlady. She was not young, yet, for a black Woman, handsom
enough; and her Daughter very pretty: I entered into a Resolution to make my Observations, and watch them all at a Distance;
nevertheless carefully concealing my Jealousy. However, I must
confess, I was not a little pleas'd, that any Thing could divert my
own Persecution. He was now no longer my Guest, but my
Landlady's, with whom I found him so much taken up, that a
little Care might frustrate all his former impertinent Importunities on the old Topick.

But all my Suspicions were very soon after turn'd into Cer-
tainties, in this Manner: I had been abroad, and returning somewhat weary, I went to my Chamber, to take, what in that
Country they call, a *Cesto*, upon my Bed: I got in unseen, or
without seeing any Body, but had scarce laid my self down,
before my young Landlady, as I jestingly us'd to call the Daughter,
rushing into my Room, threw her self down on the Floor, bitterly
exclaiming. I started off my Bed, and immediately running to the
Door, who should I meet there but my *Irish Clerico*, without his
Habit, and in his Shirt? I could not doubt, by the *Dishabillè* of the
Clerico, but the young Creature had Reason enough for her
Passion, which render'd me quite unable to master mine; wherefore as he stood with his Back next the Door, I thrust him in that
ghostly Plight into the open Street.

I might, with leisure enough, have repented that precipitate
Piece of Indiscretion; if it had not been for his bad Character, and
the favourable Opinion the Town had conceived of me; for he
inordinately exclaim'd against me, calling me Heretick, and
telling the People, who were soon gathered round him, that
coming to my Lodgings on the charitable work of Conversion,
I had thus abus'd him, script him of his Habit, and then turn'd
him out of Doors. The Nuns, on their hearing the Outcries he
made, came running to their Grates, to enquire into the Matter,
and when they understood it, as he was pleas'd to relate it;
though they condemn'd my Zeal, they pity'd my Condition.
Very well was it for me, that I stood more than a little well in the
good Opinion of the Town; among the Gentry, by my frequent
Conversation, and the inferior Sort by my charitable Distribu-

tions; for nothing can be more dangerous, or a nearer Way to violent Fate, than to insult one of the Clergy in *Spain*, and especially, for such an one as they entitle a Heretick.

My old Landlady (I speak in respect to her Daughter) however formerly my seeming Friend, came in a violent Passion, and wrenching the Door out of my Hands, opened it, and pull'd her *Clerico* in; and so soon as she had done this, she took his Part, and railed so bitterly at me, that I had no Reason longer to doubt her thorough Conversion, under the full Power of his Mission. However the young one stood her Ground, and by all her Expressions, gave her many Inquirers Reason enough to believe, all was not Matter of Faith that the *Clerico* had advanced. Nevertheless, holding it adviseable to change my Lodgings, and a Friend confirming my Resolutions, I removed that Night.

The *Clerico* having put on his upper Garments, was run away to the *Corrigidor*, in a violent Fury, resolving to be early, as well knowing, that he who tells his Story first, has the Prospect of telling it to double Advantage. When he came there, he told that Officer a thousand idle Stories, and in the worst Manner; repeating how I had abus'd him, and not him only, but my poor Landlady, for taking his Part. The *Corrigidor* was glad to hear it all, and with an officious Ear fish'd for a great deal more; expecting, according to Usage, at last to squeeze a Sum of Money out of me. However he told the *Clerico*, that, as I was a Prisoner of War, he had no direct Power over me; but if he would immediately write to the President *Ronquillo*, at *Madrid*, he would not fail to give his immediate Orders, according to which he would as readily act against me.

The *Clerico* resolv'd to pursue his old Maxim and cry out first; and so taking the *Corrigidor*'s Advice, he wrote away to *Madrid* directly. In the mean Time the People in the Town, both high and low, some out of Curiosity, some out of Friendship, pursu'd their Enquiries into the Reality of the Facts. The old Landlady they could make little of to my Advantage; but whenever the young one came to the Question, she always left them with these Words in her Mouth, *El Diabolo en forma del Clerico*, which rendring Things more than a little cloudy on the *Clerico*'s Side, he was advis'd and press'd by his few Friends, as fast as he could to get out of Town; Nuns, Clergy, and every Body taking Part against him, excepting his new Convert, my old Landlady.

The Day after, as I was sitting with a Friend at my new Quarters, *Maria* (for that was the Name of my Landlady's Daughter) came running in with these Words in her Mouth, *El Clerico, el Clerico, passa la Calle*. We hasten'd to the Window, out of which we beheld the *Clerico, Murtough Brennan*, pitifully mounted on the Back of a very poor Ass (for they would neither let, nor lend him a Mule through all the Town) his Legs almost rested on the Ground, for he was lusty, as his Ass was little; and a Fellow with a large Cudgel march'd a-foot, driving his Ass along. Never did *Sancha Pancha*, on his Embassage to *Dulcinea*, make such a despicable, out of the way Figure, as our *Clerico* did at this Time. And what increas'd our Mirth was, their telling me, that our *Clerico*, like that Squire (tho' upon his own Priest-Errantry) was actually on his March to *Toboso*, a Place five Leagues off, famous for the Nativity of *Dulcinea*, The Object of the Passion of that celebrated Hero *Don Quixot*. So I will leave our *Clerico* on his Journey to *Murcia*, to relate the unhappy Sequel of this ridiculous Affair.

I have before said, that, by the Advice of the *Corrigidor*, our *Clerico* had wrote to *Don Ronquillo* at *Madrid*. About a Fortnight after his Departure from *la Mancha*, I was sitting alone in my new Lodgings, when two *Alguizils* (Officers under the *Corrigidor*, and in the Nature of our Bailiffs) came into my Room, but very civilly, to tell me, that they had Orders to carry me away to Prison; but at the same Moment they advis'd me, not to be afraid; for they had observed, that the whole Town was concern'd at what the *Corrigidor* and *Clerico* had done; adding, that it was their Opinion, that I should find so general a Friendship, that I need not be apprehensive of any Danger. With these plausible Speeches, though I afterwards experienced the Truth of them, I resign'd my self, and went with them to a much closer Confinement.

I had not been there above a Day or two, before many Gentlemen of the Place sent to me, to assure me, they were heartily afflicted at my Confinement, and resolv'd to write in my Favour to *Madrid*; but as it was not safe, nor the Custom in *Spain*, to visit those in my present Circumstances, they hoped I would not take it amiss, since they were bent to act all in their Power towards my Deliverance; concluding however with their Advice, that I would not give one *Real of Plata* to the *Corrigidor*, whom they hated, but confide in their assiduous Interposal, Don *Pedro de Ortega* in particular, the Person that perform'd the Part of the *Tauriro* on Horseback, sometime before, sent me Word, he would not fail to write to a Relation of his, of the first Account in *Madrid*, and so represent the Affair, that I should not long be debarr'd my old Acquaintance.

It may administer, perhaps, Matter of Wonder, that *Spaniards*, Gentlemen of the stanchest Punctilio, should make a Scruple and excute themselves from visiting Persons under Confinement, when, according to all Christian Acceptation, such a Circumstance would render such a Visit, not charitable only but generous. But though Men of vulgar Spirits might, from the Narrowness of their Views, form such insipid Excuses, those of these Gentlemen, I very well knew, proceeded from much more excusable Topicks. I was committed under the Accusation of having abus'd a sacred Person, one of the Clergy; and though, as a Prisoner of War, I might deem my self exempt from the Power of the Inquisition; yet how far one of that Country, visiting a Person, so accused, might be esteemed culpable, was a consideration in that dangerous Climate, far from deserving to be slighted. To me therefore, who well knew the Customs of the Country, and the Temper of its Countrymen, their Excuses were not only allowable, but acceptable also; for, without calling in Question their Charity, I verily believ'd I might falsely confide in their Honour.

Accordingly, after I had been a close Prisoner one Month to a Day, I found the Benefit of these Gentlemen's Promises and Solicitations. Pursuant to which, an Order was brought for my immediate Discharge; notwithstanding, the new Convert, my old Landlady, did all she could to make her appearing against me effectual, to the Height of her Prejudice and Malice, even while the Daughter, as sensible of my Innocence, and acting with a much better Conscience, endeavoured as much to justify me, against both the Threats and Persuasions of the *Corrigidor*, and his few Accomplices, though her own Mother made one.

After Receipt of this Order for my Enlargement, I was mightily press'd by Don *Felix*, and others of my Friends, to go to *Madrid*, and enter my Complaint against the *Corrigidor* and the *Clerico*, as a Thing highly essential to my own future Security. Without asking Leave therefore of the *Corrigidor*, or in the least acquainting him with it, I set out from *la Mancha*, and, as I afterwards understood, to the terrible Alarm of that griping Officer; who was under the greatest Consternation, when he heard I was gone; for as he knew very well, that he had done more than he could justify, he was very apprehensive of any Complaint; well knowing, that as he was hated as much as I was beloved, he might assure himself of the Want of that Assistance from the Gentlemen, which I had experienced.

So soon as I arrived at *Madrid*, I made it my Business to enquire out, and wait upon Father *Fahy*, Chief of the *Irish College*. He received me very courteously; but when I acquainted him with the Treatment I had met with from *Brennan*, and had given him an Account of his other scandalous Behaviour, I found he was no Stranger to the Man, or his Character; for he soon confirm'd to me the Honour *Brennan* first boasted of, his considerable Family, by saying, that scarce an Assize passed in his own Country, without two or three of that Name receiving at the Gallows the just Reward of their Demerits. In short, not only Father *Fahy*, but all the Clergy of that Nation at *Madrid*, readily subscribed to this Character of him, *That he was a Scandal to their Country*.

After this, I had nothing more to do, but to get that Father to go with me to *Pedro de Dios*, who was the Head of the *Dominican* Cloyster, and Dean of the Inquisition. He readily granted my Request, and when we came there, in a Manner unexpected, represented to the Dean, that having some good Dispositions towards Mother-Church, I had been diverted from them, he feared, by the evil Practices of one *Murtough Brennan*, a Countryman of his, tho' a Scandal to his Country; that under a Pretence of seeking my Conversion, he had lay'd himself open in a most beastly Manner, such as would have set a Catholick into a vile Opinion of their Religion, and much more one that was yet a

Heretick. The Dean had hardly Patience to hear Particulars; but as soon as my Friend had ended his Narration, he immediately gave his Orders, prohibiting *Murtough*'s saying any more Masses, either in *Madrid*, or any other Place in *Spain*. This indeed was taking away the poor Wretches sole Subsistence, and putting him just upon an Equality with his Demerits.

I took the same Opportunity to make my Complaints of the *Corrigidor*; but his Term expiring very soon, and a Process being likely to be chargeable, I was advised to let it drop. So having effected what I came for, I returned to my old Station at *la Mancha*.

When I came back, I found a new *Corrigidor*, as I had been told there would, by the Dean of the Inquisition, who, at the same Time, advised me to wait on him. I did so, soon after my Arrival, and then experienced the Advice to be well intended; the Dean having wrote a Letter to him, to order him to treat me with all Manner of Civility. He show'd me the very Letter, and it was in such particular and obliging Terms, that I could not but perceive he had taken a Resolution, if possible, to eradicate all the evil impressions, that *Murtough*'s Behaviour might have given too great Occasion for. This serv'd to confirm me in an Observation that I had long before made, That a Protestant, who will prudently keep his Sentiments in his own Breast, may command any Thing in *Spain*; where their stiff Bigotry leads 'em naturally into that other Mistake, That not to oppose, is to assent. Besides, it is generally among them, almost a work of Supererogation to be even instrumental in the Conversion of one they call a Heretick. To bring any such back to what they call Mother Church, nothing shall be spar'd, nothing thought too much: And if you have Insincerity enough to give them Hopes, you shall not only live in Ease, but in Pleasure and Plenty.

I had entertain'd some thoughts on my Journey back, of taking up my old Quarters at the Widow's; but found her so intirely converted by her *Clerico*, that there wou'd be no room to expect Peace: For which Reason, with the help of my fair *Vicinos*, and *Don Felix*, I took another, where I had not been long, before I received an unhappy Account of *Murtough*'s Conduct in *Murcia*. It seems he had kept his Resolution in going thither; where meeting with some of his own Countrymen, though he found 'em

7

stanch good Catholics, he so far inveigled himself into 'em, that he brought them all into a foul chance for their Lives. There were three of 'em, all Soldiers, in a *Spanish* Regiment, but in a fit of ambitious, though frantick, Zeal: *Murtough* had wheedled them to go along with him to *Pedro de Dios*, Dean of the Inquisition, to declare and acknowledge before him, that they were converted and brought over to Mother Church, and by him only. The poor Ignorants, thus intic'd, had left their Regiment, of which the Colonel, having notice, sent after them, and they were overtaken on the Road, their *Missionair* with them. But notwithstanding all his Oratory, nay, even the Discovery of the whole Farce, one of them was hang'd for an Example to the other two.

It was not long after my Return before News arriv'd of the Peace; which though they receiv'd with Joy, they could hardly entertain with Belief. Upon which, the new *Corrigidor*, with whom I held a better Correspondence than I had done with the old one, desired me to produce my Letters from *England*, that it was true. Never did People give greater Demonstrations of Joy, than they upon this Occasion. It was the common cry in the Streets, *Paz con Angleterra, con todo Mundo Guerra*; And my Confirmation did them as much Pleasure as it did Service to me; for is possible, they treated me with more Civility than before.

But the Peace soon after being proclaimed, I received Orders to repair to *Madrid*, where the rest of the Prisoners taken at *Denia* had been carried; when I, by reason of my Wounds, and want of Health, had been left behind. Others I understood lay ready, and some were on their March to *Bayone* in *France*; where Ships were ordered for their Transportation into *England*. So after a Residence of three Years and three Months; having taken leave of all my Acquaintance, I left a Place, that was almost become natural to me, the delicious *Sainte Clemente de la Mancha*.

Nothing of Moment, or worth observing, met I with, till I came near *Ocanna*; and there occurred a Sight ridiculous enough. The Knight of the Town, I last came from, the ever renown'd *Don Quixot*, never made such a Figure as a *Spaniard*, I there met on the Road. He was mounted on a Mule of the largest size, and yet no way unsizeable to his Person: He had two Pistols in his

Holsters, and one on each side stuck in his Belt; a sort of large Blunderbuss in one of his Hands, and the fellow to it slung over his Shoulders hung at his Back. All these were accompany'd with a right *Spanish Spado*, and an Attendant *Stiletto*, in their customary Position. The Muletier that was my guide, calling out to him in *Spanish*, told him he was very well arm'd; to which, with a great deal of Gravity, the Don returned Answer, *by Saint Jago a Man cannot be too well arm'd in such dangerous Times*.

I took up my Quarters that Night at *Ocanna*, a large, neat, and well built Town. Houses of good Reception, and Entertainment, are very scarce all over *Spain*; but that, where I then lay, might have pass'd for good in any other Country. Yet it gave me a Notion quite different to what I found: for I imagined it to proceed from my near Approach to the Capital. But instead of that, contrary to all other Countries, the nearer I came to *Madrid*, the Houses of Entertainment grew worse and worse; not in their Rates do I mean (for that with Reason enough might have been expected) but even in their Provision, and Places and way of Reception, I could not however forbear smiling at the Reason given by my Muletier, that it proceeded from a piece of Court Policy, in Order to oblige all Travellers to hasten to *Madrid*.

Two small Leagues from *Ocanna* we arrived at *Aranjuez*, a Seat of Pleasure, which the Kings of *Spain* commonly select for their place of Residence during the Months of *April* and *May*. It is distant from *Madrid* about seven Leagues; and the Country round is the pleasantest in all *Spain*, *Valencia* excepted. The House it self makes but a very indifferent Appearance; I have seen many a better in *England*, with an Owner to it of no more than five hundred Pounds *per Annum*; yet the Gardens are large and fine; or as the *Spaniards* say, the finest in all *Spain*, which with them is all the World. They tell you at the same Time, that those of *Versailles*, in their most beautiful Parts, took their Model from these. I never saw those at *Versailles*: But in my Opinion, the Walks at *Aranjuez*, tho' noble in their length, lose much of their Beauty by their Narrowness.

The Water-works here are a great Curiosity; to which the River *Tagus* running along close by, does mightily contribute. That River is let into the Gardens by a vast number of little Canals, which with their pleasing *Mæanders* divert the Eye with inexpressible Delight. These pretty Wanderers by Pipes properly plac'd in them, afford Varieties scarce to be believ'd or imagin'd; and which would be grateful in any Climate; but much more, where the Air, as it does here, wants in the Summer Months perpetual cooling.

To see a spreading Tree, as growing in its natural Soil, distinguish'd from its pineing Neighbourhood by a gentle refreshing Shower, which appears softly distilling from every Branch and Leaf thereof, while Nature all around is smiling, without one liquid sign of Sorrow, to me appear'd surprizingly pleasing. And the more when I observ'd that its Neighbours receiv'd not any the least Benefit of that plentiful Effusion; And yet a very few Trees distant, you should find a dozen together under the same healthful *Sudor*.¹⁵ Where art imitates Nature well, Philosophers hold it a Perfection: Then what must she exact of us, where we find her transcendent in the Perfections of Nature?

The watry Arch is nothing less surprizing; where Art contending with Nature, acts against the Laws of Nature, and yet is beautiful. To see a Liquid Stream vaulting it self from the space of threescore Yards into a perfect Semi-Orb, will be granted by the Curious to be rare and strange: But sure to walk beneath that Arch, and see the Waters flowing over your Head, without your receiving the minutest Drop, is stranger, if not strange enough to stagger all Belief.

The Story of *Actæon*, pictur'd in Water Colours, if I may so express my self, tho' pretty, seem'd to me, but trifling to the other. Those seem'd to be like Nature miraculously displayed; this only Fable in Grotesque. The Figures indeed were not only fine, but extraordinary; yet their various Shapes were not at all so entertaining to the Mind, however refreshing they might be found to the Body.

I took notice before of the straitness of their Walks: But tho' to me it might seem a Diminution of their Beauty: I am apt to believe to the *Spaniard*, for and by whom they were laid out, it may seem otherwise. They, of both Sexes, give themselves so intolerably up to Amouring, that on that Account the Closeness of the Walks may be look'd upon as an Advantage rather than a

Defect. The grand Avenue to the House is much more stately, and compos'd as they are, of Rows of Trees, somewhat larger than our largest Limes, whose Leaves are all of a perfect Pea bloom Colour, together with their Grandeur, they strike the Eye with a pleasing Beauty. At the Entrance of the Grand Court we see the Statue of *Philip* the Second; to intimate to the Spectators, I suppose, that he was the Founder.

Among other Parks about *Aranjuez* there is one intirely preserved for Dromedaries; an useful Creature for Fatigue, Burden, and Dispatch; but the nearest of kin to Deformity of any I ever saw. There are several other enclosures for several sorts of strange and wild Beasts, which are sometimes baited in a very large Pond, that was shown me about half a League from hence. This is no ordinary Diversion: but when the Court is disposed that way, the Beast, or Beasts, whether Bear, Lyon, or Tyger, are convey'd into a House prepar'd for that purpose; whence he can no other way issue than by a Door over the Water, through, or over, which forcing or flinging himself, he gradually finds himself descend into the very depth of the Pond by a wooden Declivity. The Dogs stand ready on the Banks, and so soon as ever they spye their Enemy, rush all at once into the Water, and engage him. A Diversion less to be complain'd of than their *Tauridores*; because attended with less Cruelty to the Beast, as well as Danger to the Spectators.

When we arrived at *Madrid*, a Town much spoken of by Natives, as well as Strangers, tho' I had seen it before, I could hardly restrain my self from being surprized to find it only environ'd with Mud Walls. It may very easily be imagin'd, they were never intended for Defence, and yet it was a long time before I could find any other use, or rather any use at all in 'em. And yet I was at last convinc'd of my Error by a sensible Increase of Expence. Without the Gates, to half a League without the Town, you have Wine for two Pence the Quart; but within the Place, you drink it little cheaper than you may in *London*. The Mud Walls therefore well enough answer their Intent of forcing People to reside there, under pretence of Security; but in reality to be tax'd, for other Things are taxable, as well as Wine, tho' not in like Proportion.

All Embassadors have a Claim or Privilege, of bringing in what Wine they please Tax-free; and the King, to wave it, will at any Time purchase that Exemption of Duty at the price of five hundred Pistoles *per Annum*. The Convents and Nunneries are allowed a like Licence of free Importation; and it is one of the first Advantages they can boast of; for, under that Licence having a liberty of setting up a Tavern near them, they make a prodigious Advantage of it. The Wine drank and sold in this Place, is for the most part a sort of white Wine.

But if the Mud Walls gave me at first but a faint Idea of the Place; I was pleasingly disappointed, as soon as I enter'd the Gates. The Town then show'd itself well built, and of Brick, and the Streets wide, long, and spacious. Those of *Atocha*, and *Alcala*, are as fine as any I ever saw; yet is it situated but very indifferently: For tho' they have what they call a River, to which they give the very fair Name of *la Mansuera*, and over which they have built a curious, long, and large Stone Bridge; yet is the Course of it, in Summer time especially, mostly dry. This gave occasion to that piece of Railery of a Foreign Embassador, *That the King would have done wisely to have bought a River, before he built the Bridge.* Nevertheless, that little Stream of a River which they boast of, they improve as much as possible; since down the Sides, as far as you can see, there are Coops, or little Places hooped in, for People to wash their Linen (for they very rarely wash in their own Houses) nor is it really an unpleasing Sight, to view the regular Rows of them at that cleanly Operation.

The King has here two Palaces; one within the Town, the other near adjoining. That in the Town is built of Stone, the other which is called *Bueno Retiro*, is all of Brick. From the Town to this last, in Summer time, there is a large covering of Canvas, propt up with tall Poles; under which People walk to avoid the scorching heats of the Sun.

As I was passing by the Chapel of the *Carmelites*, I saw several blind Men, some led, some groping the Way with their Sticks, going into the Chapel. I had the curiosity to know the Reason; I no sooner enter'd the Door, but was surprized to see such a number of those unfortunate People, all kneeling before the Altar, some kissing the Ground, others holding up their Heads, crying out

Misericordia. I was informed 'twas Saint *Lucy's* Day, the Patroness of the Blind; therefore all who were able, came upon that Day to pay their Devotion: So I left them, and directed my Course towards the King's Palace.

When I came to the outward Court, I met with a *Spanish* Gentleman of my Acquaintance, and we went into the *Piazza's*; whilst we were talking there, I saw several Gentlemen passing by having Badges on their Breasts; some white, some red, and others green: My Friend informed me that there were five Orders of Knighthood in *Spain*. That of the Golden Fleece was only given to great Princes, but the other four to private Gentlemen, *viz.* That of *Saint Jago, Alacantara, Saint Salvador de Montreal,* and *Monteza.*

He likewise told me, that there were above ninety Places of Grandees, but never filled up; who have the Privilege of being cover'd in the Presence of the King, and are distinguished into three Ranks. The first is of those who cover themselves before they speak to the King. The second are those who put on their Hats after they have begun to speak. The third are those who only put on their Hats, having spoke to him. The Ladies of the Grandees have also great Respect show'd them. The Queen rises up when they enter the Chamber, and offers them Cushions.

No married Man except the King lies in the Palace, for all the Women who live there are Widows, or Maids of Honour to the Queen. I saw the Prince of *Asturia's* Dinner carried through the Court up to him, being guarded by four Gentlemen of the Guards, one before, another behind, and one on each Side, with their Carbines shoulder'd; the Queen's came next, and the King's the last, guarded as before, for they always dine separately. I observed that the Gentlemen of the Guards, though not on Duty, yet they are obliged to wear their Carbine Belts.

SAINT Isodore, who from a poor labouring Man, by his Sanctity of Life arrived to the Title of *Saint,* is the Patron of *Madrid,* and has a Church dedicated to him, which is richly adorned within. The Sovereign Court of the Inquisition is held at *Madrid,* the President whereof is called the Inquisitor General. They judge without allowing any Appeal for four Sorts of Crimes, *viz.* Heresy, Polygamy, Sodomy and Witchcraft, and when any are convicted, 'tis called the Act of Faith.

Most People believe that the King's greatest Revenue consists in the Gold and Silver brought from the West Indies (which is a mistake) for most Part of that Wealth belongs to Merchants and others, that pay the Workmen at the Golden Mines of *Potosi*, and the Silver Mines at *Mexico*; yet the King, as I have been informed, receives about a Million and a half of Gold.

The *Spaniards* have a Saying, that the finest Garden of Fruit in *Spain* is in the middle of *Madrid*, which is the *Plaza* or Market Place, and truly the Stalls there are set forth with such variety of delicious fruit, that I must confess I never saw any Place comparable to it; and which adds to my Admiration, there are no Gardens or Orchards of Fruit within some Leagues.

They seldom eat Hares in *Spain* but whilst the Grapes are growing, and then they are so exceeding fat, they are knocked down with Sticks. Their Rabits are not so good as ours in *England*; they have great plenty of Patridges, which are larger and finer feather'd than ours. They have but little Beef in *Spain*, because there is no Grass, but they have plenty of Mutton, and exceeding good, because their Sheep feed only upon wild Potherbs; their Pork is delicious, their Hogs feeding only upon Chestnuts and Acorns.

MADRID and *Valladolid*, though Great, yet are only accounted Villages: In the latter *Philip* the Second, by the persuasion of *Parsons* an *English* Jesuit, erected an *English* Seminary; and *Philip* the Fourth built a most noble Palace, with extraordinary fine Gardens. They say that *Christopher Columbus*, who first discover'd the West Indies, dyed there, tho' I have heard he lies buried, and has a Monument at *Sevil*.

The Palace in the Town stands upon eleven Arches, under every one of which there are Shops, which degrade it to a meer Exchange. Nevertheless, the Stairs by which you ascend up to the Guard Room (which is very spacious too) are stately, large, and curious. So soon as you have pass'd the Guard Room, you enter into a long and noble Gallery, the right Hand whereof leads to the King's Apartment, the left to the Queen's. Entring into the King's Apartment you soon arrive at a large Room, where he keeps his *Levee*; on one side whereof (for it takes up the whole Side) is painted the fatal Battle of *Almanza*. I confess the View somewhat affected me, tho' so long after; and brought to Mind many old Passages. However, the Reflection concluded thus in favour of the *Spaniard*, that we ought to excuse their Vanity in so exposing under a *French* General, a Victory, which was the only material one the *Spaniards* could ever boast of over an *English* Army.

In this State Room, when the King first appears, every Person present, receives him with a profound Homage: After which turning from the Company to a large Velvet Chair, by which stands the Father Confessor, he kneels down, and remains some Time at his Devotion; which being over, he rising crosses himself, and his Father Confessor having with the motion of his Hand intimated his Benediction, he then gives Audience to all that attend for that purpose. He receives every Body with a seeming Complaisance; and with an Air more resembling the French than the *Spanish* Ceremony. Petitions to the King, as with us, are delivered into the Hands of the Secretary of State: Yet in one Particular they are, in my Opinion, worthy the Imitation of other Courts; the Petitioner is directly told, what Day he must come for an Answer to the Office; at which Time he is sure, without any further fruitless Attendance, not to fail of it. The Audience being over, the King returns through the Gallery to his own Apartment.

I cannot here omit an accidental Conversation, that pass'd between General *Mahoni* and my self in this Place. After some talk of the Bravery of the *English* Nation, he made mention of General *Stanhope*, with a very peculiar *Emphasis*.

"But," says he, "I never was so put to the Nonplus in all my Days, as that General once put me in. I was on the road from *Paris to Madrid*, and having notice, that that General was going just the Reverse, and that in all likelyhood we should meet the next day: Before my setting out in the Morning, I took care to order my gayest Regimental Apparel, resolving to make the best Appearance I could to receive so great a Man. I had not travell'd above four Hours before I saw two Gentlemen, who appearing to be *English*, it induc'd me to imagine they were Forerunners, and some of his Retinue. But how abash'd and confounded was I? when putting the Question to one of 'em, he made answer, *Sir, I am the Person*. Never did Moderation put Vanity more out of Countenance: Tho' to say Truth, I cou'd not but think his Dress

7*

as much too plain for General *Stanhope*, as I at that juncture thought my own too gay for *Mahoni*. But," added he, "that great Man had too many inward great Endowments to stand in need of any outside Decoration."

Of all Diversions the King takes most delight in that of Shooting, which he performs with great Exactness and Dexterity. I have seen him divert himself at Swallow shooting (by all, I think allow'd to be the most difficult) and exceeding all I ever saw. The last time I had the Honour to see him, was on his Return from that Exercise. He had been abroad with the Duke of *Medina Sidonia*, and alighted out of his Coach at a back Door of the Palace, with three or four Birds in his Hand, which according to his usual Custom, he carried up to the Queen with his own Hands.

There are two Play-houses in *Madrid*, at both which they act every Day; but their Actors, and their Music, are almost too indifferent to be mentioned. The Theatre at the *Bueno Retiro* is much the best; but as much inferior to ours at *London*, as those at *Madrid* are to that. I was at one Play, when both King and Queen were present. There was a splendid Audience, and a great Concourse of Ladies; but the latter, as is the Custom there, having Lattices before them, the Appearance lost most of its Lustre. One very remarkable Thing happen'd, while I was there; the *Ave-Bell* rung in the Middle of an Act, when down on their Knees fell every Body, even the Players on the Stage, in the Middle of their Harangue. They remained for some Time at their Devotion; then up they rose, and returned to the Business they were before engag'd in, beginning where they left off.

The Ladies of Quality make their Visits in grand State and Decorum. The Lady Visitant is carry'd in a Chair by four Men; the two first, in all Weathers, always bare. Two others walk as a Guard, one on each Side; another carrying a large Lanthorn for fear of being benighted; then follows a Coach drawn by six Mules, with her Women, and after that another with her Gentlemen; several Servants walking after, more or less, according to the Quality of the Person. They never suffer their Servants to over load a Coach, as is frequently seen with us, neither do Coachmen or Chairmen go or drive as if they carried Midwives in lieu of Ladies. On the contrary, they affect a Motion so slow and so stately, that you would rather imagine the Ladies were every one of them near their Time, and very apprehensive of a Miscarriage.

I remember not to have seen here any Horses in any Coach, but in the King's, or an Embassador's; which can only proceed from Custom; for certainly finer Horses are not to be found in the World.

At the Time of my being here, Cardinal *Giudici* was at *Madrid*; he was a tall, proper, comely Man, and one that made the best Appearance. *Alberoni* was there at the same Time, who, upon the Death of the Duke of *Vendome*, had the good Fortune to find the Princess *Ursini* his Patroness. An Instance of whose Ingratitude will plead Pardon for this little Digression. That Princess first brought *Alberoni* into Favour at Court. They were both of *Italy*, and that might be one Reason of that Lady's espousing his Interest: tho' some there are, that assign it to the Recommendation of the Duke of *Vendome*; with whom *Alberoni* had the Honour to be very intimate, as the other was always distinguish'd by that Princess. Be which it will, certain it is, she was *Alberoni's* first, and sole Patroness; which gave many People afterwards a very smart Occasion of reflecting upon him, both as to his Integrity and Gratitude. For, when *Alberoni*, upon the Death of King *Philip's* first Queen, had recommended this present Lady, who was his Countrywoman, (she of *Parma*, and he of *Placentia*, both in the same Dukedom) and had forwarded her Match with the King, with all possible Assiduity; and when that Princess, pursuant to the Orders she had received from the King, passed over into *Italy* to accompany the Queen Elect into her own Dominions; *Alberoni*, forgetful of the Hand that first advanced him, sent a Letter to the present Queen, just before her Landing, that if she resolved to be Queen of *Spain*, she must banish the Princess *Ursini*, her Companion, and never let her come to Court. Accordingly that Lady, to evince the Extent of her Power, and the Strength of her Resolution, dipatch'd that Princess away, on her very Landing, and before she had seen the King, under a Detachment of her own Guards, into *France*; and all this without either allowing her an Opportunity of justifying her self, or assigning the least Reason for so uncommon an Action. But the same *Alberoni* (though afterwards created Cardinal, and for some Time King *Philip's* Prime Minion) soon saw that Ingratitude of his rewarded in his own Disgrace, at the very same Court.

I remember, when at *la Mancha*, Don *Felix Pachero*, in a Conversation there, maintain'd, that three Women, at that Time, rul'd the World, *viz.* Queen Anne, Madam *Mantenon*, and this Princess *Ursini*.

Father *Fahy's* Civilities, when last at *Madrid*, exacting of me some suitable Acknowledgment, I went to pay him a Visit; as to render him due Thanks for the past, so to give him a further Account of his Countryman *Brennan*; but I soon found he did not much incline to hear any Thing more of *Murtough*, not expecting to hear any Good of him; for which Reason, as soon as I well could, I changed the Conversation to another Topick. In which some Word dropping of the Count *de Montery*, I told him, that I heard he had taken Orders, and officiated at Mass: He made answer, it was all very true. And upon my intimating, that I had the Honour to serve under him in *Flanders*, on my first entring into Service, and when he commanded the *Spanish* Forces at the famous Battle of *Seneff*; and adding, that I could not but be surprized, that he, who was then one of the brightest *Cavalieroes* of the Age, should now be in Orders; and that I should look upon it as a mighty Favour barely to have, if it might be, a View of him; he very obligingly told me, that he was very well acquainted with him, and that if I would come the next Day, he would not fail to accompany me to the Count's House.

Punctually at the Time appointed, I waited on Father *Fahy*, who, as he promised, carry'd me to the Count's House: He was stepping into his Coach just as we got there; but seeing Father *Fahy*, he advanced towards us. The Father deliver'd my Desire in as handsom a Manner as could be, and concluding with the Reason of it, from my having been in that Service under him; he seem'd very well pleas'd, but added, that there were not many beside my self living, who had been in that Service with him. After some other Conversation, he call'd his Gentleman to him, and gave him particular Orders to give us a *Frescari*, or in *English*, an Entertainment; so taking leave, he went into his Coach, and we to our *Frescari*.

Coming from which, Father *Fahi* made me observe, in the open Street, a Stone, on which was a visible great Stain of somewhat reddish and like Blood.

"This," said he, "was occasion'd by the Death of a Countryman of mine, who had the Misfortune to overset a Child, coming out of that House (pointing to one opposite to us) the Child frighted, though not hurt, as is natural, made a terrible Out-cry; upon which its Father coming out in a violent Rage (notwithstanding my Countryman beg'd Pardon, and pleaded Sorrow as being only an Accident) stabb'd him to the Heart, and down he fell upon that Stone, which to this Day retains the Mark of innocent Blood, so rashly shed".

He went on, and told me, the *Spaniard* immediately took Sanctuary in the Church, whence some Time after he made his Escape. But Escapes of that Nature are so common in *Spain*, that they are not worth wondering at. For even though it were for wilful and premeditated Murder, if the Murderer have taken Sanctuary, it was never known, that he was delivered up to Justice, though demanded; but in some Disguise he makes his Escape, or some Way is secured against all the Clamours of Power or Equity. I have observed, that some of the greatest Quality stop their Coaches over a stinking nasty Puddle, which they often find in the Streets, and holding their Heads over the Door, snuff up the nasty Scent which ascends, believing that 'tis extream healthful; when I was forced to hold my Nose, passing by. 'Tis not convenient to walk out early in the Morning, they having no necessary Houses, throw out their Nastiness in the Middle of the Street.

After I had taken Leave of Father *Fahy*, and return'd my Thanks for all Civilities, I went to pay a Visit to Mr. *Salter*, who was Secretary to General *Stanhope*, when the *English* Forces were made Prisoners of War at *Breuhiga*; going up Stairs, I found the Door of his Lodgings a-jar; and knocking, a Person came to the Door, who appeared under some Surprize at Sight of me. I did not know him, but inquiring if Mr. *Salter* was within; He answered, as I fancy'd, with some Hesitation, that he was but was busy in an inner Room. However, though unask'd, I went in, resolving, since I had found him at home, to wait his Leisure. In a little Time Mr. *Salter* enter'd the Room; and after customary

Ceremonies, asking my Patience a little longer, he desired I would sit down and bear Ensign *Fanshaw* Company (for so he call'd him) adding at going out, he had a little Business that required Dispatch; which being over, he would return, and join Company.

The Ensign, as he call'd him, appear'd to me under a *Dishabileè*; and the first Question he ask'd me, was, if I would drink a Glass of *English* Beer? Misled by his Appearance, though I assented, it was with a Design to treat; which he would be no Means permit; but calling to a Servant, ordered some in. We sat drinking that Liquor, which to me was a greater Rarity than all the Wine in *Spain*; when in dropt an old Acquaintance of mine, Mr. *Le Noy*, Secretary to Colonel *Nevil*. He sat down with us, and before the Glass could go twice round, told Ensign *Fanshaw*, That his Colonel gave his humble Service to him, and ordered him to let him know, that he had but threescore Pistoles by him, which he had sent, and which were at his Service, as what he pleas'd more should be, as soon as it came to his Hands.

At this I began to look upon my Ensign as another guess Person[16] than I had taken him for; and *Le Noy* imagining, by our setting cheek by joul together, that I must be in the Secret, soon after gave him the Title of Captain. This soon convinc'd me, that there was more in the Matter than I was yet Master of; for laying Things together, I could not but argue within my self, that as it seem'd at first, a most incredible Thing, that a Person of his Appearance should have so large Credit, with such a Complement at the End of it, without some Disguise, and as from an Ensign he was risen to be a Captain, in the taking of one Bottle of *English* Beer; a little Patience would let me into a Farce, in which, at present, I had not the Honour to bear any Part but that of a Mute.

At last *Le Noy* took his leave, and as soon as he had left us, and the other Bottle was brought in, Ensign *Fanshaw* began to open his Heart, and tell me, who he was. "I am necessitated," said he, "to be under this Disguise, to conceal my self, especially in this Place.

"For you must know," continued he, "that when our Forces were Lords of this Town, as we were for a little while, I fell under an Intrigue with another Man's Wife; Her Husband was a Person of considerable

Account; nevertheless the Wife show'd me all the Favours that a Soldier, under a long and hard Campaigne, could be imagined to ask. In short, her Relations got acquainted with our Amour, and knowing that I was among the Prisoners taken at *Breuhiga*, are now upon the Scout and Enquiry, to make a Discovery that may be of fatal Consequence. This is the Reason of my Disguise; this the unfortunate Occasion of my taking upon me a Name that does not belong to me."

He spoke all this with such an Openness of Heart, that in return of so much Confidence, I confess'd to him, that I had heard of the Affair, for that it had made no little Noise all over the Country; that it highly behoved him to take great Care of himself, since as the Relations on both Sides were considerable, he must consequently be in great Danger; That in Cases of that Nature, no People in the World carry Things to greater Extremities, than the *Spaniards*. He return'd me Thanks for my good Advice, which I understood, in a few Days after, he, with the Assistance of his Friends, had taken Care to put in Practice; for he was convey'd away secretly, and afterwards had the Honour to be made a Peer of *Ireland*.

My Passport being at last sign'd by the Count *de las Torres*, I prepared for a Journey, I had long and ardently wish'd for, and set out from *Madrid*, in the Beginning of *September*, 1712, in Order to return to my native Country.

Accordingly I set forward upon my Journey, but having heard, both before and since my being in *Spain*, very famous Things spoken of the *Escurial*; though it was a League out of my Road, I resolved to make it a Visit. And I must confess, when I came there, I was so far from condemning my Curiosity, that I chose to congratulate my good Fortune, that had, at half a Day's Expence, feasted my Eyes with Extraordinaries, which would have justify'd a Twelve-months' Journey on purpose.

The Structure is intirely magnificent, beyond any Thing I ever saw, or any Thing my Imagination could frame. It is composed of eleven several Quadrangles, with noble Cloisters round every one of them. The Front to the West is adorn'd with three stately Gates; every one of a different Model, yet every one the Model of nicest Architecture. The Middlemost of the three leads into a fine Chapel of the *Hieronomites*, as they call them; in which are entertain'd one hundred and fifty Monks. At every of the four Corners of this august Fabrick, there is a Turret of excellent Workmanship, which yields to the Whole an extraordinary Air of Grandure. The King's Palace is on the North, nearest that Mountain, whence the Stone it is built of was hew'n; and all the South Part is set off with many Galleries, both beautiful and sumptuous.

This prodigious Pile, which, as I have said, exceeds all that I ever saw; and which would ask, of it self, a Volume to particularize, was built by *Philip* the Second. He lay'd the first Stone, yet liv'd to see it finished; and lies buryed in the *Panthæon*, a Part of it, set apart for the Burial-place of succeeding Princes, as well as himself. It was dedicated to Saint *Laurence*, in the very Foundation; and therefore built in the Shape of a Gridiron, the Instrument of that Martyr's Execution; and in Memory of a great Victory obtained on that Saint's Day. The Stone of which it is built, contrary to the common Course, grows whiter by Age; and the Quarry, whence it was dug, lies near enough, if it had Sense or Ambition, to grow enamour'd of its own wonderful Production. Some there are, who stick not to assign this Convenience, as the main Cause of its Situation; and for my Part, I must agree, that I have seen many other Parts of *Spain*, where that glorious Building would have shone with yet far greater Splendour.

There was no Town of any Consequence presented it self in my Way to *Burgos*. Here I took up my Quarters that Night; where I met with an *Irish* Priest, whose Name was *White*. As is natural on such Rencounters, having answered his Enquiry, whither I was going; he very kindly told me, he should be very glad of my Company as far as *Victoria*, which lay in my Road; and I with equal Frankness embrac'd the Offer.

Next Morning, when we had mounted our Mules, and were got a little Distance from *Burgos*; he began to relate to me a great many impious Pranks of an *English* Officer, who had been a Prisoner there a little before I came; concluding all, with some Vehemence, that he had given greater Occasion of Scandal and Infamy to his native Country, than would easily be wiped off, or in a little Time. The Truth of it is, many Particularly, which he related to me, were too monstrously vile to admit of any Repetition here; and highly meriting that unfortunate End, which that

Officer met with some time after. Nevertheless the just Reflection made by that Father, plainly manifested to me the Folly of those Gentlemen, who, by such Inadvertencies, to say no worse, cause the Honour of the Land of their Nativity to be called in question. For tho', no doubt, it is a very false Conclusion, from a singular, to conceive a general Character; yet in a strange Country, nothing is more common. A Man therefore, of common Sense, would carefully avoid all Occasions of Censure, if not in respect to himself, yet out of a human Regard to such of his Countrymen as may have the Fortune to come after him; and, it's more than probable, may desire to hear a better and juster Character of their Country, and Countrymen, than he perhaps might incline to leave behind him.

As we travelled along, Father *White* told me, that near the Place of our Quartering that Night, there was a Convent of the *Carthusian* Order, which would be well worth my seeing. I was doubly glad to hear it, as it was an Order most a Stranger to me; and as I had often heard from many others, most unaccountable Relations of the Severity of their Way of Life, and the very odd Original of their Institution.

The next Morning therefore, being *Sunday*, we took a Walk to the Convent. It was situated at the Foot of a great Hill, having a pretty little River running before it. The Hill was naturally cover'd with Evergreens of various Sorts; but the very Summit of the Rock was so impending, that one would at first Sight be led to apprehend the Destruction of the Convent, from the Fall of it. Notwithstanding all which, they have very curious and well ordered Gardens; which led me to observe, that, what ever Men may pretend, Pleasure was not incompatible with the most austere Life. And indeed, if I may guess of others by this, no Order in that Church can boast of finer Convents. Their Chapel was completely neat, the Altar of it set out with the utmost Magnificence, both as to fine Paintings, and other rich Adornments. The Building was answerable to the rest; and, in short, nothing seem'd omitted, that might render it beautiful or pleasant.

When we had taken a full Survey of all; we, not without some Regret, return'd to our very indifferent Inn; Where the better to pass away the Time, Father *White* gave me an ample Detail of the

Original of that Order. I had before-hand heard somewhat of it; nevertheless, I did not care to interrupt him, because I had a Mind to hear how his Account would agree with what I had already heard.

"*Bruno*," said the Father, "the Author or Founder of this Order, was not originally of this, but of another. He had a holy Brother of the same Order, that was his Cell-mate, or Chamber-fellow, who was reputed by all that ever saw or knew him, for a Person of exalted Piety, and of a most exact holy Life. This man, *Bruno* had intimately known for many years; and agreed in his Character, that general Consent did him no more than Justice, having never observed any Thing in any of his Actions, that, in his Opinion, could be offensive to God or Man. He was perpetually at his Devotions; and distinguishably remarkable, for never permitting any Thing but pious Ejaculations to proceed out of his Mouth. In short, he was reputed a Saint upon Earth. "THIS Man at last dies, and, according to Custom, is removed into the Chapel of the Convent, and there plac'd with a Cross fix'd in his Hands: Soon after which, saying the proper Masses for his Soul, in the Middle of their Devotion, the dead Man lifts up his Head, and with an audible Voice, cry'd out, *Vocatus sum*. The pious Brethren, as any one will easily imagine, were most prodigiously surprised at such an Accident, and therefore they earnestly redoubled their Prayers; when lifting up his Head a second Time, the dead Man cried aloud, *Judicatus sum*. Knowing his former Piety, the pious Fraternity could not then entertain the least doubt of his Felicity; when, to their great Consternation and Confusion, he lifted up his Head a third Time, crying out in a terrible Tone, *Damnatus sum*; upon which they incontinently removed the Corps out of the Chapel, and threw it upon the Dunghill.

"Good *Bruno*, pondering upon these Passages, could not fail of drawing this Conclusion; That if a Person to all Appearance so holy and devout, should miss of Salvation, it behov'd a wise Man to contrive some Way more certain to make his Calling and Election sure. To that Purpose he instituted this strict and severe Order, with an Injunction to them sacred as any Part, that every Professor should always wear Hair Cloth next his Skin, never eat any Flesh; nor speak to one another, only as passing by, to say, *Memento mori*."

This Account I found to agree pretty well with what I had before heard; but at the same Time, I found the Redouble of it made but just the same Impression, it had at first made upon my

Heart. However having made it my Observation, that a Spirit the least contradictory, best carries a Man through *Spain*; I kept Father White Company, and in Humour, 'till we arrived at *Victoria*. Where he added one Thing, by Way of Appendix, in Relation to the *Carthusians*, That every Person of the Society, is oblig'd every Day to go into their Place of Burial, and take up as much Earth, as he can hold at a Grasp with one Hand, in order to prepare his Grave.

Next Day we set out for *Victoria*. It is a sweet, delicious, and pleasant Town. It received that Name in Memory of a considerable Victory there obtained over the *Moors*. Leaving this Place, I parted with Father *White*; he going where his Affairs led him; and I to make the best of my Way to *Bilboa*.

Entring into *Biscay*, soon after I left *Victoria*, I was at a Loss almost to imagine, what Country I was got into. By my long Stay in *Spain*, I thought my self a tolerable Master of the Tongue; yet here I found my self at the utmost Loss to understand Landlord, Landlady, or any of the Family. I was told by my Muletier, that they pretend their Language, as they call it, has continued uncorrupted from the very Confusion of *Babel*; though if I might freely give my Opinion in the Matter, I should rather take it to be the very Corruption of all that Confusion. Another *Rhodomontado* they have, (for in this they are perfect *Spaniards*) that neither *Romans*, *Carthaginians*, *Vandals*, *Goths*, or *Moors*, ever totally subdued them. And yet any Man that has ever seen their Country, might cut this Knot without a Hatchet, by saying truly, that neither *Roman*, *Carthaginian*, nor any victorious People, thought it worth while to make a Conquest of a Country, so mountainous and so barren.

However, *Bilboa* must be allowed, tho' not very large, to be a pretty, clean and neat Town. Here, as in *Amsterdam*, they allow neither Cart, nor Coach, to enter; but every Thing of Merchandize is drawn, and carried upon Sledges: And yet it is a Place of no small Account, as to Trade; and especially for Iron and Wooll. Here I hop'd to have met with an opportunity of Embarking for *England*; but to my Sorrow I found my self disappointed, and under that Disappointment, obliged to make the best of my Way to *Bayonne*.

Setting out for which Place, the first Town of Note that I came to, was *Saint Sebastian*. A very clean Town, and neatly pav'd; which is no little Rarity in *Spain*. It has a very good Wall about it, and a pretty Citadel. At this Place I met with two *English* Officers, who were under the same state with my self; one of them being a Prisoner of War with me at *Denia*. They were going to *Bayonne* to embark for *England* as well as my self; so we agreed to set out together for *Port Passage*. The Road from St. *Sebastian* is all over a well pav'd Stone Causeway; almost at the end whereof, there accosted us a great number of young Lasses. They were all prettily dress'd, their long Hair flowing in a decent manner over their Shoulders, and here and there decorated with Ribbons of various Colours, which wantonly play'd on their Backs with the Wind. The Sight surpriz'd my Fellow Travellers no less than me; and the more, as they advanced directly up to us, and seiz'd our Hands. But a little time undeceiv'd us, and we found what they came for; and that their Contest, tho' not so robust as our Oars on the *Thames*, was much of the same Nature; each contending who should have us for their Fare. For 'tis here a Custom of Time out of mind, that none but young Women should have the management and profit of that Ferry. And tho' the Ferry is over an Arm of the Sea, very broad, and sometimes very rough, those fair Ferriers manage themselves with that Dexterity, that the Passage is very little dangerous, and in calm Weather, very pleasant. In short, we made choice of those that best pleased us; who in a grateful Return, led us down to their Boat under a sort of Music, which they, walking along, made with their Oars, and which we all thought far from being disagreeable. Thus were we transported over to *Port Passage;* not undeservedly accounted the best Harbour in all the Bay of *Biscay*.

We stay'd not long here after Landing, resolving, if possible, to reach *Fonterabia* before Night; but all the Expedition we could use, little avail'd; for before we could reach thither the Gates were shut, and good Nature and Humanity were so lock'd up with them, that all the Rhetorick we were Masters of could not prevail upon the Governor to order their being opened; for which Reason we were obliged to take up our Quarters at the Ferry House.

When we got up the next Morning, we found the Waters so broad, as well as rough, that we began to enquire after another Passage; and were answer'd, that at the Isle of *Conference*, but a short League upwards, the Passage was much shorter, and exposed to less Danger. Such good Reasons soon determin'd's us: So, setting out we got there in a very little Time; and very soon after were landed in *France*. Here we found a House of very good Entertainment, a Thing we had long wanted, and much lamented the want of.

We were hardly well seated in the House before we were made sensible, that it was the Custom, which had made it the business of our Host, to entertain all his Guests at first coming in, with a prolix Account of that remarkable Interview between the two Kings of *France* and *Spain*. I speak safely now, as being got on *French* Ground: For the *Spaniard* in his own Country would have made me to know, that putting *Spain* after *France* had there been look'd upon as a meer Solecism in Speech. However, having refresh'd our selves, to show our deference to our Host's Relation, we agreed to pay our Respects to that famous little Isle he mention'd; which indeed, was the whole burden of the Design of our crafty Landlord's Relation.

When we came there, we found it a little oval Island, over-run with Weeds, and surrounded with Reeds and Rushes.

"Here," said our Landlord (for he went with us) "upon this little Spot, were at that juncture seen the two greatest Monarchs in the Universe. A noble Pavilion was erected in the very middle of it, and in the middle of that was placed a very large oval Table; at which was the Conference, from which the Place receiv'd its Title. There were two Bridges rais'd; one on the *Spanish* side, the Passage to which was a little upon a Descent by reason of the Hills adjacent; and the other upon the *French* side, which as you see, was all upon a Level. The Musick playing, and Trumpets sounding, the two Kings, upon a Signal agreed upon, set forward at the same time; the *Spanish* Monarch handing the *Infanta* his Daughter to the Place of Interview. As soon as they were enter'd the Pavilion, on each Side, all the Artillery fired, and both Armies after that made their several Vollies. Then the King of *Spain* advancing on his side the Table with the *Infanta*, the King of *France* advanced at the same Moment on the other; till meeting, he received the *Infanta* at the Hands of her Father, as his Queen; upon which, both the Artillery and small Arms fir'd as before. After this, was a most splendid and sumptuous Entertainment; which being over, both Kings retir'd into their feveral Dominions; the King of *France* conducting his new Queen to *Saint Jean de Luz*, where the Marriage was consummated; and the King of *Spain* returning to *Port Passage*."

After a Relation so very inconsistent with the present State of the Place; we took Horse (for Mule-mounting was now out of Fashion) and rode to *Saint Jean de Luz*, where we found as great a difference in our Eating and Drinking, as we had before done in our Riding. Here they might be properly call'd Houses of Entertainment; tho' generally speaking, till we came to this Place, we met with very mean Fare, and were poorly accommodated in the Houses where we lodged.

A Person that travels this way, would be esteem'd a Man of a narrow Curiosity, who should not desire to see the Chamber where *Louis le grand* took his first Night's Lodging with his Queen. Accordingly, when it was put into my Head, out of an Ambition to evince my self a Person of Taste, I asked the Question, and the Favour was granted me, with a great deal of *French* Civility. Not that I found any Thing here, more than in the Isle of *Conference*, but what Tradition only had rendered remarkable.

Saint Jean de Luz is esteem'd one of the greatest Village Towns in all *France*. It was in the great Church of this Place, that *Lewis* XIV according to Marriage Articles, took before the high Altar the Oath of Renunciation to the Crown of *Spain*, by which all the Issue of that Marriage were debarred Inheritance, if Oaths had been obligatory with Princes. The Natives here are reckon'd expert Seamen; especially in Whale fishing. Here is a fine Bridge of Wood; in the middle of which is a Descent, by Steps, into a pretty little Island; where is a Chapel, and a Palace belonging to the Bishop of *Bayonne*. Here the Queen Dowager of *Spain* often walks to divert herself; and on this Bridge, and in the Walks on the Island, I had the Honour to see that Princess more than once.

This *Villa* not being above four Leagues from *Bayonne*, we got there by Dinner time, where at an Ordinary of twenty *Sous*, we eat and drank in Plenty, and with a *gusto*, much better than in any part of *Spain*; where for eating much worse, we paid very much more.

BAYONNE is a Town strong by Nature; yet the Fortifications have been very much neglected, since the building of the Citadel, on the other Side the River; which not only commands the Town, but the Harbour too. It is a noble Fabrick; fair and strong, and rais'd on the side of a Hill, wanting nothing that Art could furnish, to render it impregnable. The Marshal *Bouflers* had the Care of it in its erection; and there is a fine Walk near it, from which he us'd to survey the Workmen, which still carries his Name. There are two noble Bridges here, tho' both of Wood, one over that River which runs on one side the Town; the other over that, which divides it in the middle, the Tide runs thro' both with vast Rapidity; notwithstanding which, Ships of Burden come up, and paying for it, are often fasten'd to the Bridge, while loading or unloading. While I was here, there came in four or five *English* Ships laden with Corn, the first, as they told me, that had come in to unlade there, since the beginning of the War.

On that Side of the River where the new Citadel is built, at a very little distance lies *Pont d' Esprit*, a Place mostly inhabited by *Jews*, who drive a great Trade there, and are esteemed very rich, tho' as in all other Countries mostly very rogueish. Here the Queen Dowager of *Spain* has kept her Court ever since the Jealousy of the present King reclus'd her from *Madrid*. As Aunt to his Competitor *Charles* (now Emperor) he apprehended her Intrigueing; for which Reason giving her an Option of Retreat, that Princess made choice of this City, much to the Advantage of the Place, and in all Appearance much to her own Satisfaction. She is a Lady not of the lesser Size; and lives here in suitable Splendour, and not without the Respect due to a Person of her high Quality: Every time she goes to take the Air, the Cannon of the Citadel saluting her, as she passes over the Bridge; and to say Truth, the Country round is extremely pleasant, and abounds in plenty of all Provisions; especially in wild Fowl. *Bayonne* Hams are, to a Proverb, celebrated all over *France*.

We waited here near five Months before the expected Transports arrived from *England*, without any other Amusements, than such as are common to People under Suspence. Short Tours will not admit of great Varieties; and much Acquaintance could not be any way suitable to People, that had long been in a strange

Country, and earnestly desired to return to our own. Yet one Accident befell me here, that was nearer costing me my Life, than all I had before encounter'd, either in Battle or Siege.

Going to my Lodgings one Evening, I unfortunately met with an Officer, who would needs have me along with him, aboard one of the *English* Ships, to drink a Bottle of *English* Beer. He had been often invited, he said; and I am afraid our Countryman, continued he, will hold himself slighted, if I delay it longer. *English* Beer was a great rarity, and the Vessel lay not at any great distance from my Lodgings; so without any further Persuasion I consented. When we came upon the Bridge, to which the Ship we were to go aboard was fastened, we found, as was customary, as well as necessary, a Plank laid over from the Ship, and a Rope to hold by, for safe Passage. The Night was very dark; and I had cautiously enough taken care to provide a Man with a Lanthorn to prevent Casualties. The Man with the Light went first, and out of his abundant Complaisance, my Friend, the Officer, would have me follow the Light: But I was no sooner stept upon the Plank after my Guide, but Rope and Plank gave way, and Guide and I tumbled both together into the Water.

The Tide was then running in pretty strong: However, my Feet in the Fall touching Ground, gave me an opportunity to recover my self a little; at which Time I catch'd fast hold of a Buoy, which was plac'd over an Anchor on one of the Ships there riding: I held fast, till the Tide rising stronger and stronger threw me off my Feet; which gave an Opportunity to the poor Fellow, our Lanthorn-bearer, to lay hold of one of my Legs, by which he held as fast as I by the Buoy. We had lain thus lovingly at Hull together, strugling with the increasing Tide, which, well for us, did not break my hold (for if it had, the Ships which lay breast a breast had certainly sucked us under) when several on the Bridge, who saw us fall, brought others with Ropes and Lights to our Assistance; and especially my Brother Officer, who had been Accessary as well as Spectator of our Calamity; tho' at last a very small Portion of our Deliverance fell to his share.

As soon as I could feel a Rope, I quitted my hold of the Buoy; but my poor Drag at my Heels would not on any account quit his hold of my Leg. And as it was next to an Impossibility, in that Posture to draw us up the Bridge to save both, if either of us, we must still have perished, had not the Alarm brought off a Boat or two to our Succour, who took us in.

I was carry'd as fast as possible, to a neighbouring House hard by, where they took immediate care to make a good Fire; and where I had not been long before our intended Host, the Master of the Ship, came in very much concern'd, and blaming us for not hailing the Vessel, before we made an Attempt to enter. For, says he, the very Night before, my Vessel was robb'd; and that Plank and Rope were a Trap design'd for the Thieves, if they came again; not imagining that Men in an honest way would have come on board without asking Questions. Like the wise Men of this World, I hereupon began to form Resolutions against a Thing, which was never again likely to happen; and to draw inferences of Instruction from an Accident, that had not so much as a Moral for its Foundation.

One Day after this, partly out of Business, and partly out of Curiosity, I went to see the Mint here, and having taken notice to one of the Officers, that there was a difference in the Impress of their Crown Pieces, one having at the bottom the Impress of a Cow, and the other none:

"Sir," reply'd that Officer, "you are much in the right in your Observation. Those that have the Cow, were not coin'd here, but at *Paw*, the chief City of *Navarr*; where they enjoy the Privilege of a Mint, as well as we. And Tradition tells," says he, "that the Reason of that Addition to the Impress was this: A certain King of *Navarr* (when it was a Kingdom distinct from that of *France*) looking out of a Window of the Palace, spy'd a Cow, with her Calf standing aside her, attack'd by a Lyon, which had got loose out of his Menagery. The Lyon strove to get the young Calf into his Paw; the Cow bravely defended her Charge; and so well, that the Lyon at last, tir'd and weary, withdrew, and left her Mistress of the Field of Battle; and her young one. Ever since which, concluded that Officer, by Order of that King, the Cow is plac'd at the bottom of the Impress of all the Money there coined."

Whether or no my Relator guess'd at the Moral, or whether it was Fact, I dare not determine; But to me it seem'd apparent, that it was no otherways intended, than as an emblematical Fable to cover, and preserve the Memory of the Deliverance of

Henry the Fourth, then the young King of *Navarr*, at that eternally ignominious Slaughter, the Massacre of *Paris*. Many Historians, their own as well as others, agree, that the House of *Guise* had levell'd the Malice of their Design at that great Prince. They knew him to be the lawful Heir; but as they knew him bred, what they call'd a *Hugonot*, Barbarity and Injustice was easily conceal'd under the Cloak of Religion, and the Good of Mother Church, under the veil of Ambition, was held sufficient to postpone the Laws of God and Man. Some of those Historians have deliver'd it as Matter of Fact, that the Conspirators, in searching after that young King, press'd into the very Apartments of the Queen his Mother; who having, at the Toll of the Bell, and Cries of the Murder'd, taken the Alarm, on hearing 'em coming, plac'd her self in her Chair, and cover'd the young King her Son with her Farthingale, till they were gone. By which means she found an opportunity to convey him to a Place of more Safety; and so preserv'd him from those bloody Murderers, and in them from the Paw of the Lyon. This was only a private Reflection of my own at that Time; but I think carries so great a Face of Probability, that I can see no present Reason to reject it. And to have sought after better Information from the Officer of the Mint, had been to sacrifice my Discretion to my Curiosity.

While I stay'd at *Bayonne*, the Princess *Ursini* came thither, attended by some of the King of *Spain's* Guards. She had been to drink the Waters of some famous Spaw in the Neighbourhood, the Name of which has now slipt my Memory. She was most splendidly entertain'd by the Queen Dowager of *Spain*; and the Mareschal *de Montrevel* no less signaliz'd himself in his Reception of that great Lady, who was at that Instant the greatest Favourite in the *Spanish* Court; tho' as I have before related, she was some Time after basely undermined by a Creature of her own advancing.

BAYONNE is esteem'd the third *Emporium* of Trade in all *France*. It was once, and remain'd long so, in the Possession of the *English*; of which had History been silent, the Cathedral Church had afforded evident Demonstration; being in every respect of the *English* Model, and quite different to any of their own way of Building in *France*.

PAMPELONA is the Capital City of the *Spanish Navarr*,

supposed to have been built by *Pompey*. 'Tis situated in a pleasant Valley, surrounded by lofty Hills. This Town, whether famous or infamous, was the Cause of the first Institution of the Order of the Jesuits. For at the Siege of this Place *Ignatius Loyola* being only a private Soldier, receiv'd a shot on his Thigh, which made him uncapable of following that Profession any longer; upon which he set his Brains to work, being a subtle Man, and invented the Order of the Jesuits, which has been so troublesome to the World ever since.

At *Saint Stephen* near *Lerida*, an Action happened between the *English* and *Spaniards*, in which Major General *Cunningham* bravely fighting at the Head of his Men, lost his Life, being extreamly much lamented. He was a Gentleman of a great Estate, yet left it, to serve his Country; *Dulce est pro Patria Mori*.

About two Leagues from *Victoria*, there is a very pleasant Hermitage plac'd upon a small rising Ground, a murmuring Rivulet running at the bottom, and a pretty neat Chapel standing near it, in which I saw *Saint Christopher* in a Gigantick Shape, having a *Christo* on his Shoulders. The Hermit was there at his Devotion, I ask'd him (tho' I knew it before) the reason why he was represented in so large a Shape: The Hermit answered with great Civility, and told me, he had his Name from *Christo Ferendo*, for when our Saviour was young, he had an inclination to pass a River, so *Saint Christopher* took him on his Shoulders in order to carry him over, and as the Water grew deeper and deeper, so he grew higher and higher.

At last we received News, that the *Gloucester* Man of War, with two Transports, was arrived at *Port Passage*, in order for the Transporting of all the remaining Prisoners of War into *England*. Accordingly they march'd next Day, and there embark'd. But I having before agreed with a Master of a Vessel, which was loaded with Wine for *Amsterdam*, to set me ashoar at *Dover*, stay'd behind, waiting for that Ship, as did that for a fair Wind.

In three or four Days' Time, a fine and fair Gale presented; of which the Master taking due Advantage, we sail'd over the Bar into the Bay of *Biscay*. This is with Sailors, to a Proverb, reckon'd the roughest of Seas; and yet on our Entrance into it, nothing appear'd like it. 'Twas smooth as Glass; a Lady's Face might pass

for young, and in its Bloom, that discover'd no more Wrinkles;
Yet scarce had we fail'd three Leagues, before a prodigious Fish
presented it self to our View. As near as we could guess, it might
be twenty Yards in Length; and it lay sporting it self on the sur-
face of the Sea, a great Part appearing out of the Water. The
Sailors, one and all, as soon as they saw it, declar'd it the certain
Forerunner of a Storm. However, our Ship kept on its Course,
before a fine Gale, till we had near passed over half the Bay; when,
all on a sudden, there was such a hideous Alteration, as makes
Nature recoil on the very Reflection. Those Seas that seem'd
before to smile upon us, with the Aspect of a Friend, now in a
Moment chang'd their flattering Countenance into that of an
open Enemy; and Frowns, the certain Indexes of Wrath, presented
us with apparent Danger, of which little on this Side Death could
be the Sequel. The angry Waves cast themselves up into Mountains, and scourg'd the Ship on every Side from Poop to Prow:
Such Shocks from the contending Wind and Surges! Such Falls
from Precipices of Water, to dismal Caverns of the same uncertain Element! Although the latter seem'd to receive us in
Order to skreen us from the Riot of the former, Imagination
could offer no other Advantage than that of a Winding-Sheet,
presented and prepared for our approaching Fate. But why
mention I Imagination? In me 'twas wholly dormant. And yet
those Sons of stormy Weather, the Sailors, had theirs about them
in full Stretch; for seeing the Wind and Seas so very boisterous,
they lash'd the Rudder of the Ship, resolv'd to let her drive, and
steer herself; since it was past their Skill to steer her. This was our
Way of sojourning most Part of that tedious Night; driven
where the Winds and Waves thought fit to drive us, with all our
Sails quite lower'd and flat upon the Deck. If *Ovid*, in the little
Archipelagian Sea, could whine out his *jam jam jacturus*, &c. in this
more dismal Scene, and much more dangerous Sea (the Pitch-like
Darkness of the Night adding to all our sad Variety of Woes)
what Words in Verse or Prose could serve to paint our Passions,
or our Expectations? Alas! our only Expectation was in the Return of Morning; It came at last; yet even slowly as it came, when
come, we thought it come too soon, a new Scene of sudden
Death being all the Advantage of its first Appearance. Our Ship

was driving full Speed, towards the *Breakers* on the *Cabritton* Shore, between *Burdeaux* and *Bayonne*; which filled us with Ideas more terrible than all before, since those were past, and these seemingly as certain. Beside, to add to our Distress, the Tide was driving in, and consequently must drive us fast to visible Destruction. A State so evident, that one of our Sailors, whom great Experience had render'd more sensible of our present Danger, was preparing to save one, by lashing himself to the main Mast, against the expected Minute of Desolation. He was about that melancholy Work, in utter Despair of any better Fortune, when, as loud as ever he could bawl, he cry'd out, *a Point, a Point of Wind*. To me, who had had too much of it, it appear'd like the Sound of the last Trump; but to the more intelligent Crew, it had a different Sound. With Vigour and Alacrity they started from their Prayers, or their Despair, and with all imaginable Speed, unlash'd the Rudder, and hoisted all their Sails. Never sure in Nature did one Minute produce a greater Scene of Contraries. The more skilful Sailors took Courage at this happy Presage of Deliverance. And according to their Expectation did it happen; that heavenly Point of Wind deliver'd us from the Jaws of those *Breakers*, ready open to devour us; and carrying us out to the much more wellcome wide Sea, furnished every one in the Ship with Thoughts, as distant as we thought our Danger.

We endeavoured to make *Port Passage*; but our Ship became unruly, and would not answer her Helm; for which Reason we were glad to go before the Wind, and make for the Harbour of *Saint Jean de Luz*. This we attain'd without any great Difficulty, and to the Satisfaction of all, Sailors as well as Passengers, we there cast Anchor, after the most terrible Storm (as all the oldest Sailors agreed) and as much Danger as ever People escap'd.

Here I took notice, that the Sailors buoy'd up their Cables with Hogsheads; enquiring into the Reason of which, they told me, that the Rocks at the Bottom of the Harbour were by Experience found to be so very sharp, that they would otherwise cut their Cables asunder. Our Ship was obliged to be drawn up into the Dock to be refitted; during which, I lay in the Town, where nothing of Moment, or worth reciting, happen'd.

I beg Pardon for my Errors; the very Movements of Princes

must always be considerable, and consequently worth Recital. While the Ship lay in the Dock, I was one Evening walking upon the Bridge, with the little Island near it. (which I have before spoke of) and had a little *Spanish* Dog along with me, when at the further End I spy'd a Lady, and three or four Gentlemen in Company; I kept on my Pace of Leisure, and so did they; but when I came nearer, I found they as much out number'd me in the Dog, as they did in the human Kind. And I soon experienced to my Sorrow, that their Dogs, by their Fierceness and Ill-humour, were Dogs of Quality; having, without Warning, or the least Declaration of War, fallen upon my little Dog, according to pristine Custom, without any honourable Regard to Size, Interest or Number. However the good Lady, who, by the Privilege of her Sex, must be allow'd the most competent Judge of Inequalities, out of an Excess of Condescension and Goodness, came running to the Relief of oppressed poor *Tony*; and, in courtly Language, rated her own oppressive Dogs for their great Incivility to Strangers. The Dogs, in the Middle of their insulting Wrath, obey'd the Lady with a vast deal of profound Submission; which I could not much wonder at, when I understood, that it was a Queen Dowager of *Spain*, who had chid them.

Our Ship being now repaired, and made fit to go out again to Sea, we left the Harbour of *Saint Jean de Luz*, and with a much better Passage, as the last Tempest was still dancing in my Imagination, in ten Days' Sail we reach'd *Dover*. Here I landed on the last Day of *March*, 1713 having not, till then, seen or touch'd *English* Shoar from the Beginning of *May*, 1705.

I took Coach directly for *London*, where, when I arriv'd, I thought my self transported into a Country more foreign, than any I had either fought or pilgrimag'd in. Not foreign, do I mean, in respect to others, so much as to it self. I left it, seemingly, under a perfect Unanimity: The fatal Distinctions of *Whig* and *Tory* were then esteemed meerly nominal; and of no more ill Consequence or Danger, than a Bee robb'd of its Sting. The national Concern went on with Vigour, and the prodigious Success of the Queen's Arms, left every Soul without the least Pretence to a Murmur. But now on my Return, I found them on their old Establishment, perfect Contraries, and as unlikely to be brought to meet as direct Angles. Some arraigning, some extolling of a Peace; in which Time has shown both were wrong, and consequently neither could be right in their Notions of it, however an over prejudic'd Way of thinking might draw them into one or the other. But *Whig* and *Tory* are, in my Mind, the compleatest Paradox in Nature, and yet like other Paradoxes, old as I am, I live in Hope to see, before I die, those seeming Contraries perfectly reconcil'd, and reduc'd into one happy Certainty, the Publick Good.

Whilst I stay'd at *Madrid*, I made several Visits to my old Acquaintance General *Mahoni*. I remember that he told me, when the Earl of *Peterborow* and he held a Conference at *Morvidro*, his Lordship used many Arguments to induce him to leave the *Spanish* Service. *Mahoni* made several Excuses, especially that none of his Religion was suffer'd to serve in the *English* Army. My Lord reply'd, That he would undertake to get him excepted by an Act of Parliament. I have often heard him speak with great Respect of his Lordship, and was strangely surprized, that after so many glorious Successes he should be sent away.

He was likewise pleased to inform me, that at the Battle of *Saragoza*, 'twas his Fortune to make some of our Horse to give way, and he pursued them for a considerable time; but at his Return, he saw the *Spanish* Army in great Confusion: But it gave him the Opportunity of attacking our Battery of Guns; which he performed with great Slaughter, both of Gunners and Matrosses: He at the same time inquired, who 'twas that commanded there in chief. I informed him 'twas Col. *Bourguard*, one that understood the Oeconomy of the Train exceeding well. As for that, he knew nothing of; but that he would vouch, he behaved himself with extraordinary Courage, and defended the Battery to the utmost Extremity, receiving several Wounds, and deserved the Post in which he acted. A Gentleman who was a Prisoner at *Gualaxara*, informed me, that he saw King *Philip* riding through that Town, being only attended with one of his Guards.

Saragoza, or *Cæsar Augusta*, lies upon the River *Ebro*, being the Capital of *Arragon*; 'tis a very ancient City, and contains fourteen great Churches, and twelve Convents. The Church of the Lady of the *Pillar* is frequented by Pilgrims, almost from all Countries; 'twas anciently a Roman Colony.

Tibi laus, tibi honor, tibi sit gloria, O gloriosa Trinitas, quia tu dedisti mihi hanc opportunitatem, omnes has res gestas recordandi. Nomen tuum sit benedictum, per sæcula sæculorum. Amen.

FINIS

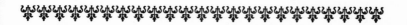

THE

HISTORY

Of the remarkable LIFE of

JOHN SHEPPARD, &c.

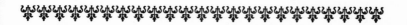

THE

HISTORY

Of the remarkable LIFE of

JOHN SHEPPARD,

CONTAINING

A particular Account of his many

ROBBERIES and ESCAPES,

Viz.

His robbing the Shop of Mr. *Bains* in White-Horse-Yard of 24 Yards of Fustian. Of his breaking and entering the House of the said Mr. *Bains*, and stealing in Goods and Money to the Value of 20 l. Of his robbing the House of Mr. *Charles* in *May Fair* of Money, Rings, Plate, &c to the Value of 30 l. Of his robbing the House of Mrs. *Cook* in *Clare-Market*, along with his pretended Wife, and his Brother, to the Value of between 50 and 60 l. Of his breaking the Shop of Mr. *Philips* in *Drury-Lane*, with the same Persons, and stealing Goods of small Value. Of his entering the House of Mr. *Carter*, a Mathematical Instrument Maker in *Wytch Street*, along with *Anthony Lamb* and *Charles Grace*, and robbing of Mr. *Barton*, a Master Taylor who lodged therein, of Goods and Bonds to the Value of near 300 l. Of his breaking and entering the House of Mr. *Kneebone*, a Woollen-Draper, near the *New Church* in the *Strand*, in Company of *Joseph Blake* alias *Blewskin* and *William Field*, and stealing Goods to the Value of near 50 l. Of his robbing of Mr. *Pargiter* on the Highway near the Turnpike, on the Road *Hampstead*, along with the said *Blewskin*. Of his robbing a Lady's Woman in her Mistress's Coach on the same Road. Of his robbing also a Stage Coach, with the said *Blewskin*, on the *Hampstead* Road. Likewise of his breaking the Shop of Mr. *Martin* in *Fleet-street*, and stealing 3 silver Watches of 15 l. Value.

ALSO

A particular Account of his rescuing his pretended Wife from St. *Giles*'s Round House. Of the wonderful Escape himself made from the said Round-House. Of the miraculous Escape he and his said pretended Wife made together from *New-Prison*, on the 25th of *May* last. Of his surprizing Escape from the Condemn'd Hold of *Newgate* on the 31st of *August*: Together with the true manner of his being retaken; and of his Behaviour in *Newgate*, till the most astonishing, and never to be forgotten Escape he made from thence, in the Night of the 15th of October. The Whole taken from the most authentick Accounts, as the Informations of divers Justices of the Peace, the several Shopkeepers above-mentioned, the principal Officers of *Newgate* and *New Prison*, and from the Confession of *Sheppard* made to the Rev. Mr. *Wagstaff*, who officiated for the Ordinary at *Newgate*.

LONDON: Printed and sold by JOHN APLEDEE in *Black-Fryers*, J. ISTED, at the *Golden-Ball* near *Chancery Lane* in *Fleet Street*, and the Booksellers of *London* and *Westminster*. (Price One Shilling.)

TO THE
CITIZENS
OF
London and *Westminster.*

GENTLEMEN,

Experience has confirm'd you in that everlasting Maxim, *that there is no other way to protect the* Innocent, *but by Punishing the* Guilty.

Crimes ever were, and ever must be unavoidably frequent in such populous Cities as yours are, being the necessary Consequences, either of the Wants, *or the* Depravity, *of the lowest part of the* humane *Species.*

At this time the most flagrant Offences, as Burning *of* Dwellings; Burglaries, *and* Highway Robberies *abound; and* Frauds *common* Felonies, *and* Forgeries *are practic'd without Number; thus not only your Properties, but even your very Lives are every way struck at.*

The Legislative Power *has not been wanting in providing necessary and wholesome Laws against these* Evils, *the executive part whereof (according to your great Privileges) is lodged in your own Hands: And the Administration hath at all times applyed proper Remedies and Regulations to the Defects which have happen'd in the Magistracy more immediately under their Jurisdiction.*

Through the just and salutary Severities of the Magistrates, publick excessive Gaming has been in a manner Surpress'd; and some late Examples of divine Vengeance have overtaken certain of the most notorious lewd Prostitutes of the Town, which together with the laudable endeavours of the great and worthy Societies, has given no small check to that enormous and spreading Vice.

But here's a Criminal *bids Defiance to your Laws, and* Justice *who declar'd and has manifested that the Bars are not made that can either keep him Out, or keep him In, and accordingly hath a second time fled from the very Bosom Of Death.*

His History will astonish! and is not compos'd of Fiction, Fable, or Stories plac'd at York, Rome, *or* Jamaica, *but* Facts *done at your Doors,* Facts *unheard of, altogether new, Incredible, and yet Uncontestable.*

He is gone once more upon his wicked Range in the World. Restless Vengeance is pursuing, and Gentlemen *'tis to be hoped that she will be assisted by your Endeavours to bring to Justice this notorious Offender.*

THE
LIFE
OF
JOHN SHEPPARD, &c.

THIS *John Sheppard*, a Youth both in Age and Person, tho' an old Man in Sin; was Born in the Parish of *Stepney* near *London*, in the Year 1702, a Son, Grandson, and great Grandson of a *Carpenter*: His Father died when he was so very Young that he could not recollect that ever he saw him. Thus the burthen of his Maintenance, together with his Brother's and Sister's, lay upon the Shoulders of the Widow Mother, who soon procured an Admittance of her Son *John* into the *Work-House* in *Bishopsgate-Street*, where he continued for the space of a Year and half, and in that time received an Education sufficient to qualifie him for the Trade his Mother design'd him, *viz.* a *Carpenter*: Accordingly she was recommended to Mr. *Wood* in *Witch-Street* near *Drury-Lane*, as a Master capable of entertaining and instructing her Son: They agreed and Bound he was for the space of seven Years; the Lad proved an early profficient, had a ready and ingenious Hand, and soon became Master of his Business, and gave entire Satisfaction to his Master Customers, and had the Character of a very sober and orderly Boy. But alas unhappy Youth! before he had compleated six Years of his Apprenticeship, he commenced a fatal Acquaintance with one *Elizabeth Lyon*, otherwise call'd *Edgworth Bess*, from a Town of that Name in *Middlesex* where she was Born, the reputed Wife of a Foot Soldier, and who lived a wicked and debauch'd Life; and our young *Carpenter* became Enamour'd of her, and they must Cohabit together as Man and Wife.

Now was laid the Foundation of his Ruin; *Sheppard* grows weary of the Yoke of Servitude, and began to dispute with his

Master; telling him that his way of Jobbing from House to House'
was not sufficient to furnish him with a due Experience in his
Trade; and that if he would not set out to undertake some
Buildings, he would step into the World for better Information.
Mr. *Wood* a mild, sober, honest Man, indulg'd him; and Mrs.
Wood with Tears, exhorted him against the Company of this
lewd Prostitute: But her Man prompted and harden'd by his
HARLOT, D——n'd *her Blood*, and threw a Stick at his Mistress, and beat her to the Ground. And being with his Master at
Work at Mr. *Britt*'s the *Sun* Ale-house near *Islington*, upon a very
trivial Occasion fell upon his Master, and beat and bruised him
in a most barbarous and shameful Manner. Such a sudden and
deplorable Change was there in the Behaviour of this promising
young Man. Next ensued a neglect of Duty, both to God and his
Master, lying out of Nights, perpetual Jarrings, and Animosities;
these and such like, were the Consequences of his intimacy with
this she *Lyon*; who by the sequel will appear to have been a main
loadstone in attracting of him up to this Eminence of Guilt.

Mr. *Wood* having Reason to suspect, that *Sheppard* had robb'd
a Neighbour, began to be in great Fear and Terror for himself.
And when his Man came not Home in due season at Nights bar'd
him out; but he made a mere jest of the Locks and Bolts, and
enter'd in, and out at Pleasure; and when Mr. *Wood* and his Wife
have had all the Reason in the World to believe him Lock't out,
they have found him very quiet in his Bed the next Morning,
such was the power of his early Magick.

Edgworth Bess having stol'n a Gold Ring from a Gentleman,
whom she had pick'd up in the Streets, was sent to St. *Giles*'s
Roundhouse; *Sheppard* went immediately to his Consort, and
after a short Discourse with Mr. *Brown* the Beadle, and his Wife,
who had the Care of the Place, he fell upon the poor old Couple,
took the Keys from them, and let his Lady out at the Door in
spight of all the Out-cryes, and Opposition they were capable
of making.

About *July* 1723, He was by his Master sent to perform a
Repair, at the House of Mr. *Bains*, a Piece-Broker in *White-Horse
Yard*; he from thence stole a Roli of Fustain, containing 24 Yards,
which was afterwards found in his Trunk. This is supposed to be

the first Robbery he ever committed and it was not long e're he Repeated another upon this same Mr. *Bains*, by breaking into his House in the Night-time, and taking out of the *Till* seven Pounds in Money, and Goods to the value of fourteen Pounds more. How he enter'd this House, was a Secret till his being last committed to *Newgate*, when he confessed that he took up the Iron Bars at the Cellar Window, and after he had done his Business, he nailed them down again, so that Mr. *Bains* never believed his House had been broke; and an innocent Woman a Lodger in the House lay all the while under the weight of a suspicion of committing the Robbery.

Sheppard and his Master had now parted, ten Months before the expiration of his Apprenticeship, a woeful parting to the former; he was gone from a good and careful Patronage, and lay expos'd to, and comply'd with the Temptations of the most wicked Wretches this Town could afford as *Joseph Blake*, alias *Blewskins, William Field, Doleing, James Sykes*, alias *Hell* and *Fury*, which last was the first that betray'd, and put him into the Hands of Justice, as will presently appear.

Having deserted his Master's Service, he took Shelter in the House of Mr. *Charles* in *May-Fair*, near *Piccadilly*, and his Landlord having a Necessity for some Repairs in his House, engag'd one Mr. *Panton* a *Carpenter* to Undertake them, and *Sheppard* to assist him as a Journeyman; but on the 23rd of *October*, 1723, e're the Work was compleat, *Sheppard* took Occasion to rob the People of the Effects following, *viz.* seven Pound ten Shillings in Specie, five large silver Spoons, six plain Forks ditto, four Tea-Spoons, six plain Gold Rings, and a Cypher Ring; four Suits of Wearing Apparel, besides Linnen, to a considerable value. This Fact he confess'd to the Reverend Mr. *Wagstaff* before his Escape from the Condemn'd Hold of *Newgate*.

Sheppard had a Brother, nam'd *Thomas*, a *Carpenter* by Profession, tho' a notorious Thief and House-breaker by Practice. This *Thomas* being committed to *Newgate* for breaking the House of Mrs. *Mary Cook* a *Linnen-Draper*, in *Clare-street, Clare-Market*, on the 5th of *February* last, and stealing Goods to the value of between 50, and 60 l. he impeach'd his Brother *John Sheppard*, and *Edgworth Bess* as being concerned with him in the Fact; and

8*

these three were also Charg'd with being concern'd together, in breaking the House of Mr. *William Phillips* in *Drury-Lane*, and stealing divers Goods, the Property of Mrs. *Kendrick* a Lodger in the House, on the 14th of the said *February*: All possible endeavours were us'd by Mrs. *Cook* and Mr. *Phillips*, to get *John Sheppard* and *Edgworth Bess* Apprehended, but to no purpose, till the following Accident.

Sheppard was now upon his wicked Range in *London*, committing Robberies every where at Discretion; but one Day meeting with his Acquaintance, *James Sykes*, alias *Hell* and *Fury*, sometimes a Chair-man, and at others a Running Foot-man. This *Sykes* invited him to go to one *Redgate's*, a Victualling-house near the *Seven Dials*, to play at *Skettles*, *Sheppard* comply'd, and *Sykes* secretly sent for Mr. *Price* a Constable in St. *Giles's Parish*, and Charg'd him with his Friend *Sheppard* for the Robbing of Mrs. *Cook*, &c. *Sheppard* was carried before Justice *Parry*, who order'd him to St. *Giles's* Round-house till the next Morning for farther Examination: He was Confin'd in the Upper part of the Place, being two Stories from the Ground, but 'ere two Hours came about, by only the help of a Razor, and the Stretcher of a Chair, he broke open the Top of the Round house, and tying together a Sheet and Blanket, by them descended into the Church-yard and Escap'd, leaving the Parish to Repair the Damage, and Repent of the Affront put upon his Skill and Capacity.

On the 19th of *May* last in the Evening, *Sheppard* with another Robber named *Benson*, were passing thro' *Leicester-fields*, where a Gentleman stood accusing a Woman with an attempt to steal his Watch, a Mobb was gathered about the Disputants, and *Sheppard's* Companion being a *Master*, got in amongst them and pick'd the Gentleman's Pocket in good earnest of the Watch; the Scene was surprizingly chang'd, from an imaginary Robbery to a real one; and in a moment ensued an Out-cry of *stop Thief*, *Sheppard* and *Benson* took to their Heels, and *Sheppard* was seiz'd by a Serjeant of the Guard at *Leicester* House, crying out *stop Thief* with much earnestness. He was convey'd to St. *Ann's* Round House in *Soho*, and kept secure till the next Morning, when *Edgworth Bess* came to visit him, who was seiz'd also; they were carried before Justice *Walters*, when the People in *Drury-Lane* and *Clare-Market* appeared, and charged them with the Robberies aforemention'd: But *Sheppard* pretending to Impeach certain of his Accomplices, the Justice committed them to *New-Prison*, with intent to have them soon removed to *Newgate*, unless there came from them some useful Discoveries. *Sheppard* was now a second time in the hands of Justice, but how long he intended to keep in them, the Reader will soon be able to Judge.

He and his MATE were now in a strong and well guarded Prison, himself loaded with a pair of double *Links* and *Basils*[17] of about fourteen pounds weight, and confined together in the safest Appartment call'd *Newgate Ward*; *Sheppard* conscious of his Crimes, and knowing the *Information* he had made to be but a blind Amusement that would avail him nothing; he began to Meditate an Escape. They had been thus detained for about four Days, and their Friends having the Liberty of seeing them, furnish'd him with Implements proper for his Design, accordingly Mr. *Sheppard* goes to work, and on the 25th of *May* being *Whitson Monday* at about two of the Clock in the Morning, he had compleated a practicable breach, and sawed of his Fetters; having with unheard of Diligence and Dexterity, cut off an Iron Bar from the Window, and taken out a Muntin, or Bar of the most solid Oak of about nine Inches in thickness, by boring it thro' in many Places, a work of great Skill and Labour; they had still five and twenty Foot to descend from the Ground; *Sheppard* fasten'd a Sheet and Blanket to the Bars, and causes Madam to take off her Gown and Petticoat, and sent her out first, and she being more Corpulent than himself, it was with great Pain and Difficulty that he got her through the Interval, and observing his Directions, was instantly down, and more frighted than hurt; the *Phylosopher* follow'd, and lighted with Ease and Pleasure; But where are they Escap'd to? Why out of one Prison into another. The Reader is to understand, that the *New Prison* and *Clerkenwell Bridewell* lye Contiguous to one another, and they are got into the Yard of the latter, and have a Wall of twenty-two Foot high to Scale, before their Liberty is perfected; *Sheppard* far from being unprepared to surmount this Difficulty, has his Gimblets and Peircers ready, and makes a Scaleing-Ladder. The Keepers and Prisoners of both Places are a sleep in their Beds; he Mounts his *Bagage*, and in less than ten Minutes carries both her and himself over this wall, and compleats an entire Escape. Altho' his Escape from the Condemn'd Hold of *Newgate*, has made a far greater Noise in the World, than that from this Prison hath. It has been allow'd by all the Jayl-Keepers in *London*, that one so Miraculous was never perform'd before in *England*; the broken Chains and Bars are kept at *New Prison* to Testifie, and preserve the Memory of this extraordinary Villain.

Sheppard not warn'd by this Admonition, returns like a *Dog to his Vomit*, and comes Secretly into his Master *Wood's* Neighbourhood in *Witch-street*, and concerts Measures with one *Anthony Lamb*, an Apprentice to Mr. *Carter* a Mathematical Instrument-maker, for Robbing of Mr. *Barton* a Master Taylor; a Man of Worth and Reputation, who Lodg'd in Mr. *Carter's* House. *Charles Grace*, a graceless Cooper was let into the Secret, and consented, and resolved to Act his Part. The 16th of *June* last was appointed, *Lamb* accordingly lets *Grace* and *Sheppard* into the House at Mid-Night; and they all go up to Mr. *Barton's* Appartment well arm'd with Pistols, and enter'd his Rooms, without being disturb'd. *Grace* was Posted at Mr. *Barton's* Bedside with a loaded Pistol, and positive Orders to shoot him through the Head, if in case he awak'd. *Sheppard* being engag'd in opening the Trunks and Boxes, the mean while. It luckily happen'd for Mr. *Barton*, that he slept Sounder than usual that Night, as having come from a Merry-making with some Friends; tho' poor Man little Dreaming in what dreadful Circumstances. They carried off in Notes, and Bonds, Guineas, Cloaths, Made and Unmade, to the value of between two and three Hundred Pounds; besides a Padesuoy Suit of Cloaths, worth about eighteen or twenty Pounds more; which having been made for a Corpulent Gentleman, *Sheppard* had them reduc'd, and fitted for his own Size and War, as designing to Appear and make a Figure among the *Beau Monde*. *Grace* and *Sheppard*, having disposed of the Goods at an Ale-house in *Lewkenors Lane* (a Rendezvous of Robbers and Ruffians) took their Flight, and *Grace* had not been since heard of. *Lamb* was apprehended, and carried before Justice *Newton*, and made an ample Confession; and there being nothing but that against him at his Tryal, and withal, a favourable Prosecution, he came off with a

Sentence of Transportation only. He as well as *Sheppard* has since confirm'd all the above particulars, and with this Addition, *viz.* That it was Debated among them to have Murder'd all the People in the House, save one Person.

About the latter End of the same Month, *June*, Mr. *Kneebone*, a Woollen-Draper near the New Church in the *Strand*, receiv'd a Caution from the Father of *Anthony Lamb*, who intimated to Mr. *Kneebone* that his House was intended to be broke open and robb'd that very Night. Mr. *Kneebone* prepar'd for the Event, ordering his Servants to sit up, and gave Directions to the Watchman in the Street to observe his House: At about two in the Morning *Sheppard* and his Gang were about the Door, a Maid-Servant went to listen, and heard one of the Wretches, say, *Da——n him, if they could not enter that Night, they would another, and would have 300 l. of his*, (meaning) Mr. *Kneebone's* Money. They went off, and nothing more was heard of them till *Sunday* the 12th Day of *July* following, when *Joseph Blake*, alias *Blewskins*, *John Sheppard*, and *William Field* (as himself Swears) came about 12 o'Clock at Night, and cut two large Oaken-Bars over the Cellar-Window, at the back part of the House in *Little-Drury-Lane*, and so entered; Mr. *Kneebone*, and his Family being at Rest, they proceeded to open a Door at the Foot of the Cellar-Stairs, with three Bolts, and a large Padlock upon it, and then came up into the Shop and wrench'd off the Hasp, and Padlock that went over the Press, and arriv'd at their desir'd Booty; they continu'd in the House for three Hours, and carry'd off with them One Hundred and eight Yards of Broad Woollen Cloth, five Yards of blue Bays, a light Tye-Wig, and Beaver-Hat, two Silver Spoons, an Handkerchief, and a Penknife. In all to the value of near fifty Pounds.

The *Sunday* following, being the 19th of *July*, *Sheppard* and *Blewskins* were out upon the *Hampstead* Road, and there stopt a Coach with a Ladies Woman in it, from whom they took but Half-a-Crown; all the Money then about her; the Footman behind the Coach came down, and exerted himself; but *Sheppard* sent him in hast up to his Post again, by threat of his Pistol.

The next Night being the 20th of *July*, about Nine, they Robb'd Mr. *Pargiter*, a Chandler of *Hamstead*, near the Halfway-House;

Sheppard after his being taken at *Finchley* was particularly examin'd about this Robbery. The Reverend Mr. *Wagstaff* having receiv'd a Letter from an unknown Hand, with two Questions, to be propos'd to *Sheppard*, *viz*. Whether he did Rob *John Pargiter*, on *Monday* the 20th of *July*, about Nine at Night, between the *Turnpike* and *Hamstead*; How much Money he took from him? Whither *Pargiter* was Drunk, or not, and if he had Rings or Watch about him, when robb'd? which, Request was comply'd with, and *Sheppard* affirm'd, that Mr. *Pargiter* was very much in Liquor, having a great Coat on; neither Rings on his Fingers or Watch, and only three Shillings in his Pocket, which they took from him, and that *Blewskins* knock him down twice with the Butt-end of his Pistol to make sure Work, (tho' Excess of drink had done that before) but *Sheppard* did in kindness raise him up as often.

The next Night, *July* 21, they stopt a Stage-Coach, and took from a Passenger in it, Twenty-two Shillings, and were so expeditious in the Matter, that *not two Words were made about the Bargain*.

Now Mr. *Sheppard's* long and wicked Course seemingly draws towards a Period. Mr. *Kneebone* having apply'd to *Jonathan Wild*, and set forth Advertisements in the Papers, complaining of his Robbery. On *Tuesday* the 22d of *July* at Night *Edgworth Bess* was taken in a Brandy-shop, near *Temple-Bar* by *Jonathan Wild*; she being much terrify'd, discover'd where *Sheppard* was: A Warrant was accordingly issued by Justice *Blackerby*, and the next Day he was Apprehended, at the House of *Blewskin's* Mother, in *Rose-Mary-Lane*, by one *Quilt*, a Domestick of Mr. *Wild's* though not without great opposition, for, he clapt a loaded, Pistol to *Quilt's* Breast, and attempted to shoot him, but the Pistol miss'd fire; he was brought back to *New Prison*, confin'd in the Dungeon; and the next Day carried before Justice *Blackerby*. Upon his Examination he Confess'd the three Robberies on the Highway aforemention'd, as also the Robbing of Mr. *Bains*, Mr. *Barton*, and Mr. *Kneebone*, he was committed to Newgate, and at the Sessions of *Oyer* and *Terminer*, and Goal delivery, holden at the *Old-Baily*, on the 12th, 13th and 14th of *August*, he was try'd upon three several indictments, *viz*. First for breaking the House of *William Philips*.

John Sheppard, of the Parish of St. *Martin* in *the Fields*, was indicted for breaking the House of *William Philips*, and stealing divers Goods, the 14th of *February* last. But there not being sufficient Evidence against the Prisoner, he was acquitted.

He was also indicted a Second Time, of St. *Clement Danes*, for breaking the House of *Mary Cook*, the 5th of *February* last, and stealing divers Goods: But the Evidence against the Prisoner being defficient as to this Indictment also, he was acquitted.

He was also indicted the Third Time, of St. *Mary Savoy*, for breaking the House of *William Kneebone*, in the Night-Time, and stealing, 108 Yards of Woollen Cloth, the 12th of *July* last. The Prosecutor depos'd, That the Prisoner had some Time since been his Servant, and when he went to Bed, the Time mentioned in the Indictment, about 11 a-Clock at Night, he saw all the Doors and Windows fast; but was call'd up about four in the Morning, and found his House broke open, the Bars of a Cellar-Window having been cut, and the Bolts of the Door that comes up Stairs drawn, and the Padlock wrench'd off, and the Shutter in the Shop broken, and his Goods gone; whereupon suspecting the Prisoner, he having committed ill Actions thereabouts before, he acquainted *Jonathan Wild* with it, and he procur'd him to be apprehended. That he went to the Prisoners in New *Prison*, and asking how he could be so ungrateful to rob him, after he had shown him so much Kindness? The Prisoner own'd he had been ungrateful in doing so, informing him of several Circumstances as to the Manner of committing the Fact, but said he had been drawn into it by ill Company. *Jonathan Wild*, depos'd, The Prosecutor came to him, and desir'd him to enquire after his Goods that had been stolen, telling him he suspected the Prisoner to have been concern'd in the Robbery, he having before committed some Robberies in the Neighbourhood. That inquiring after him, and having heard of him before, he was inform'd that he was an Acquaintance of *Joseph Blake*, alias *Blewskins*, and *William Field*: Whereupon he sent for *William Field*, who came to him; upon which he told him, if he would make an ingenuous Confession, he believ'd he could prevail with the Court to make him an Evidence. That he did make a Discovery of the Prisoner, upon which he was apprehended, and also of others since convicted, and gave an Account of some Parcels of the Cloth, which were found accordingly. *William Field* depos'd, That the Prisoner told him, and *Joseph Blake*, that he knew a *Ken*[18] where they might get something of Worth. That they went to take a View of the Prosecutor's House, but disprov'd of the Attempt, as not thinking it easy to be perform'd; But the Prisoner perswaded them that it might easily be done, he knowing the House, he having liv'd with the Prosecutor. That thereupon he cut the Cellar Bar, went into the Cellar, got into the Shop, and brought out three Parcels of Cloth, which they carried away. The Prisoner had also confest the Fact when he was apprehended, and before the Justice. The Fact being plainly prov'd, the Jury found him guilty of the Indictment.

Sentence of Death was pronounc'd upon him accordingly. Several other Prosecutions might have been brought against him, but this was thought sufficient to rid the World of so Capital an Offender: He beg'd earnestly for Transportation, to the most extream Foot of his Majesty's Dominions; and pleaded Youth, and Ignorance as the Motive which had precipitated him into the Guilt; but the Court deaf to his Importunities, as knowing him, and his repeated Crimes to be equally flagrant, gave him no satisfactory Answer: He return'd to his dismal Abode the Condemn'd Hold, where were Nine more unhappy Wretches in as dreadful Circumstances as himself. The Court being at *Windsor*, the Malefactors had a longer Respite than is usual; during that Recess, *James Harman, Lumley, Davis* and *Sheppard* agreed upon an Escape, concerted Measures, and provided Instruments to make it effectual; but put off the Execution of their Design, on Account the two Gentlemen having their hopes of Life daily renewed by the favourable Answers they receiv'd from some considerable Persons; but those vanishing the day before their Execution, and finding their Sentence irreversible, they two dropt their hopes, together with the Design, they form'd for an Escape, and so in earnest prepar'd to meet Death on the Morrow, (which they accordingly did.). 'Twas on this Day Mr *Davis* gave *Sheppard* the Watch Springs, Files, Saws, &c. to Effect his own Release; and knowing that a Warrant was Hourly expected for his Execution with Two others, on the *Friday* following; he thought it high time to look about him, for he had waited his Tryal, saw his Conviction, and heard his Sentence with some patience; but finding himself irrespitably decreed for Death, he could sit passive no longer, and on the very Day of the Execution of the former; whilst they were having their Fetters taken off, in order for going to the Tree, that Day he began to saw, *Saturday* made a progress; but *Sunday* omitted, by Reason of the Concourse in the *Lodge*: *Edgworth Bess* having been set at Liberty, had frequent Access to him, with others of his Acquaintance. On *Monday* the Death *Warrant* came from *Windsor*, appointing that he, together with *Joseph Ward* and *Anthony Upton* should be Executed on the *Friday* following, being the 4th of *September*. The Keepers acquainted him therewith, and desired him to make good use of that short Time. He thank'd them, said *he would follow their Advice*, and *prepare*. *Edgworth Bess*, and another Woman had been with him at the Door of the Condemn'd Hold best part of the Afternoon, between five and six he desir'd the other Prisoners, except *Stephen Fowles* to remain above, while he offer'd something in private to his Friends at the Door; they comply'd, and in this interval he got the Spike asunder, which made way for the Skeleton to pass with his Heels foremost, by the Assistance of *Fowles*, whom he most ungenerously betray'd to the Keepers after his being retaken, and the Fellow was as severely punish'd for it.

Having now got clear of his Prison, he took Coach disguis'd in a Night Gown at the corner of the *Old Baily*, along with a Man who waited for him in the Street (and is suppos'd to be *Page* the Butcher) ordering the Coachman to drive to *Black-Fryers Stairs*, where his prostitute gave him the Meeting, and they three took Boat, and went a Shoar at the *Horse-Ferry* at *Westminster*, and at the *White-Hart* they went in, Drank, and stay'd sometime; thence they adjourn'd to a Place in *Holbourn*, where by the help of a Saw he quitted the Chains he had brought with him from *Newgate*; and then like a Freeman took his Ramble through the City and came to *Spittle-Fields*, and there lay with *Edgeworth Bess*.

It may be easy to imagine what an alarm his Escape gave to the Keepers of *Newgate*, three of their People being at the farther End of the *Lodge*, engag'd in a Discourse concerning his wonderful

Escape from *New-Prison*, and what Caution ought to be us'd, lest he should give them the slip, at that very Instant as he perfected it.

On *Tuesday* he sent for *William Page* an Apprentice to a Butcher in *Clare-Market*, who came to him, and being Pennyless, he desir'd *Page* to give him what Assistance he could to make his way, and being a Neighbour and Acquaintance, he comply'd with it; but e're he would do any thing, he consulted a near Relation, who as he said, encourag'd him in it; nay, put him upon it, so meeting with this Success in his Application to his Friend, and probable an Assistance in the Pocket, he came to *Sheppard* having bought him a new blue *Butcher's* Frock, and another for himself, and so both took their Rout to *Warnden* in *Northamptonshire*, where they came to a Relation of *Page's*, who receiv'd and Entertain'd them kindly, the People lying from their own Bed to Accommodate them. *Sheppard* pretending to be a *Butcher's* Son in *Clare-Market*, who was going farther in the Country to his Friends, and that *Page* was so kind as to Accompany him; but they as well as their Friend became tir'd of one another; the *Butchers* having but one Shilling left, and the People poor, and Consequently unable to Subsist two such Fellows, after a stay of three or four Days, they return'd, and came for *London*, and reach'd the City on *Tuesday* the 8th of *September*, calling by the way at *Black-Mary's-Hole*, and Drinking with several of their Acquaintance, and then came into *Bishopsgate street*, to one *Cooley's* a *Brandyshop*; where a *Cobler* being at Work in his Stall, stept out and Swore *ther was* Sheppard, *Sheppard* hearing him, departed immediately. In the Evening they came into *Fleet-street*, at about Eight of the Clock, and observing Mr. *Martin's* a Watchmaker's Shop to be open, and a little Boy only to look after it: *Page* goes in and asks the Lad whether Mr. *Taylor* a *Watchmaker* lodg'd in the House? being answer'd in the Negative, he came away, and Reports the Disposition of the Place: *Sheppard* now makes Tryal of his old Master-peice; fixeth a Nail Peircer into the Door post, fastens the Knocker thereto with Packthread, breaks the Glass, and takes out three *Silver Watches* of 15 l. value, the Boy seeing him take them, but could not get out to pursue him, by reason of his Contrivance. One of the

Watches he Pledg'd for a Guinea and Half. The same Night they came into *Watch-street*, *Sheppard* going into his *Master's* Yard, and calling for his Fellow 'Prentice, his Mistress heard, knew his Voice, and was dreadfully frightened; he next went to the *Cock and Pye Ale-House* in *Drury-Lane*, sent for a Barber his Acquaintance, drank Brandy and eat Oysters in the view of several people. *Page* waiting all the while at the Door, the whole Neighbourhood being alarm'd, yet none durst attempt him, for fear of Pistols, &c. He had vow'd Revenge upon a poor Man as kept a Dairy-Cellar, at the End of *White-Horse-Yard*, who having seen him at *Islington* after his Escape, and engag'd not to speak of it, broke his Promise; wherefore *Sheppard* went to his Residence took the Door off the Hinges and threw it down amongst all the Man's Pans, Pipkins, and caus'd a Deluge of Cream and Milk all over the Cellar.

This Night he had a narrow Escape, one Mr. *Ireton* a Sheriffs Officer seeing him and *Page* pass thro' *Drury-Lane*, at about Ten o'Clock pursu'd 'em, and laid hold of *Page* instead of *Sheppard*, who got off, thus *Ireton*, missing the main Man, and thinking *Page* of no Consequence, let him go after him.

Edgworth Bess had been apprehended by *Jonathan Wild*, and by Sir *Francis Forbes* one of the Aldermen of *London*, committed to the *Poultry-Compter*, for being aiding and assisting to *Sheppard* in his Escape; the Keepers and others terrify'd and purg'd her as much as was possible to discover where he was, but had it been in her Inclination, it was not in her Power so to do, as it manifestly appear'd soon after.

The People about the *Strand*, *Witch-street* and *Drury-Lane*, whom he had Robb'd, and who had prosecuted him were under great Apprensions and Terror, and in particular Mr. *Kneebone*, on whom he vow'd a bloody Revenge; because he refus'd to sign a Petition in his behalf to the *Recorder* of *London*. This Gentleman was forc'd to keep arm'd People up in his House every Night till he was Re-taken, and had the same fortify'd in the strongest manner. Several other Shop-keepers in this Neighbourhood were also put to great Expence and Trouble to Guard themselves against this dreadful Villian.

The Keepers of *Newgate*, whom the rash World loaded with Infamy, stigmatiz'd and branded with the Title of Persons guilty of Bribery; for Connivance at his Escape, they and what Posse in their Power, either for Love or Money did Contribute their utmost to undeceive a wrong notion'd People. Their Vigilance was remarkably indefatigable, sparing neither Money nor Time, Night nor Day to bring him back to his deserv'd Justice. After many Intelligences, which they endeavour'd for, and receiv'd, they had one which prov'd very Successful. Having learnt for a certainty that their Haunts was about *Finchly Common*, and being very well assur'd of the very House where they lay; on *Thursday* the 10th of *September*, a posse of Men, both of Spirit and Conduct, furnish'd with Arms proper for their Design, went for *Finchley*, some in a Coach and Four, and others on Horseback. They dispers'd themselves upon the *Common* aforesaid, in order to make their View, where they had not been long e're they came in Sight of *SHEPPARD* in Company of *WILLIAM PAGE*, habited like two *Butchers* in new blue Frocks, with white Aprons tuck'd round their Wastes.

Upon *Sheppard's* seeing *Langley* a Turnkey at *Newgate*, he says to his Companion *Page*, *I see a Stag*; upon which their Courage dropt; knowing that now their dealing way of Business was almost at an End; however to make their Flight as secure as they could, they thought it adviseable to take to a Foot-path, to cut off the pursuit of the *Newgate Cavalry*; but this did not prove most successful, *Langley* came up with *Page* (who was hindermost) and Dismounting with Pistol in Hand, commands *Page* to throw up his Hands, which he trembling did, begging for Life, desiring him to *Fisk* him, *viz.* (search him,) which he accordingly did, and found a broad Knife and File; having thus disarm'd him, he takes the *Chubb* along with him in quest of the slippery *Ele*, *Sheppard*; who had taken Shelter in an old Stable, belonging to a Farm-House; the pursuit was close, the House invested, and a Girl seeing his Feet as he stood up hid, discover'd him. *Austin* a Turnkey first attach'd his Person. *Langley* seconded him, *Ireton* an Officer help'd to Enclose, and happy was the hindermost who aided in this great Enterprise. He being shock'd with the utmost Fear, told them he submitted, and desir'd they would let him live as long as he could, which they did, and us'd him mildly; upon searching him they found a broad Knife with two of the Watches as he had taken out of Mr. *Martin's* Shop, one under each Armpit; and now having gain'd their Point, and made themselves Masters of what they had often endeavoured for, they came with their *Lost Sheep* to a little House on the *Common* that sold Liquors, with this Inscription on the Sign, *I have brought my Hogs to a fair Market*; which our two unfortunate *Butchers* under their then unhappy Circumstances, had too sad Reason to apply to themselves. *Sheppard* had by this time recover'd his Surprize, grew calm and easy, and desir'd them to give him Brandy, they did, and were all good Friends, and Company together.

They adjourn'd with their Booty to another Place, where was waiting a Coach and Four to Convey it to Town, with more Speed and Safety; and Mr. *Sheppard* arriv'd at his old Mansion, at about two in the Afternoon. At his a-lighting, he made a sudden Spring; He declar'd his Intention was to have slipt under the Coach, and had a Race for it; he was put into the Condemn'd-Hold, and Chain'd down to the Floor with double *Basils* about his Feet, &c. *Page* was carried before Sir *Francis Forbes* and committed to the same Prison for Accompanying and aiding *Sheppard* in his Escape. The prudence of Mr. *Pitt* caus'd a Separation between him and his Brother the first Night, as a Means to prevent any ensuing Danger, by having two Heads, which (according to our Proverbial Saying) *are better than one*.

The Joy the People of *Newgate* conceiv'd on this Occasion is inexpressible, *Te Deum* was Sung in the *Lodge*, and nothing but Smiles, and Bumpers, were seen there for many Days together. But *Jonathan Wild* unfortunately happen'd to be gone upon a wrong Scent after him to *Sturbridge*, and Lost a Share of the Glory.

His Escape and his being so suddenly Re-taken made such a Noise in the Town, that it was thought all the common People would have gone Mad about him; there being not a *Porter* to be had for Love nor Money, nor getting into an Ale-house, for *Butchers; Shoemakers* and *Barbers*, all engag'd in Controversies, and Wagers, about *Sheppard*. *Newgate* Night and Day surrounded with the Curious from St. *Giles*'s and *Rag-Fair*, and *Tyburn Road* daily lin'd with Women and Children; and the *Gallows* as carefully watch'd by Night, lest he should be hang'd *Incog*. For a Report of that nature, obtain'd much upon the Rabble; In short,

it was a Week of the greatest Noise and Idleness among Mecha-
nicks that has been known in *London*, and *Parker* and *Pettis*, two
Lyricks, subsisted many Days very comfortably upon *Ballads* and
Letters about *Sheppard*. The vulgar continu'd under great Doubts
and Difficulties, in what would be his Case, and whether the *Old
Warrant*, or a *New One* must be made for his Execution, or a New
Tryal, *&c.* were the great Questions as arose, and occasion'd
various Reasonings and Speculation, till a News Paper, call'd the
Daily Journal set them all to Rights by the Publication of the
Account following, *viz.*

'*J. Sheppard* having been Convicted of Burglary, and Felony, and
received Sentence of Death, and afterwards 'Escap'd from *Newgate*;
and being since Re-taken'; we are assur'd that it must be prov'd in a
Regular, and *Judicial* way, that he is the same Person, who was so Convicted and made his Escape, before a Warrant can be obtain'd for his
Execution; and that this Affair well be brought before the Court at the
Old Baily the next Sessions.'

This was enough; People began to grow calm and easy and got
Shav'd, and their Shoes *finish'd*, and Business returned into its
former Channel, the Town resolving to wait the *Sessions* with
Patience.

The Reverend Mr. *Wagstaff*, who officiated in the absence of
the *Ordinary*, renew'd his former Acquaintance with Mr. *Sheppard*, and examin'd him in a particular manner concerning his
Escape from the Condemn'd Hold: He sincerely disown'd, that
all, or any, belonging to the Prison were privy thereto; but
related it as it has been describ'd. He declar'd that *Edgworth Bess*,
who had hitherto pass'd for his *Wife*, was not really so: This was
by some thought to be in him Base, and Ungenerous in that, as
she had Contributed towards his Escape, and was in Custody on
that Account, it might render her more liable to Punishment,
than if she had been thought his Wife; but he endeavour'd to
acquit himself, by saying, that she was the sole Author of all his
Misfortunes; That she betray'd him to *Jonathan Wild*, at the time
he was taken in *Rosemary-Lane*; and that when he was contriving
his Escape, she disobey'd his orders, as when being requir'd to
attend at the Door of the Condemn'd-Hold by Nine, or Ten in

the Morning to facilitate his Endeavours, she came not till the Evening, which he said, was an ungrateful Return for the care he had taken in setting her at Liberty from *New-Prison*; and thus Justify'd himself in what he had done, and said he car'd not what became of her.

He was also Examined about Mr. *Martin's* Watches; and whether *Page* was privy to that Robbery; he carefully guarded himself against uttering any thing that might affect him, peremptorily declar'd him Innocent of that, as well as of being privy to his Escape, and said, that he only out of Kindness, as being an old Companion, was resolv'd to share in his Fortunes after he had Escap'd.

He was again continually meditating a second Escape, as appear'd by his own Hardiness, and the Instruments found upon him, on *Saturday* the 12th, and *Wednesday* the 16th of *September*, the first Time a small File was found conceal'd in his Bible, and the second Time two Files, a Chisel and an Hammer being hid in the Rushes of a Chair; and whenever a Question was mov'd to him, when, or by what Means those Implements came to his Hands; he would passionately fly out, and say, *How can you? you always ask me these, and such like Questions;* and in a particular manner, when he was ask'd, Whether his Companion *Page* was an Accomplice with him, either in the affair of the Watches, or any other? (he reply'd) *That if he knew, he would give no direct Answer*, thinking it to be a Crime in him to detect the Guilty.

It was thought necessary by the Keepers to remove him from the Condemn'd-Hold to a Place, call'd the *Castle*, in the Body of the Goal, and to Chain him down to two large Iron Staples in the Floor; the Concourse of People of tolerable Fashion to see him was exceeding Great, he was always Chearful and Pleasant to a Degree, as turning almost every thing as was said into a Jest and Banter.

Being one *Sunday* at the Chapel, a Gentleman belonging to the *Lord Mayor*, ask'd a Turnkey, Which was *Sheppard*, the Man pointed to him? Says *Sheppard, yes Sir, I am the* Sheppard, *and all the Goalers in the Town are my Flock, and I cannot stir into the Country, but they are all at my Heels* Baughing, *after me, &c.*

He told Mr. *Robins*, the *City Smith*, *That he had procur'd him a*

small Job, and that whoever it was that put the Spikes on the Con-
demn'd-Hold was an honest Man, for a better peice of Metal, says he,
I never wrought upon in my Life.

He was loth to believe his frequent Robberies were an Injury
to the Public, for he us'd to say, That *if they were ill in one Respeƈt,*
they were as good in another, and that though he car'd not for Working
much himself, yet he was desirous that others should not stand Idle,
more especially those of his own Trade, who were always Repairing of
his Breaches.

When serious, and that but seldom, he would Refleƈt on his
past wicked Life. He declar'd to us, that for several Years of his
Apprenticeship he had an utter abhorrence to Women of the
Town, and us'd to pelt them with Dirt when they have fell in his
way; till a *Button-Mould-Maker* his next Neighbour left off that
Business, and set up a Viƈtualling-house in *Lewkenhors-Lane,*
where himself and other young Apprentices resorted on *Sundays,*
and at all other Opportunities. At this House began his Acquaintance with *Edgworth Bess.* His sentiments were strangely alter'd,
and from an Aversion to those Prostitutes, he had a more favourable Opinion, and even Conversation with them, till he Con-
traƈted an ill Distemper, which as he said, he cur'd himself of by a
Medicine of his own preparing.

He inveigh'd bitterly against his Brother *Thomas* for putting
him into the Information, for Mrs. *Cook's* Robberry, and pretended
that all the Mischiefs that attended him was owing to that
Matter. He acknowledg'd that he was concern'd in that Faƈt, and
that his said Brother broke into his Lodgings, and stole from him
all his Share and more of the acquir'd Booty.

He oftentimes averr'd, that *William Field* was no ways concern'd in Mr. *Kneebone's* Robbery; but that being a Brother of
the Quill; *Blewskin* and himself told him the particulars, and
manner of the Faƈts, and that all he Swore against him at his
Tryal was False, and that he had other Authority for it, than
what came out of their (*Sheppard* and *Blewskin*) Mouths, who
aƈtually committed the Faƈt.

And moreover, that *Field* being acquainted with their Ware-
house (a Stable) near the *Horse-Ferry* at *Westminster,* which
Sheppard had hir'd, and usually resposited therein the Goods he

stole. He came one Night, and broke open the same, and carried off the best part of the Effects taken out of Mr. *Kneebone's* Shop.

Sheppard said he thought this to be one of the greatest Villanies that could be acted, for another to come and Plunder them of Things for which they had so honourably ventur'd their Lives, and wish'd that *Field*, as well as his Brother *Tom* might meet with forgiveness for it.

He declar'd himself frequently against the Practice of *Whidling*, or *Impeaching*, which he said, had made dreadful Havock among the *Thieves*, and much lamented the depravity of the *Brethren* in that Respect; and said that if all were but such *Tight-Cocks* as himself, the *Reputation* of the *British Thievery* might be carried to a far greater height than it had been done for many Ages, and that there would then be but little Necessity for Jaylors and Hangmen.

These and such like were his constant Discourses, when Company went up with the Turnkeys to the *Castle* to see him, and few or none went away without leaving him Money for his Support; in which he abounded, and did therewith some small Charities to the other Prisoners; however, he was abstemious and sparing enough in his Diet.

Among the many Schemes laid by his Friends, for the preserving himself after his Escape, we were told of a most Remarkable one, propos'd by an ingenious Person, who advis'd, that he might be Expeditiously, and Secretly convey'd to the Palace at *Windsor*, and there to prostrate his Person, and his Case at the Feet of a most Gracious Prince, and his Case being so very singular and new, it might in great probability move the Royal Fountain of unbounded Clemency; but he declin'd this Advice, and follow'd the Judgment and Dictates of *Butchers*, which very speedily brought him very near the Door of the *Slaughterhouse*.

On the 4th of *September*, the Day as *Joseph Ward*, and *Anthony Upton* were Executed, there was publish'd a whimsical Letter, as from *Sheppard*, to *Jack Ketch*, which afforded Diversion to the Town, and Bread to the Author, which is as followeth, *viz*.

SIR,

I Thank you for the Favour you intended me this day: I am a Gentleman, and allow you to be the same, and I hope can forgive Injuries; fond Nature prompted, I obey'd, Oh, propitious Minute! and to show that I am in Charity, I am now drinking your Health, and a *Bon Repo* to poor *Joseph* and *Anthony*. I am gone a few Days for the Air, but design speedily to embark; and this Night I am going upon a Mansion for a Supply; it's a stout Fortification, but what Difficulties can't I encounter, when, dear *Jack*, you find that Bars and Chains are but trifling Obstacles in the way of your Friend and Servant"

From my Residence in   JOHN SHEPPARD.
Terra Australi incognito.

P.S. Pray my Service to Mr. *Or—— di——y* and to Mr. *App——ee.*

On *Saturday* the 10th of *October*, *Anthony Lamb*, and *Thomas Sheppard*, with 95 other Felons were carried from *Newgate* on Shipboard, for Transportation to the Plantations; the last begg'd to have an opportunity given him of taking his final Leave of his Brother *John*; but this was not to be Granted, and the greatest Favour that could be obtain'd, was that on the *Sunday* before they had an Interview at the *Chapel*, but at such a distance, that they neither saluted, or shook Hands, and the Reason given for it, was that no Implements might be convey'd to *Sheppard* to assist him in making an Escape.

This, Caution seem'd to be absolutely necessary, for it appear'd soon after that *Sheppard* found Means to release himself from the Staples to which he was Chain'd in the Castle, by unlocking a great Padlock with a Nail, which he had pickt up on the Floor, and endeavour'd to pass up the Chimney, but was prevented by the stout Iron Bars fix'd in his way, and wanted nothing but the smallest File to have perfected his Liberty. When the Assistants of the Prison, came as usual with his Victuals, they began to examine his Irons; to their great Surprize they found them loose, and ready to be taken off at Pleasure. Mr. *Pitt* the Head Keeper, and his Deputies were sent for, and *Sheppard* finding this Attempt entirely frustrated, discover'd to them by what means he had got them off; and after they had search'd him, found nothing, and Lock'd and Chain'd him down again: He took up the Nail and unlocked the Padlock before their Faces; they were struck with the greatest Amazement as having never heard, or beheld the like before. He was then Handcuff'd, and more effectually Chain'd.

The next Day, the Reverend Mr. *Purney Ordinary* of the Place came from the Country to visit him, and complain'd of the sad Disposition he found him in, as Meditateing on nothing, but Means to Escape, and declining the great Duty incumbent upon him to prepare for his approaching Change. He began to Relent, and said, that since his last Effort had prov'd not Successful, he would entertain no more Thoughts of that Nature, but entirely Dispose, and Resign himself to the Mercy of Almighty God, of whom he hop'd to find forgiveness of his manifold Offences.

He said, that *Edgworth Bess* and himself kept a little Brandy-shop together in *Lewkenhors-Lane*, and once sav'd about Thirty Pounds; but having such an universal Acquaintance amongst Theives, he had frequent calls to go *Abroad*, and soon quitted that Business, and his Shop.

On *Friday* the 2d, of *October* his old Confederate *Joseph Blake* alias *Blewskin*, was apprehended and taken at a House in St. *Giles's* Parish by *Jonathan Wild*, and by Justice *Blackerby* committed to *Newgate*. *William Field* who was at his liberty, appearing and making Oath, that *Blewskin* together with *John Sheppard* and himself, committed the Buglary and Felony in Mr. *Kneebone's* House, for which *Sheppard* was Condemn'd.

The Sessions commencing at the *Old-Bailey* on *Wednesday* the 14th of *October* following, an Indictment was found against *Blewskin* for the same, and he was brought down from *Newgate* to the *Old-Bailey* to be Arraign'd in order to his Tryal; and being in the Yard within the Gate before the Court: Mr. *Wild* being there Drinking a glass of Wine with him, he said to Mr. *Wild*, *You may put in a word for me, as well as for another Person?* To which Mr. *Wild* reply'd, I cannot do it. *You are certainly a dead Man, and will be tuck'd up very speedily*, or words to that effect: Whereupon *Blewskin* on a sudden seiz'd Mr. *Wild* by the Neck, and with a little Clasp Knife he was provided with he cut his

Throat in a very dangerous Manner; and had it not been for a *Muslin* Stock twisted in several Plaits round his Neck, he had in all likelyhood succeeded in his barbarous Design before *Ballard* the Turnkey, who was at Hand, could have time to lay hold of him; the Villain trumph'd afterwards in what he had done, Swearing many bloody Oaths, that if he had murder'd him, he should have died with Satisfaction, and that his Intention was to have cut off his Head, and thrown it into the Sessions House-Yard among the Rabble, and Curs'd both his Hand and the Knife for not Executing it Effectually.

Mr. *Wild* instantly had the Assistance of three able Surgeons, *viz.* Mr. *Dobbins*, Mr. *Marten* and Mr. *Coletheart*, who sew'd up the Wound, and order'd him to his Bed, and he has continu'd ever since, but in a doubtful State of Recovery.

The Felons on the Common Side of *Newgate*, also animated by *Sheppard's* Example, the Night before they were to be Shipt for Transporation, had cut several Iron Bars assunder, and some of them had saw'd off their Fetters, the rest Huzzaing, and making Noises, under pretence of being Joyful that they were to be remov'd on the Morrow, to prevent the Workmen being heard; and in two Hours time more, if their Design had not been discover'd, near One Hundred Villians had been let loose into the World, to have committed new Depredations; nothing was wanted here but *Sheppard's* great Judgment, who was by himself in the strong Room, call'd the *Castle*, meditating his own Deliverance, which he perfected in the manner following.

On *Thursday* the 15th of this Instant *October*, at between One and Two in the Afternoon, *William Austin*, an Assistant to the Keepers, a Man reputed to be a very diligent, and faithful Servant, went to *Sheppard* in the strong Room, call'd the *Castle*, with his Necessaries, as was his Custom every Day. There went along with him Captain *Geary*, the Keeper of *New Prison*, Mr. *Gough*, belonging to the *Gate-house* in *Westminster*, and two other Gentlemen, who had the Curiosity to see the Prisoner, *Austin* very strictly examined his Fetters, and his Hand-Cuffs, and found them very Safe; he eat his Dinner and talk'd with his usual Gayety to the Company: They took leave of him and wish'd him a good Evening. The Court being sitting at the *Old-Bailey*, the Keepers and most of their Servants were attending there with their Prisoners: And *Sheppard* was told that if he wanted any thing more, then was his Time, because they could not come to him till the next Morning: He thank'd them for their Kindness, and desir'd them to be *as early as possible*.

The same Night, soon after 12 of the Clock Mr. *Bird*, who keeps a Turners-shop adjoyning to *Newgate*, was disturb'd by the Watchman, who found his Street Door open, and call'd up the Family, and they concluding the Accident was owing to the Carelessness of some in the House, shut their Doors, and went to Bed again.

The next Morning *Friday*, at about eight Mr. *Austin* went up as usual to wait on *Sheppard*, and having unlock'd and unbolted the double Doors of the Castle, he beheld almost a Cart-load of Bricks and Rubbish about the Room, and his Prisoner gone: The Man ready to sink, came trembling down again, and was scarce able to Acquaint the People in the *Lodge* with what had happen'd.

The whole Posse of the Prison ran up, and stood like Men depriv'd of their Senses: Their surprize being over, they were in hopes that he might not have yet entirely made his Escape, and got their Keys to open all the strong Rooms adjacent to the *Castle*, in order to Trace him, when to their farther Amazement, they found the Door ready open'd to their Hands; and the strong Locks, Screws and Bolts broken in pieces, and scatter'd about the Jayl. Six great Doors (one whereof having not been open'd for seven Years past) were forc'd, and it appear'd that he had Descended from the Leads of *Newgate* by a Blanket (which he fasten'd to the Wall by an Iron Spike he had taken from the Hatch of the *Chapel*) on the House of Mr. *Bird*, and the Door on the Leads having been left open, it is very reasonable to conclude he past directly to the Street Door down the Stairs; Mr *Bird* and his Wife hearing an odd sort of a Noise on the Stairs as they lay in their Bed, a short time before the Watchman alarm'd the Family.

Infinite Numbers of Citizens came to *Newgate* to behold *Sheppard's* Workmanship, and Mr. *Pitt* and his Officers very readily Conducted them up Stairs, that the World might be convinc'd there was not the least room to suspect, either a Negligence, or Connivance in the Servants. Every one express'd the greatest Surprize that has been known, and declar'd themselves satisfy'd with the Measures they had taken for the Security of their Prisoner.

One of the Sheriffs came in Person, and went up to the *Castle* to be satisfy'd of the Situation of the Place, &c. Attended by several of the City Officers.

The Court being sat at the *Sessions-House*, the Keepers were sent for and Examin'd, and the Magistrates were in great Consternation, that so horrid a Wretch had escap'd their Justice. It being intended that he should have been brought down to the Court the last Day of the *Sessions*, and order'd for Execution in two or three Days after; if it appear'd that he was the Person Condemn'd for the breaking Mr. *Kneebone's* House, and included in the Warrant for Execution, &c.

Many of the Methods by which this miraculous Escape was effected, remain as yet a Secret, there are some indeed too Evident, the most reasonable Conjecture that has hierto been made, is, that the first Act was his twisting and breaking assunder by the strength of his Hands a small Iron Chain, which together with a great Horse Padlock, (as went from the heavy Fetters about his Legs to the staples) confin'd him to the Floor, and with a Nail open'd the Padlock and set himself at Liberty about the Room: A large flat Iron Bar appears to have been taken out of the Chimney, with the Assistance thereof 'tis plain he broke thro' a Wall of many Foot in Thickness, and made his way from the *Castle* into another strong Room Contiguous, the Door of it not having been open'd since several of the *Preston* Prisoners were Confin'd there about seven Years ago: Three Screws are visibly taken off of the Lock, and the Doors as strong as Art could make them, forc'd open. The Locks and Bolts, either wrench'd or Broke, and the Cases and other Irons made for their Security cut assunder: An Iron Spike broke off from the Hatch in the *Chapel*, which he fix'd in the Wall and fasten'd his Blanket to it, to drop on the Leads of Mr. *Bird's* House, his Stockings were found on the Leads of *Newgate*; 'tis question'd whether sixty Pounds will repair the Damage done to the Jayl.

It will perhaps be inquir'd how all this could be perform'd without his being heard by the Prisoners or the Keepers; 'tis well known that the Place of his Confinement is in the upper part of the Prison, none of the other Felons being Kept any where near him; and 'tis suppos'd that if any had heard him at Work, they would rather have facilitated, than frustrated his Endeavours. In the Course of his Breaches he pass'd by a Door on his Left belonging to the *Common-Side* Felons, who have since Curs'd him heartily for his not giving them an opportunity to kiss his Hand, and lending them a favourable lift when his Hand was in; but that was not a Work proper for Mr. *Sheppard* to do in his then Circumstances.

His Fetters are not to be found any where about the Jayl, from whence 'tis concluded he has either thrown them down some Chimney, or carried them off on his Legs, the latter seems to be Impracticable, and would still render his Escaping in such Manner the more astonishing; and the only Answer that is given to the whole, at *Newgate* is, *That the* Devil *came in Person and assisted him.*

He undoubtedly perform'd most of these Wonders in the darkest part of the Night, and without the least Glimpse of a Candle; a word, he has actually done with his own Hands in a few Hours, what several of the most skilful Artists allow, could not have been acted by a number of Persons furnish'd with proper Implements, and all other Advantages in a full Day.

Never was there anything better Tim'd, the Keepers and all their Assistants being obliged to a strict Attendance on the Sessions at the *Old Bailey*, which held for about a Week; and *Blewskin* having confin'd *Jonathan Wild* to his Chamber, a more favourable opportunity could not have presented for Mr. *Sheppard's* Purposes.

The Jaylors suffer'd much by the Opinion the ignorant Part of the People entertain'd of the Matter, and nothing would satisfie some, but that they not only Conniv'd at, but even assisted him in breaking their own Walls and Fences, and that for this Reason too, *viz.* That he should be at Liberty to instruct and train up others in his Method of House-Breaking; and replenish the Town with a new set of Rogues, to supply the Places of those Transported beyond Sea.

This is indeed a fine way of Judging, the well-known Characters of Mr. *Pitt*, and his Deputies, are sufficient to wipe of such ridiculous Imputations; and 'tis a most lamentable Truth, that they have often-times had in their Charge Villains of the deepest Die; Persons of Quality and great Worth, for whom no Entreaties, no Sums how large soever have been able to interfere between the doleful Prison, and the fatal Tree.

The Officers have done their Duty, they are but Men, and have had to deal with a Creature something more than Man, a *Protæus*, Supernatural, Words cannot describe him, his Actions and Workmanship which are too visible, best testifie him.

On *Saturday* the 17th, *Joseph Blake*, alias *Blewskin*, came upon his Tryal at the *Old Bailey*: *Field* gave the same Evidence against him, as he had formerly done against *Sheppard*; and the Prisoner making but a triffling Defence, the Jury found him Guilty of Buglary and Felony. The Criminal when the Verdict was brought in, made his Obeysances to the Court, *and thank'd them for their Kindness.*

It will be necessary that we now return to the Behaviour of Mr. *Sheppard*, some few Days before his last Flight.

Mr. *Figg* the famous Prize Fighter comeing to see him, in *NEWGATE*, there past some pleasant Raillery between them; and after Mr. *Figg* was gone, *Sheppard* declared he had a Mind to send him a formal Challenge to Fight him at all the Weapons in the strong Room; and that let the Consequence be what it would, he should call at Mr. *Figg's* House in his way to Execution, and drink a merry Glass with him by way of Reconciliation.

A young Woman an Acquaintance of his Mother, who wash'd his Linnen and brought him Necessaries, having in an Affray, got her Eyes beaten Black and Blue; says *Sheppard* to her, *How long hast thou been Married?* Replyes the Wench. *I wonder you can ask me such a Question, when you so well know the Contrary*: Nay, says *Sheppard* again, Sarah *don't deny it, for you have gotten your Certificate in your Face.*

Mr. *Ireton* a Bailiff in *Drury-Lane* having pursued *Sheppard* after his Escape from the Condemn'd-Hold with uncommon Diligence; (for the safety of that Neighbourhood which was the chief Scene of his Villainies) *Sheppard* when Re-taken, declared, he would be even with him for it, and if ever he procur'd his Liberty again, *he would give all his Prisoners an* ACT OF GRACE.

A Gentleman in a jocose way ask'd him to come and take a Dinner with him, *Sheppard* reply'd, *he accepted of the Invitation, and perhaps might take an opportunity to wait on him*; and there is great Reason to believe he has been as good as his Word.

He would complain of his Nights, as saying, *It was dark with him from Five in the Evening, till Seven in the Morning*; and being not permitted to have either a Bed or Candle, his Circumstances were dismal; and that he never slept but had some confus'd Doses, he said he consider'd all this with the Temper of a Philosopher.

Neither his sad Circumstances, nor the solemn Exhortations of the several Divines who visited him, were able to divert him from this ludicrous way of Expression; he said, *They were all Ginger-bread Fellows*, and came rather out of Curiosity, than Charity; and to form *Papers* and *Ballads* out of his Behaviour.

A *Welch* Clergyman who came pretty often, requested him in a particularly Manner to refrain Drinking; (tho' indeed there was no necessity for that Caution) *Sheppard* says, Doctor, *You set an Example and I'll follow*; this was a smart Satyr and Repartee upon the *Parson*, some Circumstances consider'd.

When he was visited in the *Castle* by the Reverend Mr. *Wagstaff*, he put on the Face only of a Preparation for his End, as appear'd by his frequent Attempts made upon his Escape, and when he has been press'd to Discover those who put him upon Means of Escaping, and furnish'd him with Implements, he would passionately, and with a Motion of striking, say, *ask me no such Questions, one File's worth all the Bibles in the World*.

When ask'd if he had not put off all Thoughts of an Escape and Entertain'd none but those of Death, would Answer by way of Question, not directly, whether they thought it possible, or probable for him to Effect his Release, when Manackled in the manner he was. When mov'd to improve the few Minutes that seem'd to remain of his Life; he did indeed listen to, but not regard the Design and Purport of his Admonition, breaking in with something New of his own, either with respect to his former Accomplices, or Actions, and all too with Pleasure and Gayety of Expression.

When in *Chapel*, he would seemingly make his Responses with

9

Devotion; but would either Laugh, or force Expressions (when as an Auditor of the Sermon) be of Contempt, either of the Preacher, or of his Discourse.

In fine, he behav'd so, in Word, and Action, (since re-taken) that demonstrated to the World, that his Escape was the utmost Employ of his Thoughts, whatever Face of Penitence he put on when visited by the Curious.

An Account of SHEPPARD'S Adventures of five Hours imme-
    diately after his Escape from *Newgate*, in a Letter to his Friend.
    DEAR FRIEND!

Over a Bottle of *Claret* you'll give me leave to *declare it*, that I've fairly put the *Vowels* upon the good Folks at *Newgate*, *i.o.u.* When I'm able, I may, or may not discharge my *Fees*, 'tis a *Fee-simple*, for a Man in my Condition to acknowledge; and tho' I'm safe out of *Newgate*, I must yet have, or at least, affect, a *New Gate* by Limping, or Turning my Toes in by making a right *Hand* of my *Feet*. Not *to be long*, for I hate *Prolixity* in all Business: *In short*, after *Filing*, *Defileing*, *Sawing*, when no Body *Saw*. *Climbing* (this *Clime in*) it prov'd a good *Turner* of my Affairs, thro' the House of a *Turner*. Being quite past, and safe from *Estreat* on Person or Chattels, and safe in the *Street*, I thought Thanks due to him who cou'd *Deliver hence*; and immediately (for you must know I'm a *Catholick*) to give Thanks for my Deliverance, I stept amongst the *Grey-Fryers* to come an joyn with me, in saying a *Pater-Noster*, or so, at *Amen-Corner*. The *Fryers* being *Fat* began to *Broil*, and soin after *Boild up* into a Passion to be disturb'd at that time of Night. But being got *Loose* and having no Time to *Lose*, I gave them good Words, and so the Business was done. From thence I soon slip'd through *Ludgate*, but was damnably fearful of an *Old Bailey* always lurking thereabout, who might have brought me to the *Fleet* for being too *Nimble*, besides, I was wonderfully apprehensive of receiving some unwelcome *Huggings* from the *W . . . n* there; therefore with a step and a stride I soon got over *Fleet-ditch*, and (as in Justice I ought) I prais'd the *Bridge* I got over. Being a *Batchelor*, and not being capable to to manage a Bridewell you know. I had no Business near *St. Brides*, so kept the right hand-side, designing to *Pop* into the *Alley* as usual; but fearing to go thro' there, and *harp* too much on the same *String*, it gave an *Allay* to my Intention, and on I went to *Shoe-lane* end but there meeting with a *Bully Hack* of the Town, he wou'd have shov'd me down, which my Spirit resenting, tho' a *brawny Dog*, I soon *Coller'd* him, fell Souse at him, then with his own Cane I *strapp'd* till he was force to *Buckle* too, and hold his *Tongue*, in so much he durst not say his *Soul* was his own, and was glad to pack of at *Last*, and turn his *Heels* upon me: I was glad he was gone you may be sure, and *dextrously* made a *Hand* of my *Feet* under the *Leg-Tavern*; but the very Thoughts of *Fetter-Lane* call'd to mind some Passages, which made me avoid the *Passage* at the end of it, (next to the Coffee House you know) so I soon whip'd over the way, yet going along two wooden *Logger-heads* at *St. Dunstan's* made just them a damn'd Noise about their *Quarters*, but the sight of me made perfectly *Hush* in a *Minute*; now fearing to goe by *Chance-a wry-Lane*, as being upon the *Watch* my self and not to be *debarr'd* at *Temple-Bar*; I stole up *Bell-Yard*, but narrowly escap'd being *Clapper-claw'd* by two Fellows I did not like in the Alley, so was forc'd to goe round with a design to *Sheer-off* into *Sheer-Lane*, but the *Trumpet* sounding at that very time, alarm'd me so, I was forc'd to Grope my way back through *Hemlock-Court*, and take my *Passage* by *Ship-Yard* without the Bar again; but there meeting with one of our trusty Friends, (all Ceremonies a-part) he told me under the *Rose* I must expect no *Mercy* in *St. Clement*'s Parish, for the *Butchers* there on the *Back* on't would *Face* me, and with their *Cleavers* soon bring me down on my *marrow* Bones; you may believe I soon hastened thence, but by this time being Fainty and night Spent, I put forward, and seeing a *Light* near the *Savoy-Gate*, I was resolv'd not to make *Light* of the Opportunity, but call'd for an hearty Dram of *Luther* and *Calvin,* that is, *Mum* and *Geneva* mix'd; but having Fasted so long before, it soon got into my Noddle, and e'er I had gone twenty steps, it had so intirely *Stranded* my Reason, that by the time I came to *Half-Moon-Street* end, it gave a *New-Exchange* to my Senses, and made me quite *Lunatick*.

However, after a little Rest, I stole down *George-Passage* into *Oaf-Alley* in *York-Buildings*, and thence (tho' a vile Man) into

Villiers-Street, and so into the *Strand* again, where having gone a little way, *Hefford's-Harp* at the Sign of the *Irish-Harp*, put me a *Jumping and Dancing* to that degree that I could not forbear making a *Somerset* or two before *Northumberland-House*. I thought once of taking the *Windsor* Coach for my self *John Sheppard*, by the Name of *Crook*——but fearing to be *Hook'd* in before my Journey's End, I stept into *Hedge-Lane*, where two Harlots were up in the *Boughs* (it seems) *Branching* out their Respects to one another, through their Windows, and People beginning to gather thereabout, I ran *Pelmel* to *Piccadilly*, where meeting by meer chance a *Bakers* Cart going to *Turnham-Green*, I being not *Mealy Mouth'd*, nor the Man being *Crusty* I *wheel'd* out of Town.

I did call at *Hammersmith*, having no occasion directly. I shall stay two or three Days in that Neighbourhood, so, if you Direct a letter for Mr. Sligh Bolt, to be left with Mrs. *Tabitha Skymmington* at *Cheesewick*, it's Safety will *Bear Water* by any *Boat*, and come *Current* with the Tyde to

Dear B O B

Yours from the Top
of *Newgate* to the Bottom

J. SHEPPARD.

P.S. If you see *Blewskin*, tell him I am well, and hope he receiv'd my last—I wou'd write by the *Post* if I durst, but it wou'd be, certainly *Post-pon'd* if I did, and it would be *stranger* too, to trust a Line by a *Stranger*, who might *Palm* upon us both and never Deliver it to *Hand*.

I send this by a *Waterman*, (I dare trust) who is very Merry upon me, and says he wou'd not be in my *Jacket*.
Saturday Octob. 17, 1724.

We shall conclude with what had been often observ'd by many Persons to *Sheppard*; *viz.* That it was very Imprudent in him to take Shelter in the City, or the adjacent Parts of it, after his Escape from the Condemn'd Hold; and withal to commit a *Capital Offence*, almost within Sight of *Newgate*, when his Life and all was in such Danger. His Reply was general, *viz.* That it was his Fate: But being ask'd a particular Reason for his not taking a longer Rout than the City, and the Neighbouring parts: pleaded Poverty as his Excuse for Confinement within those Limits; at the same time urging, that had he been Master at that time of five Pounds, *England* should not have been the Place of his Residence, having a good Trade in his Hands to live in any populated Part of the World.

FINIS

THE

MEMOIRS

OF

Maj^r. *Alexander Ramkins,*

A

HIGHLAND OFFICER,

Now in Prison at

A V I G N O N, &c.

THE

MEMOIRS

OF

Maj^r. *Alexander Ramkins,*

A

HIGHLAND OFFICER,

Now in Prison at

AVIGNON.

BEING

An Account of several remarkable Adventures during about
Twenty Eight Years Service in *Scotland, Germany, Italy,
Flanders* and *Ireland*; exhibiting a very agreeable and in-
structive Lesson of Human Life, both in a Publick and
Private Capacity, in several pleasant Instances of his
Amours, Gallantry, Oeconomy, *&c.*

LONDON: Printed for *R. King* at the *Queen's-head,* and
W. Boreham at the *Angel* in *Pater-noster-row,* 1719.

Price 1*s.* 6*d.* Stich'd, and 2*s.* Bound.

9*

THE
PUBLISHER TO THE READER

I Think it proper to inform the Reader that these Papers were deliver'd into my Hands by a near Kinsman of the Authors, who lately came from the Southern Parts of France *His Design in imparting these Memoirs to me, was (as I quickly perceiv'd) to know my Sentiments of the Performance. It seems the Gentleman had been sour'd by* French *Practises, and was willing that the World should be no longer a Stranger to what was the ground of his distast. The Author appears very well qualify'd for his Task, and opens a Scene of Politicks which the good natur'd part of Mankind will scarce think human Race capable of. Those that are acquainted with the Person of Major Ramkins, assure me, that the late King James never had a more active and diligent Servant, and that he was one never wanting in his Station. If I am of a contrary Opinion to the Publick in judging these Remarks worthy of the Press, 'tis what I do not at present find my self convinc'd of. One Benefit at least may be expected from 'em, that they will induce all true Britains to be cautious, and not imbark themselves in a foreign Interest for the future, if not for the sake of their Country, at least for their own Sakes. I will not anticipate the Contents, but only take the freedom to acquaint the Reader in General. That it will be one of the greatest Paradoxes in future Ages to read, that the Court of St. Germains should have been a Sleep, and impos'd upon for Twenty Eight Years successively, unless their being trick'd by the greatest of Politicians, be a Circumstance to take off from the Surprize.*

THE
MEMOIRS
OF
Alexander Ramkins, &c.

I WAS NOT above Seventeen Years of Age when the Battle of
Gillycranky was fought between the Two Highland Generals, the
Lord Viscount *Dundee* and *Mackay*. And being then a Stripling at
the University of *Aberdeen* and understanding that several Clans
were gathering into a Body in defence of King *James* II I sold my
Books and Furniture of my Lodgings, and equipp'd my self to
observe the Martial Call, I found my self prompted with. I arriv'd
in a few Days near the Field of Battle, and joyn'd my self with a
broken Body of Men who were making up towards the Mountains to recover themselves after the Fatigue of Battle. The
Noviceship I went through in the *Highlands*, was no improper
Foundation for the course Method of living I have been since
engag'd in for above Twenty Seven Years; during which Time,
I have run through all those Hardships which are incident to one
who seeks a Preferment in Fire and Smoak.

While I strolled about in the *Highlands*, it was my good
Fortune to be under the Tuition of an old Officer, who let me
into many of those little Secrets which are not unserviceable to
such as Design to make the whole Earth the Theatre of their Life;
but what I chiefly valued this old Gentleman's Conversation for,
was the Happiness I had to be a Hearer of some of his Politick
Lessons, of which he was a great Master, having furnish'd himself
by Fifty Years Practice, with the best Idea's of that kind.

Upon a certain Day when our Party were out, some upon
Foraging, and others to get Intelligence, I being alone in a Cottage
with this old Captain, and being desirous to know his Opinion of
the Affairs of *Europe* in general, as also what was like to be the

Issue of that Cause we had undertaken. The old Captain willing to satisfy my Curiosity as far as his Skill would reach, pulled out some Remarks he had made upon the Year 1640. Observe, *says* he, Child what I say to you, 'tis a Maxim never to be neglected among Politicians to keep up Divisions in an Enemies Country; you may, perhaps, imagine that this will be a short Game that is a playing, but depend upon it my Grey Hairs will not see an end of it. I allow the King of *France* has declar'd himself a Friend to King *James* II; He is a very powerful Prince, and if he would turn his Forces this Way, and be upon the Defensive near Home, a few Months would bring the War to a Period. But that Monarch has things in his Head which I must not mention. There will be great Skirmishing in the Dominions of *Great Britain*, but no decisive Action if *Lewis le Grand* can hinder it. He takes Cardinal *Richlieu*'s Conduct for a Precedent. It would have been no difficult Task for the *French* to have joyn'd their Forces with King *Charles* I. and have made a short Hand of that Contest between the King and Parliament; but that Politick Cardinal instead of this Method, had Emissaries in the *English* Cabinet to exaggerate Matters between them. The same Method has been observ'd by that Nation ever since; and if *Lewis le Grand* does not make a Politick Use of King *James* II. without doing him any real Service, I shall be very willing to correct my self, and cancel that Paragraph in my Observations.

This was the first Politick Lesson I was entertain'd with by my old Master; which, though at that time my want of Experience did not permit me thoroughly to comprehend, yet since, a Resemblance of Circumstances has often reviv'd it my Mind; nor could I ever be well reconcil'd to that Piece of Morality, That it was a laudable Practice to set People by the Ears together.

The hopes of being releas'd, is the best Support to Men in Misery, and our small Body of Three Hundred Men wou'd not have remain'd so long under Discipline, if Expectation had not been nourish'd with daily Alarms of Assistance from *France*. Our commanding Officer was Romantickly Loyal, and look'd upon every little Hill we scrambled over, as an impregnable Fortress, from whose Summit he often took occasion to Harangue us, as if the Eyes of all *Europe* were upon us, and the Fate of the Three

Kingdoms hung at our Swords Points. But the Truth was, I believe, we were unknown to all Mankind, and if those Villages we march'd by cou'd but secure the Cattle from us, the State was in no great Danger from our Quarter.

As for the Hopes of being assisted from *France*, though our Commander neglected no Pains to instill such a Belief into the Generality of the Soldiers, in order to prolong his Reign in that honourable Post he enjoy'd, yet I read it plainly in my old Captain's Forehead, that *France* was not accustom'd to open their Treasures in countenancing Chimerical Adventures, and that the most we could expect from thence, would be a small *Dunkirk* Privateer, with a Hogshead or two of Brandy to keep the Cause alive, while he was pushing on his Conquests in other Parts of the Globe, in which the Glory and Interest of *France* was more immediately concern'd. For my own Part, as I was resolv'd to pursue my Fortune in the way of Arms, and finding that there was no appearance of *Scotland*'s being a Place of Action, so I advis'd with my old Master what course I should steer to answer the Ends of my Call. The old Gentleman, though he might have deterr'd me from such an Undertaking, by proposing himself as an Instance how little cou'd be gain'd that way, having nothing to show for near Sixty Years Service in the War, but a Bundle of Politick Remarks drawn from the false Steps he and others have made in endeavouring to make their Fortune, yet since every Man must spin out his Thread of Life one way or other, and that that was most likely to succeed well to which a Person found himself most inclinable, so he humour'd my present Dispositions; but at the same time, counsell'd me to Transport my self over to the Continent, where I might meet with something worthy my Curiosity. Islands, *says he*, are commonly won and lost in a Day, nor will they afford you that variety of Stratagems which will make you perfect in the Art of War. After this I only waited for a fit Opportunity to quit the Service I was in, for though I was no farther engaged than in the Quality of a Gentleman Volunteer, yet a Strain of Honour would not permit me to forsake my Companions, unless some more plausible Reason occurr'd to me than what I could invent at that Time. But it was not long before an occasion offered it self to put my Project in Execution.

By moving too and fro our little Army, I was within Twenty Miles of my Mother's House, (for my Father had been dead some Years) having therefor first communicated my Design to my old Master, whom I intended to invite along with me, if he approv'd of my Undertaking.

In conclusion, Things were order'd so, that the old Captain, with myself, and another, were detatch'd out towards the Coast to get Intelligence, and that Night about Eleven we agreeably surpriz'd my Mother who had for several Months been lamenting the Loss of her darling Son, whom she suppos'd to be kill'd at the Battle of *Gillycranky*; for she had not justly inform'd herself of the precise Time I ran away from the College at *Aberdeen*.

I had Two elder Brothers, who both inherited the martial Spirit of our Family, had been a long time absent from Home; one of them was prefer'd in the Emperor's Army in *Hungary*, the other belonging to the Guards of King *James* II follow'd his Fate into *France* and *Ireland*, and afterwards was kill'd in *Ireland*. My father had three small Lordships, which we were equally to be Sharers of, allowing proportionably for my Mothers maintenance, with a Thousand Pounds to be rais'd to marry our only Sister.

Now, as it was my Intention to Travel and gain Experience in the World, so my old Captain put it into my Head to raise a Sum of Money upon the Credit of my Land, assuring me it would prove my best Friend upon all Occasions, for that the World had but a very mean Opinion of Merit when strip'd of other Advantages to recommend it. This Affair took up more Time than my warm Temper could well bear, and the Lawyers threw in so many Delays, that had not the old Captain (who was well acquainted with Business' been at my Elbow to forward Things, I might have lost my Vocation of being a Soldier before any Agreement cou'd have been made. But after two Months were expir'd, I found my self Master of fifteen Hundred Pound, the Price of my share of Land after the Deductions made for my Mother and Sister; Twelve Hundred Pounds I lodg'd with a Banker at *Amsterdam*, the other Three was employ'd for an Equipage, and to supply my Necessities in the Tour I design'd to take. The old Captain I intended to take along with me to be my Guide as well as Adviser; for I saw so many Perfections in him, which the ungrateful World had neglected, That I judg'd it would be an honourable Omen in one that was beginning the World, not to let him leave the Stage of Life unrewarded: But as his Years had render'd him incapable to attend me in my Rambles, so Death came in to release him, and this worthy Person was taken from me about Ten Days before the Time I had fix'd for my Travels. However, I must not let his Memory die, but give the World an Account of him as far as I cou'd gather from the Gentleman when he was disposed to Answer to Questions concerning himself, in which he always behaved himself with a well guarded Modesty.

I learn'd from him, That his Father was the Head of a Clan which was one half cut off by *Oliver Cromwell*, and the other half Transported into the *West-Indies*, with the fifteen Hundred *Scots*, that were condemn'd thither to Slavery by the Protector. My Friend being at that time about Twelve Years old, chose rather to share his Fathers Fate, and view the Western parts of the Worlds, than fall into the Hands of a Person who would stain the Beauty of his tender Mind, by giving him an unsuitable Education. After he had buried his Father in *Virginia*, he took the Opportunity of a *French* Vessel to pass over to *Brest*, and so to *Paris*, who by the Assistance of a *Scotch* Nobleman, who was acquainted with his Family, he pick'd up a liberal Education, and made himself Master of the *French* and *Latin*, and having it in his Election whether he wou'd engage himself to the Church or follow the Camp, he chose the latter, and after some Months spent in the Academy, he enter'd himself among the *Gens d' Arms*, and made very useful Observations in two or three Campaigns in *Germany*, in the last of which he was taken Prisoner and seduc'd into the Emperors Service by some of his Countrymen, who persuaded him the *Germans* were more accustom'd to advance Strangers than the *French*. In a little time he was observ'd by his Colonel to be a Person of Parts and Resolution, and so was gradually advanc'd from a Cornet to a Captain of Horse; and as a Man of Spirit and Action never wants Opportunity to shew himself, so this Gentleman met with many brave Adventures in the way of Soldiery, which some time he would occasionally recount to me, but they would be too tedious to insert in these

Remarks. When King *James* II came to the Crown of *England*, he desired to throw up his Commission, it being suggested to him, that the Prince stood in need of some old experienc'd Officers to model an Army he was raising. Upon this Prospect he pass'd over to *England*, but being destitute of Acquaintance he loiter'd about the Court, till one of the Duke of *Berwick*'s Retinue, who had heard of him at the Siege of *Buda*, made the King acquainted with him. So he was order'd down into *Scotland* with the Promise of a Colonels Commission, but the Revolution following soon after, he acted only as a Captain of Foot at the Battle of *Gillycranky*.

But to cut short this Digression, the time now drew near that I was to undertake my intended Ramble, and indeed it was high time; for it being whisper'd about in the Neighbourhood that I had been in Arms for King *James* II. *Home*, as the saying is, *was too hot a Place for me*; so I sent my Servant to enquire for a Conveniency to pass over to *Flanders*, and in two Days I was provided with a *Roterdam* Vessel, and so with very little Ceremony took leave of my Mother, who though she was unwilling to part with me, yet she prefer'd the lesser Danger to the greater, and rather wish'd me expos'd to the Waves, than to the Insults of my Enemies at Home.

The Wind blew very fresh, but tacking about too much to the *North East*, it drove us upon Shore with that violence that we were oblig'd to put in twice to Land, once at *Scarborough*, and again at *Yarmouth*.

At this latter Place, a Pragmatical Searcher came aboard us with an Air of Authority as if he design'd to visit my Trunks; but one of the Sailors informing me that this was stretching his Commission, for he ought not to search after any Goods unless the Cargo was design'd for that Port, so I ridded my self of this Spark with a Half-Crown Piece; for I had no mind to enter much into a Parley with him lest he might discover my *Highland* Expedition, for Fear never wants Apprehensions. After two Days stay in this Port, the Wind proving favourable, we were not very long in making a Trip to *Roterdam*, where I only refresh'd myself a few Hours, and pass'd on to *Amsterdam* to visit my Bank, and settle a Correspondence as to Returns of money.

I met with nothing in this City that made any Impression upon me to stay any longer than settling the small concern of Money I lodg'd there. The hurry of Business was too Mechanical an Entertainment, for one whose Head was filled with high Flights of Honour, Sieges, Battles, and other such like Sports. The *French* Army at this time lay upon the *Rhine*, and my Design was to make that Way. When I arriv'd there, I found they had surrounded *Mentz* in order to Besiege it. I was glad to begin my first Campaign with so glorious an Undertaking, not doubting, but a great deal of Bravery would be shown where the Flower of the Houshold was design'd for Action; but before I could make any Advantage of this Occurrence, I was to make my self known to some Person of Character who might introduce me so as to be a Spectator of that noble Siege. At last I met with a *Scotch* Gentleman, who rid in among the grand Molquetains, who being fully inform'd of my Warlike Dispositions, assur'd me he would put me into the readiest Method he cou'd to gain Experience; but when he inform'd me that I must not pretend to great Things on a sudden, and that I had at present only two Things in Election, either to carry a Musquet in a Common Foot Regiment, during the Siege, or which he wou'd rather advise me to (in case I had Money to be at that expence) to go to *Strasburgh* and put my self under Discipline for six Weeks or two Months among the *French* Cadets.

I must confess this was a great balk upon a double account: It not only depriv'd me of the Satisfaction of seeing the Siege carried on, but it was a sensible check to my aspiring Humour, to think what Drudgery I was to undergo before I could be regarded by the World; but when I reflected on what I had often heard the old Captain (I buried in the *Highlands*) say upon this Head, it made me easier under the Disappointment, and the next Day I went on to *Strasburg*, and enter'd my self among the Cadets. 'Tis in the Nature of a College, where young Gentlemen are instructed in the Rudiments of War.

During my stay at *Strasburg* I omitted no opportunity of improving myself as to the *French* and *High Dutch* Fortifications, and other Parts of the Mathematicks which were useful in War. I was also present at some Lectures of Politicks which were given to those more advanc'd in Years, in which they handled the Interest of Nations, and brought down their Reflections to the present Times. This I look'd upon as an excellent Method of educating young Officers; for it qualify'd them to be serviceable to their Country under a double Capacity; that is, as well to Argue as to Fight for it, and defend it equally with their Tongue and Sword.

I remember an Antient Marquis who had a Superintendency over this Academy, entertaining us one Day with the Motives of the present War, and running up the Cause to its Original, laid it before us in this manner: *That the Monarchs of* France *wou'd look upon themselves as injur'd by the rest of the Princes of* Europe, *till the imperial Diadem was restor'd to* France, *who were first Possessors of it in the Person of* Charles the Great; *that they had made several pushes in all Ages to recover it, but without Effect; that while the* English *had footing in* France, *they were too lazy to extend their Conquests upon the Empire of the* West; *and when they had chased out the* English, *and were rid of that Incumbrance, the House of* Austria, *by the vast Acquisitions of the* Low Countries, *and joint Power of* Spain, *sat so hard upon 'em, that* France *was not in a Capacity to make any Advances towards recovering their Right to the Empire: What therefore they had been upon these latter Years, was to make a strong Party among the Electoral Princes, and by degrees secure a Majority in the Imperial Diet, in order to set aside the House of* Austria, *and settle the Imperial Crown upon the* French Line, *as it was in the Beginning.* To this he added, *That this invincible Monarch,* Lewis XIV, *had made considerable Advances of late Years, especially in bringing over several Electors, and now the Chapter of* Cologn *to chuse Cardinal* Fustenberg *for their Archbishop, who though a Native of* Germany, *yet was a* Frenchman *by Interest, and had given his Word to be very Industrious in settling the Imperial Dignity upon the House of* Bourbon. *And this Election of Cardinal* Fustenberg *being contested by the Emperor and Pope Innocent* XI. *was the Motive of the present War; for they put up the Duke of* Bavaria's *Brother in opposition against him.*

This Account of the occasion of the present War, vary'd very much from the Idea we in *Scotland* had of Affairs. We were made to believe, That the King of *France* being a zealous Roman Catholick Monarch, had engag'd himself in a War against the Allies, meerly upon a Religious Motive, to re-establish King *James*, who was dethron'd upon no other Account but because he was a Roman Catholick. But I have since found by comparing Matters, that the Revolution in *England* was not the Occasion, but the Consequence of the War between the *French* and the Allies; for the Emperor, &c. understanding that King *James* II, was drawn into a Scrape by the *French* King, and that he made a Property of him to carry on his Ambitious Designs; 'tis not to be wonder'd at, if they prefer'd the general Good of *Europe*, and immediate Safety of their own People to the private Good of King *James* II. who had been so indiscreet as to expose himself to Ruin by giving into a *French* Project. However this unpolitick Management proved very lucky to *France* upon a double Account; for tho' they had begun a War upon the disedifying bottom of Ambition, it was afterwards consecrated in mny Peoples Thoughts, under a Colour of justifying a dethron'd Roman Catholick Prince, besides the Advantage of causing a considerable Diversion by fomenting a War in the Three Kingdoms of *Great-Britain*; for as for re-establishing that unfortunate Prince in his Throne, though I was a long Time of Opinion *France* really design'd it; yet since I have been convinc'd by undeniable Arguments, that it neither was his Interest to bring it about, nor that he ever seriously attempted it. I must own it was never very Intelligible to me, not even in my very darkest State of Bigottry for the *French* Interest, that the Emperor, the King of *Spain*, and Duke of *Savoy*, with many other Roman Catholick Princes, nay, the Pope himself should all fail in their Duty and Zeal for Religion, and the King of *France* (who was remarkable upon other Occasions for sacrificing it to Politick ends) should be the only one in *Europe* that wou'd stand up for it. It was not so in the Infancy of the *Dutch* Republic, when *France* concurr'd with the Seven Provinces to have them torn from the *Spanish* Monarchy, and by the same Assistance, enabled 'em to make head against the Church. It was not so when a Frown of *Oliver Cromwell* cou'd oblige *France* to lay aside the charitable Maxim of Royal Protection, and send *Charles* II. and his Brother the Duke of *York*, out of their Territories by an Infamous Condescension. But *James* II. had forgotten

the Affronts offer'd to the Duke of *York*, and I suppose had a
Mind to make a second Tryal of *French* Hospitality, and whether
they would be more obliging to him in his old Age, than they
had been in his Youth. Neither is this plausible Pretence of de-
fending a Prince injur'd upon the Score of Religion, very consistent with their Conduct, in regard of the *Turk*. To maintain
a Catholick Prince at St. *Germains*, and support the Enemy of
Christianity at *Constantinople* with great Remittances of Moneys,
and a constant Supply of Engineers; is a piece of State Casuistry
above my Comprehension, and Prince *Eugene* had a great deal
of Reason to knock his Breast, and hold up his Hands to Heaven,
when he saw *French* Engineers dragg'd out of *Turkish* Mines in
Hungary with *Agnus Dei*'s, and Relicks about their Necks as
Ensigns of *Lewis* XIV's Christianity, and Zeal for the Church.

But to proceed to my own concerns. As soon as the Time was
expir'd, I propos'd to my self to stay in the Academy at *Strasburgh*,
I provided my self with the Equipage of a grand Musketeer, and
for a Present of 50 Pistols, and the strength of good Recommendation from my Countrymen, I was admitted to ride among
'em. But here I had a fresh Difficulty to struggle with. My
Countrymen finding me pretty flush of Money, and that I was
very generous, was as observant as a Spaniel, and so very Officious
both early and late, that I found it impracticable to steal an Hour
of Privacy to recollect my self, in order to model my Conduct
after the best Precedents I met with in the course of the Day; and
what made me yet more uneasy, he was not content to visit me
alone, but had often a second or third with him; who as they
were very obliging in informing me of the Methods of living
in a Camp, so they was always very *adroit*, and gave me the
Preference upon all Occasions; but then as I engross'd all the
Ceremony of the Day, so I was thrown into unavoidable Circumstances of paying them for their Attendance. This constant
Charge, though in Time it would have made me weary of acting
the Grand Signior, yet I could better have bore with it, had I not
smelt a Design they had to strip me of my Bank I had at *Amsterdam*; for I was so unguarded in my Conduct as to have acquainted
my Countrymen with my Money concerns, which he and his
Associates had already devour'd in their Imagination, and

wanted but a fit Opportunity to draw me in at Play, and so at
once put me upon a Level with themselves and other Soldiers of
Fortune: But being aware of the Trap that was laid for me, my
whole Study was how to disengage myself from this Gang, so
as to give no Suspicion that I understood their meaning; for this
I imagin'd might be the ground of a Quarrel, and to perhaps have
worse Consequences than if they really had strip'd me of my
Substance. Arm'd with this Caution, I receiv'd 'em in the usual
manner, but still kept off when a Motion was made either of high
drinking or playing deep; for no Man is secure, when either
Liquor or Passion gains the Ascendent over him. But this State
of Violence could not continue long, sometimes I was at a loss
for an Excuse to baffle their Importunity, other times I found
them dispos'd to represent me as of an uncomplying Temper, so
that there was no way left but either to draw or withdraw, for I
saw plainly that if I staid among them a Quarrel would ensue.
This Consideration, with the unheard of Devastation I saw in the
Palatinate made by the *French* Troops, gave me a Surfeit of the
Rhine. I am not Ignorant that no Part of the World is free from
Sharpers, but I thought in another Place I might better resist
their first Onset, and let them gain no ground upon me, while
Rule I here neglected for want of Experience. And now I was
oblig'd to make a Call upon my Banker at *Amsterdam* for Two
Hundred Pounds, resolving not to break the remaining 1000
Pound Bulk, unless upon some extraordinary Emergency. I had
sometime before intimated to my Officers and Comrades the
Design I had to quit the Service upon the *Rhine*, assuring them it
was not out of any Disobligation, having experienced their
obliging Temper upon all Occasions; but as I understood King
James was at the Head of his Army in *Ireland*, so I look'd upon my
self in some Measure inexcusable if I serv'd in a foreign Army,
when I might contribute more immediately to succour my
Prince. My Reasons were applauded, and I not a little content to
depart without giving Disgust. Without delay therefore I posted
to *Paris*, where I design'd to make no very long stay, only what
was necessary to recover my self from the Fatigue of the Campaign,
and satisfy my Curiosity in taking a View of that noble City. I
was happy in one thing during my stay here, that I was agreeably

surpriz'd with the fight of my only Sister, whose Husband being
under some malignant Court Influence, was oblig'd to withdraw
with his Family out of *Scotland*. *Paris* is a Place like all other great
Cities, where Persons of all Conditions and Characters may
spend their Time agreeably, if that useful Trifle call'd Money be
not wanting. Hitherto I had no occasion to be Melancholly upon
that Score; for though I was not furnish'd to make any extraordinary Figure, yet being only a single Person, and as yet never
launch'd out into any Extravagances, so within my narrow
Sphere, I made a decent Appearance. But as no Man is prosperous at all Times, so it was not long before I found my self
engag'd in an Affair which very much troubled my Repose, and
which I would willingly have compounded for with my *Amsterdam* Bank. The Business was this, my Eldest Brother before he
went with King *James* into *Ireland*, made some stay at *Paris* and
St. Germains, where he was order'd to collect some Recruits of the
Three Nations, which he was to conduct over in the Quality of a
Route-Captain. Now as he was a Person who had seen very much
of the World, and was somewhat addicted to Gallantry and
Intriguing with the Fair Sex, so he could not remain long in a
Place without Publishing some Marks of his Vocation that way.
It happen'd that a young Lady who lodg'd in the same House
with him, had occasion to pay a visit to her Acquaintance; my
Brother observing her in a Posture to go out of the House alone,
offer'd to usher her to the place she design'd for. The Lady with
the usual *French* Freedom and obliging Air, made him a Courtsey,
and accepted the Offer. When he complied with this Piece of
Civility, he took his leave, and return'd to his Lodgings. From
this Accident my Brother dated an Intrigue. The Ladies Carriage
(which by the way was nothing but what is customary there upon
a slender Acquaintance) encourag'd him to make Advances; the
next Step he made was to drink Tea with her in her Chamber,
and afterwards he invited her to the *Opera*. But the young Lady
as she was strictly Virtuous, never gave way to none of these
Freedoms, but in the Company of her Landlady or her Daughter,
who were both Prudes. In the mean time a Relation of this
Gentlewoman's, who was a Lieutenant in the Regiment of
Navarre came up to *Paris*, and had not been long in Town before

he was inform'd by some busy Noddle, that his Cousin was either upon the Point of being married, or what was rather suggested to him, that one Captain *Ramkins* a *Scotch* Officer, who lodg'd in the same House, had dishonourable Designs upon her. Now as Persons never want Arguments to induce them to take things in the worst Sense, (tho' I will not avouch for my Brothers Intention) so the *French* Officer being of a suspicious and also a fiery Temper, wanted no body to exasperate him. He took it for granted the Thing was so, and taking Coach he came to his Kinswoman, and after having attack'd her with a great deal of scurrilous Language, he waited not for her Reply, but flung away to find my Brother in order to cut his Throat. My Brother was then at St. *Germains* receiving his last Orders from the Secretary for his departure for *Ireland*, but return'd that Night to *Paris*. His Landlady at his Return gave him a Note, which she said was deliver'd to her by the Post. The Contents were a double Surprize to him, first a bold and daring Challenge, and again, he neither knew whom he was to meet, nor upon what Account, only the Time and Place were mention'd. Thus doubtful with himself what Course to take, he acquainted his Landlady with the Subject of the Letter, but she was also at a loss, having neither seen the Lady's Relation, nor heard that he was come to Town, otherwise it might have created some Suspicion. But after Supper, according to Custom, she went up to have an Hours Chat with the young Lady, and among other Things, mention'd the odd Letter Captain *Ramkins* had receiv'd that Evening; the Lady suspecting what the matter really was, gave the Landlady sufficient Intimation by the Consternation she was in, that she was not unacquainted with the Occasion of that Letter. In the mean time, my Brother was gone to consult with some of his Acquaintance how he should behave himself in this juncture: Some advis'd him to neglect it as a sham Challenge, whereby some of his Acquaintance being merry dispos'd had a mind to divert themselves; others judg'd it might be a Design to Assassinate him upon account of some old Grudge now worn out of his Memory; in conclusion, 'twas order'd that he should present himself at the Place mention'd in the Challenge, and in case it was a real Thing, and that he escap'd with Life, a Horse should be ready to ride

Post to *Brest*, whether he and his Recruits were order'd to take
Shipping. But that he might not Alarm his Lodgings, he spent the
remainder of the Night in the Tavern with his Friends, a fitter
Preparation than praying for the Work he was about. About
Five in the Morning he set out towards the Place of Battle, half a
dozen of his Acquaintance following him at a convenient distance,
to wait for the Issue, and to see Justice done in case he was
assaulted against the usual Method of Duelling. When he came
to the Place apointed, he saw a young Gentleman walking and
musing under a Hedge with his Arms a Kimbo, whom he rightly
judg'd to be his Man. When he came within Speech of him, the
French Officer stop'd and ask'd him if his Name was not *Ramkins*,
and whether he had not receiv'd a Note the Evening before upon
such an Occasion? my Brother made no other Reply, but that he
took himself to be the Person, and that he would indite an Answer
with the Point of his Sword; for though, said he, I am a Stranger
both to you and the occasion of this Trouble you have given me,
yet as I take you to be a Man of Honour, so I suppose you think
your self injur'd to that degree, that Satisfaction either cannot or
will not be given any other way, and therefore I am here ready to
make up this mysterious Quarrel after the Method you have
made choice of. It sometimes happens that Peace is struck up
between Two Nations Sword in Hand; but my Brother's Antagonist was too warm to stand a Parley and act the Part of a
Plenipotentiary; upon which, without making the least Reply,
he whips off his Cloaths into his Shirt, and open'd his Breast to
show his Adversary he scorn'd to take any ungenerous Advantage. My Brother was also honourable upon the same score; for
though he wore a short Buff Waiscoat without Skirts according
to the Fashions of those Times, and which might have deadened
a Push, yet he threw it off and put himself upon the Level with
his Adversary in all respects, so to it they went. My Brother
found himself much superior in Strength and Vigour, and that in
all probability he cou'd Command his Adversary's Sword,
paried with him a considerable Time, and put by several Pushes
without attempting the Gentleman's Life, but finding him Resolute, and that one of them must fall, he made one home Thrust,
and drove his Sword quite through his Adversary's Body, falling

upon him at the same time; and thus fell this unfortunate young Gentleman a Victim to his ungovernable Passion.

It appear'd afterwards, that this *French* Officer having been often play'd upon by several in his Regiment, that he had been two Years among them and never yet made any Experiment of his personal Courage, told them at his going up to *Paris*, That they should here in a little Time he had qualify'd himself by killing his Man. Now it is suppos'd he thought the *British* Nation, not being fam'd for their Skill in handling the Sword, he had an excellent opportunity of showing his Manhood, and the Advantage of making his escape when he had done the Fact, because little or no Enquiry wou'd be made after a Stranger. My Brother being convinc'd his Adversary was incapable to Rally, made haste to gather up his Cloaths, exchanging the Evangelical Advice of *burying* the dead, to that natural Precept of *Self-preservation*, and I must leave him pursuing his Journey towards *Brest*, to return to his Lodgings, and give an account how this Catastrophe came to affect me at my coming to *Paris*.

The young Lady who was the Innocent occasion of this unfortunate Accident, took little Rest after she was inform'd of the Contents of the Note left by her Kinsman, and her Concern grew upon her when she understood Captain *Ramkins* was out of his Lodgings all Night; thus she remain'd under great Inquietudes till Three a Clock the next Day, when she, with her Landlady and Daughter, took a Coach privately and drove directly to the Place where the Gentlemen were to meet according to the Contents of the Letter. They discharg'd their Coach upon a pretence of taking a Walk in the Fields, and after a small Tour the Landlady's Daughter put her Foot into a Cake of clotted Blood, but it was so chang'd, as to the Colour, that she could not well distinguish what it was, but at a little distance finding a Glove, and several Blades of Grass ting'd with a Vermillion Dye, being press'd down and ruffled as it were with some Cattle weltring and tumbling about. They had a strong Suspicion one of the Gentlemen had ended his Days upon the Spot, and to clear their Suspicion, they walk'd back into the City till they arrived at the *Petite Chastelet*, which is a publick Room in the Nature of a Guard Bed, where all Corps are expos'd to view and whither

People usually go in quest of any of their Friends, or Acquaintance that are wanting. And here the young Gentlewoman was quickly satisfy'd that her Cousin's Rashness had brought him to his End. This Accident happening not long before I came to *Paris*, the Discourse of it was very fresh, and what occasion'd me to have an account of it at my first Arrival, was my Lodging at the same House with my Brother, it being the usual Lodgings for *English* and *Scotch*. 'Tis true that Landlady and her Daughter where removed to *Orleans*, where they had an *Estate* belonging to their Family, but the young Lady, Cousin to the deceas'd Officer, was still in her old Apartment. I had not been above three Days, but my Name began to be known as well by the Direction of some Letters I receiv'd out of *Germany*, as by other means there are of having such Things divulg'd. The young Lady was not so struck with the Horror of the Name of her Cousins Murtherer, as not to have the Curiosity to peep at me as I came in and out of my Lodgings, and the more, because I had so great a Resemblance to him both as to Figure and Features, that without any extraordinary Skill in Physiognomy, she might conclude I was either his Brother or some near Relation. Now whether my Brother's Cavaliers Carriage had left an Idea in the Lady's Head which she could not conveniently part with, or her Inquisitiveness after me was only a Female Curiosity, I am not able to determine, but it was very unfortunate to me to have been so near a Kin to one she admired in case it was so, or that her Inquisitiveness should make me so publick; for I had not been in *Paris* above Eight Days, but the Archers or City Guards took me out of my Bed at Four a Clock in the Morning, and carried me to Prison upon strong Suspicion of being that very Captain *Ramkins* who had kill'd the *French* Officer in a Duel. Captain *Ramkins* I certainly was call'd at my own Request, having taken that Travelling Name as all Independent Gentlemen do, who cannot tell well what Title to give themselves upon the Road. My case had no very good Aspect at the beginning. There were so many Circumstances to render me suspected, that though I was satisfy'd my Life was not in Danger, yet it was an easy Thing to perceive it wou'd be both a troublesome, and also a chargeable Spot of Work. The first Thing I did was to send for my Brother-in-law, whom I employ'd

as my Solicitor, to lay a true Narration of the Fact before the
King's Attorney. My Counsel advis'd me to *Subpœna* the young
Lady, who wou'd be a material Witness that I was not the Captain *Ramkins* chargeable with the Fact, which she seem'd willingly
to acquiesce to; but some of the deceased Friends endeavour'd to
invalidate her *Affidavit*, upon a pretence, that there was too great
an Intimacy between her and Captain *Ramkins*. However, to put
the Contest upon an Issue which would allow of no Reply, I
procured the Testimonies of several Officers in the Army, that I
was actually upon the *Rhine* when the Duel was fought at *Paris*,
besides the corroborating Evidence of several *Irish* Gentlemen
who liv'd in *Paris* and at *St. Germains*, who were ready to offer
their Oaths I was not the Man. 'Tis incredible to think what
Pains the deceas'd Gentleman's Relations took to destroy me,
though I have the Charity to think they judg'd I was the Person
they sought after, though it is somewhat unintelligible they
wou'd not Credit the young Lady their Cousin. This Affair
help'd me off with the greatest Part of my ready Money, for 'tis a
Blessing which attends all Law-Suits, that the Gainer is oblig'd
to refund to the Lawyers what he recovers from his Adversary,
and for my part, I pay'd pretty dear for an Authentick Copy of
my Innocence; and the Carriage of the Court to me was such, as if
I had been particularly favour'd in not being hang'd instead of my
Brother.

After this troublesome Business was over, I began to enjoy
my self a little in the Diversions of *Paris*; and by the Assistance of
my Brother-in law, I had a good Guide in him to view several of
the Curiosities that City abounds with, though I cannot say I
took any extraordinary relish that way, for my Thoughts being
chiefly upon War, I digested other Matters as a nice Appetite does
improper Food. It was my Intention to go over to *Ireland*, and to
made that undertaking less chargeable to me, I endeavour'd to
procure a Commission, which was no difficult matter at that
Time, especially to one who was provided with a little Money
to facilitate the Grant. I did not stick much upon the Nature of
the Commission, for my Years, and small Experience could make
no very extraordinary Demands; so I was Registred as a Lieutenant, which I, according to the usual Custom, upon receival

dexterously improv'd into Captain. Indeed I had very lofty Expectations, and the Affairs of King *James* went so well at that time in *Ireland*, that there was not a Footman who follow'd that Prince, but look'd upon his Fortune as made.

These Considerations put me and some others upon a Project of transporting our selves to the *North* of *England*, where King *James* had a very strong Party, and we were inform'd that immediately upon the Reduction of *Ireland*, as before, the whole Strength of his Army wou'd power in upon *England* that way. A Day was fix'd to put my Design in Execution, but falling into Discourse a little after with a Person of Experience, he intimated that the Business wou'd not be so near over in *Ireland* as I imagin'd; for I can assure you, says he, Three Expresses have arrived lately at *Versailles*, to solicit the *French* Court for Cannon and Ammunition, without which it wou'd be impossible for King *James*'s Forces to become Masters in *Ireland*, but that the *French* were so dilatory in this Affair upon some Politick Views, that it was great Odds that Nation wou'd be quickly recover'd by King *William*'s Forces. This was a misterious Insinuation to one of my small Experience, for my shallow Brain told me, Expedition was the Business of War; whereas I found afterwards it was the Interest of *France* to spin on the *Irish* War, and to order Things so, that King *William* should always have an Army employ'd there; for they look'd upon it as a Chimerical Notion, that the War could be carry'd on into *England*, or that an *Irish* Army was capable to reduce *England*; for *France* knew very well their own Designs of not intending to send any *French* Troops to joyn them in *England*.

I own I never entirely forgot the Reflexion that Gentleman made upon the present Posture of Affairs; but yet I cannot say I assented to his Opinion, however, it wrought so much upon me as to alter my Resolutions of going directly into the *North* of *England*; for I govern'd my self by this Dilemma, that in Case *Ireland* was not reduc'd till I came there, I might have the Opportunity of having a share in the Reduction, but if it was, the Passage between the *North* of *Ireland* and *England* was very short. Upon this Bottom I began my Journey, I took Shipping at *Brest* and landed at *Cork*, pursuing the rest of my Journey by Land, upon account of the Danger I was inform'd of in going by Sea;

for that several *English* Men of War guarded the narrow Seas between *Dublin* and *Holy-head*. When I came into King *James's* Army, my first Enquiry was after my Brother, whom you may be sure I entertain'd in the first place with the Consequence of his Duel at *Paris*; and though he often sigh'd to reflect upon his Misfortune in being the occasion of the *French* Officer's Death, which might have been honourably avoided; yet he laugh'd plentifully, when he heard the Part I had afterwards in that Melancholy Farce; and rally'd me home when I insisted upon Charges and desired to be reimburs'd with Sixty *Louis d'Ors*, which that Affair had cost me upon his Account; all the Satisfaction I could get was, that he thought I put a greater Value upon my being his Brother, than to think it over-rated at that trifling Sum: The Life of a Brother, said he, is the only thing that can answer for a Brotherly Affection.

The Scene of Affairs in *Ireland* was very much alter'd upon raising the Siege of *London-derry*; Men and Arms were imported from *England* on all Sides to make Head against King *James*, and several bloody Skirmishes happen'd in several Parts of the Kingdom. It wou'd make a Volume to account the Marches and Counter-marches both Parties made in that irregular Country to attack and avoid one another. But where ever it was my Lot to engage, the general Complaint was a want of Money, Ammunition and Arms; this (as it cou'd not be otherwise) made us unsuccessful under many promising Advantages. We had Men enough, and those not destitute of Zeal or Courage; but to expose themselves Naked against Arms and Discipline, was a desperate way of Engaging. But *France* still went upon the old Politick Scheme to gain Advantages upon the Continent by dilatory Proceedings in King *James's* Affairs; for unless this was their Prospect, was it not a supine Piece of Management to suffer a Body of near Thirty Thousand brave Men to lie unarm'd in the Field above half a Year, when *France* had Magazines and Stores to furnish above a Million of Soldiers? But as King *James* was not only to be the *Dupe* of their great Monarch, but the Sport and Game of his Ministers, besides a general Topick of refusing him an Assistance upon the Politick Motive of prolonging the War. It seems the Chief Minister of State had some private Ends in these dilatory Proceedings, and King *James*'s Cause in *Ireland* was also to be sacrific'd to this Gentleman's Resentments. The Case was this, *Lewis* XIV upon great Importunity, and to put a Gloss upon, and lay deep Colours upon his Politicks, condescended so far, as to order five or six Thousand despicable Foot Soldiers for King *James*'s Service in *Ireland*, with a General at their Head, who had been more accustom'd to lead up a Country Dance than an Army, and better qualify'd to break a Jest than look in upon an Enemy. This General, however, was according to King *James*'s own liking, though contrary to the Chief Minister's Design, who wanted that Post for a Relation of his own. This undesign'd Affront of King *James* in preferring *C. L.* to the Minister's Favourite, lost the Battle of the *Boyne*, and perhaps all *Ireland*; for the Chief Minister would neither send Arms nor Money to supply that brave Body of Men, but threw them into the Circumstances of either dying unreveng'd, or saving their Lives by Flight. The History of that Battle has so many Eye Witnesses still alive for me to dwell upon it; I shall only make bold to relate what my Fate was upon that unfortunate Day, and how inglorious *France* withdrew the sham Succours they sent *King* James. My Post was to Head a Company of *Fingalian* Granadiers, who were plac'd in an Orchard which hung over a Defilee, through which we expected the Enemy would march after they had pass'd the River. I make bold to stile my Company Granadiers, because they were design'd to be so when first rais'd, but were now arm'd rather like Pioneers than Grenadiers; we had not above a dozen Grana-does, no Bayonets, and several without any Fire-arms; and if the Chief Men of the Action were no better equipp'd, 'tis easy to guess how the Gross of the Army was provided. According to our Expectation, a Party of the Enemy fell into the Trap, and what Shot we had, we let it successively fly at them out of the Orchard; in the mean time, we heard a great Noise behind us, and turning my self about, I saw the Orchard almost surrounded with Horse, which I expected were some of our own Party coming up to support us, but found them to be a Squadron of the Enemy, who immediately summon'd us to yield, or we must expect the last Fate of War. There was no time to Parley, upon which I made a Sign to the Commanding Officer of the Enemy not to proceed to Slaughter, and so out of Twenty Two Men with which I defended that Post, Nine of us fell into the Enemies Hands, the rest dying bravely in the Engagement. Our Entertaintment was what is usually with Prisoners of War, Hunger and hard Lodgings, but in a little Time being remov'd to *Dublin*, Things were better with me; I had the Liberty of a large Prison and civil Usage. And here it was I met with an excellent Friend, who never fail'd those who make Application to him, I mean a small Bank of Money which my Brother left me, and which I had sent to *Dublin per* Bill from *Newry*, that I might run no hazard of being plunder'd in case of a Defeat, and in this I have often applauded my own Caution, that though I have frequently hazarded my Life, I never risqu'd my Substance; if Death happen'd, I was certain of being provided for; and if Imprisonment, I had what wou'd make my Captivity easy, and perhaps, purchase my Enlargement.

'Tis not a being in a Battle that makes a Person a capable Judge how to describe it; every Officer has his Post which he must not depart from, and though he may be able to describe the Situation of the Troops before an Engagement, yet afterwards during the Fight, there is so much Noise, Smoak and Confusion, that for my part, I scarce can give a true Narration of what happen'd within a dozen Yards compass. Upon this Account, I cannot tell in what manner the *French* Troops behav'd themselves, but I was inform'd they made a tollerable Stand against King *William*'s Army, but that they quickly chang'd it into a running Fight, and very dexterously convey'd both King *James* and themselves out of Danger, and in a little time out of the Kingdom, directing their March to the next Seaport Town, which was not in the Enemies Hands, from whence they found their way Home. If these Troops were serviceable at the *Boyne*, they certainly might have been much more useful, if they had remain'd and assisted the *Irish* the remainder of the War; but they had shown themselves, and that was enough to answer the politick Ends for which they were sent. 'Tis suppos'd after this Defeat at the *Boyne*, that King *James* was aware of the *French* Politics, and so would ne'er think of returning in Person again into *Ireland*, it being abundantly sufficient if he left two or three active Generals among 'em to Alarm the Enemy and do the Drudgery of the *French* Court, in making a Diversion to favour his Conquests in other Parts of the World. But to return to the Series of my own Story, I had now obtain'd Liberty of the City of *Dublin* upon Paroll, and spent my Life pretty agreeable, especially when I understood that a kind of a Cartel was fix'd, and there was no Danger of a Halter. My long stay in *Dublin* brought me acquainted with several General Officers of King *William*'s Army, who were my Countrymen and well acquainted with my Family. The great Respect they showed me, was, as I perceiv'd at long run, in order to debauch me from King *James*'s Service; but it was not in my power at that time, to remove the Scruples I was entangled in as to the Revolution; besides I had other Motives urgent enough not to engage in the *English* Service, till I had seen a little more Abroad. But in the midst of all the Disasters I met with, nothing affected me with a more sensible Grief than the Thoughts of *Lewis* the XIVth's Insincerity, for though it only rid my Mind in the Nature of a Scruple or first Impression, yet I found it grow daily more and more upon me, and often in the height of my Diversions it lay upon my Stomach like an indigested Meal; yet at the same time I durst not mutter the least of this Matter to the greatest Confident I had in the World; for I was sensible what would be the Consequence of such a Liberty of Speech, and that nothing less than perpetual Imprisonment in the *Bastile* must have atton'd for the Crime, and that King *James* wou'd have look'd upon himself as oblig'd to have justify'd the Conduct of *France*, though perhaps he lay under the same Jealousies with myself in regard of *French* Politics. How often have I, when I have been alone, exaggerated my Folly in engaging in a Cause, which the principal Agent never design'd to bring to an Issue? but then again I have corrected my self for giving way to a false Impression, and condemning the Conduct of so many Thousands who had more Experience than I could lay claim to, and yet willingly went all the Lengths of the *French* Court. Now as I always had a great Respect for Men of Years and Experience, so I was re- solv'd to silence all the Scruples relating to *French* Politicks, and see an end of the *Irish* War, not so much under the Influence of a *French* Power (which never did any real Service to King *James* in

Ireland) but because so many worthy Gentlemen eagerly pursue the Cause, whom I had Reason to think were better Judges of such high Matters than my self. And what in the next place I was to undertake, was how to be releas'd from my Confinement, in which I cou'd find no Difficulty besides a breach of Paroll, my Person being every Day at Liberty, but understanding that several Persons in the same Circumstances with my self, were partly conniv'd at when they made their Escape. I took the same Method, and rather chose to walk off, than wait to be exchang'd, or Bribe for my Enlargement. Perhaps the Reader will expect here to be entertain'd with the remaining Part of the *Irish* War, especially where I was employ'd; but he must be content to be inform'd in General, That as I made it a Law with my self ne'er to omit any Occasion of improving my self in the Art of War, so I took particular care not to be upon any Foreign Duty in the Day of Action. I was wounded at the Battle of *Aghram*, where I had one of my Legs broke, and lost two Fingers with the cut of a Sabre. I was at the first Siege of *Limerick*, and help'd to surprize the Enemy's flying Camp and Provisions they were carrying to supply the main Army that was carrying on the Siege. Afterwards I entred the Town, and remain'd there during the Siege, having the Liberty to pass over into *France* with the rest of the *Irish* Troops upon the Articles of *Limerick*; but there was one remarkable Passage happen'd to me during the Siege of that Town, which I cannot dispense with my self to pass over in Silence; it was rather a casual Matter, than a Design laid, however it equally answer'd the end. At one of the Sallies, in which we design'd to overthrow a Mount they had made to raise a Battery upon, after a smart Engagement, it being in the Night, I had the opportunity to step aside and strip a *Dutch* Granadier, and immediately putting on his Cloaths I mingled my self with the Enemy's Battalions as they drew back towards their Camp, thus unperceiv'd I had the opportunity the next Morning to view their Works and make my Remarks. But now I was somewhat at a loss how to make a hand of this Stratagem and get back into the Town, nor was I less concern'd how to avoid being discover'd as not belonging to the Enemy; but the Confusion they were in the next Day in burying their Dead and repairing their Works, made me pass undiscover'd till Night, so about Nine at Night when it was throughly dark, I stole to that Side of the Town which lies next to the Sea, and swimming over undiscover'd, I crept under the Wall, and calling softly upon the next Centinel, I inform'd him who I was, bidding him call to the Captain of the next Guard, and bring a Rope and two or three Soldiers to hall me up. I was very welcome to the Garrison, for 'twas suppos'd, I was either kill'd or taken Prisoner in the Sally. This Stratagem, though I had no Design in it at our attacking the Enemy, it being only a sudden Thought, yet it had a very good Event; for the next Sally we made, as I had observ'd, the weakest Part of the Besiegers Works, so I lead a Party of Resolute Men that way, who lost no Time, but levell'd all their Works, and dragg'd a considerable Booty into the Town.

The Wars of *Ireland* being at an End, and the Articles of *Limerick* Sign'd, about 15000 regular Troops were Transported into *France*, besides several Thousands of others, who all proved as useful to the Monarch of *France* in his Wars in *Italy*, *Spain*, *Germany*, &c. as they had been in making a Three Years Diversion in *Ireland*, so happy was *France* in making a Politick use of King *James*'s Misfortune, that *Lewis* XIV was much a greater Gainer by his being Banish'd, than if he had remain'd in the quiet Possession of his Throne. And now there were several Specula-tions, what Method the *French* King wou'd take to make the World believe he had a Design to reinstall King *James*. The most direct Means was to attempt a Descent, but this was impractic-able by the way of *Ireland*; for if an Army of 30000 Men cou'd not keep it when they were actually in Possession of it, there was no likelyhood of their succeeding in a Descent, nor was it prob-able, that *France* would add more Force to them who had so often refus'd them when they were in Circumstances to receive. The most favourable Interpreters of the *French* King's Politicks, began now to think he had laid all Thoughts of a Restoration aside. King *James*'s Troops were employ'd and scatter'd where they were useless upon that Design, and his Court was modell'd, as if nothing more should be attempted. However it was thought convenient still to carry the Juggle on, and several Methods were made use of to seduce the poor Jacobites in *England* and *St. Ger-*

mains, that their Work was still going on. Great Respect was shown to the Court of *St. Germains* by his Most Christian Majesty, with repeated Assurances to stand by them: In the mean time I was permitted to leave the Army, and solace my self for two or three Months at *Paris*, where, by the Assistance of my old Friend ready Money, I made my self very acceptable. It was my Happiness hitherto never to be engaged in an Intrigue with the Fair Sex; for though several of my Station have diverted themselves that way with much prejudice to their Business, yet I was always so bent upon War, that I cou'd never find spare Hours for such trifling Conversation, for that was the Notion I had of it. A general Whining and Pining away for a Trolloping Girl, was to me a very awker'd and inconsistent Piece of Pageantry; however, I had been often told by Persons of Experience, that no Man had so just an Idea of the World, as he that had been well hamper'd and sower'd by a Love Intrigue; for though Women appear to be only Spectators, and to bear no Sway in the Politicks of the World, yet underhand, the Fate of Kingdoms often hung at their Girdles, and the wisest of Princes often hazarded the Repose of his People for an Hours Dalliance with some Coquet and diverting Creature of the fair Sex. I cannot tell well how it happen'd, but I suppose by not resisting the first impressions of this kind, I found my self far gone in an Intrigue, and that without either Thought or Design; but I understood afterwards that a Breach of Idleness being espy'd in my Conduct, the Roving Deity seiz'd the Advantage and enter'd Sword in Hand. The Gentlewoman who drew me into this Snare, was no otherwise my Acquaintance than by an accidental Visit; but I was so much a Philosopher, as to know that where there is a Sympathy of Humours, all other Considerations are neglected, and a *Turk* with those Advantages, is as capable to make a Conquest as a *Christian*. I had at my first entrance upon the Stage of the World made a double Promise to my self, the one was never to hearken to a Love Affair till I had acquired a Stock of Experience, and Money to make that Passion Serviceable and of real Use in an honourable Way; the other was not to graft upon a Foreign Stock; but I was forc'd to humble my self under a violation of both these Purposes; for the Object of my Passion was a *Spanish* young Lady though of *Irish* Extraction, her Family Transporting themselves thither about the middle of Queen *Elizabeth's* Reign. Now I had two or three Difficulties to struggle with relating to this Affair: in the first place, I had not as yet imparted the Secret to the young Lady; again, my Brother's Example gave me grounds to think I cou'd not avoid a Quarrel with some of her Relations; but what chiefly frighted me, was the Plague of Wedding, in case we were both of a Mind, for a keen Hound is not easily call'd off from a hot Scent, till he has either caught or lost his Game. In the midst of these Perplexities, I judg'd 'twou'd be a wise Part to disclose my self to some Persons of Experience in these Matters; for in all the Skirmishes and Sieges I had been at, they never threw me into such a Consternation and Absence of Thought; and accordingly I met with an old Adept in these Affairs. When he heard my Case, after two or three Turns he approach'd me with the serious Air of a Physician, and I thinking he had Design to feel my Pulse, I offer'd him my Hand, which he only shook very gently, saying, Young Man, all the Comfort I can give you is, that you must buy your Knowledge by Experience as I and many others have done before you. All Advice is lost upon a Person in Love. Should I advice you to quit the Enterprize, I know you would not do it. A Halter or an *East-India* Voyage may do you Service in Case you are refused. In a Word, whatever I advised you to you will certainly do the contrary; However, that you may be said to have lost your Time in coming hither, hasten to the young Lady, tell her in a Franck Cavalier way how Things are with you; give all the vent you can to your Passion; if it blows over, you will be a wary Man hereafter, if it ends in Wedlock, any Body will inform you of the Consequences. While the old Gentleman was entertaining me with this Lesson, my Head grew so dizy, as if some invisible Hand had turn'd it round like a Gigg, so I left him abruptly, and went directly to my Lodgings to Bed, but to this Day I cannot tell, whether I went a Foot or in a Coach my Head was in such a Confusion. The next Morning finding my ideas better rang'd, I propos'd to seize the first Opportunity to let the Lady understand the Difficulties I struggled under upon her Account; but the Nature of our Visits was such, that I cou'd not do it any otherwise than by Letter: Thus when I had once broke the Ice, and that too with a fair Prospect of making Advances, in the next Place I gain'd the Maid by the usual Methods that such Creatures are render'd Obsequious, and under her Conduct methoughts I sail'd prosperously on without the least Rub to my suppos'd Happiness; 'tis true I was at a constant Charge of Presents, Treats, and now and then a Serenade according to the *Spanish* Customs. But I remember at one of these Midnight Scenes of Gallantry, I saw something that gave me a great deal of Uneasiness; drawing up my Musick under the Lady's Window, besides her Face, which was at the Casement wide open, I saw the Reflexion of a Periwig move towards the Corner of the Window; this made me vehemently suspect somebody had a better place in her Affections than my self, for there was no Male kind belonging to the Family, her Father and Brother, as she told me at other Times, being in *Spain*, to take care of some Effects they expected by the Flota from the *West Indies*. However, I endeavour'd to smother this Impression of Jealousy, attributing the Mistake to the Circumstances of Night, Candle Light, or some other false Medium that might ground it, so I was resolv'd to take no notice of it at my next Visit. But it was not long before I met with another Occasion of Jealousy, which cou'd not so easily be banish'd out of my Head. Sitting in the Chocolate House, a young Gentleman was giving himself Airs with a Snuff-box, which to my Eye (and it was my Interest to observe it very narrowly) appear'd to be the very same I had some time before presented the Lady with, and as an aggravating Circumstance, in taking Notice of the Gentleman's Periwig, it had the same Form with the Reflexion I saw up in the Lady's Chamber Window, *vid.* a flat Top, neither rais'd nor parted in the Middle, which spoke it to be a Piece of *English* Furniture. The Sight of the snuff-box drew all my Blood into my Heart, and left my pale Cheeks to account for the Consternation, wherefore not able to contain my self had I kept my Ground, I flung out of the Chocolate House, not unobserv'd by the Company to be in some Disorder; but when they look'd out of the Window and saw me stand gazing in the middle of the Street, (for my Motion thither was purely Animal, having no thought whither I was going) it encreas'd their Surprise. However, at three Steps I was got again into the Chocolate House, and with a galliard Air, addressing my self to the Gentleman with the Snuff box, *Sir*, said I, *I confirm the Gift, and may all sniffling Fools that are in Love be serv'd like me*. I allow'd no Time for a Reply, but bolting again into the Street, it came into my Head that perhaps two Snuff-boxes might be so much alike, as not to observe the difference without confronting 'em. This Thought gave me a Curiosity to step into a Toyshop, where I desired to have a Sight of the newest fashion'd Snuff-boxes, and when among others, I saw above half a Dozen exactly like that I had made the Lady a Present of, a Secret Confusion spread it self over my Soul to have given way to such Suspicions. The Matyrdom accustom'd by such like Thoughts as these being the usual Entertainment of Persons in my Condition, and I having read in several Moralists, *That there can be no true Love without a Mixture of Jealousy, which two rose proportionably, and that Jealousy was the greatest Plague of Human Life*. These Considerations, I say, made me Struggle hard to throw off the Tyranny I groan'd under, and it happen'd very luckily for me that within a few Days after the young Lady was sent for into *Spain*, so that I had in Election either to throw up all my Expectations in *France*, and follow her, or Moralize a Week or two; upon the Disappointment, and so recover my self again to my Senses, which I quickly did by spending my Time in a Treatise of Algebra and Fortifications. As for the Lady she parted without any Reluctance, and it mortify'd me sensibly, that what I had made a Study and Business of, was only her Diversion and Amusement; but I kept my Resolution never more to divert my self that way, till I was effectually tramell'd.

And now I was preparing to visit *Italy*, where some of the *Irish* Forces were then employ'd, and my Company expected me; but before I set out, I had a mind to inform my self better of a certain Report wisper'd at *St. Germains*, That in a little Time King *James* would make another Push, and that a Descent in *England* was certainly in Agitation. Now I was at a Loss how to be truly inform'd of this Matter; the King's Fleet rendevouzing upon the Coast of *Normandy*, and several Battalions marching that way, look'd something like a Descent, but this was not sufficient to convince me, who knew that such Alarms were often given upon a quite different Score, to what the Generality of

People had in View. However, the *French* laid strong Colours upon this Preparative; first they gave out, That they had bribed most of the *English* Fleet, so there wou'd be no Danger from that Quarter nor Body to oppose the Descent; again, King *James* set forth a solemn Manifesto, inviting all his Subjects to rise and take Arms, granting an Amnesty only to such as were specify'd in his Proclamation, and to put the last Stroke to this Master-piece of Policy; the King himself was perswaded to appear at the Head of some Troops upon the Coast of *Normandy*. The Pill thus guilded, was swallow'd by every Body; I own I was my self charm'd with the Beauty of the Project, and it look'd so like the dawning of a Restoration, that I was resolv'd to make Interest with our General, that I might not return to my Company upon the Borders of *Italy;* but rather accompany my Prince, and contribute more immediately to conclude the happy Work. While these Matters were in Agitation, I had an Invitation to see the Palace and Gardens of St. *Clou*, from an old Acquaintance, whom I knew an Officer upon the *Rhine*, but now was one of the Duke of *Orlean's* Secretaries. This Gentleman, as we walk'd in St. *Clou's* Gardens, being inquisitive how I had spent my Time since our last parting, and how my Affairs stood at present, I gave him a short Narration of my Travels and Actions, telling him I was now a Captain of Foot, and had a Promise of a Lieutenant Colonels Commission the next Vacancy, but that I design'd to throw up my Pretensions, and accompany King *James*. The Gentleman surpriz'd at what I said, I suppose Sir, said he, you must have a fair Prospect of a Place at Court to put it at Ballance with a Lieutenant Colonels Commission, and then turning his Discourse into Raillery, or perhaps says he, you are so taken with the beautiful Enclosures of *Normandy*, as to think a Tour in that Country will recompence all other Losses. No Sir, said I, but I am in hopes, that as I am one who have been useful to his Majesty in several Capacities, so being near his Person in the Descent, if it prove Successful, as no Body seems to question, so I shall be more in his Majesty's Eye, and in fairer Prospect of climbing, than if I were doing him Service at a Distance. Well, Sir, said he, I am sorry our former Intimacy does oblige me to use the Freedom of disabusing you of this vulgar Error of most of King *James's* Subjects. I cannot blame

10*

them for being desirous to return Home, but they are so Infatuated in their Zeal that way, that they imagine every Step our Monarch takes, tends immediately towards their Master's Restoration; believe me, old Friend, Kings have commonly long Heads, and 'tis well known *Lewis* XIV has led all *Europe* through so many Politick Mazes for these Forty or Fifty Years, that he never lets any Body know he is doing a Thing till 'tis in a manner done. All Masters in Politicks look one way and Row another. I own the Preparatives upon the Coast of *Normandy* look like a Descent, but there are false Attacks upon Kingdoms as well as upon Towns: You are not Ignorant that King *William* is now at the Head of a powerful Army in *Flanders*, and that our King is not so well provided there as he expected; Now if King *William* receives the Reinforcement he expects out of *England* and *Scotland*, it will give him that Superiority, that *France* will not be able to make the last stand on that Quarter; so that 'tis no Secret for us at *Versailles*, that all this Alarm of a Descent upon *England*, is a meer blind to make a Diversion, and to hinder the Transportation of the *British* Forces. But you Jacobites and *English* are so ragingly dispos'd, to give every Thing a favourable turn towards King *James*'s Cause, that I have frequently observ'd, there can scare be two Men of War sent out of any Port of *France*, let it be towards the *Indies*, *Mediterranean*, or other Places, but you make a Descent of it. But as I insinuated Sir, I am glad I have the Opportunity to set you to Rights as to this Affair, that you may not risque a seeming promising Fortune, by catching a Shadow. The Thoughts of having King *James* made such a Tool of, would not permit me immediately to be civil to the Gentleman, and return him Thanks for the seasonable Advice; however, after I had recollected my self, I did my Duty in that Respect: But the Idea he gave me of his Masters Politicks left a Deep Resentment on my Soul. Afterwards, as I return'd to *Paris*, I ruminated upon this Subject, and I saw a thousand Contradictions and Improbabilities in the pretended Descent. The Troops design'd for this Business was very few, and the worst in *France*; the King's own Subjects were not to be employ'd, unless a few Straglers; besides there were no Transportships, nor in fine, any Thing that look'd like an Attempt to Conquer three Potent Kingdoms. King *William* had in a manner the whole Kingdom in his Design at his Descent, he also had the *English* Army secur'd to him, he brought over 15000 Veterans in a Fleet of 600 Sail, but this sham Descent was destitute of all these Advantages. I don't question but *Lewis* XIV, as he proposed an End in this Politick Amusement, so it answer'd accordingly; but as for poor King *James*, I know no Benefit either He or his Friends reap'd from it, besides the Fatigue of a *Norman* Progress, and having all the Jacobites in *England* imprison'd, fin'd, and plunder'd; so that to gain a few Acres of Land to *France*, *England* must be exasperated to let all the Laws loose upon both Protestants and Roman Catholicks that were Well-wishers to King *James*. And yet though the French Court obtain'd their Ends in one Respect, they suffer'd from the Hand of Providence in another. I wou'd not be thought to pry with too much Curiosity into the hidden Paths of Providence, otherwise I should be apt to judge that the Destruction of the *French* Fleet at the *Hague*, look'd somewhat like a Judgment from Heaven for amusing an unfortunate Prince with a false Prospect of Happiness, and yet that loss has been sometimes objected to King *James*, as marr'd upon his Account, so dextrous are the *French* in turning Things to their own Credit.

After this you may well imagine I took a new Resolution not to part with the Prospect I had of making my Fortune in the Post I was in, joyning Company therefore with three or four more Officers who belong'd to the same Army in which I serv'd, we set out with all Expedition. I don't remember to have been better diverted upon the Road, since I first knew what it was to Travel; one of our Company was a *Provincial*, and the very Quintessence of Wit and Gaiety. There was not the most trivial Occurrence but he dexterously made use of it to divert us, particularly at a small Village within a Days Journey of *Lions*. The Bailiff of the Village coming to our Inn to gather a kind of Tax (as it happen'd to be a Day pitch'd upon for that end) for the Relief of the Poor, the *Provincial* Gentleman being deputed, the Steward of our Company, fell into some Discourse with the Bailiff in the Kitchin. Among other Things, the Bailiff being mellow, gave him to understand, that though his Mien and Equipage was not extraordinary, yet he was the Chief Man in the Town, and

immediately represented the King's Majesty, so that if any of the
Company were of Quality, it was his Business to show them that
Respect which was due to them. The *Provincial* had a good Cue
to give us a Comical Scene, which all was contriv'd upon the
Spot, to drive away a deep Melancholy from one of our Company, who had not spoke a Word in two Days. With that he
took the Bailiff aside, Sir, said the Person, we all attend here on
the Prince of —— Eldest Son, who is going to Travel into *Italy*.
Had there been a Garison here, it ought to have been drawn up at
his Entrance, and the Keys of the Town deliver'd to him; but
since you are not so provided, you may exert yourselves as much
as you can; I suppose you have Musick in the Town? yes Sir said
the Bailiff, we have three Violins, a grand Bass, and a Citherne.
Do you never exhibit any Plays says the *Provincial*, or other
Antick Performance? No replies the Bailiff, but we have a Sport
that comes very near it, which we entertain the Country with
twice a Year, *viz.* at *Easter* and *Whitsunday*, and the Parts are now
fresh in the Actors Memory. This will do says the *Provincial*, but
see all Things are ready to give the Young Prince the Diversion
immediately after Supper, because he durst not sit up very late.
As for the Prologue, wherein you are to Address your selves to his
Highness, I will furnish you with the Method and Form in which
it must be spoke by the Schoolmaster of the Town. Now all this
was carried on in Privacy from us, tell we were call'd out one by
one, all excepting the Chagrin Gentleman, who lay dozing in an
two arm'd Chair, to whom we were instructed to pay a singular
Respect to during Supper, to blind the Matter. And now the
whole Village was drawn about the Inn, to have a Sight of the
young Prince. After Supper all the Tables and Chairs were remov'd; the Bailiff enters with his Staff, and according to Information given him, Kneels down and pays his Respects to the
suppos'd Prince; After him comes in the Actors in their proper
Dresses; and then the School-master, who open'd the Farce with
a Comical Address made by the *Provincial* Officer, which in every
Line hinted at some Passage of the Melancholy Gentleman's Life,
but with such an Ambiguous turn, and yet home to the Man,
that it was an excellent Piece of Diversion, to observe the variety of
Motions in the Princes Countenance, who thought all to be

Witchcraft and Inchantment. The Force being over, and we left to our selves, the *Provincial* returning up Stairs from conducting his Troop to the Door, Well, Gentlemen, says he, how do you relish your Diversion? *Et vous Monsieur le Prince*, if this will not bring you to your self, you shall be Dethron'd at *Lyons*, and put upon a Level with the rest of the Company; for he that pretends to put on a starch'd reserv'd Air upon a Journey, make himself a Prince by his Distance, and so must either lose his Dignity by being good Humour'd, or pay the Reckoning like a Prince, and that we have Decreed shall be your Choice the Remainder of the Journey. The *Provincial* gain'd his End, for either this comical Accident was the Occasion, or the Term of the Gentleman's Melancholy was expired; for afterwards he put on a gay Temper, and proved tollerable Company.

We cou'd not content our selves with a single Nights Lodging in *Lyons*, that City is furnish'd with too many Rarities for the amusement of Strangers, not to partake of a little more of their Money than any Vulgar Inn upon the Road. And as we none of us desired to carry more with us than what wou'd Answer our Travelling Expences, so we joyn'd in a Resolution to divert our selves one Week or ten Days in that Populous Place. I had a Recommendation from *Paris* to an *Irish* Clergyman, who was a Prependary here, and a Person of Repute. This Gentleman wou'd oblige me to take a Bed with him during my stay there, which I was very unwilling to accept of upon Account of my Company, however, he said that would be no Inconvenience, since I might take my freedom with them all the Day, in case I wou'd favour him with my Company half an Hour before Bed time in the Evening. I perceiv'd this Goatly Clergyman was of a different Stamp to the Generality of his Countrymen, and had a true Idea of the *French* Politicks, for discoursing one Night upon the Subject of a Restoration, and finding I was a Person he might deliver his Mind freely to. Certainly, *said* he, never Prince was more the Game of Politicians and Fools than King *James* II. His own Friends at home threw him out of his Throne by their forward and indiscreet Management, and now he is bubbled with daily Hopes of Recovering it, when in reality there was never any Design to bring it about. But King *James* will always be King *James*, and

Judge every Man Honest, who does but pretend to be so; for pray, gave me leave Sir, will it pass for a seizable Story in future Ages. That *Lewis* XIV should make War in order to Restore *James* II and keep above 40000 Men in constant Pay, and never employ any of them that way. Twenty thousand Horse would have laid the Three Kingdoms desolate in a few Weeks, but was there so much as one single Dragoon employ'd that way? Was not King *James* forced to melt his Canon and debase the Coin with it, whilst *Lewis* XIV could send vast Remittances to *Constantinople* to Support the *Turk?* Were not 300000 Men driven like Sheep from the Banks of the *Boyne* for want of Arms, while what wou'd have furnish'd a Million of Men, were Rusting in the Magazines of *France?* Were not the Highlanders constantly neglected, and fed with nothing but Promises, till they were reduc'd from a Victorious Army to a Troop of Banditti? Have not the Lives and Fortunes of Thousands in *England* payed very dear for these *French* Politics, by being encourag'd to rise up and Precipitate themselves into Ruin, by the Motions of Fleets and Armies upon sham Pretences of making Descents. I own Sir, I am transported when I find an Opportunity to vent my self upon this Subject. Had *Lewis* XIV been streightned by the Allies, he might have some pretence of not affording so much Assistance as otherwise he might; but in the last War, he was always Victorious both upon the *Rhine* and in *Flanders*, and if after the Battle of *Steenheer, Fleurs, Landen,* and Victories at Sea, besides the vast number of Towns he reduced, he did not think fit to employ his Arms towards restoring King *James*, I must take the Liberty to think the War was not begun upon his Account, nor that it can be judg'd the Interest of *France* (unless they act against their own interest, which they are too wise a Nation to do) to have him re-establish'd. But all this, Sir, I speak under the Rose; the Honour of the *French* Court is too much touch'd by such Reflections as these to suffer them to go unpunish'd if I should be discover'd. But I conclude from my worthy Friend at *Paris* who gave me your Character, that I might use any freedom in your Company. It may perhaps look like Ingratitude in me to reflect upon a Person by whose Benevolence I possess this Post I have in the Church, which does not only afford me a decent Maintenance, but the Opportunity of obliging a Friend, but as I was a greater sufferer in *Ireland*, by giving too much into *French* Projects, so I look upon both this or any other Kindness they can do me, as a piece of Restitution. The Frank and open Satyr of this Clergyman against the *French* Conduct was very agreeable to my Temper, and I was not backward in seconding him in the same Key. But while we were entertaining our selves with these dismal Reflections, a Servant knock'd at the Chamber Door, so the Gentleman step'd to know his Business, and after about half a Quarter of an Hour return'd again. I have been, says he, this Fortnight engaged in a very troublesome Affair, which is like to have an ill Consequence to the Party concern'd. Here is, says he in Town an *Englishman*, who has, as he informs me, been studying at a College of that Nation of *Rome*, but for want of Health is oblig'd to break off his Studies, to have the Benefit of his own Country Air, which the Physicians prescribe to him as the only Remedy to patch up his decaying Constitution: But the poor Gentleman, about Three Leagues out of Town, as he was steering his Course towards *Paris*, and so Homeward, met with a very unfortunate Accident. Walking on the Road about half an Hour before Sun setting, he was overtaken by a Gentleman who kept pace with him, and ask'd him among other Things how far he design'd to Travel that Night, the *Englishman* told him he was a Stranger to the Stages upon the Road, but he believ'd he should take the Opportunity of the next Inn, for that it began to grow late. The *French* Man appear'd very obliging in his Conversation, and told him he should have been glad of his Company, but that he was oblig'd to turn off on the Right Hand to a Friends House, whither he was going to divert himself a Day or Two. They had not gone a Hundred Rood farther, but he stop'd and desired the *English*-man if he wou'd take a pinch of Snuff, and then look'd backward and forward with an ominous Countenance, he Collar'd the *Englishman*, and drawing a small Pistol out of his Pocket, without any farther Ceremony, he cry'd *Ou la vie, ou la Bourse*. The Business was quickly over, and the *Englishman* robb'd of all his Stock, which was to the value of Nine Pounds *English*, besides a little Box of *Roman* Coin, which were small Pieces of Money he kept for Counters. The Foot-pad, after he had got his Booty, alters his Course, and turns back towards *Lions*, charging the *Englishman* not to pursue him, nor yet go forward till he saw him out of Sight; for if he did, he wou'd certainly return upon him and deprive him of his Life as well as his Money. There was no arguing the Case, and the Surprize was so great, that had there been any way of escaping this Accident, 'tis probable it wou'd not have occurr'd at that time.

As soon as the Villain was out of sight, the *Englishman* loitered his Time too and fro till it was dark, and then return'd backward towards *Lyons*, hoping to meet either with Credit or Charity for a small Sum to bear his Charges home, but not being able to reach the Town that Night, he put in at a poor Cabaret, where he open'd his dismal Condition to the Master of the House, who being a very Compassionate Man, promis'd to entertain him *Gratis* that Night, and conduct him to *Lyons* the next Morning. His first Application was to me; I promis'd to get him some Relief in a Day or Two, and the mean Time I procur'd him a Lodging. The next Day coming up a Street which leads to my House, he accidently cast his Eyes into a Habadasher's Shop, where he saw a Person sitting upon a Stool at the side of the Counter chaffering for a Hat; his Back, and a Silk Bag his Wigg was tied up in, had so much the Resemblance with the Person that rob'd him, that he stood gazing into the Shop so long, that the shop-keeper step'd to the Door, and call'd to him if he would come in and please to buy any Thing, upon which the Gentleman upon the Stool turning himself about to look out of the Shop, he was known to be the same Man who had committed the Robbery, and being in a Consternation to see the Person he had assaulted stand directly before the Shop, he threw down the Hat he had in his Hand, and leaving his Money upon the Counter, bolted out of the Door; but the *Englishman* immediately alarm'd the whole Street, and the Rogue was taken and carried before a Magistrate. In the mean time I was sent for to assist the *Englishman* in the Narrative of this Fact. At first the Footpad denied he ever saw the Person, and as for the Money it cou'd not be sworn too; but the Box with little Roman Pieces being found upon him, he cou'd not stand that Proof, besides, it appears he can give no Account where he was the Evening of the Robbery, and the Innkeeper upon the Road, is positive he was one of the Persons which pass'd by his House that Evening; and to compleat all, several Persons who came in to see him out of Curiosity, depos'd, that he is very like the Man, by Description, has follow'd that Road several Years. To conclude, the *Englishman* only stays in Town now to be Witness against this *Malhoneux*. Hanging is certainly his Doom; but if other Suspicions are made out, of his being that noted Offender, who had infested the Road for a considerable Time, it will be his Fate to be broke upon the Wheel. However, the *Englishman* has recover'd most of his Money, but he will be forc'd to expend it on Charges; but I will see to ease him in that Point. I was very much edify'd with this Clergyman's Generous and Christian Temper in being obliging and endeavouring to do good to every Body. But now the Time drew near that we were to leave *Lyons*, we had but one Day more to stay, and that the *Irish* Prebendary challenged to himself, desiring I and my Companions would accept of a small Treat and Dine with him. We had every thing that was good in its kind, but he wou'd not press his Wine upon us, for the Churchman's Character, was not to be Sacrific'd to the Soldiers Appetite; for he who urges the Glass too far, if he is not himself suspected of Insobriety, is certainly obnoxious to the immoral Part of the Ceremony.

When an Army is not upon Action, the Camp is a tedious Place to spend a Mans time in; but we, who are Subjects of *Great Britain*, had some additional Circumstances to make our Time lie heavy upon our Hands; For my own part, I always look'd upon my self as a banish'd Man, and my Thoughts always look'd homeward. There are a great many Charms in some sort of Delusions, especially, if they flatter Inclination. It was now almost grown into a settled Opinion with me, that *France* would never make any farther Attempt to restore King *James*, than by way of Amusement, to drive on some other Project; and yet upon the least Intimation of a Descent, my Inclinations willingly carry'd me over to another Belief: And of this my wavering Temper I soon after gave a very remarkable Instance. My Brother-in-law inform'd me by Letter from *Paris*, that there was a deep Design laid to make us all Happy in a little Time, so he advised me to make what haste I could, for that now the Sea was dividing, and the Children of *Israel* were upon their march to the *Land of Promise*. Immediately I answer'd the Summons, and gave into the Advice by taking Post, and had the Satisfaction to Sup with my Brother in five Days time. The very next Day I went to St. *Germains*, where I was glad to find every thing in such forwardness. The King was preparing himself to go to *Callis*, where a considerable Body of Men were Rendevouzing, as 'twas generally believ'd, in order to be transported into *England*; where in and about *London*, several Persons were privately engag'd, and ready with Arms to receive the King at Landing. In the Town of St. *Germains*, several Persons dispos'd of their Lodgings and Furniture and turn'd them into Money for this Expedition. The Day came that the King was to take leave of the Queen, and here I was resolv'd to play the Physiogminist, and observe in their Countenances, whether I cou'd see any thing that look'd like a Descent, for I did not think it improbable, but the King by this time might be so far habituated to the *French* Politicks, as to concur to be made a Fool of, and I was not the only one of that Opinion, that the King himself was let into the Secret, and knew very well his Journey to *Callis*; and hovering about the Coast, was only to keep back ten Thousand *English* and *Scotch*, whose Presence, that Campaign, would have done the *French* no kindness in *Flanders*. An old Project; and thus much I read both in the King and Queen's Face, for neither at parting, nor afterwards, did the Queen signify that Disturbance which she could not have conceal'd, had the Project been real. I need not give the Reader any farther Account of this Matter for it shewed it self upon the Kings returning to St. *Germains*. Had this Design been attended with no worse Circumstances than harassing a Monarch, and fooling his Subjects at *Paris*, and St. *Germains*, it might here be regarded as an Innocent stroke of Politicks, though very disobliging and improper; but if we look on the other side the Channel, it had occasion'd very Cruel and Barbarous Consequences. Those unfortunate Gentlemen who went upon the Strength of this sham Project to raise Men, provide Arms and Horses, and attempt seizing of King *William*'s Person, are dear Instances of *French* Policy; for 'tis not to be suppos'd that *Church*, *King*, Sir *William Perkins*, Sir *John Friend*, Sir *John Fenwick*, or half a hundred of their Adherents, wou'd either have attempted the Conquering of three Kingdoms, or been discover'd by any of the Confederacy, had not the *French* both encourag'd 'em and left 'em in the lurch.

It was observable after this Peregrination, that King *James* began to ride with a very loose Rein, and throwing the Bridle in the Neck, managed his Concerns with a great deal of Indifference. He saw clearly how fatal a Thing it was for one King to fall into the Hands of another; and that under the plausible Cloak of Hospitality, and Royal Protection, a Person might be lull'd a Sleep in the Arms of an Enslaver. When Princes are detain'd Prisoners, they generally wear all the Symptoms of their Royalty besides that of Freedom, which cannot be distinguish'd so much by the Eye as, the Judgment; and if some of King *James*'s Subjects regarded their Master with the same Compassion at the Castle of St. *Germains* as if he had been in the *Bastile*, there was very little Difference to be found besides the largeness of the Enclosure. And if King *James* has not often been heard to let drop Expressions as if he regarded himself no otherwise than a Politick Prisoner, I am very much misinform'd by those who constantly attended his Person. The denying him his own Guards, the number of Spies he had upon all his Actions, the Uneasiness he often shew'd that he cou'd enjoy no Privacy, are Circumstances that smell very strong of a Prison. However, the Pretence of protecting a Person in Distress, was a noble Sham, and so well dress'd up, that the Generallity ne'er look'd through the Disguise. The Salary allow'd him, and frequent Protestations of standing by him with unpolitic Heads, were look'd upon as undeniable Proofs of *Lewis* XIV.' Sincerity; but those who were better acquainted with *French* Stratagems, easily pull'd off the Vizard. King *James* fell into the Hands of *France*, and was a rich Opportunity in the *French* Hands, from whence they might raise a Thousand Advantages. He was too great a Treasure to be parted with only upon good Terms. A Tool no less useful to make a Diversion in time of War, than to obtain a beneficial Article at the Conclusion of Peace; and if upon the Foot of this Maxim he was not thrown into one side of the Scales at the Peace of *Reswick*, when *France* cou'd have no other Motive but being gratified with an Equivalent for the disclaim of his Title, I shall own my self a Stranger to the Spirit and Design of that Treaty. Two things surpris'd all *Europe* upon that Treaty, the first was, that *France* should be so inclinable to hearken to a Peace after a War, in which he had always been successful. The other was, that no regard shou'd be had to King *James*, not so much as to be admitted to speak, though *France* pretended to have undertaken the War meerly upon his Account, and that his Quarrel seem'd to be the only Circumstance to justify his Conduct in the War. The Hopes of gaining Time to work his Ends upon *Spain*, will easily account for his forwardness in clapping up a Peace, and giving up more Towns than he had been Master of by by the War; for thus like a through pac'd Politician, he humbled himself by little Condescensions to the Feet of the Allies, and sacrifices these Excrescencies of his Glory, in hopes very speedily to make good all such Deficiences by the larger Acquisition of *Spain*: But nothing will answer the other Part of People's Expectations. *Lewis* XIV had often made solemn Protestations, that as the War was principally undertaking to do right to K. *James*, so Peace should not be made unless he was consider'd; and unless it were a few near the Person of *Lewis* XIV who were in the Secret concerning the Design upon *Spain*, there was not a Man in *France* but who had a better Opinion of their Monarch's Honour, than to think he wou'd desert King *James* the Second's Cause in so scandalous a Manner, as not to admit his Plenipotentiaries to speak at *Reswick*: Yes, so undefensible was the Conduct of *France* upon this Head, that they commonly own'd they were asham'd to look any that belong to the Court of St. *Germains* in the Face, since all their lofty Protestations for restoring King *James* ended in the self-ended Design of securing the *Spanish* Monarchy in the House of *Bourbon*. And thus poor King *James* had implicitely devoted himself to the *French* King's Politicks, first by suffering himself to be led blindfolded, and after he had pull'd off the Veil, (though some will have it he died with the Film upon his Eyes) caress'd the Opportunity, and made it a principal Ingredient among those Misfortunes which he was in hopes to raise his Merits hereafter, and if he question'd the *French* King's Sincerity, he either durst not tell him, or scrupled to publish his Insincerity.

These were the melancholly Meditations with which the more

discerning part of King *James's* Friends often entertain'd themselves, but great care was taken that no such Language shou'd reach the *French* Court. Their Honour was too nearly touch'd to pass over such Reflexions in that severity and remarkable Punishment. I took my self to be pretty Cautious upon such like Subjects, yet upon this last pretended Descent, King *James* being inform'd that I had express'd my self very improperly upon the Matter, so as to blame the Dilatory Methods of *France* upon his Account, I was order'd to be Prisoner in my Lodgings, but releas'd after two Days Confinement, with a threatning Charge, never more to reflect upon the *French* King's Conduct. I do not remember where I spoke the Words, or in what Company, but I believe I might make a loose upon their Management who prefer'd the *French* to the King's own Subjects upon this Expedition; adding withal, that it look'd as if such Persons had no Design the Project should take Effect, but this was enough to shew I had a jealous Mind.

About this Time my Company, with the rest of the Regiment, was order'd down into *Flanders*, and having been a considerable Time absent I was commanded to attend there. My Brother-in-law who was one of the Robe in his own Country, and unacquainted with the Wars, yet was moved with a certain Curiosity to see a Campaign, and tho' much against my Sister's Will, resolv'd to accompany me into *Flanders*; yet his Principal Motive was to make a Halt at *Doway*, whither he had been invited some time before by a near Relation belonging to the *Scotch* College in that University. We went together in the *Cambray* Coach, and after a short stay at *Doway*, we proceeded on to the Army, which then was under that expert and resolute General the Duke of *Luxembourg*. It was certainly a kind impulse of Heaven that gave me my Brother for a Companion upon this Occasion; for an Action happening soon after, viz. the famous Battle of *Launden*, where it was my Misfortune to be dangerously wounded. I had the Satisfaction of my Brother's Company and Assistance during a tedious Sickness, which was the Consequence of my Wounds. The *French* were no great Gainers by this Battle, though they at long run routed the Enemy, and kept the Field; for besides the great loss they sustain'd during the Attack, which far exceeded that of the Allies, the Victory was not well pursu'd. It was my Post to reinforce a Party of *French* Fusiliers, who were order'd to Storm the Intrenchmenent, in which Service a Bullet was lodg'd in my Shoulder, which besides disabling me on one Side, the loss of Blood I suffer'd was so great, that I was not able to support my self, but drop'd down and had been trampled to Death under my own Mens Feet, had not a strong Body'd Drummer hurried me out of the Croud upon his Back; but he carried me off with such Precipitation, that one of the Enemies Troopers seeing me at a Distance, and thinking me to be somebody of Consequence, sprung after me upon his Gelding, and carried both me and the Drummer into a Village on the left Hand of the Attack, where several Squadrons were posted. The commanding Officer who was a Colonel of the *English* Guards, finding, I was of the *British* Nation, order'd me to be laid in a Barn with a Centinel to guard me, and the Surgeon of the Regiment was immediately call'd for to dress and tie up my Wounds. I had not been in that Lodging above an Hour, but the Village was attack'd by the *French* Gens d' Arms, and there was a Tryal of Skill between the Flower of both the Armies, in which Action the *French* at last were Superior, so I was releas'd, but it was equal to me in the Condition I was in whose Hands I fell into, for I had so many fainting Fits which succeeded one another, that I expected not to survive any of 'em. My Brother, whom I desired to go to *Loraine* during the Action had a Mind to be a little nearer, so remain'd with the Baggage, but met not with me till the next Day, that we both went in a Waggon to his Lodgings in *Loraine*, where I was confin'd three Months before I was able to Travel.

In this Retirement it was that I began to be very Serious: A Soldiers Life has many Occurrences which are not very reconcileable to strict Morality. To comprize my own Character in relation to Christianity, I was neither a Saint nor a Devil. The Pains I felt were very Sharp, and hindred my Rest; my Blood was heated and boiling up to a Fever, which being agitated with daily dressing my Wounds, it requir'd a skillful Physician and a good Regimen in the Patient, to stave off a Fit of Sickness. My Brother prov'd an excellent Nurse, and had he not us'd a great deal of Reason in keeping me from improper Nourishment, the Game would quickly have been up with me. I was also waited upon several times by a worthy Clergyman, who neglected not to give me Penitent Hints to have regard to the main Concern; I return'd him Thanks, and gave him to understand I would make use of him when there was more urgent Occasion. When I began to grow a Valetudinarian, and that my Wounds began to heel up, I had the Liberty to drink *Loraine* Beer, which is much celebrated in those Parts. As yet I had drank nothing but Tissans and such like Decoctions, which being very mild upon the Palate, did not give content to the inward dryness and thirst I felt by the loss of Blood. But I quickly repented this Indulgence of tasting the Beer, I took such deep Draughts that I relaps'd into a dangerous and most violent Fever, in which I acted all the Parts of a dying Man, besides making my Exit; I was delirious above three Days, which though it was but a melancholly Sight in it self, yet I behav'd my self so various in my rambling Discourse, that it occasion'd no small Diversion to such as were present, and had no immediate concern in my Welfare. I besieg'd Towns, rally'd scattered Forces, accepted Challenges, wandered over the *Alpes*, and pass'd over several Seas without Ships; I was in the Orchard at the Boyne, under the Walls of *London Derry*, and diverted with the fine Rode to *Lions*, and what I thought I should never have in my Head again, some amorous Ideas, though very faint one's, discover'd themselves, and I was heard to talk of Snuff-Boxes, Periwigs, and *Spanish* Ladies. My Brother who heard me, and to whom I had discover'd that Intrigue, burst out into a Laugh when he heard me name Snuff-Boxes; for this was enough to make him believe the Passion was not dead in me, which he horded up to rally me with.

During this Entertainment which I gave the Spectators, my Brother had sent for the Priest, but I was then in a very improper State to settle Accounts in Relation to the next World. However, the Gentleman approaching my Bed, and calling upon me to hear whether I could return a rational Answer. He bid me lift up my Heart to God, and call upon my Redeemer. But I, as I suppose, taking him to be one of my Sergeants, bid God — D—n him for a Rascal, why had he not been with me before? for the Colonel had order'd a Review shou'd be made at Eleven a Clock.

The Priest shrugg'd up his Shoulders, sprinkled me with Holy Water, and retir'd to the Window, where my Brother and the Physician were attending my Fate. When my Delirious Fit was over, which was about an Hour afterwards, I turn'd my Eyes towards the other Side of the Room, where I saw three Persons leaning in the Window with their Backs towards me; and not being entirely recover'd from my Delirious State, I fancied my self a Prisoner at *Constantinople*, and that my Brother, the Physician, and the Priest, were three Mutes sent to Strangle me; but in an Instant or two I return'd to my self, and discover'd whose Hands I was in. This was a terrible Attack, and the Enemy had made such a Breach, that I desired to wisper a Word with the Priests, telling him I wou'd Capitulate next Morning about Eight a Clock. Afterwards I recover'd very leisurely, and took great Care not to be too bold with the *Lorain* Beer. My Phician advised me not to remove from that Place till I was perfectly establish'd, assuring me there was not better Air in all the *Netherlands*. I follow'd his Advice, for I cou'd not think him prompted to give it me through Avarice, for he was so very moderate in his Fees, that I thought my self oblig'd at our parting to make him a handsome Present. My Brother who was a Man of Letters, and very curious in his Enquiries, had a good opportunity during our stay here to get acquainted with several learned Men of this University. One of the first account was Dr. *Martin* an *Irish* Clergyman, who had a lively Genious and was also a Person of great reading. In the mean time my Sister at *Paris* began to grow impatient for her Husband, but she bore his Absence the better when she understood how useful he had been to me during my Sickness. However, we made bold to Trespass a little further, by taking a turn round the Country. It was not a Journey entirely of Pleasure, for I was oblig'd to go to *Amsterdam*, there being a stop put to the Interest of my Mony, so I was resolved to see that Matter rectify'd. So having obtained a Pass from the Allies, under the Quality of two *Scotch* Merchants we began our Journey. When I came to *Amsterdam*, I was very much surpriz'd to understand the odd Occasion of my Money being stop'd. It seems a Countryman, of mine who had fish'd out something of my Concerns, and saw me fall at the Battle of *Launden*, had Counterfeited a Deed in the

Nature of a Will, which imported, that all my Effects in *Amsterdam* were left to him, he being my Brother, and demanding it as his due. The Banker had the Deed perus'd by several Persons, it had a great appearance of being Authentick, and my Hand was so inimitably clap'd to it, that when compared with what was certainly known not to be Counterfeit, 'twas impossible to discover the Difference. Now the Banker desired this pretended Brother of mine to have Patience till he had an account from *Paris* whether or no I was dead, and the general Report being that I was kill'd at *Launden*, this was the occasion that the Money was neither paid to my Correspondent nor to my Sham Brother. This Point once clear'd, I was resolv'd to find out the Person who had personated my Brother, that I might bring him to condign Punishment, as also to clear a Suspicion I had, that my Servant had a Hand in it, for otherwise I thought it impossible one that was a Stranger should know whose Hands my Money was in. In the first place I cunningly interrogated my Servant at a distance, and found enough by his Countenance that he was not entirely Innocent, however, not being able to prove it upon him, I in the next place made a diligent Search after my Sham-Brother; for he had told the Banker at his last Visit that he wou'd return again in Seven or Eight Days, and Six of 'em were now expired. The Gentleman was as good as his World. He came to the Banker with a good Assurance, and demanded both Principal and Interest. I was then at my Lodging, but being sent for, I was strangely surpris'd to see the Clerk of my Company, who was also a Sergeant, metamorphos'd into my Brother. He shrunk two Inches lower at the Sight of me; but dissembling the matter, I am glad to see thee alive Sergeant said I, for I took it for granted you were kill'd at the Battle of *Launden*; and I, reply'd the impudent Villain, thought you had, otherwise I had not been here: but if you please, noble Captain, to walk into the next Tavern and give me leave to wait upon you, I will discover to you the occasion of my coming to *Amsterdam*. My Fears as to my Money being now all over, I comply'd with the Rascal, and went along with him. But he dress'd up such a Narrative in favour of his good Intention, and strengthen'd it with such plausible Circumstances, That he and my Servant, whom he confess'd to be one of the Party, had no other Intention but to get the Money out of the Banker's Hands for the Use of my Relations; for that they had Reason to suspect I had made no Will, and so no body wou'd have a Right to demand the Money. Now though this Stratagem was very probably all a Fiction, yet it wrought so much with me, that I did not Prosecute either of 'em; for as I was acquainted with both their Friends in *Scotland*, so I had some regard for them, and dismiss'd them to go home or whither they pleas'd, not thinking it safe to entertain Persons who had been involved in such mysterious Practices.

My Affairs being settled at *Amsterdam*, we had the Curiosity to see *Antwerp*, which is a City where a Stranger may employ his Time very agreeably, for a longer Term than we cou'd conveniently spend there. We lodg'd at a House where an *English* Nobleman also had an Apartment. He had been in that City about two Months, kept a handsome Equipage, was very young, and a well bred Gentleman, of great value among the Ladies, and had he been able to support the Character he bore at first appearance here, it would have convinced the World there is very little difference between a Footman and a Nobleman, where neither Sense nor Money are wanting to carry on the Resemblance. I must anticipate the dismal Exit of this unfortunate Gentleman which happen'd not till about two Years afterwards. While he was in his Splendour at *Antwerp*, and cou'd answer every bodies Expectations as to Money matters, it was not any Mans Business to pry into his Pedigree; but when his Conduct began to be observ'd, and taken Notice to be full of Shuffling and Demurs in the Payment of small Bills, there was a Jealousy spread about the Town that the Lord G—— would prove a Cheat, so his Credit began to sink in the Shops, but it held up still among the Ladies, where a handsome Personage, and a charming Tongue is often ready Money. But it was not long before he began also to be suspected from this Quarter; his Visits were not so frequent, his Treats much more sparing; and especially one Lady, who was his greatest Admirer, and most capable to make Him Happy on all Accounts, was oblig'd to expose him, and make this Phantom of Nobility evaporate. In the frequent Visits he pay'd this Lady, he had observ'd a very handsome Diamond Ring upon her Finger, which was no less remarkable for its uncommon Form, than intrinsick Value, at a low Estimate being judg'd to be worth 80 *l.* Sterling. The Gentleman had often thrown out a great many Compliments upon it, which usually tended towards extolling the Ladies Judgment and Fancy in the choice and ordering of that Jewel, for she wanting to her self, let him and every body else know, it was a Thought of her own. The Gentleman in the midst of one of his Panegericks upon this little Charmer, begg'd the Favour of the Lady that he might borrow it for a Day or two till he had shewn it a Jeweller, for he design'd to have one made in the same Form. The Lady was not a little pleas'd that her Fancy was like to become a Pattern to the Town, willingly drew it off her Finger, not in the least suspecting any Trick, for as yet his Fame was untouch'd. I think he made two or three Visits without returning the Ring, pretending the Workman was dilatory in taking a Pattern; but 'tis suppos'd he wanted time to prepare himself for a Flight, and brush off with the Ring. However, none of these Suspicions enter'd the Ladies Head, he not being her Aversion. About three or four Days after, a Lady visiting her, told her the *English* Nobleman had parted with his Chariot, pawn'd his best Suit of Cloaths, and that his Credit was not only very low, but it was suppos'd he wou'd in a Day or two be oblig'd to Decamp, or take up his Quarters in a Jail. 'Tis obvious to imagine that the first Thing that came into the Ladies Mind upon this Occasion was her Diamond Ring; but, as she confess'd afterwards to a Friend, the Compassion she had for the Gentleman's Circumstances had so large a Place in her Heart, that she does not remember to have had any concern upon her in Relation to the Jewel; from whence we may gather that Evil Fate that hangs over some Persons Heads, for had but this unfortunate Person pursu'd the Interest he had with that Lady, whilst he was in flourishing Circumstances, he might easily have carried it to the *non plus ultra*, and became Master, of 15000, as she her self own'd when she recover'd her Passion and began to think calmly. However, the Diamond Ring was not to be neglected, for though she had been willing to have parted with her Interest in it to Succour the Gentleman in Distress, it was too large an Alms, and would perhaps have been judg'd by the World rather an Instance of her

Forwardness and Indiscretion than of her Charity. Her Friends before advis'd her to demand the Ring, which she did that Evening, but understood he had pawn'd it for the full Value; upon which she was (though much against her Inclination) oblig'd to Arrest him, and had him clap'd up in Prison: But however, she was a very kind Jailor. It is a Custom, having the Force of the Law in the *Netherlands*, that when a Debtor is kept in Prison, it shall be at the Charges of the Creditors; in which also they observe a kind of Proportion, that a Gentleman is to be allow'd like a Gentleman, and a Mechanick is to be content with a smaller Allowance. The Lady comply'd very willingly with the Custom, and her Prisoner being reputed a Person of Quality, it was an excellent Disguise to show her Liberality. But afterwards being weary of the Charge, and finding by the Information of several *Englishmen* that pass'd thro' *Antwerp*, that her Prisoner was not the Person he pretended to be, but a meer Sharper and Knight of the Post, she slacken'd in her Charity, and gradually brought him down to a common Allowance, and at last discharg'd him. His Life after that was a meer Romance; He first went into *Gaunt*, here he took up a large Apartment of four or five Rooms well furnish'd, which he sold after a Fortnight, taking an advantage of the Landlady's Abscence. With the strength of this Plunder, he made a Figure for two or three Months at *Brussels*, where he fought a Duel with *H. S.* an *English* Gentleman. This Accident drove him from *Brussels*, but finding he was not secure in the *Spanish Flanders*, he crossed the Lines, spent the remainder of his Substance at *Lisle*, and he directed his Course to *Dunkirk*, from whence 'tis said he design'd to take Shipping for *England*. But here he finish'd his Misfortunes as I was inform'd upon the Spot, by a Merchant who resided in that Town, and saw his Exit. This *English* Merchant walking upon the Key according to Custom, observ'd a young Gentleman walking in a Melancholy Posture, and thinking he knew him, though the poor Dress he was in would not suffer him to make a positive Judgment; however, he stept up towards him, and upon a nearer View, was convinc'd he was the Person he took him for. This Merchant had been acquainted with him at *Antwerp*, when he bore the Character of an *English* Nobleman and lived with great Splendor. The

Gentleman more dash'd, as I suppose, to jump upon one who had heard of his Tricks, than for the meanness of his Circumstances, told the Merchant he was an unfortunate Man, and Things were now so desperate with him, that he had no way left to relieve himself but by a Halter. The Merchant having a charitable regard for his Circumstance, though he knew him to be a very undeserving Object, told him, he wou'd provide him with a Lodging and Diet till he had a Return of Money, the Gentleman answer'd frankly he expected no Returns, nor did he know of any Body that wou'd Assist him, nor cou'd he make any Demands. This Account encourag'd the Merchant to be more Charitable, so he conducted him to an Inn, desiring the Master of the House to furnish him with Diet and Lodging till further Orders. Two Days after, the Merchant coming to Visit him about Ten in the Morning, when they imagin'd he was still in Bed, a Servant being sent up to call him, he was hang'd upon the Beam, in one Corner of his Chamber. The Merchant had a great Curiosity to find out the Pedigree of this Romantick Gentleman, but cou'd get no Authentick Account. I told him I was inform'd at *Antwerp*, that he was Footman to a Person of Quality, and that he had robb'd his Master, and fled into the *Netherlands* to escape Justice, which made him always unwilling to think of returning Home.

The Peace of *Reswick* was a ratifying King *James*'s Abdication, and enrolling in the *French* Archives, what was before declar'd in the Convention at *Westminster*. It was now no Time to expostulate with *Lewis* XIV. why he had concluded a Peace without mentioning the Person upon whose Account he had began the War? The Titular King of St. *Germains*, and the Real one at *Whitehall*, were not irreconcileable, and the continuation of the Pension was regarded as an unquestionable mark of the *French* King's Sincerity, and the unthinking Crew spoke well of the Master that cramm'd them, never dreaming that they were but fatten'd for Slaughter, and that under the Disguise of Succouring their Persons, he might Prey upon their Interest. The *Spanish* Monarchy was what *France* had in their Eye by the Peace of *Reswick*, and the Restoring of King *James* was decreed to be the Motive of a War when they came to a Rupture. Upon the Decease of the King of *Spain*, *Lewis* XIV diverted Europe with a fresh Scene of Politicks. He convinc'd 'em, that what he had done at *Reswick* was a meer Decoy to gain Time and Breath, and bring greater Designs about. The Allies saw clearly he had been jugling with two Sham Treaties of Partition, but was underhand working to engross the Whole, and that the Son and Father at St. *Germains* were always to serve to the same Purposes, and stand in the first Line of his *Manifesto*, to make the War plausible, and raise Factions in the Territories of *Great-Britain*. This was Fact, for no sooner were *Things* ready in *Spain* and *Flanders*, but King *James* II departed this Life, which opportunity the *French* Monarch snatched, and in a studied Royal Transport, exalted the young Striplings Expectations at St. *Germains* by a solemn Protestation, that he wou'd never sheath his Sword till he saw him upon the Throne of his Ancestors, by which I suppose he understood no more than that titular Inauguration which was settled upon his Father at the Peace of *Reswick*. For had not the Affair of the *Spanish* Monarchy prompted *France* to this generous Declaration in Favour of the Son, 'tis highly probable the *Gallick* Sword wou'd have rusted in the Scabbard, as it was lock'd up by the Treaty of *Reswick*, nor had it been now drawn but upon a more beneficial Provocation, than restoring King *James*, for if it was the Interest of *France* to let the Father sit down quietly with the Title, nothing cou'd supervene to give the Son the Reality. Upon this Basis the War was renewed again on both Sides, and the Juggle was kept on with the Court of St. *James*'s, and great Pains were taken by the Emissaries of *France*, to buoy up King *James*'s Friends both at home and abroad, that *Lewis* XIV was Sincere, and wou'd exert himself sooner and later in their Cause.

The World needs not be put in Mind what Service King *James* II, Troops did to *France* during the War, every Action spoke their Bravery, but the grand Reform that was made upon the Peace was a sorry recompence for their Service. *France* wou'd not entertain 'em, and a Halter was their Doom if they return'd Home. This was an odd way of obliging King *James*; I speak not so much upon my own account, (though I was reduc'd at the same Time) because I had a Sufficiency elsewhere to keep me from Starving; but it was but a melancholly sight to behold poor Men strolling upon the Road, not knowing which way to

direct their Course, and begging Alms through those Towns in
which a little before they had Triumph'd in Victory. But the
Rod is often thrown away and burnt after the Child is Whip'd.
Upon this Occasion it was that I took leave of *Mars*, resolving to
make use of this Interval of Peace, to satisfy an old Curiosity to
see *England*, a Place as yet I never had beheld. Some Acquaintance
I had contracted at *Dunkirk*, made me willing to take Shipping
there, besides the hopes I had of decoying a pleasant Gentleman
for my Companion, and upon my Arrival I found him in a good
Humour, so we set Sail about three in the Morning, and came
under *North Foreland Point* about seven the same Day. The Master
of the Vessel, though he was an old Coaster, was not willing to
trust himself among the Flats in a dark Moon, so we lay at Anchor
all Night, and in the Morning by peep of Day, the Wind being
pretty favourable, we weigh'd and pursu'd our Voyage up the
River; but being a little too soon for the Tyde, we struck upon a
Sand Bed, and oblig'd to remain ther till the Rise of the Water. I
was all alone in the Master's Cabin when this Accident happen'd,
but being very intent upon a Book, I was not sensible whether
we mov'd or stood still. A Lady who was with the rest of the
Passengers upon Deck coming hastily down, Sir, said she. Do you
sit quietly here and we are struck upon a Sand-Bed? Madame,
said I, I did suppose such a Thing, but the Tyde will cast us off.
You suppos'd such a Thing, said she, Why, Sir, we shall certainly
be drown'd, come let us to Prayers. I was not very much accustom'd to the Sea, yet I imagin'd there could be no great Danger as
long as we had a flowing Tyde, and that it did not blow a Storm:
Had the Water been ebbing and a Storm ensu'd upon it, 'tis
probable our Ship, being none of the strongest, might have been
beaten to Pieces among those Sands. However, I step'd upon
Deck to see how Things went; there was a profound Silence
every where, the Passengers were scatter'd here and there looking
one at another, but not speaking a Word; the Master was walking
with his Arms across without Fear, but not without Concern in
his Countenance: I ask'd him how he came to be mistaken in the
Tyde? he answer'd, Accidents would happen'd sometimes, but
there was no Danger. Then running on in a Strain of Sailors Cant,
he said, God was at Sea as well as at Land, that the Lord wou'd

protect 'em if they did but put their Trust in him, and love him as they ought. In the middle of this moral Lesson, the Ship was gently wafted off the Sands by the Tyde, and Sails being abroad spread, the Ship sail'd merrily along. 'Twas surprizing to observe the Alteration in every bodies Countenance; the Women began to Laugh and Giggle; the Men began to rally one another for want of Courage; the Sailors began to raise their Note higher and higher, and the Master of the Ship turn'd his Sermon into a Volley of Oaths and Curses against his Crew; and thus in an instant, from a profound Silence we recover'd our selves again to Noise and Hurry. That Day brought us to *Gravesend*, where we took Boat, and so arriv'd safe at *London*, though I was not very well pleas'd with those small Boats People usually pass in from *Gravesend* to *London*, for I understood they were often Overset by sudden Gusts of Wind which blow from the Shoar.

London is a Place above my Description, and though I lost no Time the six Months I remain'd there, to view what Curiosities were to be seen, yet 'tis probable many Things worthy of Observation escaped my Diligence. I took a particular care not to make my self Public, but pass'd at my Lodgings under Disguise of a Merchant, yet abroad I acted the Marquess, not to be depriv'd of the Means of introducing my self into the best of Company. I found they were much divided in *England* as to the *French* Politicks; some were of Opinion that *Lewis* XIV was serious in King *James*'s Cause, but these were Persons who had no Notion of Foreign Affairs, and judg'd of Matters according to their first Appearance; for others who had studied the Interest of Nations, and how their Pretensions lie in regard of one another, had no Notion of the *French* King's Sincerity, either towards King *James*, or any other Prince he dealt with, and there is not one Instance I have mention'd in these Memoirs, in order to demonstrate the Infatuated State of the Court of St. *Germains*, but I heard it frequently urg'd to the same purpose, by the most intelligent Persons, as well Friends as Enemies to King *James*. While I was diverting my self at *London*, I receiv'd a Letter from *Paris*, that there was a Lieutenant Collonel's Place vacant, which I might easily be promoted to in Case I wou'd be at the trouble to, make use of what Interest I might reasonably Command. But I quickly understood, that by my Interest was meant my Money, so employing my *Amsterdam* Stock that way, I might very probably by a *French* Piece of Civility, live to want both my Money and a Commission. I return'd a thousand Thanks to my Friends for their Diligence in my Absence, but told 'em, I had rather wait till another War broke out, and their would be more choice of Promotions, and I might please my self, because I was somewhat curious what Regiment I engag'd in.

It was a tedious Journey to go into *Scotland* by Land, otherwise I was very much disposed to see my own Country once more, and apprehending besides, there might be some Danger upon account of being engaged in the *French* Service during this late War. I laid these Thoughts aside, and contented my self with making a small Tour Twenty or Thirty Miles distance from *London*, in which Progrination I saw *Windsor, Greenwich, Hampton-Court*, and some other Places of Note. But in one of these Jaunts, I had like to have paid very dear for my Curiosity. The Neighbourhood of *London* is much infested with Highwaymen, and if a Gentleman rides not with Pistols, 'tis very probable he will be attack'd. Unacquainted with these Customs, the Day I went to *Windsor*, I had in Company with me an *Irish* Gentleman; we made use of nothing but common Hacks, nor had any other Arms but our Swords; about the middle of *Honslow Heath* we met two Gentlemen well mounted, who pass'd by us unsuspected, but turning suddenly upon us again, with each of 'em a small Pistol cock'd, they very civilly demanded our Money. Gentlemen, said I, I am a Stranger; no Gentlemen said they, come quickly deliver what you have, we are in a publick Road, and can't stand arguing; but finding us a little Dilatory, they whip'd the Bridles from our Horfes, cut our Garths, and so dismounted us; and so I and my Companion were very dexterously strip'd of what they found in our Pockets, which was all I had about me, but my Friend reserv'd two or three Guineas in his Fob. When they had finish'd their Business, they gallop'd different ways cross the Heath, and left us like a couple of Asses, to drive our Horses to the next Town, and carry the Saddles under our Arms; but by the Invention of our Garters, and some other such like Tackle, we halter'd our Steeds till we cou'd refit our selves better. What we lost was but a Trifle, and 'twas done in so small a space of Time, that appear'd like a Dream or passing Thought. It was happy either for us or them, that this happen'd in the Morning when our Heads were cool, for had they attack'd us when warm'd up with good Liquor, I believe I should have had little regard to those Pop-guns they threatened us with. When we came to the next Town, and gave the People an account of our Disaster; the Landlord of the Inn ask'd us, if we had ever been upon that Road before, and we inform'd him this was the first time, then said I have Authority to enroll you as Freemen upon the small Fee of each a Bottle of Wine, and this I take to be no Imposition, because I am plac'd here in a convenient Part of the Country to advance a small sum to such as are robb'd of all they have, and cannot pursue their Journey; so Gentlemen, if that be your Condition, I have a couple of Guineas ready for you, which I will lend upon Honour, but in Case it be not a clean Robbery, what you have conceal'd from the Diligent Highwaymen is the Landlord's Fee as far as each a Bottle of Wine. This Merry Landlord I thought was very conveniently posted to divert People after their Misfortunes, we never went about to examine him, whether his Demand was customary, or only a Piece of shire Wit, and an extempory Instance of his prolifick Genius, but sat down, and made our selves most immoderately drunk. The Landlord discanted very copiously upon the ancient and modern Practise of Robbing upon the Road, and seem'd very much inclin'd to lessen the Crime. Formerly, said he, no Body robb'd upon the Road but base scoundrel Fellows; but now 'tis become a Gentleman-like Employment, and young Brothers of very good Families are not asham'd to spend their time that way; besides the Practise is very much refin'd as to the manner, there's no Fighting or Hectoring during the Performance, but these Gentlemen approach you decently and submissive, with their Hat in their Hand to know your Pleasure, and what you can well afford to support them in that Dignity they live in: 'Tis true, says he, they often for Form sake have a Pistol in their Hand, which is part of their riding Furniture; but that is only in the Nature of a Petition, to let you know they are Orphans of Providence just fallen under your Protection. In a Word, demanding Money upon the Road, is now so agreeably perform'd, that 'tis much the same with asking an Alms. The poor Beggar wou'd rob you if he durst, and the Gentleman Beggar will not rob you if you will but give a decent Alms suitable to his Quality. I thought my time so well spent to hear this Landlord plead in favour of Padding, that I told my Companion I had often known the time that I wou'd have willingly have parted with more Money than I was strip'd of upon the Heath, to have some Melancholly Thoughts driven away by such a merry Companion.

The Time drawing near that I prescribed to my self to remain in *England*, we were now advis'd to return by the short Sea, which we perform'd without any Let or remarkable Accident. I have observ'd towards the beginning of these Memoirs, that the War begun in 1688, was undertaken in Defence of Cardinal *Fastenberg* to the Electorate of *Cologn*; the next War was for the Mornarchy of *Spain*, but the Restoration of King *James* was always a material Article, and a very useful Circumstance of the War. I need not acquaint the Reader how *France* was reduced in this last bloody War, her best Troops ruin'd, incapable to win a Battle, every Campaign carry'd two or three of their best Towns, the Nation dispirited, and Credit sunk, and nothing but a dismal Scene of Poverty and Misery: And yet in the midst of all this Misery, (as the *Spanish* Beggars are said to strut about in their Cloak and Bilboes at their Side) so this Gasping Monarch had the Assurance not only to talk of making a Descent, but actually equipp'd a small nimble Fleet with a Body of Men, and persuaded the Pretender to go upon the foolish Errand, as if he cou'd have any prospect of Conquering the Three Kingdoms, who was in danger every Moment of having his Capital Sack'd and himself turn'd out of his Throne. Cou'd there be a more Romantick Undertaking, or more unintelligible in all its Circumstances, than the Pretender's Descent upon *Scotland*? The deluded Youth was carry'd to the Coast of *Scotland*, but upon what Design, is a Secret to this Day. He was made to believe at his departure from *Dunkirk*, that *Scotland* was dissatisfy'd to a Man upon account of the Union, and that it wou'd be an easie matter to Conquer *England* by putting himself at the Head of a *Scotch* Army; but when he desired to be landed to put the Project in Execution, the *French*

General told him, he had Orders from his great Master, that there should be no Landing. Now whether this was part of the old Game, and only in Order to make a Diversion, or to surprize *Edinburgh* Castle, where most of the Specie of *Scotland* was said to be lodg'd at that time, is various alledg'd by Men of Speculation. That there was no appearance of succeeding in the main, is pretty plain from many Circumstances. *England* with their Allies at that Time were in a Capacity to spare 50000 Men, against which a few poor scrambling *Highland* Foot, wou'd but have made a very bad Resistance. I am not willing to think *France* would send Princes a Pilfering, or that the Pretender was design'd to steal the Money out of *Edinburgh* Castle, a Stratagem much more decently committed to some Partisan, or three or four *Dunkirk* Privateers. So I think it more suitable to the Prudence, and for the Honour of the *French* Court, to mention this design'd Descent only as a Diversion to amuse and employ the *British* Troops at Home, that they might not annoy the Enemy in *Flanders.* But how this Affair will be reconcil'd to that Affection and Friendship *Lewis* XIV. seem'd to have at that time for the Pretender, I am at a loss, with the rest of Mankind, to account for, since it was exposing him to the greatest of hazards for a Trifle, and throwing up the Cause at once, had he fallen into the Hands of his Enemies, and 'tis not the least Miracle of his Life that he escap'd them. I was invited to have gone abroad with the Pretender upon this Expedition, being than Free, but the Project appear'd to me so full of Inconsistencies, I have frequently since enlarg'd upon my own Politicks and Foresight in that Affair.

Thus much I must say for the Jacobite Party, never were Men more baffled and rallied oftner upon Projects or Hopes, but the unwholesome Diet never turn into the Substance, but infects the Body with peccant Humours, which now and then are discharg'd by Phlegbotomy, and then they turn to a Gangreen by Amputation. Jacobitism (I speak of it in relation to the strong Hopes they have of succeeding by a *French* Power) is an uncurable Distemper. I have often wonder'd to hear Persons, otherwise of great Penetration and Sense, grow constantly Delirious upon this Topick. The Wagers that have been lost upon that very Prospect wou'd have purchas'd him a little Kingdom. Time has open'd a

great many People's Eyes; but there is a set of Men who are en-
slaved to the *French* Projects, and so far infatuated, that nothing
can cure them. If fooling him with sham Descents, neglecting all
Opportunities of assisting, if banishing him, excluding him by
solemn Articles, will not satisfy 'em as to this Particular, 'tis my
Opinion they wou'd not be convinc'd, if they should see *France*
chaffering for his Head, and finish the Twenty Eight Years old
Politicks with 100000 *l.* being what is set upon it. There is no
extraordinary difference between disposing of another Man's
Right, and disposing of his Person. There was a Time when
France gloried in the Ostentatious Title of being the Assylum of
distress'd Monarchs, and I remember I was once dispos'd to have
almost deify'd their Monarch upon that Score; but when I took
the Frame of his Politics, and examin'd every Wheel and Spring
by which they moved, I rescued my self from the Prejudices I
had been nurs'd up in; and though I always pursu'd the same End,
yet I was a constant Enemy to their Method, which I was convinc'd were all directed another Way, and that a Restoration
upon a *French* Footing was a Chimerical Project, and that if it
had taken Effect by their Arms, *England* must have had another
Doomsday-Book, and have suffer'd once more under an Arbitary
Discipline, more dreadful than that of *William the Conqueror*, from
whom *England* has been struggling to retrieve her self ever since.

I had formerly made a Resolution with my self not to hearken
to a Love-Intrigue, but upon a Prospect of putting an end to such
Amusements. The long time I had been out of the Army, gave
me several Opportunities to make Enquiry after a Person who
was capable of making me happy in that Respect. I took a singular
Care when any Thing was offer'd that way, to consult my Reason
more than my Passions, and had fix'd before my Eyes, the per-
plex'd State I liv'd in those Weeks I held a Correspondence with
the *Spanish* Lady. 'Tis a dangerous practice when a Person shuts
his Eyes among Precipices, and neglects Consultation where the
Choice is hazardous. There liv'd in *Paris* a Collonel's Widow,
neither very young, nor very handsome. The intimacy I had with
her Husband, who was kill'd in *Italy*, brought me first acquainted
with her. Her discreet Carriage in a great variety of intricate Circumstances had often Charm'd me. There was no Difficulty in a

marriage State, but she had struggled with it; a morose Husband, the Death of an only Child, the Gripes of Poverty when her Consort was in the Army and lavish'd away his Income, were great Tryals in which she always Triumph'd, and wore a stoical Constancy without any Reservedness. She had a large Pension allow'd her for Life, upon account of her Husband's Merits, who had done great Service during the Wars. Under these Circumstances I attack'd, rather like a Judicious than a Passionate Lover. The Method I took with her, was quite different to what I observ'd in pursuing my *Spanish* Mistress. There was no Balls, Treats, nor Serenading, we both knew the World too well, either She to expect, or I to offer her such Entertainments. In a Word, our whole Discourse when I visited ran upon Oeconomy and Morals. It was not long before she understood my Meaning, and that my repeated Visits tended towards Marriage. She alledg'd several Things to divert me from it; that she was tired with being an Officer's Wife, which oblig'd either to a rambling Method of Living, or to labour under great Inconveniences, and that I, perhaps, might not make the best of Husbands, that State being a Lottery full of Blanks. I had nothing more pertinent to alledge upon this Occasion, than to assure her, that during my Absence in the Army she should never be unprovided with what would make her easie, and for being a good Husband, I gave her all the Assurances that such a Matter was capable of, and at the same time made her the Compliment, that in case any misunderstanding should ever happen between us, her approv'd Conduct and Discretion would certainly declare me Guilty. In conclusion, I put on the Trummels, and never question'd but I had made the most prudential Choice that any Person could do; but there is something in Woman-kind which can never be found out by Study or Reflection. 'Tis only Experience that can School a Husband, and can give him a true Idea of that mysterious Creature; for in less than Twelve Months my Thousand Pounds which I had so carefully kept unbroke at *Amsterdam* was all dispos'd of, my Soldiers Pay being my only Subsistance for myself and Family, my Wife reserving her own Income for Pin-mony; my Credit very low, my Days very irksome upon many accounts, and I who had hitherto appear'd with Assurance in Company, because of my Money-merit, was now Neglected; for every Tradesman began to smell out my Poverty. I am of Opinion it would do Posterity no kindness, if I shou'd discover how I came to be ruin'd by a Prudent Wife, for no Body wou'd Credit me. If I should advise 'em to trust no Woman living, so as to give her full Scope upon an Opinion of her Conduct. I took my self to be as wise, upon this Head, as any Man living. It had been my Study above twenty Years. There is a secret Devil in every Woman, which is often Conjur'd down by a Husband's Temper; and though many Men may pass for bad Husbands by their Morose Carriage, 'tis less prejudicial, than that Indulgence which few Women have Discretion to make use of. My Wife's first Husband was represented as not very kind to her, whereas his less obliging Temper was the Effect of his Judgment, and a touch of Skill he had in managing a Woman, whom Caresses wou'd have exalted into Impertinence, &c.

I would not be understood so upon this Subject, as if we lived unhappily as to our Affections; no, we regarded each other as two inseparable Companions, not only whose Interest it was not to be at variance, but we really did affectionately love each other. I cou'd not so much blame her as my self for if Children, Servants, &c. make a loose from their Duty, who are chiefly to be blam'd, but such gentle and restraining Methods did not curb 'em, but let 'em feel they had Reins in their Hands. Thus hamper'd in Wedlock, I had nothing to give me ease but that three parts of Mankind were in the same, if not in a much worse Condition. However, to make our Circumstances tollerable for the future, I perswaded my Consort to abridge her self of some superfluous Charge which we cou'd not well bear any longer. First we disposed of our Coach, and then our Acquaintance was reform'd of Course; by Degrees a multitude of modish Visitors dwindled away into two or three formal Matrons, which at last ended in a Decent Apartment in a Monastery, where she spent her Time agreeably enough when I was in the Camp. Hitherto the main matter which pall'd all my Joys, was the impossibility of a Restoration, which now was much lessen'd by the concurrence of Domestick Evils, and the Cares which attend a married State. Yet when I seriously reflected upon the Conduct of *France* in regard of King *James* and the Pretender, I have often observ'd my self to sweat and fret my self into a violent Fever with the very Thoughts of it; but I never was so sensibly touch'd upon this Head as after the Battle of *Malplacket*. which was follow'd with the Surrender of several Towns, so that there was nothing but the poor Barrier of *Landrecy* left to save the Capital, and by Consequence, the Kingdom of *France*. The *French* King having now play'd away all his Leading Cards, was now put to his Trumps. He attempts the Treacherous and Needy Ministers with long Bags of *Louisdo'rs*, which were all ineffectual when his Arms cou'd do no more.

'Tis fresh in every true *Britains* Memory, what strange Methods were taken to bring about the Peace, which quickly after ensued. I shall only mention as much of that Affair as is requisite to make it manifest, That *France* had no consideration for the Pretender's Interest during that Treaty. The War was begun upon account of the *Spanish* Monarchy; *France* was reduc'd to the last extremity, and could hold out no longer, now the Consequence shou'd have been for *France* to have surrender'd up King *Philip*'s Title; but on the contrary it was secur'd to him, and by what any one can conjecture on the Equivalent, that the Pretender should be banish'd *France*, and herafter neither directly nor indirectly be assisted by Force: Nay, so eagerly was *France* bent upon this Project of securing *Spain*, *France*, and neglecting the Pretender, that 'tis well known he refus'd to be concern'd with those in *England* who were willing to restore the Pretender. I shall not pretend to dive into the late Queen's Secrets, and how she was dispos'd that way. 'Tis well known she was not over real for the *Hanoverian* Succession, and that the Pretender's Interest was the only one in competition with it. But where was the *French* Zeal for the Pretender, when he had the Generalissimo and his Arms, the Secretary, the Treasurer, *&c.* all at his Devotion, and if the Pretender was not actually restor'd at that Juncture, the Remora cou'd be no where but on the *French* Side, who had a longer reach in their Politicks than the Restoration of the Pretender. They saw clearly bringing that about wou'd create a Civil War in *England*, and be an occasion of renewing in *Germany*; now their Business was a sudden Peace, and a quiet Possession of *Spain*. And this is the real Spirit of Politics that govern'd the *French* at the Peace of *Utrecht*.

This kind of Management so disconcerted all the Pretenders Party who then govern'd the Queen, that they flew all in Pieces, astonish'd not to find the *French* insist upon the Pretender's Right, as they had laid the Design. They inform against one another, and by their unseasonable and discontinued Animosities threw the Queen into an Agony of Fear, which afterwards usher'd in the Agony of Death. In the mean Time *France* smil'd at the disorder, and hugg'd themselves in the noble Project of having lost every Battle in that Bloody War, and yet obtain'd what they fought for, as they had always been Victorious, whilst the poor Pretender was so little consider'd by *France*, that tho' the Ministry was ready to assert his Title, yet *France* wav'd it and subscrib'd to his Banishment, least that Affair should ruin the Main Project.

But what I am in the next place going to observe, will make clear that *France* was not only unwilling to be active in assisting the Pretender, but that they were scrupulous upon the Point, and made it their Business to disswade him from any such Attempt. I remember I was my self in *Lorain*, when the News of the Queen's Decease was brought the Pretender by a Servant of *L.P.* He was no Stranger to the Interest he had just before with the Ministry, who still were most of 'em in Power. A Ship lay ready for him to waft him over, but he was arrested in his Journey by the *French* King's Orders, and threatened by *M. T.* with the Bastile, if he did not return forthwith to *Lorain*, otherwise considering the After-acts of the Gentlemen then in Play, he would very probably been at St. *James's* several Days before King *George* left his Palace at *Hanover*. This was so shocking a Treatment from the grand Protector of distress'd Monarchs, that the Queen Mother then at *Chalonois* said this was a Key to all the mask Politics which had been acting 27 Years, and the very Thought of it threw her into such a Consternation, that she has never since recover'd it. I know 'tis pretended that *Lewis* XIV was now grown more scrupulous than formerly; he had been in sticking to the Letter of Treaties. I shall not dispute whether passing through the Country without assisting the Pretender, cou'd be wrested by any Logick to be acting in his Favour. But if *Lewis* XIV, was scrupulous, he ought to have been so when he grew nearer his End; for 'tis pretended by those who are willing to represent him as always a Friend to King *James*, that in despute of the Articles of *Utrecht*, he came into the Measures of the Duke of *Ormond*, Lord *Bolinbroke*, the Earl of *Mar*, &c. and had not Death in the mean time taken him off, wou'd have furnish'd 'em with all Things necessary to have made a Head against King *George*. This, I say, is confidently reported by *Lewis* XIV's Admirers. But then they will have the inconsistancy to account for, why he shou'd not scruple to raise an Army to succour the Pretender, who a little before scrupled to let him pass'd with a Couple of Servants, through his Country. For my own Part I am enclin'd to believe he never was so much his Friend, but died as he cou'd, a juggler, and that if he sign'd any thing in form of the late Insurrection 'twas in one of his delirious Fits which were not infrequent in his latter Years. If the Regent be a just Interpreter of his Actions.

And to come home to the present Time, has not *France* still the same regardless Dispositions towards the Pretender? Are they not ready to enter into any Engagement whatever to stand by the Articles of *Utrecht* to the greatest nicety? I know it has been aprised about, that *France* was in the Design against King *George*; but as the Regent reply'd very pertinently to the Earl of *Stairs's* Memorial. There needs no more convincing Proof that *France* has not been meddling, than to understand that both in *Scotland* and *England*, the Rebels have been destitute both of Arms and Money? The Custom-house Officers of *Great-Britain*, have no Authority to search *French* Ships as they go out of their own Ports, and had it not been an easy Matter to have sent what Arms they pleas'd into *Scotland?* What occasion was their for the Pretender to have sculk'd so long upon the Shoar, and stolen privately out of one of their Havens, if the Regent had encourag'd him.

It was no Secret to me and several others above Twenty Eight Years ago, that *France* was never sincere in this Affair; but as their Projects came nearer to a Conclusion, they took less care to conceal the Secret. Till they had a Prospect of settling the *Spanish* Monarchy in the House of *Bourbon*, they were loud and high in their Demands concerning King *James*; but the Hopes they conceiv'd that way, made 'em clap up a Peace at *Reswick*, and lay King *James's* Interest to Sleep. When the *Spanish* Project was ripe, and the Wealth of the *Indies* ready to drop into their Lap, and that they were actually to be put into Possession of it, the Allies were amused with two Partition Treaties, and the Pretender sacrific'd to the same Politicks at the Treaty of *Utrecht*. Yes he was neglected, despised, banish'd out of *France*, forc'd out of *Lorain*, a free State, threaten'd at *Avignon*, a Sanction never yet violated, and now he and his Adherents are preparing themselves to be thrust into the Jaws of the *Turk*, unless the Regent out of Pity deliver him up in hope of the 100000 *l.* and finish the Character of succouring distress'd Monarchs, by being the Occasion of losing his Head on *Tower-Hill*, rather than being Impail'd at *Constantinople*.

But before I dismiss this Matter, I am to account for several Things, which will argue the Court of St. *Germains* guilty of the greatest Ingratitude, unless they acknowledge the endless Obligations they lie under to *France*. Has he not fed a distressed People almost Twenty Years, and that two in a Royal and Princely Manner? Did he not entertain above 15000 *Irish* Troops who were dismiss'd *Ireland* by the Treaty of *Limerick?* Has he not constantly pay'd all the Respect imaginable to the Court of St. *Germains?* promis'd King *James* upon his Death-bed, he wou'd never desist? assur'd the Son he wou'd draw his Sword, and it should ne'er be sheath'd till he had fix'd him in his Throne? Has he not made several chargeable Attempts to make good his Promise? Such Panegyricks as these have often Rung in my Ears, when the *French* were bent upon extolling the Religious Disposition of the Monarch in protecting an unfortunate Prince; and the Expedient was not unserviceable in regard of the generality of the People who easily were blinded with the glaring Object. But let us take this Oeconomy to pieces, and examine every Wheel and Spring; for my part, I can regard this boasted Liberality no otherwise than a very imperfect Restitution. Did not K. *James* both Ruin himself and Thousands of Families meerly by going into *French* Measures. I heard the Court of *France* was oblig'd to feed all the Posterity of that unfortunate misled Multitude, who have been deluded this Twenty Nine Years by their Politicks. 'Tis what I believe what the loosest of their Casuists wou'd not refuse to oblige 'em to upon a fair hearing of the Case. But that the Entertaining the *Irish* Troops shou'd be mention'd as an Instance of *French* Charity, is a very Remarkable piece of Assurance. The *Swiss* and other States are consider'd with large annual Pensions for the Privilege of Listing Men, besides double Pay during the Time of their Service; but the *Irish* and all the rest of King *James*'s Subjects, poor Fools, must think themselves happy to bear the brunt of every Siege and Engagement, for half Pay, be regarded as Beggars, living upon Charity, be reform'd and abandon'd when they are no further useful. The Honour purchas'd by these distress'd People at *Cremina, Luzara, Spireback, Almaza, Friburg, &c.* have merrited better Articles, and the Blood they have lost is a large disbursement for the Expences at St. *Germains.* A few *French* Compliments paid once a Week at St. *Germains,* is but a poor recompence for a ruin'd People, especially when the Origin and Motive of their Misfortunes are look'd into. And the Gasconades and Politick, Promises made both to the Father and the Son of never sheathing the Sword with the Sham Attempts in their Favour, will be recorded in Antiquity, not as Arguments of his Christianity, but strong Lines of Policy how a Prince is to make use of all Occurrences to promote the welfare of his own People, nothing, being more successful in such junctures, than a Pretence of Religion, and assisting Persons in distress.

Having brought my Remarks to this Period, I design'd to have drop'd my Pen immediately, but considering that a Judicious Reader will expect I should advance something by way of Principle to justify the Reflexions I have made. I must add a Word or two more concerning the unjust, as well as unpolitick Proceedings of those who have been deluded by a Foreign Power to bring Destruction to their own native Country. And in the first place I must deliver my Thoughts as to the Cause in General. The Question of Hereditary, was not so well clear'd at the Revolution, but that many very discerning and well meaning Men might be drawn into a Belief, that lineal and immediate Right was part of the Divine Law, and so not dispensable. This was my Opinion in the Beginning, and it was a Principle which carried me through the Wars this Twenty Nine Years in Favour of King *James,* even at those Times, when I was fully convinc'd that *France* had no real Design to re-establish him. But afterwards when I began to look narrowly into the Question of Hereditary Right, and saw that the Notion of *Jure Divino* was only an assum'd Principle to buoy up the Faction. I by Degrees slacken'd in my Zeal, and having no other Nation of Government, then by submitting to the Supream National Power, where the Law of God was silent, I found this an effectual Means to quiet my Conscience. However I still persisted and follow'd the Pretender's Cause, the Success of the Roman-Catholick Interest provoking me to it: For I imagin'd that Salvo ought to weigh down in Practise, where other Matters relating to Succession were still under Controversy; but when I took under serious Consideration the Practise of our Ancestors, and how in all Ages both Church and State came frequently into Non-Hereditary Measures, where I run over the String of Disappointments King *James* had met withal by the Politic Management of *France*. When I reflected what Misery had befallen, and was like to befall these Kings by adhering to the besoted Notion of Hereditary Right, I put the whole Controversy upon the Issue of Religion, and it plainly appear'd to me, that no Roman Catholick was oblig'd to oppose the Revolutionary Measures in Conscience, much less in Policy. I was fully satisfy'd in the first Part of the Enquiry by that unanswerable Piece lately printed, call'd, *A Roman Catholick System of Allegiance.* As for the latter Part, let the Tory and Roman Catholick Party sum up their Losses since 1688, and it will convince 'em how foolishly they acted. Thus settled in my Principles in regard of Loyalty, I design'd to pay an intire and unlimited Obedience to the present Constitution; as to my Religion, which I own is not conformable to that by Law Establish'd. I will make a discreet Use of that Indulgence the Government is pleas'd to allow; and if Providence thinks fit to make me Suffer upon that Score, no rational Man will blame my Zeal till he does convince me of my Mistake.

FINIS

1. Boswell, *Life of Johnson*, ed. Hill & Powell (Oxford, 1934), iv. 333–4.
2. Op cit. (Princeton, 1941), p. 218.
3. Op. cit. (London, 1711), i. 346.
4. See James Sutherland, *Background for Queen Anne* (Methuen, London, 1939), pp. 182–200.
5. P. 288.
6. P. 289.
7. Boswell, *London Journal 1762–63*, Introduction.
8. Stauffer, *Art of Biography in 18th-century England*, p. 217. Cf. Ramkins's *Memoirs*, pp. 311–12.
9. P. 285.
10. P. 293.
11. P. 296.
12. P. 325.
13. Pp. 290, 294, 319.
14. P. 289.
15. A. W. Secord, *Studies in the Narrative Method of Defoe* (New York, 1963), p. 203.
16. Carleton's *Memoirs*, p. 94; *Journal of the Plague Year* (Everyman edn.), p. 63.
17. Pp. 124, 177.
18. P. 67.
19. Hester L. Piozzi, *Observations and Reflections made in the course of a journey through France, Italy, and Germany, 1789*, ed. Herbert Barrows (Ann Arbor, 1967), p. 35.
20. P. 196.
21. *Daniel Defoe*, ed. James T. Boulton (Batsford, London, 1965), pp. 255–57.
22. Pp. 32, 60, 159.
23. Pp. 136, 58, 52.
24. Francis Coventry, *History of Pompey the Little* (London, 1750), p. 10.
25. Pp. 236, 238, 246.

Those interested in the complex bibliographical details of Defoe's works should consult J. R. Moore's *A Checklist of the Writings of Daniel Defoe*, Bloomington, 1962. The text used of *Memoirs of an English Officer* is that of the third issue, issued 27 May 1728. Moore points out that Carleton himself, while he did not write the book, 'hung around the press while it was being printed, and . . . was responsible for some "ffoists" of his own, including the utterly irrelevant conclusion of the book'. The text of *Ramkins* is the original one, issued 9 December 1718. That of *Sheppard*, likewise, is from the first issue of 1724.

Defoe's spelling and punctuation have been left unaltered, but the modern 's' has been substituted for the old long 's', the spelling of proper names has been regularized, and obvious errors have been silently corrected.

BIBLIOGRAPHY

Few of Defoe's voluminous works are now in print, and there is no 'collected' edition now available except, rarely, in second-hand bookshops. All Defoe's longer fiction, however, is now in print, in most cases in several editions. The best introductory books about him are: J. Sutherland, *Defoe* (1937), 1951; Ian Watt, in *The Rise of the Novel*, 1957; J. R. Moore, *Daniel Defoe, Citizen of the Modern World*, 1958. An exceptionally fine introductory selection is J. T. Boulton, *Daniel Defoe*, 1965.

1. *String . . . Bow:* single file . . . in an arc.
2. *Curtain:* in a fortification the curtain is that part of the wall that connects the bastions or gates.
3. *Fascines:* brushwood.
4. *vivacity:* quickness of perception.
5. *Rate:* class of vessel according to strength.
6. *Matrosses:* artillery soldiers immediately below gunners in rank, who acted as their mates.
7. *Antichronism:* contradiction in chronology—here an anticipation.
8. *native sympathy:* the Duke of Berwick was James II's bastard by Arabella Churchill, Marlborough's sister.
9. *casemets:* chambers built into the thickness of ramparts, used for various purposes such as, here, storage of powder.
10. *Hough:* hamstring.
11. *flash'd:* slashed.
12. *Picarons:* rogues.
13. *Rattle:* idle chatterer. O.E.D. lists the first use of this as 1742.
14. *Fleer:* deceitfully civil grin.
15. *Sudor:* watery exudation (usually of sweat).
16. *guess: Person* thus the text.
17. *Basils:* leg-irons.
18. *Ken:* house.